Stephen
Sept '18.

The Dead Scholar

The Dead Scholar

A Quin and Morgan Mystery

John Moss

ANNE MCDERMID AND ASSOCIATES LIMITED

Copyright © 2013 John Moss
ISBN 978-0-9918238-2-6
Also available as an ebook

ANNE MCDERMID AND ASSOCIATES LIMITED

chapter one

Professor Kurtz, He Dead

Philosophers Walk is a fold in the landscape of downtown Toronto, replete with unkempt shrubbery, mottled grass, and intrepid stands of light-starved smog choked trees. A brick pathway meanders from the modest gates at Bloor Street to a formal entry off Hoskin beside Trinity College. Spaces among clusters of foliage provide sanctuary for exhibitionists, lairs for lovers, lookouts for voyeurs, retreats for the disaffected. On the east side, the Walk is flanked by nondescript walls along the back of the Royal Ontario Museum and, on the west, by service entrances to a dishevelled collection of buildings representing one of the great universities of the world. Philosophers Walk is a favourite haunt for strolling professors in the liberal arts who are close to retirement.

Miranda Quin stood in a small grove just off the

pathway, contemplating the corpse of an elderly gentleman dressed with the expensive shabbiness of a long-time academic. Morning traffic had not yet risen to a din and the university was only beginning to waken into its midsummer calm, but the air was already fetid, the trees drooped overhead, the grass was sere. Despite the early hour, Miranda could feel beads of sweat gather under her breasts. She wasn't wearing a bra.

The dead man leaned against a tree in a sitting posture, with a book spread open across his drawn-up legs. He seemed comfortable, were it not for the fact he was dead. He might have been merely the victim of genteel dementia, an old man who had wandered through the darkness in search of a good place to read and then died. He might have known the book by heart and was avoiding the distractions of light.

Miranda glanced down at herself, she grimaced at the incongruity of wearing a little black dinner dress in the early morning and looked up to see the equally strange apparition of her partner, David Morgan, as he ducked under the yellow plastic tape and walked towards her. He was dressed in running shorts and a grungy T-shirt, drenched in sweat.

"What do you think?" she asked as he squatted beside the dead man and cocked his head, trying to penetrate the pall of death.

"Murdered."

"Yeah, he's been posed *post mortem*."

"His cravat is much too tight. Who wears a cravat?" Morgan looked up at her. "A professor," he said, answering his own question. "Renaissance specialist. English Department."

"Morgan?" Like most people, including himself, she used his last name only; his first was a kind of secret, to be used with discretion.

"It's the book. *Sylva Sylvarum*."

"And?"

"Francis Bacon. A facsimile copy."

"A facsimile?"

"No self-respecting scholar would expose an authentic edition to the morning dew?"

"He's dead, Morgan. He might not have had a choice."

"He was killed by a book lover. Who else would kill a Renaissance bibliophile but another bibliophile? Avoiding all possible puns, a Bacon lover. Both of them, probably."

"And is Bacon your newest area of expertise?"

"Not yet."

Miranda, who had been leaning over to see the book, was suddenly aware her neckline was gaping. She crouched down on the opposite side of the victim. Morgan's body gleamed with sweat and his dark brown hair glistened black, the grey strands obscured by dampness.

"Morgan?"

He looked over at her and smiled enigmatically. He waited for her to find the words, shifting his weight over clenched knees.

"Okay," said Miranda, "since when are you a runner?"

"First time out."

"Really." she said, standing up.

He rose to his feet, facing her. "I bought the shoes a month ago. Woke up this morning, I had a dream about running." No, he thought, he had dreamed about falling.

"I think of you more into mind games."

"Running is very cerebral."

"And you just happened to be running through Philosophers Walk and by pure serendipity strode into the middle of a crime scene?"

"Synchronicity. The uncanny coincidence—synchronicity, not serendipity."

"But a lucky turn of events."

"Not for Professor Kurtz."

"Who?"

"Him." He nodded towards the corpse at their feet.

"You know who he is?"

"Didn't recognize him at first—he's changed."

"He's dead."

"You don't remember him?"

"He was probably retired by the time I came along."

"Four and a half years."

"What?"

"You're four and a half years younger. We're contemporaries," said Morgan.

"Getting there."

"I like your shoes."

"Cole Haans. Moderately expensive."

"The duty officer told me you were here."

"So much for synchronicity!"

"Or serendipity."

"Bad date?" He smiled.

"Something like that. Is his name really Kurtz?"

"Yeah. 'Mr. Kurtz, he dead.'" Morgan huddled down again close to the body, feeling a little awkward, aware that he hadn't yet learned the urban athlete's disdain for decorum.

Miranda squatted beside him, knees together and cocked to the side in an effort to maintain decorum of her own, despite a hemline too short for the occasion. Amused by their mutual self-consciousness, she looked sideways at Morgan and chortled. He smiled back, at a loss about what she found humourous but pleased to share in the good-natured intimacy, notwithstanding the corpse and the scurry of forensic specialists moving through the undergrowth all around them.

Professor Kurtz on closer examination did not look very comfortable. An elaborately dramatic gesture on the part of the killer, placing the corpse with his book open to the night under a chestnut tree, seemed in the stifling light of morning a macabre and awkward contrivance, trivializing death. Or trivializing the professor. An act of defiance? Or of contempt? Perhaps both.

"He does look familiar," said Miranda. "Kind of a prototype for the fusty professor."

Morgan noticed, even dead, Professor Kurtz revealed the sallow fleshiness of a sedentary life. His hair was silver and carefully long about the ears and neck. His beard was epicene rather than robust, yet his eyebrows were voluminous, like clusters of wind-blown fluff caught on strands of barbed wire.

He tried to recall the sound of the professor's voice. It was a phlegmatic rumble, he was sure. A harrumphing drone. He could summon descriptions to mind but not the voice itself. A ragged clatter of consonants, the slurping of vowels; very Germanic, although the Professor had declared himself to have originated in the suburbs of Scarborough.

Most Canadian faculty members in the English Department in Morgan's student days affected a lisping Oxford accent. Americans on campus vocalized with crisp mid-Atlantic enunciation that suggested a BBC television newsreader or landed gentry from the Scottish Highlands. Kurtz, as an heir to Erasmus, apparently preferred the vocal disguise of a continental European—ironically, since his exact area of expertise was Francis Bacon, an Englishman.

Kurtz apparently yearned to feel at home in an era when it still seemed possible to know everything.

In Morgan's final year at university, he had thought Bacon was the epitome of cool. Here was a contemporary of Shakespeare whose eclectic intelligence, omnivorous curiosity, and unfettered imagination offered a perfect model for Morgan's own undisciplined but energetic mind. Unfortunately, between their alliance across time loomed the imposing figure of Professor Dieter Kurtz.

Morgan had the temerity to write several term essays on Bacon without the benefit of scholarly mediation—in other words, he did not defer to such critics in the field as his worthy professor but preferred to engage directly with Bacon himself. Kurtz acknowledged Morgan's stellar insights with a series of A minuses, and showed his disdain by writing nothing at all on the returned papers.

Gazing at the rigid features of the old man with a twinge of nostalgia, Morgan recalled the iron-grey eyes that had glowered at him when he went to Kurtz's office to appeal his final grade.

"It's from Shakespeare," he said, without looking up.

"What?"

"Fusty, it's from fustilarean."

"Morgan, have you any idea how strange it is to hear a grown man in early middle age, dressed in tiny little shorts, brand new shoes, and an odiferous T-shirt, using such a big word?"

"I'm forty, more or less."

"More. And I'm mid-thirties, give or take. What's your point?"

"No one is middle-aged these days. That was our parents' generation. We just get older."

In spite of herself, she thought he looked good in running shorts.

"Thank you," he said, apparently reading her mind. "You get to wear skirts in hot weather."

"Morgan, how little you know." She paused before stating the obvious: "It's a dress."

Morgan brushed a mosquito from his bare thigh, which made him feel vulnerable.

They rose to their feet simultaneously, eying each other with a playful wariness. They were fully cognizant of the corpse at their feet but each also recognized their mutual need to approach murder obliquely. It was not for lack of compassion but, rather, because of it—enforcing a distance, leaving them open to intuitive leaps and abstract conjecture.

Sometimes bystanders were dismayed by what seemed an inappropriate attitude or lack of focus but colleagues held them in sufficient regard that their being dressed for a dinner date or a road race while attending an early morning murder scene would elicit no more response than wry appreciation for their eccentricities.

"Of course, in heat like this," she said, "if a woman's not going anywhere in a hurry, she can stand with legs apart, like this, and if there's a breeze…"

He blew gently through pursed lips.

She nodded and winked. "In case you hadn't noticed, the art of wearing a skirt, or a dinner dress in the morning, is this—you have to look natural. Fake that, the rest is easy. Being a woman is not an arbitrary calling, you know, it's a vocation."

They were standing close and Morgan stepped back several feet to admire the shape of her thighs against the thin material of her dress. She retaliated by staring at the front of his shorts. At least they weren't that satiny synthetic that clings. Embarrassed, he wandered off inside the arbitrary perimeter of the crime scene marked by yellow tape.

It was as if nothing beyond the tape was of forensic interest while everything within was possible evidence. *Crime seldom works so neatly,* he thought. *But you have to establish limits. Otherwise, there would be no end to the implications of murder.*

Morgan gazed in apparent distraction first one way, then another, then moved back closer to Miranda and after an awkward moment of silence addressed her with what he offered as the most natural question in the world. "Have you ever read Augustine?"

"Who?" she asked, baffled by hearing the name without a context.

"Saint Augustine."

"Morgan, I'm Anglican."

"You guys believe in saints."

"I'm lapsed."

"I was only wondering if you'd ever read Augustine's *City of God*."

"And you have I suppose. You're a fallen Presbyterian. Is it a page-turner?"

"How come I'm fallen and you're lapsed?"

"Theology, Morgan."

"Do you ever dream that you're falling?"

"Fallen, yes. Often. Sometimes deliciously. Falling, no. You were dreaming about falling for Saint Augustine?"

"The best sex is spiritual," said Morgan as if he doubted it. "That's what *The City of God* is about. Or maybe *The Confessions*. Seems more likely."

"Sounds like a lady's man off his game."

"I dreamed I was falling. I think it was me. And I liked it. I wonder what's taking the coroner's people so long?"

"Hot morning, everything's slow. Except you, the running man."

He grinned at her shyly, as if he had been caught doing some inconsequential thing the wrong way and she had gently admonished him.

And she felt vaguely betrayed that her partner of nearly a decade had taken up an activity demanding such focused commitment. She was placated, however, by the thought that anyone not embarrassed to admit dreaming about sex and a fifth century saint wasn't entirely beyond redemption.

Absent-mindedly, Morgan turned and wandered away again, as if he were looking for something but could not decide what it was. Miranda watched him, tough and boyish, vulnerable in his strange attire and yet confident, then glanced at the dead man. Morgan hadn't picked up on her suggestion that, yes, she did dream she was fallen, and for a moment she felt tingly.

She liked that he hadn't asked her details about last night's date or why she had spent most of the night in the office. It was no big deal. She dressed for dinner and never undressed. End of story.

She glanced over at her partner. He might not be much of a runner but he was in remarkbly good shape. *He walks everywhere. Never drives if he can avoid it. Eats better than most single men his age. Probably unconsciously does isometrics while reading his esoteric tomes or googling arcana.* She returned her attention to her own body. She knew when she felt good she looked good .

She crouched down again to examine the body of Professor Kurtz more closely and whimsy immediately gave way to morbidity.

How distinct is the skin of the dead, she thought. *How suddenly depthless it seems. Like classical sculpture.* She savoured the allusion.

The name of the sculptor Praxitiles came to mind. A couple of millennia later, stone breathed, Michelangelo wrapped flesh around bone and covered it with marble skin so sheer the veins pulsed and sinews gleamed.

Miranda had never been to Italy.

She rose to her feet and smoothed her dress. She had recently been loved by an expert in art history. She had once fancied philosophy a reasonable occupation for an inquiring mind. Of course she knew who Saint Augustine was. She was surprised Morgan wouldn't know she knew.

She plucked the neckline of her dress away from her skin and drawing her lower lip tight over her teeth she blew breath down her cleavage. For a moment she felt strands of coolness between her breasts, until moisture gathered in warm beads and slid to her midriff. She scratched and the material of her dress came away damp with perspiration. It was one of those sultry Toronto days when seniors and people with respiratory problems were urged into air-conditioned malls. And Morgan picked this of all days to start running!

Despite the absurd incongruity of his costume at a murder scene, she thought, looking over at him, he was dressed appropriately for the heat. But it was not only his fanciful outfit that attracted her eye, or his way of going, his sure and fluid movement. It was interesting to watch him think.

There he was, wandering, absorbed in abstraction.

That was what he did; he started at the periphery and worked inward, gathering odds and ends of information, floating them among random hypotheses, until the chaos resolved. Through what? Intuition, induction, informed elimination of the extraneous? And *she* started at the centre, she began with the evidence at hand and made her way out to the margins, deducting from one thing, another, and another, building a discursive structure of inevitability.

Morgan in fact was thinking about plunging through the air the previous night. As he had fallen, shards of glass drifted beside him at the same velocity, catching edges of light, and the name of Saint Augustine hovered close by, the letters of the words in fluttering wisps of gold and green. At the exact moment of impact, Morgan's eyes had flashed open. He could taste blood. He swung his legs over the side of the bed. In the heat of the early morning, the hardwood floor had felt cold to his feet. He ran a finger across his teeth and gums, then examined it in the light rising to his sleeping loft from below. There was no blood.

He thought of himself as a recovering Calvinist; why dream of a Catholic saint? Looking in the bathroom mirror he had been almost surprised when the eyes that met his were his own.

Miranda shifted her gaze to the victim. Professor Kurtz offered himself up as a curiosity; there seemed no urgency surrounding his death. The book and his posture were sinister and yet whimsical, deflecting the dread normally aroused by the dead. He might have once been an attractive man, she couldn't be sure. She found his faded cords and tweed jacket a charming affectation, especially in the stifling heat. He must have been in his late seventies, maybe into his eighties, but he was one of those old men who carry age with distinction. His beard trimmed close to his face, in conjunction with his rampant eyebrows, implied a perverse vanity, an arrogant awareness of himself as a sexual being because of his advanced years, not in spite of them.

A stray hair in his beard caught her eye, a wiry strand darker than the rest, lying perpendicular to the shorn white stubble.

She took a pair of tweezers and a plastic envelope from a small kit in her purse and lifted the loose hair to examine it against the light before tucking it away for analysis. It appeared to be a human pubic hair, although unlikely to have come from the victim. The thought of free-floating pubic hairs forced her to stifle a gag reflex.

She preferred to think the hair was somehow connected with the old man's death, rather than being the airborne detritus from a fumbling midnight tryst upwind. Murder, she could deal with. Sex was more complicated.

chapter two

Jane Latimer

Miranda was about to call Morgan to share her discovery when a commotion along the cordoned-off path caught her attention. A woman of about her own height and age, but dressed in brief running clothes and glistening like a goddess, was creating a scene. If Morgan was a neophyte runner, this was an athlete in peak condition. As Miranda walked over, the woman recognized her to be a person in authority and immediately adjusted her voice to a collegial whisper, as if the uniformed officer were no longer a consideration. "I know this man," she said, casting her eyes briefly in the direction of the corpse.

"Good," said Miranda.

"I need to get in there."

"I'm afraid you can't jog through a crime scene," Miranda responded.

"But that person is in there," the woman challenged, her voice rising lightly as she motioned towards Morgan—who, from a bystander's perspective, looked ridiculously out of place in his own skimpy outfit, fully engaged in contemplation.

"Yes he is," said Miranda. "He's a detective."

"Oh." The woman shrugged.

"Just why do you want to get closer?"

"Well, I need to be sure it's him. I need to be sure he's dead. I need to see if that's a book in his hands, it looks like it from here. I need to see what it is?"

"That's a lot of needing. You are?"

"An associate of the deceased—Jane Latimer. I'm a professor of Renaissance literature."

"Here?"

"Pretty much anywhere." She smiled at what must have been a private joke. "Yes, at this university, on the grounds of which I now find my access prohibited."

"Not at all," said Miranda. "The campus is entirely yours, apart from this small corner."

"Was he reading Francis Bacon?"

Miranda looked at her carefully but refrained from answering.

Jane Latimer glanced at her and looked away. She had piercing eyes which life-lines crinkling at the edges made curiously attractive.

There was an awkward silence between them.

"You'd better come in." Miranda said. She spoke as if she were inviting a vampire to cross the invisible threshold of vulnerability. She motioned to the officer.

"I'm Detective Sergeant Quin," she said.

The woman strode past her and through the web of police technicians straight to the dead man. She had a spring in her step that Miranda unconsciously emulated as she followed behind.

Jane Latimer seemed not the slightest intimidated by the presence of death as she gazed down at the corpse, her own vitality lending the scene an air of comic absurdity. Yet there was a tension between her and Professor Kurtz, intimations of a long-standing relationship that wasn't about to achieve closure simply because one of them was alive and the other was very much not.

As Morgan ambled over to join the two woman, he admired the constrained passion exuding from the interloper's scantily clad and athletic physique. She ignored him, she stared at the dead man's face as if trying to memorize his features in final repose. Or was it a silent rebuke for taking death as a refuge? Her apparent openness was hard to read.

"Professor Latimer, this is my partner, Detective Sergeant Morgan." Miranda wondered at her impulse to define their relationship. "Morgan, Professor Latimer was out jogging." As if that wasn't self-evident. "She knows him."

"Running, Professor Latimer was running, not jogging."

His eyes travelled quickly from the woman's head to her feet and back again. She smiled, accepting his frank appraisal as a compliment.

"And you are a runner, too," she observed. Morgan

held himself a little more erect and smiled in return.

Miranda felt strangely outside the club. *One day, and he's an athlete*, she thought. *Joggers are runners, but apparently runners aren't joggers.*v*Both get to wear cool clothes and sweat in public.*

"Just starting," he said with ingenuous modesty that somehow implied he had been off the road temporarily and had now resumed his natural calling. "And what's your connection? You were colleagues?"

"Yes and no. Dr. Kurtz retired a dozen years ago, the year I was hired. But he stayed around as a Professor Emeritus—the university supplied him with office space, he had the use of research facilities, and he was ostensibly available for consultation."

"Ostensibly?" Miranda queried.

"He was to be avoided when possible. He was a bit of a bastard," said Jane Latimer, looking down at the corpse.

"So much for speaking well of the dead," said Morgan.

"I am," said Jane Latimer. "If I told you what I really thought, you'd probably arrest me on the spot." She smiled graciously. "He was a difficult man, especially with graduate students. He didn't see undergraduates, but grads submitted to his condescension because he was an unavoidable authority in his field."

"An awkward trade-off," said Miranda.

"And apart from anything else he was a sexual predator."

"At his age?" Miranda exclaimed.

"They're the worst. Nothing beats an antique academic with intellectual authority, diminished prowess, and an over-wrought libido."

"Fascinating," said Miranda, finding the whole notion of a superannuated predator repulsive.

"Power and impotence, they're a dreadful combination. And the old bastard didn't discriminate, so long as they were smart. That's what counted, they had to be intellectually worthy—he never messed with mediocrity, or so he said in more than one disciplinary hearing."

"Was he actually successful?"

"With predation? Who knows. Perhaps not."

"And his other colleagues?" asked Morgan. "Did they dislike him as well?"

"He was the most arrogant scholar I have ever encountered, man or woman, in my entire career."

"That's a 'yes,' I take it."

"Can you think of any of them who would want him dead?" Miranda asked, aware that her question might seem redundant.

"Who wouldn't?" It was the expected response.

"And what about Bacon?" Miranda asked.

Jane Latimer bent down and looked at the leather-bound book in Kurtz's hands. "May I see it," she said, reaching out, but careful to avoid actually touching the book.

"Let me," said Miranda. Withdrawing a pair of disposable gloves from her purse, she put them on and tried to lift the book from the dead man's grasp but his fingers were clenched and she had to peel them back, one by one, until he suddenly relinquished his grip and the book fell across his lap and slipped onto the grass. She picked it up carefully, aware there might be fingerprints on the leather cover, and held it out for Professor Latimer to observe.

Jane Latimer turned her head this way and that, and then asked Miranda to open the cover, and to her own surprise, Miranda did, realizing there was something almost conspiratorial in the way they had admitted this woman to the heart of the crime scene. It was as if the three of them had mutual interests in the murder, even if their motives were entirely different.

The woman bent close and began to blow gently across the pages, watching several flutter by before they settled open at the title page.

"It's not real," she said. "It's a nineteenth century facsimile."

Morgan stifled a triumphant cough. Miranda caught his eye, giving him the satisfaction of her acknowledgement. Jane Latimer stood upright, plucking her damp singlet away from her body and taking a deep breath that had the effect of drawing the material even more tightly across her breasts. Both Morgan and Miranda were intensely responsive to her physicality and in consequence more aware of their own.

"Someone's having a bit of a laugh, I think." Miranda and Morgan exchanged glances, unsure of what the joke would be. "He prided himself on only reading Bacon in the original editions."

"And?"

"For him to be reading a facsimile, not bloody likely. He wouldn't be caught dead—well, not usually." She paused for effect. "It would be like catching him riding a bus, something he claimed never to have done in his entire life."

"A strange man," said Miranda.

"A dead scholar," said Morgan. "Sounds familiar doesn't it? There was a Hardy Boys mystery called something like that: The Dead Scholar's Society."

"And a medieval play," said Jane Latimer, and then apparently as an afterthought, she added: "Kurtz devoted his life to establishing a German connection."

"Between?"

"Bacon and an arcane text called *Fama Fraternitatis*. Published under the pen name, Christian Rosenkreuz."

Jane Latimer leaned closer to Miranda to get a better look at the book, and as she did so her breast burned into Miranda's bare arm. Miranda instinctively flinched and even as she did she was aware the contact was unintentional and grimaced at her own awkwardness. She reached out to steady Jane who seemed to have been set off balance by Miranda's reflexive action. The book fell to the ground again. Both women reached for it but Jane Latimer scooped it up in both hands in an intuitive action. She immediately handed it to Miranda, who took it from her, feeling somehow a little embarrassed by their brief contretemps, and repressed her instinct to brush away particles of grass and dirt.

"So, a facsimile," said Morgan. "The killer was an academic elitist. There can't be many people around, Professor Latimer, who would get the joke, if that's what it is."

"A dozen," she responded.

The precision of her answer struck Morgan as fustilarian. "A dozen?" he exclaimed.

"That would constitute the remaining membership of The Bacon Society. Twelve members, living. One dead."

"The Bacon Society?"

"Canadian Bacon! That's also a joke. Kurtz was a charter member and president-for-life."

"With a dozen disciples. Sounds vaguely familiar. Would you happen to know who they are?" said Miranda.

"I would," she responded.

"Are they so well known?" Morgan asked.

"It is not a secret society."

"You were a member."

"I am. Actually, I have been recording secretary since the day I was hired by the university. And as there was no vice-president—it didn't seem necessary because it never occurred to anyone that Kurtz might relinquish control—or die, I suppose—it will be my executive decision to turn over our membership list, should you want it."

"Interesting. You worked closely with him," said Miranda, "but you disliked him."

"Intensely. Members of the Bacon Society share a mutual love for Francis Bacon *and* a profound loathing for Dieter Kurtz."

Jane Latimer seemed to be enjoying the situation. Every few moments during their conversation she would glance down at the dead man's face, or run her eyes along his length, as if in death his body had become a landscape feature of Philosophers Walk, while his personality was already anecdotal and his spirit, such as it was, had evaporated like a wisp of malodorous vapour.

"The original Bacon Society was founded in 1886," she said, rising to what she seemed to feel was her responsibility to explain. "A woman by the name of Constance Potts published a book proving Bacon wrote Shakespeare's entire canon. The society was an instrument to promulgate her findings on the spurious authorship."

"And that's what you all believe?" asked Morgan, incredulous. "Bacon wrote Shakespeare, and Shakespeare was only a front man?"

"Yes, of course, and that Bacon was the eldest illegitimate son of Elizabeth I, by her lover, Robert Dudley, the Earl of Leicester."

"You can't be serious!"

"No, I am not serious. Otherwise we'd be the Constance Potts Society. But many out there in the world do believe such things. That is what fascinates about Bacon. He's like Elvis. His eccentric passage through life fostered myths and fantastical conceits. He was the quintessential Renaissance man, he was immersed in antiquity and the first modernist, a universal genius who undertook to know all things knowable, and to illuminate all mysteries with the light of reason. Afflicted with an exceptionally high forehead, but devilishly handsome when wearing a hat. Brilliant writer, radical thinker, morally elastic, an ambitious rogue, simply irresistible."

She stopped talking, not because she had nothing to say, but as a rhetorical device. She bent from the waist to stretch or tighten a lace. Miranda looked at Morgan across her upended bottom, which was poised between them. Jane Latimer seemed clearly relaxed in their company despite the corpse at their feet who had brought them together. Miranda had already taken the position that she liked Jane Latimer. She did not realize this until she saw in Morgan's eyes that he had done the same.

Straightening languorously, their interlocutor checked their eyes and smiled, apparently recognizing that they had assimilated their new knowledge about the irresistible Francis Bacon. Then she suggested, as if it were a social invitation, that they meet at her office later in the morning. "I'll print up the membership list," she said. "It's as good a place to start as any."

Miranda bristled momentarily at the proprietorial directive but wrote down the office address. Jane Latimer reached across the prostrate corpse and shook her hand. "I'd better get to the shower before I catch my own death. See you later, Detectives."

Miranda turned to her partner. "Morgan, why don't you run on with Professor Latimer for a bit. See how it's done. Get yourself cleaned up and I'll meet you back here in an hour."

Morgan grinned, surprisingly shy. "Do you mind," he asked.

"Not at all," the woman responded. "Run me over to the gym."

Jane Latimer took a half step and froze, by her dramatic gesture urging the other two to do the same. A curious bee hovered indolently in the column of air between them, savouring, perhaps, the sweet odour of sweat or, possibly, the residual scent of Miranda's wildflower shampoo. Miranda gently pushed her hand through the air, encouraging the bee's departure without any show of aggressiveness. Instead of leaving, the bee lighted lazily on her arm just above the wrist. Miranda held her arm up to eye-level, curious to see the bee closer. Morgan peered at it, although keeping his distance. Suddenly, Jane Latimer swiped at the bee without actually touching it. Miranda grimaced as the bee flinched, lurched, lifted and hovered briefly before Morgan whacked it in mid-air and it rose in a brief arc and fluttered in free-fall to the ground.

"I'm sorry," said Jane Latimer. "I was afraid it would sting you."

"Well, it did," said Miranda, staring at the tiny welt on her arm. "After you belted it."

"I'm so sorry. I don't think I actually touched it. Does it hurt?"

"Not much," said Miranda. "I grew up in the country," she added, as if the significance was self-explanatory. She reached into her purse and removed a Swiss Army knife which she handed to Morgan. He flicked open the blade and handed it back to her.

"My God," Jane Latimer exclaimed. "You're not going to bleed yourself, that's only for snake bites, isn't it?"

"No," Miranda laughed. "If you scrape the stinger off sideways, you avoid squeezing the venom into your flesh. Look closely," she said, holding her wounded forearm up to the sunlight. "See the little wad on the end of the stinger, that's her guts still pulsing away. The stinger's barbed, so once she committed, she was a goner. Tore the insides right out of her."

"She?"

"The workers are all female. The drones are male, or the males are drones, whichever. They just hang around the queen, hoping for sex."

"Here, let me do that," said Morgan, reaching to take the knife back from her and grasping her arm as if he were about to amputate.

"No thank you," said Miranda, emphatically. "The pleasure is mine."

Holding the knife with a flourish, she scraped across the welt while the other two leaned closer, and all three watched as the tiny stinger with its grotesque little bundle of throbbing abdominal muscles was pulled clear and floated away on the steel.

"Fascinating," said Jane Latimer. "I can't tell a bee from a hornet from a wasp."

"Hornets and wasps have straight stingers," Morgan said, with what Miranda perceived as a mixture of gravitas and bemusement. "They can withdraw from an attack and fight again. Actually, the bee doesn't have to die when she stings. Her stinger isn't barbed, it's a sort of spiral affair. If you were to let her thrust away, she'd eventually withdraw on her own and fly off quite pleased with herself. But, of course, no one waits."

"Meanwhile," said Miranda, "My arm bloody hurts and the bee is dead and Professor Latimer is the killer." She paused. "I doubt she'd have stung me without the incentive, poor thing."

"Sorry," said Jane Latimer. She was comfortable with their banter, even though the rules were still unfamiliar.

"We should go," said Morgan. "I saw the photog taking a picture of us. Guess what's going to be featured on the cover of the *Police Gazette* next week?"

"The what?" said his new running partner as they began to withdraw, leaving Miranda to her own devices.

"A scurrilous newsletter. Appears at Headquarters from time to time," he explained as they moved out of earshot, ducking under the yellow cordon and breaking into a slow run down the path into the heart of the sprawling campus.

Miranda found herself smiling. Often she was proprietorial about Morgan; not jealous but hesitant to share him, particularly with a woman so exceptionally attractive. But something about Jane Latimer set her at ease. The woman's sensual vitality made Miranda more aware of herself. She suddenly shook her head, embarrassed to be maundering off like the narrator in a historical romance.

chapter three
Ellen Ravenscroft

Miranda's attention reverted to Professor Kurtz whom she regarded now with increased curiosity. Anyone capable of evoking hostility from a band of loyal cohorts was worthy of considerable interest in his own right, quite apart from his current condition as the victim of a murder that was shrouded in whimsy.

Realizing that she still held the leather-bound book gingerly in her hands, she manipulated it into a secure position poised between a crooked arm and her breast while fumbling in her purse for a plastic bag that proved too small to contain it. The book slipped from her grasp and fell for a third time. She retrieved it, noticing it now had grass stains and a smudge that must have come from her own sweat.

"Damn," she mumbled to herself.

Miranda was usually meticulous in her treatment of forensic materials. Fortunately, it was only a facsimile, not a first edition. But of course it was still evidence.

"Here," said a familiar voice from off to the side and a hand reached out, proffering a more appropriate plastic wrap. "Tell me that wasn't your partner running off down the yellow brick road."

"It was," said Miranda, turning to address Ellen Ravenscroft, the medical examiner from the Coroner's Office who had just appeared on the scene with her crew. "Thanks," she said, bagging the book. "He's off for a romp with his new best friend."

"Who is who?"

If Jane Latimer seemed intuitively to accentuate the bond between Miranda and her partner, Ellen Ravenscroft had the opposite effect. She was a flirt, and like most flirts, she was dangerous.

"Come on, love, who is she? And since when has Morgan taken up sport, if that's what you call it, running like Toto in heat."

"Isn't she beautiful, though?"

"No," Ellen Ravenscroft replied. "She exudes sensual well-being, she is in exceptionally good condition from what I saw when I managed to tear my eyes away from Morgan, but she's not beautiful. You are beautiful, Miranda. I, even, can, on occasion, be beautiful. That woman is merely healthy."

"My goodness," said Miranda, feeling a brief wave of regret sweep through her for anything negative she might have been thinking about Ellen, and feeling relief when the wave rolled over on itself and receded, leaving her more wary than ever, and at the same time liking her more than before.

"Okay, love, let's take a look at your boyfriend, here."

"Don't be disgusting."

"I am, aren't I. Does he have a name yet?" The two women squatted down, one on either side of the body. The hot still air was beginning to pick up the odour of death.

"Professor Kurtz, late of the English Department. Renaissance specialist."

Ellen Ravenscroft offered a smile of satisfaction, as she always did when working on someone she considered her social equal. *The British class system dies slowly in a Canadian climate.* Donning latex gloves, she prodded delicately at first and then with deliberate force, exploring the body surface in ways that revealed to the trained mind an intimate morphology of the devolving world inside.

She stood and called the police photographer to take close-ups. Miranda withdrew to a vantage where she could observe procedures without being part of the scene. She was surprised to see the medical examiner loosen the cravat very carefully and then work it free from around the dead man's neck. When Ellen tilted the head back so that the photographer could get a clear shot of the throat area, Miranda's mind clicked into a deductive mode, seeking a resolution to explain the variants in procedure.

Normally, the body would be removed from the scene with as little disturbance as possible, so that analysis of clothing, of wounds, and of conformation imposed by *rigor mortis* and trauma could occur under controlled conditions at the morgue.

Ellen walked over to Miranda. "If you're through, we'll wrap him to go."

"He's all yours."

"Send over the paperwork when you can. I don't think there's much urgency but I'd like to get him on ice. I'm assuming you've already removed his wallet."

"No, we didn't touch him."

"But you know who he is?"

"A retired professor. Famous in limited circles."

"Dieter Kurtz. I've heard the name. I thought he was dead years ago. He must be in his eighties."

"Late seventies, I think; according to Judy Garland."

"Judy? Oh, Dorothy and Toto."

"Professor Jane Latimer."

"That's who she told you she was. Careful, love. You can never trust the pathologically healthy."

"I'll remember that, and that it came from a coroner."

"He's luscious, Miranda. When are you going to share him."

Miranda narrowed her eyes and stared at Ellen, wondering if she already had.

"He's really not your type," she said. "He's alive."

"Ouch!"

"Sorry," said Miranda and immediately regretted her apology. The ME's vulgarity was her awkward response to assumptions about them both being women in the same situation: single, professionals in their late thirties, and deeply committed to careers centred on death. Lascivious chatter is less about romance than frustration, she thought with unavoidable empathy. "Given his new playmate," she said as a conciliatory gesture, "I'd say we're both out of the running, so to speak."

"Runners are miserable bed-mates, you know. Their legs twitch. At least I'm only thrashing about when I dream of sex. Or when I'm in the act by myself."

"Yeah," said Miranda, resisting the impulse to say, I actually know what you mean. "He's really not the lothario you think."

"If he was, I wouldn't bother. I'm not needy enough to keep company with a lady's man—as Leonard Cohen described himself. With irony. Lord help us, I hope with irony."

"Morgan's tough as they come and he smiles intuitively at babies and people with deformities and he snarls at young mother's with cigarettes in their mouths and if they're nursing their babies he confiscates their smokes and grinds them out on the pavement, and—"

"In real life he's Clark Kent."

"Yeah, but he's super in bed."

"In your dreams."

"No, in yours," said Miranda, feeling she had somehow managed to stand by her partner and yet play the game.

"So what do you think? You've got to wonder how she just happened on the scene?"

"Yeah, and she couldn't wait to tell us he was a total bastard. And that she was among his closest friends."

"Nice."

"So what were you doing, taking off his cravat? Do you think he wasn't strangled?"

"He probably died of asphyxia but, no, he wasn't strangled. The discolouration around his neck was minimal and there wasn't much swelling. Blood had already stopped flowing by the time someone tied him in paisley. He was positioned against the tree after death; the book was set up in his grasp before *rigor* set in. He didn't die here. Have forensics do another sweep of the area, expand the crime scene a bit. And he didn't struggle much, maybe a kick or two and a shudder. He's looking pretty good for his age. I'd say he died cheerfully, or at least with dignity, at the hands of an acquaintance."

Miranda's mind wavered with conflicting possibilities. There was no dignity in dying, and certainly none afterwards. She realized that Ellen was wrong, that the murder had occurred within arm's reach of his present position. Even a strong assailant would have left scuff marks on the ground if he had been dragged or carried, and dirt on his clothing would have indicated a radical shift in his posture. There were light grass-stains on the knees of his trousers, as if he had been doing a bit of impromptu gardening, and the elbow patches on his jacket showed residual discolouration that might have come from long hours of reading with his head propped up among dusty stacks of antiquarian books. Possibly he had fallen to his knees in the face of impending death, possibly he had tumbled forward onto his outstretched arms. Miranda checked his hands for dirt or abrasions but they were clean.

She accepted that the pose and the book were a post-mortem humiliation inflicted for the private satisfaction of the assailant, and had little to do with his actual death

Ellen and Miranda were often at odds, but Miranda knew enough not to dismiss the medical examiner out of hand when her insights strayed from the morgue into the investigative sphere. There were no absolute boundaries, only limits of knowledge. Perhaps Ellen was right, the victim embraced his demise with grace and decorum. But why, then, Miranda chuckled to herself, was his fly unzipped?

The book had been shading his lap and his drawn up legs cast his groin area in rumpled shadows, but as the coroner's people began to unfold the corpse, it became clear the man's zipper was down, even though his pants were done up at the waist and his brown elasticized belt was buckled.

"Whoa!" she exclaimed, holding her hand up for the removal procedure to stop.

"Yeah," said Ellen Ravenscroft. "How about that, love. The old bugger was having it off in the woods."

"I don't think so," said Miranda. "I'd say he was taking a pee."

"Strange, then," said Ellen. "He must have expired *in medias res*." She reached out with a pencil and carefully pushed back the outer flap of the fly. There, exposed, was the pitiful cap of a wizened penis, greyish purple, like the nub of a night-blooming mushroom. "He didn't have time to get it back all the way in. No urine stains, though," she said, bending down to look closer. "No semen. Just the little one-eyed fellow lingering for a last look around."

"Circumcised," Miranda observed.

Ellen nodded for the removal to continue and the two women stood silently watching as the body was laid out in the folds of a black plastic bag that was then sealed and placed on a stretcher to be maneuvered by hand down Philosophers Walk onto the campus. The black mariah was parked on Hoskin Street, waiting to take him away one last time from the university that had apparently been the centre of his arcane and predatory life.

"Where to from here?" said Ellen. "Can I give you a lift?"

"Thanks. I walked up from Headquarters. I think I'll hang around. I told Morgan I'd wait for him."

"Maybe I'll keep you company."

"I'll tell him you said hello."

"Okay, then. And love, maybe you should go home and change. You look like a bit of a whore, especially the pumps."

"Late date with a lawyer."

"That explains everything, of course. Remember, if you want to share him—Morgan, not the lawyer—you know where to find me."

"Yeah, the morgue. That's a real come-on."

"Yes, well, I bet I see more naked men than you do."

"Lucky you."

"And I don't have to listen to them. Oh God, I haven't been with a living one for ages. What's it like? Do you remember?"

"Just barely! Go away."

"Call me sometime. We'll share our misfortunes."

"Oh, fun. I'm sure to do that."

"Bye, love."

"Bye now," said Miranda as the medical examiner gathered her things and prepared to leave. "Get back to us when you can."

"For sure," said Ellen and walked away, slipping from Miranda's mind even before passing out of sight. They were circumstantial acquaintances, they would pick up their banter when next they met but neither would inhabit the thoughts of the other in the meantime, except as foci for their professional functions. Miranda brushed a persistent mosquito from her arm without trying to kill it and looked around towards the Bloor Street end of Philosophers Walk, anticipating Morgan's return.

chapter four
Felix Swan

Morgan turned slowly in the shower, draping his exhausted body with fine lines of water. Caught up in conversation, he and Jane Latimer had run around King's College Circle three times before he dropped her off at the gym and headed for home in the Annex. Altogether, he had probably not run more than three miles, but he was drained from the heat and had not yet learned about proper hydration. Water drizzling against his skin seemed to compensate for the absence of moisture within, but his blood felt thick in his veins and his heart fluttered at the unfamiliar strain. Waves of darkness and light played like the aurora borealis against the inside of his skull. He was not at all sure that running was an appropriate activity for a man of his disposition.

Without fully drying himself, he wrapped a

bath-towel around his waist and walked through to the living room where he flopped down on the blue sofa.

He shut his eyes and in moments was soaring through the light with Saint Augustine at his side. Morgan could not make out his companion's features and yet he could see him grinning with the smug satisfaction of a man who had known many women before his conversion to the celibate life, which happened by the grace of God to coincide with his diminished appeal and dwindling appetite. Morgan was no longer falling, but the earth was spinning beneath him at runaway speed and he doubted he could ever find himself if he landed.

Good grief, he thought, and opened his eyes. He didn't know how long he'd been asleep. He walked into the kitchen and took a deep slug of skim milk straight from the carton.

Miranda would be waiting. He got dressed and hurried out to meet her. They had a murder to deal with, the death of a man despised by his closest friends, a man with a Germanic accent from the suburbs of Toronto, a sexual predator who had devoted his life to a seventeenth century philosopher and who died in a scrubby canyon formed by the back of a vast museum and service entrances to a university of corporate proportions.

Miranda sat on the carpet with her back against the sofa, left leg crooked low to the side and the other drawn close against her body, as she reached around with both arms to clasp her right foot in her hands and admire the crimson lustre on the finely trimmed nails. This particular contortion was her form of yoga; it pleased her to be supple enough to do her own pedicures. Sometimes in the winter she would indulge in a professional job but the truth was, she enjoyed doing it herself, if only for the satisfaction of being able to fold neatly into unnatural positions. Many women her age couldn't do it.

When Morgan had not returned in a reasonable time, she asked an officer to tell him she had gone home to clean up, implying she had worked through the night. The officer scrutinized her and smiled.

My God, thought Miranda, nothing is private. Having squelched her erstwhile suitor's expectations because she was not that desperate and not wanting to face an empty apartment, she had actually been at her desk when the call came in. She felt righteously indignant when the officer gave a knowing wink and told her she would let Morgan know.

Miranda had a morning television show turned on so low she didn't have to pay attention to the chatter of people sitting around a table being friends in discrete time segments. She had noticed while showering one nail had been chipped. She dabbed at it with remover and skimmed it clean with a Q-tip. She began to apply a base coat, careful not to get remover on her fingernails, which were done in a much less flamboyant but complimentary shade and holding up well. Adjusting the pads between her toes, isolating the nail under restoration, she leaned forward across her upraised leg to blow it dry with her breath. She could feel the muscles on her back tighten and her rib-cage crunch into her lower abdomen. *Maybe she should be doing pedicures more often.*

Selecting the right colour from a box displaying innumerable varieties of red—she sometimes bought new polishes just to add to the colour collection—she sat back to let the undercoat dry a bit more when there was a knock on the door. It could only be Morgan, since no one else would be so presumptuous as to slip by the security door at this time of day, and the building superintendent would ring, not knock, or at least he would knock less aggressively. She hobbled over to let him in.

Before the door was fully open, she turned and hobbled back to her position on the floor by the sofa. "So, where were you?" she said cheerfully.

"Fell asleep," he answered, closing the door behind him and following her into the living room where he sat opposite, trying in spite of himself to see what she had on, apart from the extra-large T-shirt featuring a generic wind-swept pine on a rocky promontory and emblazoned with the words, "Who Killed Tom Thomson?" And probably no bra.

He couldn't be sure whether she was wearing feather-weight shorts or flared knickers, chunked up between her legs as she continued her pedicure, seemingly unaware of his covert gaze. Neither of them talked. The television conversation continued low in the background. Both of them became absorbed in what she was doing, twisting gracefully in a lithe knot to apply the brilliant moist red to her renegade nail. Her concentration in such a trivial activity fascinated him, and he realized that that must be the point. The only equivalent he could think of was shaving. It takes the same mindless attention, but shaving was a matter of elimination, not adornment. Sometimes, he thought, men were impoverished, without the transcendent rituals women built into their lives.

After waiting for the polish to dry, she stretched her legs in front of her, leaned forward to pluck out the cotton wads, then sat back and wriggled her toes in a salute to her admiring eye. Morgan sank back into his chair, feeling he could now relax.

"We're due at Jane Latimer's office in an hour," he said. "Do you think they'll be dry by then."

"It's only eleven o'clock. And it's dry already. I'm set to go when you are, just let me throw on some clothes."

She got up almost prissily and walked out of the room, only flaunting her rear with a twitch at the very last moment before passing out of his sight-line, knowing he would be watching. "Let's go on foot," he called after her. "I need more exercise."

"How did it go, running with the goddess of sweat," she asked, leaning her head around the doorframe. "Could you keep it up?" She ducked back out of sight. He could hear a disembodied giggle.

"Sort of," he said. "But I couldn't talk at the same time. She 'glided effortlessly' and I 'trudged doggedly.'"

"Like Toto."

"What? Who?"

"Nothing. She's as good as she looks, eh?"

"Yeah, she's a runner. I might be rethinking the whole idea, I'm not sure, you know, do I want to do marathons, really? Takes time. You've got to train every day."

"I'll go for a run with you, Morgan. Maybe tomorrow. Don't give up so soon."

"I'm not giving up, I'm re-prioritizing. Let's go, I need to disperse the lactic acid."

"Lactic acid," said Miranda, coming out into the living room. "She must have given you a real work-out."

"Yeah," he mumbled. "Let's go."

As he ushered her towards the door in a gesture of misplaced chivalry, since it was her apartment and her door to close, he glanced down at her bottom, looking for a panty-line. Brief cut, he thought. She had been wearing shorts with those underneath. The mild excitement sustained from his prurient curiosity faded. As she stood aside for him to walk by her into the corridor, he resisted the impulse to give her arm a companionable squeeze and sauntered ahead towards the stairs, prepared to descend jauntily, like Gene Kelly, despite the pain in his legs.

By the time they arrived back on campus at the University of Toronto, they had reviewed the case from several perspectives.

"Do you think she did it?" said Morgan, referring to his running cohort.

"I have an open mind," Miranda responded. "Yeah, I'd say there's a possibility. But we'll never build a case until we establish motive. Not liking the guy hardly qualifies. Even despising him doesn't make it. And don't forget, she wanted us to know she hated him. That's almost a declaration of innocence. And why the book, the pose, the penis."

"The what!"

"The penis. His fly was unzipped, you couldn't see until they moved him, and his little fellow was poking through his underpants. I think he was having a pee."

"No way. Men don't do it like that—"

"What?"

"Take out what you call 'the little fellow' through their underwear fly. They slide it out a leg hole pulled to the side. It would retreat automatically if he stopped in mid-pee. And there'd be dribbles. If he was wearing boxers, of course, maybe not."

"Sounds devious to me. Why do they put flies in, if nobody uses them?"

"They're designed by women, or men who sit to pee."

"Do men do that?"

"Actually, yes. Those of us confident enough in our manhood. Middle of the night, it's easier than turning on the lights and you avoid splashing your feet."

"Yuck."

"So what was he wearing?"

"Briefs, I think. We'll check with Ellen."

"Ravenscroft, she's on the case? Great."

"She's on your case, Morgan."

"Not."

"Oh yes she is. If you're ever in need—"

"I'm always in need."

"Well, so is she."

"Not likely, love."

"Morgan, why the cravat?"

"I'd say it was his, it goes with the outfit. We'll find more about his fashion sense when we check out his home."

"But why tighten it to simulate strangulation. We don't actually know what killed him."

"I thought you said asphyxiation."

"Yes, but that covers a lot of territory."

"Could he have been stung by bees? You were."

"With a little help from our friend, Jane Latimer."

"It's unlikely, I suppose. They don't fly at night.

"And bees wouldn't arrange the book, the casual pose, *etcetera*."

"Why in Philosophers Walk of all places?"

"Maybe that's where he liked to hang out. Bees can be bought in bulk, you know. You get a little package with workers and a queen. My Dad used to get them by mail. Mrs. Pannabaker at the Post Office hated it."

"He kept bees?"

"No, he was an activist in the Bees Liberation Army. He imported them from Florida and set them free. Yes, he kept bees."

"You said there was a stray hair in his beard. Not his."

"I don't think it was his. Of course if he was peeing and then touched his face?"

"You're very focused on urination, Miranda."

"The guy was found with his pecker askew. What's a woman to think."

"Yeah," he mumbled. "Why not." They were walking along a narrow upstairs corridor in Jesus College, when he stopped suddenly and said, "Do you know they spell

Philosophers Walk without an apostrophe. Like, it's not possessive, the walk of philosophers. It's an activity—philosophers, they take walks. It's on the university maps as something philosophers do."

"And that's significant because?"

"It is," he said.

They were outside a door marked with a small brass plaque, *Dr. Jane Latimer, Associate Professor of English*. There were cartoons posted on the door culled mostly from the *New Yorker* and the newly defunct *Punch*, all relating one way or another to the Renaissance or esoteric scholarship.

Miranda knocked on the door and it immediately swung open to reveal a huge man hulking just inside who immediately thrust out his hand, grasping hers before she offered it and shaking firmly and relentlessly, relinquishing his grasp only when she determinedly withdrew, after which he reached past her to clasp Morgan's hand in both of his and began working it equally assiduously until Morgan too had to extricate himself forcibly from the man's grip. All the while, the big man was humming with compliments so facile Miranda could not believe even he took them seriously. And still, he was a good judge of character…

"… heard so much about you both and when I knew I was coming to Toronto, I thought, I'm coming to the home of the crimefighters *extraordinaire*, it's an honour, you are brilliant just brilliant and not academics, you have a reputation even at Princeton, may I call you David, David, thank you, and Miranda, you are even more beautiful than your photographs, the two of you just go together, you're so smart, it's exciting, such a relief to know there are bright people out there solving terrible crimes, you are charming, *charmant*, Miranda, I just love your smile, you reveal so much and so little—"

"This is our new Rector, Professor Felix Swan," Jane Latimer interrupted as she maneuvered around the looming figure and drew them into her office. The Rector was sweating profusely, his lank brown hair was plastered against his voluminous skull, his teeth glistened and his full lips were flecked with saliva, the residue from his loquacious salutation. Looking at Jane in acknowledgement of his introduction, his face immediately collapsed from prattling Buddha into a mask of authority. Then he turned to Miranda and a grin exploded on his face as drops of moisture dripped from his pale eyebrows. He grasped her hand again, ignoring Jane Latimer.

"We really must be friends," he said. "You and I and David. You know so many interesting people in Toronto, I'm sure you must. You will have to come to dinner. Since my mother died, quietly I might add, in her sleep, I've become something of a gourmet cook. Please say you'll come, we'll arrange it some time, I don't have my daybook, but we'll set a date soon. You do have the most wonderful smile."

Miranda tried to tune him out and in spite of herself found his unctuous gallantry almost attractive. Recognizing his conquest, Felix Swan abruptly turned to Morgan and touched him as if brushing off a fleck of lint from the front of his shirt, then let his hand rest briefly on his shoulder and spoke in a conspiratorial voice. "David, we'll have to have a few drinks and a giggle, man to man. I need to know you, to find out what the real David Morgan is like."

Heaven help us, thought Morgan but he only responded with a tight smile and moved closer to his erstwhile running partner who, acknowledging the awkwardness, finally took charge of the conversation.

"Professor Swan," she asserted in a voice strident enough it might almost be calling him to order, "Professor Swan is the newest member of the Bacon Society. He has been an adjunct for years, from his Princeton aerie, but when he joined us this year as our new Rector, he immediately signed on as a full fledged Baconian."

"Professor Latimer misleads you a little. I was a member of the Princeton Bacon Ensemble, and an associate of the Canadian conclave, not an adjunct. I have known Dieter Kurtz for decades and decades. He came to lecture at Princeton as my guest. Several times. A great man, a great man and a great loss. As you may know already, he was my mentor when I was an undergraduate here."

"You were a student at U of T? When?" asked Morgan.

"Oh years before you, dear boy. You see, I know your biography. Years and years ago. Like you, I am a citizen of Toronto. I so much admire how in spite of your background you've made such a name for yourself."

"Only if you read the crime sheets," said Morgan.

"Oh David, you're the most famous son of Cabbagetown, I'm sure of that, I'm sure. You and Hugh Garner, but he died before you were born."

"In 1979, actually."

"Well, never mind."

Swan shuffled a little to the side so that Miranda could get past him and join the other two near Jane Latimer's desk. As she sidled by, she glanced down and noticed his gargantuan feet, clad in highly polished worn black shoes. It must be difficult to find shoes his size. Poor man. The leather's cracked but they're gleaming. There's something touching about that.

"Felix, would you like me to get you a chair?" their host inquired.

"No thank you, Professor Latimer," he responded, bristling at her familiarity in front of people from outside the profession. "I believe I would rather stand." He leaned against one of her bookshelves which quaked for a moment as his massive frame sought equilibrium. "You just carry on with your meeting, Professor, I'm here *ex officio*, so the speak. Over to you."

"Actually," said Miranda, "we'll conduct the interview, if you don't mind." Her tone indicated she did not much care whether he minded or not. "You may stay if you'd like, Dr. Swan, although we'll need to speak to you in private later on."

Her presumption of authority in what he regarded as his personal fiefdom confused him. "Yes, of course," he said, shifting his full weight into balance as the bookcase teetered and came to rest. "I will just listen quietly, I like to know what is going on under my jurisdiction."

Morgan shot him a threatening glance. The brobdignagian hulk, his white shirt plastered against pink skin where his jacket was gaping open as it draped from his shoulders like a ill-fitting cape, moved back a pace and then halted, obviously deciding to stand his ground. Morgan turned, dismissing him like errant musak.

Jane Latimer took up her place behind the desk. For a few moments there was silence, apart from the shuffling of the Rector behind them, while Miranda and Morgan sat down and began looking over copies of the Bacon Society membership list, Jane Latimer having considerately made two for their convenience. She watched as both of them came to the one name universally recognizable to non-academics. Lionel Webb. Among the wealthiest men in the world. A communications magnate whose father had been a newspaper baron before him and whose grandfather on his father's side was elevated to a hereditary peerage during World War I, when he had been a senior advisor to the British government on colonial affairs. This was at a time when colonials were sorely needed and astoundingly expendable.

"Webb?" said Morgan. "The man is synonymous with *anonymous!*"

"Pardon?" said Miranda.

"If a great work of art goes at auction to an anonymous buyer, you can be sure there's a good chance it's him. He bought that Vermeer last month for twenty million—"

"Dollars?"

"U.S. He appears to be what you might call a pathological collector."

"And he's a member?" said Miranda, addressing Jane

Latimer.

"Yes he is," chimed in Felix Swan from behind them. "A wonderful man, he's just the nicest. If you want to meet him, I think I could arrange it."

"Thank you," said Miranda, without turning around. "I doubt we'll pay him a social call. There's been a murder, Mr. Swan. We'll make our own arrangements."

"Rector," said Swan.

"Pardon?"

"Dr." said Swan.

"Oh."

"Professor," said Swan.

"We get the idea," said Morgan.

"But David, of course, you must call me Felix, you must. I just so much hate the word Mister. Mister, Mister, Mister. That was my father's name. I went to Princeton to escape being Mister." As it seemed no one was interested, his voice trailed off into ruffled quietude.

"Mr. Webb is a member in good standing," said Jane Latimer. "Of course, he could call himself Lord Webb, if he cared to. Lord Ottermead, actually. But Mister seems preferable in Canada. He really is quite nice, once you get to know him. Pathological is rather unkind, , Detective Morgan. He has an insatiable appetite for cultural masterworks because he can afford to feed it. They will all go to museums eventually. So will his first editions of Bacon's *Novus Organum* and *De Augmentis Scientarum*."

"They're in lovely condition," said Swan from behind them. "Absolutely pristine."

"Absolutely pristine. I would have thought that was

redundant," said Morgan, swinging around in his chair. "Like 'dead corpse,' 'as I live and breathe,' 'or really lifelike.'"

"Saxon and Norman," said Swan. "'Cease and desist,' 'assault and battery,' 'break and enter.' Collateral damage from the Norman invasion."

"Linguistic anomalies relating to conquest," noted Jane Latimer.

"But *absolutely* and *pristine* are both Norman. They're different parts of speech, and the latter includes the former but not the former, the latter,'" said Miranda with pellucid clarity suggesting hers was the last word on the subject.

"Of course," said Swan, wounded. "One must resort to the vernacular sometimes to be understood." He intended his tone to be authoritative. He was a language specialist, Morgan had strayed into his territory, and Miranda added insult to injury with her linguistic acumen. Still, as he dripped sweat like a rain forest it was hard to take him seriously. Morgan only smiled and turned away.

"In fact," said Jane Latimer mischievously, "only at our last meeting the Rector was saying he'd die to own those very editions. Then, I believe, Professor Swan, you amended your declaration, 'I'd kill for those books.' I believe that's what you said. It was a pregnant moment, since each of us suspected any one of us might do the same. Still, it was the Rector who gave the sentiment wings, so to speak."

"Then aren't I fortunate it was Dieter Kurtz who died. Not Lord Ottermead—Lion, to his friends."

"I've read that he hates when people call him Lion," said Morgan.

"Oh really," said Felix Swan, sweating.

"Yes," Jane Latimer concurred, "I believe he does."

Miranda, shifted around in her chair to stare Swan in the eye. "You'd kill for a first edition of Bacon, would you?"

"Just something one says, dear Miranda. A figure of speech. You really must get to know me better."

"Oh, I shall," she said, then turning to Jane Latimer, she asked, "Did Professor Kurtz own any first editions?"

"Yes, in fact he possessed a very valuable copy of *Sylva Sylvarum*."

"That was the facsimile he was holding."

"He owned an original of the same. I imagine it's still in his house. He kept it in a controlled-environment case, humidity and temperature set to optimum conditions. Lionel Webb helped him set it up; the cabinet is a miniature version of Lionel's own cabinet of curiosities, his *sanctum sanctorum* with its computerized weather. The facsimile was someone's joke."

"As you said before," observed Morgan. "And Rector Swan. Would you have killed for that as well, Professor Kurtz's original edition."

"I am not inclined to violence, I have an international reputation."

"Is that an alibi?" said Miranda. "Or a character reference?"

"Reputation in what," asked Morgan.

"Medieval linguistics. It's a very esoteric field,

detective. But a man of your cerebral capacity would find it exciting, if you knew something about it."

"Perhaps I do."

"Oh!" said Swan, perplexed and suddenly wary, as if the detective's lack of academic credentials might conceal an intelligence to match his own. "You have gone up in my estimation," he added, conferring what he was evidently unaware was a nasty backhanded compliment.

"Thank you," said Morgan. "We'll have to do lunch some day and discuss the great vowel shift. I would love to explore your mind."

"Oh that would be exciting," said Swan, "of course, we must."

Jane Latimer and Miranda stared intently at Morgan, one admiring his social dexterity, and the other his casual deceit. Both women instinctively realized he knew nothing about 'the great vowel shift' or medieval linguistics, or whether or not Webb despised the name *Lion*, but they were charmed by how easily he penetrated the corpulent Rector's armour of superficiality to connect with the raw ego beneath. Generally, a flatterer is wary of flattery, but Morgan had found the way in.

Swan smiled and harrumphed and shuffled, first towards Miranda, touching the back of her chair and giving it a little shake, then, tipping his wispy wet forelock to Morgan and nodding gravely to Jane Latimer, he backed out of the room, mumbling that he would be available in his office but he had very important matters to attend to and meetings to conduct, so perhaps they could make an appointment with his secretary, and certainly they would sometime do lunch. The room seemed to breathe a palpable sigh of relief when he left.

chapter five

More About Bacon

Morgan closed the door. He sat down again beside Miranda, facing Jane Latimer who leaned over her desk with the narrow window backlighting her in a radiant glow. Even fully clothed in a modest blouse, she exuded sensuous good health, despite the stifling humidity. Her office was not air conditioned; the building was more than a hundred years old, built when late Victorianism prescribed style over comfort, with the result that air circulation was minimal, even with the windows open—which hers had not been in a generation.

"Well," she said in a stage whisper, "you have now met our redoubtable Rector, Professor Dr. Felix Swan."

"He's an interesting specimen," said Miranda. "His mood jumped around like a toad on a stove. Did he leave annoyed or are abrupt departures part of his charm?"

"A man never more appreciated than by his absence," said Morgan with dry good humour.

"And capable of murder," said Jane Latimer with an ambiguous cadence that might have meant she was making an assertion but possibly that she was asking a question, opening the subject to further discussion.

"As most of us are," said Miranda, " given the—"

"—opportunity—" Morgan chimed in.

"The circumstances. Why are you so chipper?"

"It must be the early morning run. Nothing stimulates the phagacites like a good workout at the break of day."

"The phagacites?" queried Jane Latimer, who thought she knew the arcane vocabulary of exercise and hyper-nutrition better than most.

"George Bernard Shaw," said Miranda. "It's a nonsense word, I don't remember which play. Neither does Morgan. Is Swan always that giddy?"

"No, but your achievement profile lies outside his range of influence, he was confused. He can be as smooth as a stealthy enema."

"Pardon?"

"He slips in with the most explosive results."

"You really don't like him!"

"Sometimes the only way to catch a man's character, find the right metaphor and stick with it."

"So he's known as 'the stealthy enema' by others as well?" said Miranda.

"I didn't coin the phrase, if that's what you mean, but I could give you a few others. Rector Felix Swan elicits vulgar epithets the way some people invite accolades. Is he actually a suspect?"

"Well, yes, although not on the A-list."

"And am I on the A-list?"

Miranda gazed into the woman's eyes. *She's enjoying this.* Morgan was sitting back in his chair, surveying the office artifacts, the requisite posters on either side of the window, the antiquated map of London with the Thames snaking through like a giant reptile, incongruously contained in a burnished aluminum frame. And the books. There were many books, it was a small office and the two side walls were teeming with books, some lying horizontally stacked over the vertical rows which on some shelves were two deep. The woman blinked several times and Miranda realized she was waiting to be interviewed.

"It would seem your name is at the top," Miranda responded cheerfully, pointing to the membership list she had been provided with, which had Jane Latimer's name on the first line, accompanied by the title, 'Acting President.' Instead of enjoining their host to reveal more of herself, however, Miranda shifted the conversation back to Felix Swan. Whatever might be discovered about Jane Latimer, it would not be done in her presence. The woman was too wily to reveal more than she wished.

"How did he end up the Rector of Jesus College?"

"He was invited."

"Exactly what does the rector of a college do?" asked Morgan.

"In our case, he's the CEO, the president."

"I thought rector was a religious function," said

Morgan. "So he's the boss."

"He is. There's a Board of Regents, and a Chairman of the Board. Lionel Webb. We're a secular college although we do have a chaplain. This year it's a Hindu, no beef in the cafeteria, lots of veggie burgers and chickpea meatballs."

"So Jesus is secular," said Morgan.

"Jesus might be surprised," said Miranda.

The other two looked at her blankly for a moment, then burst out laughing, while she glowed with her small triumph and took the lead in steering the conversation back to Swan.

"How does he do it, doesn't everyone see through the blather and slather?"

"You make him sound like a Clydesdale," Morgan observed appreciatively.

"He's relentlessly ambitious," said Jane. "His peers are stepping stones, which he kicks aside as he uses them to ford the river of his various dreams. He's universally despised by those he passes and adored by all ahead, the ones who count. He'll get where he has to go, no matter how many corpses are left in his wake."

"So to speak," said Miranda.

"So to speak."

"And you're not worried you might be among them."

"Not yet. I'm useful to him."

"How so?"

"Not as a scholar. He outweighs me. Pun intended. But he is in the thrall of the Bacon Society, and I am a power to be reckoned with among Baconites."

"Not Baconians?" said Morgan.

"The choice is academic."

"So to speak."

"I use them interchangeably. Bacon was a Freemason. Felix I think is a Mason. He sometimes betrays a sense of morbid confraternity with Bacon, as if their connection is beyond mortal grasp. It can be quite scary. He thinks of me as the high priestess, although God knows my reverence for Bacon is not the least bit mystical."

"The Masonic Lodge?" said Miranda. "Like the Rotary Club?"

"More like the Rosicrucians and Opus Dei. Masons are Shriners who achieve a certain degree of belonging and then qualify for admission to the most secret brotherhood of them all, where they establish a transcendent connection with the living and the dead."

"Like the Mormons," Morgan interjected. "The Church of Jesus Christ of Latter Day Saints, they baptize the dead."

"No," said Jane Latimer. "Quite the opposite. The Mormons are benevolent, even if their efforts seem futile; they perform rituals to welcome the departed into God's grace, the more the better. That's why they're genealogically obsessive, they're saving our ancestors, one by one, name by name. By contrast, the Masons are a closed order. The chosen few, bound by arcane rituals, descended through alchemical rites from the ancient builders of the pyramids, the stonemasons who died with the secrets of their order intact."

"Or were killed to make the tombs of their lords safe

for the dead," offered Morgan.

"Or found it a privilege to join them in death," said Miranda. "They sound like a cult, I always thought they were demented Rotarians."

"Those are Shriners. They ride around on their scooters in parades, behaving like prepubescents on speed. But once they cross over, flaunting their outer child becomes a disguise, classic misdirection for their weird solemn pursuits into the unfathomable depths."

"I thought you paid to get in, to make your way through the ranks. Like the Scientologists," said Morgan.

"You pay and you receive instruction, it's the same with virtually all cults and religions in the Western world, you ante up cash or obeisance or both," said Jane Latimer with authority.

"How do you know about the Masons," Miranda interjected.

"Bacon," said Jane Latimer. "You can't be a Baconian without coming face to face with Freemasonry. I wish I could say I used to lie on the floor in the upstairs hall of our mansion when I was a girl and listen through the stove-pipe vent to my father and his cronies whisper their terrible secrets."

"Why?" said Morgan.

"Oh, just to be more interesting."

Morgan and Miranda looked at her. She seemed interesting enough without fabricating a gothic childhood.

"Bacon was also a Rosicrucian," she said. "To be a scientist, in his day, was to be a philosopher and a mystic. He was both, he took all knowledge to be his province, and that included the works of man, of course, and of nature and the occult and the regions of darkness where they all intersect."

"What was Kurtz's interest in him? You said something about a German connection, a mystic text." Morgan remembered from his own studies about Bacon's mysticism, but he was not sure why a scholar of Kurtz's stature would pursue what seemed an apparent tangent. Perhaps that's how scholarship works, he thought. Through tangents, lacunae, detours, and dead-ends.

"Dieter Kurtz was convinced that Bacon was the true author of *Fama Fraternitatis*."

"Which was the Rosicrucian holy book and written in German."

"Yes, written in German. That was not a problem. Bacon was an educated man of his time, conversant in various languages."

"Enough to write a book"

"It's possible. It's not a holy book, exactly. It's more of a translation, drawing ancient arcanum through the darkness of time into a contemporary European idiom."

"Bringing the Rosicrucians back to life?"

"So to speak."

"By someone who called himself—?"

"Christian Rosenkreuz. It could have been Bacon."

Miranda decided once again to bring the conversation around to Felix Swan and the subject of their inquiry. In order to take control, she was uncharacteristically abrupt. "Do you think the Rector would be capable of murder?"

"As you said yourself, anyone could kill, depending on the circumstances."

"Could you?"

"Oh yes, I think so," she responded without hesitation. "There are times when I would like to eliminate Felix Swan, for example."

"I hope you're being ironic. Is he really so odious? Could you as easily have got rid of Dieter Kurtz? Is your animosity towards Swan personal or professional?"

"No, yes, possibly, and both."

"You are not being ironic; he really is odious; you could be a murderer; and your dislike of the Rector spans worlds?"

"Precisely. But I have an alibi, so Kurtz may have expired with a little help from his friends, yes, but not me, I was at home asleep."

"That's not generally considered an alibi," said Miranda.

"Oh, it could be," she responded with an insinuating smile.

"You were not alone?"

"If I was not alone, would I be sleeping?"

"So you were alone?"

"Why don't we wait and see whether or not an alibi is necessary," said Jane Latimer.

Miranda shrugged. She could not resist pursuing her curiosity about Felix Swan. The man seemed obviously a sycophant, so lacking in sincerity as to be ludicrous. There was something vulnerable about him, but also a meanness that protruded here and there like effulgent sores on a dimpled complexion. He was someone with an unwieldy physique who nurtured, teased, and gamboled with his ego in public like a small man walking a Rottweiler. He had very big feet, like Elvis.

"How did he get to be Rector?" she asked.

"As I said, he was invited. He has a very good reputation in his field and proven administrative skills. He was a local boy who made good at Princeton. It was kind of a homecoming."

"The prodigal returns," Morgan suggested, proving again that while he was sitting back in his chair and gazing about the room he was paying attention.

"Hardly the prodigal. I gather he led a sheltered life with his widowed mother, never squandered time or money, took her to live with him in New Jersey, and when he came back to Jesus he brought her ashes to the old family home in Rosedale, where he still resides."

"And?" said Miranda.

"And there's a rumour he might have been given a bit of an assist to leave Princeton."

"As in, they sent along letters extolling his virtues because they no longer wanted him around?" said Miranda.

"Something like that."

"Do you know why?"

"A thing about boys."

"Really?"

"Who knows. When he was appointed, rumours gathered momentum, I shouldn't be telling you this, old-timers talked about when he had been here as an undergraduate, how he and Kurtz had been awkwardly close, sort of an unnatural alliance that may have involved young boys—you want me to go on? I'm not sure whether this is relevant or just slanderous. It's serious enough, though, that there are rumours he is, you know, leaving Jesus."

"A crisis of faith?" said Morgan.

"Jesus the College," said Jane Latimer. "A crisis of confidence."

"He just arrived," said Miranda. "Do you suppose Professor Kurtz was in some way blackmailing him?"

"Whatever for," asked Jane Latimer, seemingly caught off guard. Then, recovering quickly, she said: "The university community is tolerant of most aberrations, so long as they don't interfere with research or teaching. And why? What could Kurtz possibly want from Felix Swan?"

"I think we'll need to have another talk with the Rector," said Morgan, rising to his feet. "He's moving inexorably towards the A-list."

"Why don't you go downstairs and make an appointment," said Miranda, letting her voice rise on the final syllables to convey bemusement at Swan's irritating self-importance. "I'll follow you down in a bit. I want to go over the rest of this list." She turned to Jane Latimer: "Can you spare me a little more time."

"Well, of course," was the response, and Miranda immediately realized she had once again handed narrative control to the professor. "There are several names in particular that will interest you."

"I'm off, then," said Morgan from the door. "Thanks

for the run. We'll keep in touch."

"You're most welcome, David. It was fun." She paused. "Say, if you two are free tonight, I wonder if you'd like to attend a most relevant party. It's our year-end gathering of the Bacon Society. The academic year, of course, not the calendar year." Then, to sweeten the invitation, she added, "It's at Lionel Webb's in Rosedale. The Bridle Path."

"*A most relevant party*, oh wow!" said Miranda. And they chortled in unison as an indication that none of them was overly impressed, while implicitly confessing to a common curiosity about the inordinately rich.

"You sound like Jill," said Morgan from his transitional posture, lounging against the door frame. "Oh wow, I've never heard you say 'oh wow' in your life."

"You haven't *heard* my whole life, Morgan."

"Is Jill your daughter?" asked Jane Latimer with an air of surprise. "I didn't know you were—oh, but of course, maybe you're ..."

Miranda and Morgan glanced at each other. How had this woman insinuated herself so comfortably into their lives when in fact she knew so little about them? She was, after all, a key source in a murder investigation and a possible suspect.

"She's my ward, she goes to Branksome Hall."

"Day student?"

"Boarder."

"What a great experience. I went to boarding school, hated every minute until it was over and I've missed it ever since."

"Where?" asked Miranda.

"Here. Havergal. Branksome and Havergal were notorious rivals. Still are, I believe."

"Yeah," said Morgan. "Well, I've to got work to do. I'm good for tonight if you are, Miranda. You make the arrangements." He walked off down the empty corridor whistling the Colonel Bogey March as a lingering gesture of goodbye.

"Quite the man, your partner. I'm not sure if running is his destiny."

"Don't tell him that or we'll never get him off the streets."

"Likes a good challenge, does he?"

"Can't resist. Are you a Toronto grad, too?"

"You mean, as well as Felix Swan?"

"And Morgan and myself, we both went here. Victoria College, but at different times. He's much older."

"Much."

"Nearly five years."

"I would have thought more."

"Thank you. You graduated from U of T?"

"I did my Bachelor's and Master's here, then went to Cambridge for a D. Litt."

"And took up running in the meadowlands along the Cam."

"You know your way around Cambridge, do you?"

"No, but I took a Romantics course, way back when. I remember Byron and his buddies went rambling beside the River Cam, with pauses for trysts and for plunges into its pristine depths."

"There's a place called Byron's Pool, upstream at Grantchester. It's not very deep, you can pole your way around in a punt. And it's not exactly pristine. And not very deep. You can touch bottom but you can't see it."

"Did you do it?" said Miranda, apparently out of the blue. "Did you kill Dieter Kurtz ? It would make life easier all around if you spoke up. We'd help you build a case for justifiable homicide."

"Why?"

"Good question. Forget I said that. Did you?"

"No, of course not. But thanks for your offer."

chapter six

Various Persons Of Interest

Miranda sat back in her chair and scrutinized this woman who was both ally and adversary. She knew Jane Latimer was hardly about to confess, but if she had indeed murdered Kurtz and was amusing herself in the aftermath, Miranda too could play the game, lead her on with affable banter, until sooner or later she would let down her guard, let something of the truth slip through. Meanwhile, Jane Latimer was a valuable resource, to be exploited with wit, not interrogation. Unless forensics came up with some revelation to deflate her aplomb, she was superb in the controlled delivery of information, a match for any interrogator.

Professor Latimer shuffled papers on her desk, drawing Miranda's attention back to the point of her inquiry.

"Who is Li Po?" said Miranda, picking his name from

the list for its mellifluous incongruity.

"Professor Po, you will like him."

"That's not the point," she responded testily. She was worried that the members of the Bacon Society might be of more interest than the murder of their erstwhile leader. Had she been influenced by Jane Latimer's representation of the victim as a thoroughly unlikable character? Was she being drawn into sympathy with a murderous cabal, influenced by the pathology of people who wished him dead? Was she precariously close to complicity, herself? Miranda played with the rhetoric of paranoia for a moment, then relaxed. In an effort to soften her retort, she added: "It's necessary to keep a suspect at arm's length, if you're ever to penetrate the armour of innocence."

"And I suppose innocence is armour for guilty and not guilty alike. Li Po is innocence personified, a lovely old man with a wispy white beard, a soft voice that tinkles and eyes like a raptor that betray wicked intelligence beneath an aura of passive gentility."

"A fulsome description. Thank you." This woman is interpreting reality for me, thought Miranda. "Wasn't Li Po a poet?" she asked.

"That was a different Li Po," said Jane Latimer. "Ming Dynasty. Our Li Po is a philosopher, a specialist in European literatures, but at heart a philosopher. He is retired. He taught all his life at the University of Lanchou, except during the Cultural Revolution when he worked as a farm labourer."

"Then how on earth did he get here?"

"He has a nephew, Yijun Sung, who owns a restaurant

in Chinatown. He brought the old man over to live with him. He helps a little."

"In the restaurant?"

"He is very fond of his nephew, who doesn't realize what a sacrifice his uncle made, abandoning an honourable old age in the land of his birth to reaffirm the ancestral legacy of his brother's progeny."

"In other words, each of them thinks he's made a sacrifice for the other."

"Exactly."

"I'd like to meet this Li Po. He's next on the list, after Hermione MacGregor. Right above Felix Swan. Who is followed by Hermione McCloud. Two Hermiones. Extraordinary. Are they similar?"

"Same age, both female, each vies with the other in her devotion to Bacon, same Presbyterian backgrounds, both single, elderly—I think they'd qualify as spinsters—both sharp as two tacks in a barrel, and as utterly different in personality as you could possibly imagine."

"The two Hermiones. Cold-blooded killer doesn't come immediately to mind when I think of even one Hermione. Nor when I think of Professor Li Po, for that matter."

"Ah, but Hermione Mac was once in counter-intelligence—during the war."

"World War Two?"

"Yes."

"Good grief, how old is she."

"They're both well into their seventies."

"She must have been a child spy."

"She was, she was eighteen at the end of the war."

"And Hermione McCloud."

"Hermione M, she's a sweet old thing, she was charged with murdering her mother but never convicted, the charges were dropped."

Miranda was briefly nonplussed, but managed to ask: "Was it euthanasia?"

"So they said."

"Large inheritance?"

"Apparently."

"But you say she's a sweet old thing?"

"She's a dear."

"And Hermione the Spy, what about her?"

"Hermione Mac, she's tart, as in acerbic, biting, caustic, scathing, mordant."

"Ah. I would have thought the spy would be serene, and the mother-killer mordant. How did the mother die?"

"Drowned in a bathtub. Or electrocuted. Anyway, it was in the bathtub."

"Tell me, do each of these people on your list own original copies of Bacon?"

"Oh no, not at all. They would all like to, of course. I imagine any one of us would sell our souls for an original in mint condition."

"Even you?"

"Especially me, but then, I don't place all that much value on my soul."

"What about Li Po?"

"Absolutely. He was a professor of European

literatures. We amuse him, he insists Western art records our desire to be whatever we are not. He is a man who has seen much, and he finds in early printed texts just the right balance of artistry and accessibility—limited accessibility, of course, since not more than a few thousand people in England could read when Bacon was writing."

"So it's the book, he likes, more than the content."

"I would say a characteristic of the Society is our shared appreciation of the book, both open and closed. The thing and what it contains."

"Does Li Po own any early texts of his own?"

"Not unless he left them in China. When he is given an original edition to examine, he holds it like a souvenir of a long lost child. It is touching, how sad his love is for such a beautiful thing."

"You say he has seen much. Was it during the rise of the Red Guard?"

"He is old. As a student he is said to have been on the Long March with Mao Zedong. He saw many die when they retreated 10,000 kilometres across China on foot, and after the war and the Japanese occupation he waded with Mao through fields full of corpses to political triumph, and then he retired to Lanchou. I think he found the brutality of the Cultural Revolution tolerable in comparison. So I was told."

"By whom?"

"Dieter Kurtz. There was a curious bond between the two old men, they shared terrible secrets. We knew by the impenetrable walls they would build around their private discourse; they let no one in, no one."

"Yet Kurtz told you."

The woman's eyes flashed for an instant, then turned limpid. It was enough. For the first time, Jane Latimer revealed that her armour could be breached.

"Are you up for a late lunch?" she asked, rising from behind her desk in the time-honoured gesture of drawing an interview to a close.

"What did you have in mind?" Miranda was intrigued by the other woman's need to maintain control.

"We'll meet Li Po. Let's pick up Morgan and walk over to Chinatown for dim sum."

"Good," said Miranda. "And we're on for tonight. Do you want to give me the address and the time."

"Why don't we meet and go together," said Jane Latimer. "About seven-thirty. I'll call Webb and let him know I'm bringing friends."

"Tell him who we are."

"Of course."

"That we're detectives investigating the murder of Dieter Kurtz, that we're coming on business."

"Of course."

Much as Miranda would like to have attended the meeting of the Bacon Society as an uncompromised guest or, better yet, as a fly on the wall, she recognized the impropriety, not to say legal compromise, of not declaring her purpose for being there.

"I'll call when I get back from lunch," said Jane Latimer in a reassuring tone that Miranda found slightly grating. "Let's go and see how your partner made out with Felix Swan."

"Heaven forbid," said Miranda and they both feigned a grimace of revulsion.

The two women walked down the dreary corridor, which had been painted institutional ochre before they were born, and descended the stairs, coming out opposite the Office of the Rector from which Morgan was just emerging.

"Ah, there you are," called Swan, as if their whereabouts had been in doubt. "David was telling me you're coming to Lion's tonight. Delighted. Delightful. I'll call and make the arrangements, Jane, don't you bother."

"Make sure he understands we're coming on police business," said Miranda, interrupting his flow of chatter before Jane Latimer had a chance to recover the initiative.

"Of course, of course, but it will be social as well. He's such a dear man, a wonderful host, even if you solve the murder over *hors d'oeuvres*, he'll make you feel it was planned in advance, the gathering of the coven, just for your benefit. Can I take you to lunch? The Faculty Club has excellent food and fine paintings, Emily Carrs and a lovely Tom Thompson, a classic in the vernacular style."

"Thank you," said Jane Latimer, arousing a brief look of puzzlement on the Rector's face. It had not occurred to him that the invitation might include her. "We have other plans, sorry, so kind, see you tonight." She grasped Morgan's arm and steered him towards the exit, with Miranda following close beside, leaving Felix Swan with a faint damp smile on his face, filling the door frame like an abandoned Buddha.

"That was a close call," said Jane Latimer as the main

door to Jesus College closed in their wake with an ambivalent groan. Miranda and Morgan flanked her at the top of the steps, each sharing her relief. The building rose up behind them, a gothic monstrosity looming forward as if it were going to reach out and enfold them in its demonic embrace. As they stood together, momentarily gathering their bearings, the door burst open and a dishevelled young woman was disgorged into their midst, stumbling against not one but all three.

"Oh my God," she mumbled and disengaging from her interceptors jounced down the stone stairs, two at a time, and disappeared around the dense shrubbery that disguised the front of the building as an institutional edifice and not some architectural beast slouching towards the centre of campus.

"That," said Jane Latimer, "was Jennifer Pluck."

"I'm sure it was," said Miranda. "Who is Jennifer Pluck?"

"Let's tear ourselves away from this place," Jane Latimer responded, starting down the steps ahead of them. "If we don't get to the Golden Dragon soon, there'll be nothing left to eat."

"I take it we are about to meet Li Po," said Morgan.

"How did you know?" said Jane Latimer, leading the way across University Circle.

Miranda nodded affirmation and asked again: "Who is Jennifer Pluck? You said her name as if we should know her."

"You will. She's a post-doctoral fellow, a *protégé* of Felix Swan. You'll meet her tonight."

"Her name is not on the list," said Miranda.

"Oh, it is, it should be, let me see, no it isn't. None of us noticed there are only eleven names. Yes, her name should be on."

"Does she always behave like that?"

"Like what? Like she's in a perpetual state of panic, like a woman distraught by a haunting of horrors, pursued by demons or worse? Yes, she's always like that. And invariably she's in disguise."

"Disguise?" said Miranda.

"Wears her hair in the worst possible way, bad glasses, slumps impossibly, dresses in clothes from a bargain bin at Wal-Mart. But she's the proverbial hidden beauty, everyone knows if she stood up straight, had a good bath, dressed right, and smiled, she'd be stunning. And Pluck knows it too, that's what makes it a disguise and not just bad grooming."

"Not much of a disguise, if everyone knows it's a disguise," Miranda observed.

"I'm looking forward to meeting her," said Morgan.

"You already have."

chapter seven

Li Po

The Three of them strode side by side along College Street, then down Spadina past the multicultural curiosity shops and vegetable stands into the heart of Chinatown. Morgan loved the rich unfamiliar smells and the flamboyant ethnicity and yet he was uneasy, surrounded by colours and odours and sounds that defined themselves in his mind by their difference from the Toronto he had grown up in. *Maybe I need sensitivity training*, he thought, without finding the notion embarrassing.

"Did the Rector have an alibi," Miranda asked him as they rounded the corner onto Dundas, walking beneath a welter of neon signs with Chinese characters and flashing arrows. English and the Roman alphabet were suddenly effaced in the dazzle. This was alien territory and they were outsiders.

"Yeah," he responded over the din. "Says he was working on campus in the Robarts Library. Most of the night. Said there should be witnesses. The only time the Rector can keep up with his scholarly work, he told me, is when the world sleeps."

"So he may or may not be able to prove he was there."

"And he ever so delicately suggested the onus was on us to prove otherwise. Since there were no charges, it wasn't his responsibility to prove where he was. He thought that was amusing, how the system works to the villain's advantage."

"And is he the villain?" asked Jane Latimer, holding the street-level door of the Golden Dragon open.

Morgan and Miranda stood aside to let her precede them up shabby stairs sandwiched between dingy pastel walls. Miranda caught his eye and narrowed her own eyes, cautioning him not to relax. Morgan grimaced in return, a good-natured indication that he was fully aware of their roles.

"Possibly he is," he responded. "The villain," he clarified. "Given your helpful list, we'll work by a process of elimination. And when the list is done, if we still haven't solved the case, we'll make up another list of our own. Are there any more Jennifer Plucks?"

"?"

"Names left off."

"Not on purpose." Jane Latimer looked back and smiled, then pulled open the large glass door at the top of the stairs that led into a vast and opulent dining room appointed in scarlet and ebony, well-lit and bustling, with stainless steel trolleys rolling among a virtual labyrinth of gleaming black tables that were piled with steam-baskets and small porcelain bowls of food and propelled by an army of women, a room designed to celebrate the senses without distracting from the business at hand, which was the consumption of a profuse variety of bite-size morsels, a room in which they appeared to be the only non-Chinese.

Morgan leaned over and unaccountably whispered into Miranda's ear, "The Rector and I, we talked mostly about Saint Augustine." He let his voice trail off as a tall young man hurried over to them and greeted Jane Latimer effusively. He was dressed in the kind of modified tuxedo favoured by restaurateurs even in the middle of the day,

"You are here to see my uncle?" he said. "Or to have dim sum? Perhaps both? It is good to see you, Professor. For your friends, is this their first time to the Golden Dragon? You are most welcome, ladies and gentleman. Please, follow me." And he led them in a small procession through the sumptuous maze to an empty table near the kitchen doors.

"Here is excellent. You will have your first choice of food and it is more quiet for conversation." He indicated with a sweep of his hand the clatter and rumble that filled the room with an air of the carnivalesque. "I will tell my uncle that Professor Jane Latimer is here, he will be pleased."

As the young man, presumably Yijun Sung, disappeared into the kitchen, Miranda could not help but notice the resounding clatter surging through the swinging doors and wondered if this, indeed, was a good place to talk. Were they being parked out of the way?

Anticipating Miranda's concern, Jane Latimer had already risen to her feet. She looked around, spied another free table away from the doors, and led the others towards it. "Here," she said. "This is better. And I don't think anyone will have trouble finding us. We do stand out in the crowd." They sat down and almost immediately a woman appeared from behind them with a large pot of green tea and three small cups which she placed without undue ceremony in front of each, along with chopsticks and a rice bowl.

"You like sticky rice," she announced, nodding sagaciously, as if this was something she was sure of, learned in the brief time she had been in Canada. Westerners invariably want rice wrapped in lotus leaves and never ever ask for chicken feet.

"Thank you," said Jane, who had assumed the role of host although Miranda and Morgan were quite comfortable with the rituals and delicacies of dim sum.

As trolleys in rapid succession appeared at their table and they loaded up with plates of shrimp, chicken, and pork bits wrapped in rice-flour packets to accompany their sticky rice, they were hardly aware that a slight elderly man had appeared close by and stood waiting to be noticed once the culinary commotion subsided. When Miranda saw him, she realized it was Li Po and that his apparent reticence was due neither to courtesy nor timidity, but to the natural refinement of a man interested more in observing the world than interrupting its flow.

Miranda rose to her feet, bowed slightly, and held out her hand, which the small man took with a smile of genuine interest and, clasping it firmly between both of his, gave it a gentle but deliberate squeeze, while bowing slightly in return.

"Professor Li Po," exclaimed Jane. "Please, will you join us, I want you to meet my friends."

"Professor Jane Latimer. It is always good to see you. Please, please sit down. If I may I will just have a cup of your tea. These friends are from the Police Department, I expect." He gestured over his shoulder and almost immediately a cup was placed in front of a chair beside Morgan, whom he addressed as he sat down. "You will want to interview me about the untimely death of Professor Kurtz. Please, continue eating, enjoy your dim sum. I will sit here with you and we will consider the weather until you are finished. Then we will discuss death as you please."

"I am Detective Sergeant Miranda Quin," said Miranda, intrigued by his recognition of their police status, but even more by the fact that he knew about the murder. It would not have been in the morning papers. She had not noticed a television crew on the scene when she left. Perhaps a local radio station had carried the story. So distinct did Chinatown seem from the rest of the city, it fascinated her that news from the outside had penetrated the boundaries of ethnic difference so quickly. "This is Detective Sergeant Morgan," she continued, then added, "I suppose that's what Canadians talk about when there's nothing to say, isn't it? The weather."

"Or hockey, Detective Quin. Everyone everywhere talks about weather. In Canada, perhaps with more gravity than other places. The weather here is not so serious as you think. No monsoons, few hurricanes or tornadoes, the occasional hot spell. And in winter, cold like hell." He chuckled at his own mastery of the colloquial idiom. "We will learn more about each other discussing the weather than by interrogation, perhaps. There is no hurry. Time will wait."

"Time is impatient," said Morgan, mouthing a *shu mai* dumpling. He spoke with sufficient gravitas to make his pomposity seem ironic.

"I was not being so profound," Li Po responded. "It is we who are impatient."

Miranda looked from one to the other. Was this an exchange of Zen postulations or of fortune cookie insights? She had no desire to risk looking foolish by throwing in a quip of her own.

Jane Latimer displayed no such reticence. "I would think time is the sound of a stone falling in a bottomless well," she offered.

So it *is* a game of metaphors, thought Miranda. *Time is a clock face without hands*. She said nothing.. *Why do we give clocks human characteristics?*

Since no-one had any further reflections on the nature of time and human consciousness, they lapsed into a cursory discussion of the brutality of Toronto's current heat wave. From there, the discussion easily shifted to Francis

Bacon.

"How did a man from Lanchou become so interested in a seventeenth century English philosopher-scientist?" Miranda asked Li Po, and in the brief pause while he considered his response she went on, "Did you study in Europe, perhaps?" Then, for a reason she could not fathom, she further added, "At the Sorbonne?"

Li Po said, almost to himself, placing the words in oral italics, "*They are ill discoverers that think there is no land, when they can see nothing but sea.*' Francis Bacon wrote that. Yes, I studied at the Sorbonne for one year. And at Oxford for one year and at Freiberg. I was going to spend one year in Rome as well, but it was necessary for me to return to China."

She must have read about him and forgotten, she thought. Morgan might have recognized a French inflection to the old man's English, even a nuance of the Sorbonne, he had an impeccable ear for such things. But Miranda knew she would not.

"I was interested in Francis Bacon before I travelled from China. There was no one who articulated so well that period of radical change in Western civilization by which even in childhood I was so mesmerized."

Like so many academics who adopt English as their second language, he spoke with a formal precision that made the ordinary seem exotic. Miranda looked at him with expectation, encouraging him to go on.

"Europe crept slowly from the lingering darkness of the Middle Ages, you see, while the Ming Dynasty was flourishing. Europe entered a period of wonder, the cult

The Dead Scholar

of progress began that has lasted to the present day. The Ming era was perhaps a high point in Chinese civilization, but for you, this was a new beginning. You perceived yourselves to be born again, a re-naissance based on misapprehensions of the classical past."

Miranda felt like she was back in the lecture halls as an undergraduate. Actively listening, passively receiving. *Passive-attentive, it sounds like a syndrome.* She smiled.

"Your bleak and mystical construction of God was no longer the answer to everything. There was a period of short duration when you hovered between the old and the new, the only time, perhaps, in your history when the world exceeded the limits of your imagination."

Miranda played with the phrase, letting it unravel, less sure what it meant the more she thought about it—*when the world exceeded the limits of imagination.* She glanced at Morgan. They would have to discuss this over coffee at Starbucks. He was toying with the same phrase, she was certain; she realized it was her partner's attentiveness as much as her own that encouraged the old man to continue.

"I was entranced by that brief epoch of infinite genius—before the Enlightenment took hold, before science declared awe and the sublime to be obsolete. The time of Michelangelo and Shakespeare, Leonardo and Erasmus and Bacon. You went from understanding the world through religion to forcing it into submission with technology and what you curiously describe as 'humanism.' I wanted to study the transition. You are a curious people; I wanted to study you at your best."

"Oh dear," said Miranda. "The best is over?"

"Do you consider us a people?" said Morgan. "I suppose we talk about the Chinese the same way, erroneously, I'm sure—but the Western World? We have murdered more of our own people in the last century than," he paused, "than imaginable. That would seem to give the lie to Euro-American kinship."

"Not so," Li Po responded with a professorial air of authority. "The innumerable millions who died in Western wars were victims of internecine squabbles, the quarrels of siblings. Even Japan, Japan's ferocity in World War Two was born out of a mimic mutation, the Westernized East—"

"I'm not sure many Japanese would agree."

"They were China's enemy, they and the British; the outsiders, and we were our own enemy—the overlords—the burden of the past—our enslavement to history."

"Professor Li Po is a patriot," Jane Latimer interceded, "and a distinguished scholar. He has published widely on Bacon in English and French, and in German and Italian."

"And in Chinese," said his nephew, Yijun Sung, who had stopped at his uncle's shoulder to see if the service was acceptable and the food without notable flaws.

"Perfect," said Morgan. "Excellent."

With that, Yijun Sung moved away, gliding in his black dinner jacket through the maze from table to table, at each making the same delicate inquiry in a gesture of entrepreneurial hospitality.

"I do not talk about things of my own past," said

Li Po. "In China, to do so is like trying to remember a dream. Sometimes, it is best to leave the past in the past. And here, I do not talk about such things because no one is interested. My nephew, he belongs to the Chamber of Commerce. You have made me loquacious, Detective Morgan, Detective Quin. Not careless, however. There is nothing to hide, or to hide from. Perhaps you would like to discuss murder now."

"For a start, how did you know Dieter Kurtz was murdered?" asked Miranda.

"One hears such things very quickly," Li Po responded solemnly. "The death of a great man is felt by everyone; the death of a legendary professor on Philosophers Walk resounds through the ether." He smiled, evidently pleased with his wry observation.

"Professor," said Miranda, with a wry smile of her own, "I think you find humour in your colleague's murder."

"Of course, Detective Quin, murder allows for a great deal of humour, depending on the victim, the circumstances, and who is having the discussion."

Miranda thought of the sometimes sinister humour in Agatha Christie, or between herself and her partner.

"Humour can be a profound response to an untimely death," he continued. "It can be an evasion of responsibility or of the mortal condition, itself. It can be a reasonable acknowledgement of the absurd."

"We see a lot of that," said Morgan.

"What?" said Jane Latimer.

"Absurdity, death by murder is invariably absurd."

"Depending on your perspective," said Li Po. "Death

is perhaps nothing, but dying is absurd."

"Exactly," said Morgan. "Did someone phone to tell you?"

"Professor Jane Latimer emailed the news of our colleague's passing," said Li Po. "There is no mystery."

"No," said Jane Latimer. "I did not." The two of them looked at each other and a shadow of puzzled concern crossed their faces.

"Now there *is* a mystery," said Morgan.

"I assumed it was you," said Li Po to the Acting President of the Bacon Society.

"No," she responded emphatically. "It wasn't."

"Did you receive a similar message?"

"I don't know, I haven't checked, I was with them."

Miranda and Morgan both sipped their tea, waiting for clarity.

"We could look on my nephew's computer. Can you access your e-mail from here?"

She nodded in the affirmative. "If it was a Bacon Society mailing, it could have been from anyone on the list," she explained, apparently as much to herself as the others.

"I believe that is not the case," said Li Po. "It seems it was not from me and it was not from you. And it is most unlikely that it was from Professor Dieter Kurtz."

Miranda leaned back to address them both. "You have a Bacon chat room?" she asked.

"No," Jane Latimer explained. "Not exactly. It is a closed forum. We are each set up to do multiple mailings to the entire group. Any and all of us have immediate access to the others. We chat among ourselves."

"Then it won't be difficult to trace the murder announcement," said Miranda. "Our people should be able to track it down."

"Eavesdropping is not beyond the realm of possibility," said Morgan. "It could be from an outsider, a homicidal hacker with esoteric proclivities."

"Even I have problems imagining someone spying on discussions of seventeenth century texts," said Jane Latimer. "Most people might find debates on Renaissance teleology, taxonomy, and gossip not of much interest. Not when they could be checking out penis extenders and inflatable dolls."

"Let's see if Professor Li Po's nephew will let us use his computer," said Miranda.

She looked up and Yijun Sung was standing at Li Po's side, having apparently responded to his uncle's need without an overt summons.

"Yes, of course," said Yijun Sung. "Follow me please." He led the way and the other four trooped after him through the big swinging doors into the kitchen, through a small army of cooks and assistants, through crates and boxes piled high with Chinese labels emblazoned on their sides, and into a small office at the back. When the door closed behind them, they were in another world. It could have been the office of a rising executive on Bay Street, except there was no outside window.

"It's here," exclaimed Jane Latimer, after appropriate maneuvering on the computer to access her e-mail account. "Look at this:

Professor Dieter Kurtz will be unable to participate in the conclave this evening at the home of Mr. Lionel Webb as he was struck off the rolls last night on Philosopher's Walk. All others, presumably, will be in attendance. A light dinner will be served."

"Sounds almost like Webb, reaffirming a previous invitation," said Miranda. "Who else would say, 'a light dinner will be served.'"

"Oh, any of us,' said Jane Latimer. "That's standard procedure, even down to the wording. Of course, a light dinner at my place might be chips and dips; at Webb's it will be *canapés* and *hors d'oeuvres*."

Miranda leaned forward, examining the screen for a return address, then reached over and pressed 'print.' A brief whirring preceded the emergence of a single sheet from the printer which she scanned, then passed over to Morgan who examined it for a moment, folded it, and handed it back for her to put in her purse.

"There's no indication who it's from," Morgan observed. He seemed to drift off for a moment, then pronounced, "There's an archness about the language that suggests it came from someone trying to sound like an academic. Contrary to what you've suggested, Profesor Li Po, I expect it will be from Kurtz."

"What!" exclaimed Miranda.

"Whoever did this isn't stupid," said Morgan. "He, or she, as the case may be, would know how easy it is to trace an e-mail to its origin. If it were me, I would send from Kurtz's computer, the one source that leads to a very dead end. Check the time the message was received. I'll bet it's before the body was even discovered."

"6:04:32. You're on a roll, Morgan. Now which computer? Did he have one in his office and one at home?"

"I think it's time we check out both," he said. Pulling three twenties from his wallet, he handed them to Yijun Sung. "Thanks very much for lunch," he said.

"Don't you want a receipt, Detective? I am sure Metropolitan Toronto would reimburse your expenses." Yijun Sung tucked the money into a top drawer in his desk and proceeded to write out a bill for sixty dollars.

"I don't think it cost that much," said Miranda, reading the figure upside down.

"Of course," said Yijun Sung, opening the drawer and handing Morgan a twenty. "We do not want to be accused of fraudulence." He wrote out another receipt, including a brief text in Chinese script, and tore up the first. "Thank you so much for your patronage, Detectives. I hope you will return some time when you are able to enjoy the food."

"Oh, but we did," said Miranda.

All five were now standing, although Yijun Sung remained behind his desk. Among tables he was a restaurateur, but in this room he was an executive. He nodded graciously to Morgan and Miranda and Jane Latimer. Li Po gave his assurance he would see them at Lionel Webb's and shook their hands with the firm and gentle grasp of a natural gentleman.

Out on the street, Miranda confided in a soft voice, "He hardly seems capable of murder." Then, realizing she was addressing Jane Latimer as well as Morgan, she qualified her statement, "Professor Li Po seems very nice. It would be a shame if he were the killer."

"But possible," said Jane in her ambivalent tone that hovered between posing a question and making a declaration. "Possible," she repeated.

Miranda turned to her and held out her hand. "There is no A-list or B-list, everyone qualifies. Thank you so much for your help. I have your address—we'll pick you up at seven-thirty."

She was leaving no doubt that this was the end of their extended interview. Whichever direction Jane Latimer might choose to get back to her office, Miranda's body language indicated that she and Morgan would be going the opposite way. There was a moment's hesitation, then their new friend and possible murder suspect smiled, squinted at Morgan in what might have passed for a wink and walked off along Dundas Street, back towards the university campus.

chapter eight
Jennifer Pluck

When they arrived at Kurtz's home, not far from where Morgan lived in the Annex and as easily within walking distance to the university as it was to Police Headquarters, they had parsed the lunch conversation as meticulously as grammarians looking for flaws in a counterfeit text. While Professor Li Po had seemed a wise old man misplaced in a world of cultural compromise, both agreed there was an element of menace in his facile inscrutability. He was too easily amused by death. His guileless poise apparently concealed a past washed in blood.

And they agreed that Jane Latimer's quiet manipulation of the investigation, while perhaps more helpful than she realized, was transparently self-serving. But to what end, that puzzled them: to conceal her own guilt, to implicate others, to obscure the truth? To lead them to the killer, to lead them away, to explain the moral necessity of an old scoundrel's violent death? At this point, answers begged questions.

"You know," said Morgan as they paused on the sidewalk in front of a small brick house painted solemn grey, with a sign posted on the door indicating it was a secured site pending police investigation. "Begging the question means avoiding the question, not asking for it."

"What on earth are you talking about?"

"I was thinking, we seem to be accumulating answers but we don't know the right questions, they're beggared."

"Morgan, what does go on in your mind?"

"They always get it wrong on the CBC, they talk about something begging the question, and they mean just the opposite, they mean something implies a particular antecedent, it doesn't, begging the question means—"

"David."

"You never call me David."

"Let it drop."

"Let what drop?"

"Thank you."

"Do we have a key."

"The door should be open. Forensics were over this morning. There should be a cop on duty."

"I don't see anyone." He tried the door. It was locked. "They've been and gone. Do you want to call for a key? Let's check out back, see if we can get in?" He was already on his way along the narrow walkway at the side of the house before she could respond.

The screen-door at the back was ajar and the inner door into the kitchen was unlocked. Miranda followed him in. The kitchen was immaculate. They knew Kurtz lived alone, but this was like a display in a home show. It was as if no one lived here at all. There was no food out on the counter, not a can or a bottle or a bag, not so much as a salt shaker or a butter dish.

Taped to the refrigerator door was a piece of folded blue notepaper inscribed with a flourish of dark letters: *antiquitas saeculi juventus mundi.*

Morgan opened the refrigerator. It was well stocked with items all placed in an orderly fashion, butter in the butter cove, cheese in the cheese drawer, vegetables in the crisper, everything layered top to bottom in the appropriate temperature planes.

He closed the fridge door. Someone else might have posted a comic strip or a political cartoon. Not Professor Kurtz, he apparently had little need to share casual homilies or no one to share them with. Despite the Germanic lettering, the note was in Latin.

"What do you make of this," he asked Miranda. *Antiquitas saeculi juventus mundi.* The maddening thing about Latin was how familiar it looked even when it remained unintelligible.

She mouthed the words, thought for a minute, then explained: "'Antique football sale on Monday.'"

"Close," he said, having pulled the note away from the door and opened it up. They spoke very softly in deference to the emptiness of the house. "Says here it's from Bacon's *The Advancement of Learning*. It means 'ancient times were the youth of the world.' Actually, Bacon's full title is *The Proficience and the Advancement of Learning*."

"Good for you," said Miranda.

"Nice reversal, isn't it. We are the oldest people who have ever lived, measuring from the beginning. Antiquity was our youth. The oldest is youngest. The father is child to the man."

"Morgan, I get it."

"Why *football*?"

"Juventus is a football team, Morgan. Italian. I think from Turin."

"How on earth do you know that."

"Dated a soccer fan."

Miranda opened several cupboards. Dishes were stacked neatly and unopened condiments were arranged in receding rows—he obviously bought in multiples. Spices in little cans were arranged alphabetically, separate from the similar arrangement of herbs. Miranda had never known anyone to cull out their herbs from their spices.

Moving along a hall towards the front of the house, Morgan peered to the right, into an austerely appointed dining room with blond furnishings, then he opened a door to the left. It was a broom closet, with several brooms, some still with their bristles wrapped. He opened the next door and was met by an hysterical gasping for breath as a woman seated on the toilet stared at him in wide-eyed horror.

"Oh my God," her voice rattled, "my God, you scared me. Get out."

"Miss Pluck, I presume," said Morgan with feigned nonchalance, not sure how best to extricate himself from the scene without seeming excessively prudish.

"Shut the fucking door," she said.

"Yes, of course," he said, and having already stepped into the room he stepped back and pulled the door sharply towards him so that he was standing with it square in his face as Miranda grasped his arm and turned him around.

"I believe I have just met Miss Jennifer Pluck," he said.

Miranda reached past him and rapped her knuckles with authority on the door. "Miss Pluck, we're police, we'd like to talk to you."

There was a flushing sound, and a click of the door lock, then another click as it was unlocked again, then the door opened a crack and then all the way. Jennifer Pluck stood framed in the doorway as if the room behind were a private sanctuary. She seemed surprised that it was they who regarded her as the interloper, but not at all surprised that they knew who she was.

"Would you mind telling us what you're doing here," Miranda asked with modulated severity, this in response to the young woman's look that somehow managed to convey both fear and defiance? Jane Latimer had been off the mark about her; she certainly was a picture of dishevelment but she was not in need of a bath. In fact, her wild array of clothing, her skin and her hair, were immaculate, affirming the impression that she was in disguise, projecting at the least a borrowed personality.

"I have got a key," said the young woman. "How did *you* get in?"

"This house is posted, Miss Pluck. It's part of a police investigation. Homicide. But of course you knew that, you know Professor Kurtz was murdered. Why do you have a key?"

"Did you come in through the back?" said Jennifer Pluck, looking over Miranda's shoulder, noting the door to the yard was still open, her mind working furiously to assimilate the shift in the facts to include their intrusion. She was obviously not a person accustomed to coping with sudden changes of circumstance. Morgan was behind her as she addressed Miranda. She turned her head without turning her body so that her long hair draped over her face as she peered up into his eyes, searching for, what, sympathy, forgiveness, he could not be sure.

"Dr. Felix Swan asked me to come over, the Rector of Jesus College, I saw you leaving his office, he wanted me to see if Professor Kurtz's cabinet was secure."

"His cabinet? His Bacon first edition?" said Morgan. "And why would he send you to do that?"

"Professor Kurtz could be careless sometimes."

"That seems unlikely," said Miranda, "given his fastidious housekeeping style."

"He'd sometimes forget things."

"Like the care of a prized possession?"

"We were worried it might have been…" she paused, searching for the appropriate word.

"Stolen?" Miranda suggested.

"Contaminated," she said. "Compromised."

"You were worried the police might damage it?"

"He just asked me to check."

"Is the key yours or Dr. Swan's," said Morgan.

She glared at him, then receded into herself before answering, "It is my key, I sometimes help Professor Kurtz with his research."

"Is he, or was he, still active in his field?" asked Miranda.

The young woman glowered, as if incredulous that such a question would need to be answered, and simply observed, "He died with his reputation intact."

"As a scholar," Miranda said, leaving her statement hanging, incomplete.

Jennifer Pluck shifted nervously, edging towards Morgan so that he moved backwards and the three of them worked their way down the hall as they talked, past the dining room, until they were standing at the base of the stairs with the living room open to the side. "I do not think," she was saying, "I don't think it is appropriate for me to comment on him as a person, he was complex, he needed people around him and behaved abominably when they were; he lived in isolation, he had a wide circle of acquaintances; as far as I know he had no friends. He was a man defined by innuendo and he seemed to thrive on that, wrapping himself in a mystique of gossip and rumour. You know this already, you have talked to people who knew him longer than I did, and I have no idea what was true and what was not, I paid no attention, I didn't care."

"Did you dislike him?"

"Of course. Not as much as I dislike Felix Swan, but certainly I did. He insisted on it."

Morgan regarded this nervous articulate unkempt young woman without seeming to stare, assessing her weird blend of arrogance and self-deprecation as a role she was playing out in her mind like a game of solitary 'Dungeons and Dragons,' where she got to define all the parts as versions of herself.

"He *wanted* to be disliked?" Morgan said, not sure where to go with what seemed a perceptive if clinical assessment of the dead man's personality.

"Would loathing be too strong?" asked Miranda. "You will appreciate the difficulty, Miss Pluck ..."

"Jennifer. It appears we are in a relationship of sorts, so I'm Jennifer."

"I'm Detective Quin, Miranda. This is Detective Morgan. He doesn't have a first name."

"Isn't it David?"

"How did you know?"

"I asked the Rector, he told me who you were. That's what I do, I'm a graduate student, I research. Post-doctoral, actually, but the instinct to be subservient dies hard."

"The implication being, once you're a professor, someone else does your research." Miranda seemed to be taking her more seriously than the young woman wished.

"Not really. Bitching is instinctive, it's a survival mechanism among those of us labouring for accolades with no pay in Middle Earth."

"Tolkien?"

"Purgatory. Neither devils nor angels; we're the company of the damned, the depressed, the despised."

"You could say you have an aptitude attitude, Dr. Pluck," said Miranda.

"Jennifer. It'll vanish if I get a tenured appointment."

"You've also expressed what I think could safely be called loathing for Felix Swan."

"Not enough to kill him, either."

"Either!" Miranda could not resist a quick smile at her response. "You're sure?"

"No," said the young woman, drawing out the word as if savouring it in brief contemplation. "But he's not dead yet, is he?"

"What about Kurtz?" said Miranda.

"What, could I kill him? Too late."

"You are not exactly grief stricken."

Jennifer Pluck swung her head low, around and up, so that her carefully uncoiffed hair surged away and then settled back against her skull more neatly than before.

"In mourning? No, I suppose I'm not. Have you found anyone who is? I imagine old Li Po would have expressed a kind sentiment. Jane Latimer is probably relieved; now she gets to be president. Who else have you met? Rafe and Porrig, no, they'll be amused. You'll like them. Everyone does. Lord Lionel Webb and his young protégé, Sir what's-his-name, no I don't think so. Marie Lachine, I doubt it—*elle n'aimait pas le grand morceau de merde, mais, Mademoiselle, elle est*, you know, too fastidious to let herself lose emotional control. Who does that leave? Felix, the sweating swan, I imagine he's pleased. Ah, Simon Sparrow, well, you will meet Simon Sparrow, I understand you are coming to Webb's this evening. I don't know whether Simon will even focus on the old man's demise, timely or not. His mind's too busy reinventing himself. Yes, and the two Hermiones, I'm sure neither of them give a damn whether Kurtz is alive or dead; no, not true, they enjoyed glaring at him during our meetings, that's something they have in common as well as their names, their ages, their sex, their lack thereof, and their passion for Francis Bacon. So now you have it: not much grieving amongst the lot of us!"

"Thank you for the inventory," said Miranda. "And for the insights. As I was saying, you will appreciate the difficulty in narrowing a field of suspects, none of whom seems to place any value on the dead man's life."

"I'm sure if a victim has only one enemy your job is much easier."

"But then there's no mystery," said Morgan, "and if there's no mystery, there's no urgency, and if there's no urgency there's no need for us."

"Have you ever read Augustine's *City of God*," she asked, as if it were the most natural question in the world to address to a police detective who has caught you compromised on a toilet. "Or Heidegger, that's Heidegger in a nutshell: *the authentic life must be lived in the shadow of death*."

"That's not quite what I was saying," said Morgan, scrambling in his mind to recall anything he might know about Heidegger, beyond the fact that he was a

Nazi apologist, or about Augustine, except that he was an interloper in recent dreams, an unwelcome Catholic saint soaring among fragments of a Protestant sensibility shattered by doubt.

Miranda regained control of the situation by reiterating her original query. "Let's come back to why you are here, Miss Pluck. Apart from testing the plumbing, your mission was to check on the stability of a manuscript cabinet. That seems rather flimsy as justification for violating a police warrant."

"It is not a manuscript. A manuscript is written by hand. This is a first edition of *Sylva Sylvarum*. Print-set for W. Lee, *'to be sould at the Great Turks Head next to the Mytre Taverne in Fleetstreet.'* Why else would I be here?"

Her last statement implicitly challenged Miranda, as if the young woman were delivering a riddle to be solved, the resolution of which would unlock dark secrets that might explain murder but would also reveal the psychological complexity of the human heart. She had a way about her that made the mundane ominously portentous—and, Miranda noted, vice versa, she could make the profound seem off-hand and banal.

This nervous, clever, tousled person struck Morgan as perversely attractive while Miranda, responding to the same features of personality and demeanor, found her intriguing but vaguely repulsive—inexplicably, like human genitals. She wondered if Morgan found her the same way.

That it was up to them to determine some nefarious purpose for her being in Kurtz's house, that she felt she had given them adequate explanation, rankled with Miranda and amused Morgan. Why should Jennifer Pluck feel obliged to sort out what must seem an amusing jig-saw puzzle, especially if she knew what the picture would be from the cover of the box?

For the first time, Morgan wondered at the possibility of a conspiracy. Perhaps the elimination of their President was a Bacon Society group project.

"Where is this cabinet?" Miranda decided to override her antipathy; more would be gained by connecting with the young woman.

Jennifer Pluck led them to an upstairs study. There, in an atmosphere defined by rows of books and other relics of a scholarly vocation, against a wall beside the door at the farthest extreme from a window that was completely obscured behind heavy blue-black velvet drapes, was a glass box perched on a metal chest, and inside the box was a very old book, open to display the frontispiece and title page.

"That's it," said Jennifer Pluck as she leaned over the glass surface to read the humidity and temperature gauges inside the box. Standing upright and moving back so the other two could see the book, she pronounced, "Safe and secure. I'm sure the Rector will be relieved. I haven't been here in a couple of months."

"Were you actually worried about it."

"Not that it wouldn't be here. I was concerned about its condition—the humidity and temperature are supposed to adjust automatically, but Professor Kurtz would sometimes forget to check."

"Jennifer," said Miranda. "Does the condition of this book really mean that much?"

"Yes, it does. To me, for sure."

"How so?"

"I do not believe in God."

"Excuse me?"

"God."

"I heard you, but?"

"This book, things like this make us less alone. I can hear Shakespeare's words and feel the immediacy of a human consciousness that's been dead for four hundred years. Or I can look at this book and myriad souls look back and they welcome me among them, Jennifer Pluck from nowhere, Ontario. And if Shakespeare, the individual human being, is unknowable, well here, in front of us, Francis Bacon is not, we connect—this is not about Bacon's immortality but my own."

Her eyes glistened as she glanced from Miranda to Morgan and back again, so needing to be understood they both felt her peculiar vulnerability was being offered as a gift.

She picked up a small lacquered box from a shelf beside the cabinet and toyed with it, before holding it out to them.

"It's beautiful, isn't it? Chinese, Ming Dynasty."

Morgan took the proffered box in his hands and examined the breathtaking simplicity of its design, the depth of its sheen. He passed it to Miranda. She moved the narrow lid back and forth in its track, fascinated by the fine engineering of such a tiny and elegant vessel.

"It is beautiful," Jennifer repeated, "and full with the promise of stories. Like the book. It makes us connect."

"What was it used for?" asked Miranda, gazing into the gleaming darkness which made the box seem infinitely empty.

"Vanity," said Jennifer. "Perhaps for a potpourri, powdered perfume, perhaps. It has the smell of flowers and honey."

Miranda sniffed at the box and passed it back to Jennifer Pluck who replaced in on the shelf.

"It is not the uses that speak to us," she said. "It is the thing itself, the beauty of the thing that reaches out."

"Continuity," said Morgan.

"Community," she responded.

"Beyond time," said Miranda.

"Beyond death."

"Some would argue that that is the function of art," said Miranda.

"And some would say the same of religion," said Jennifer Pluck. "But this isn't art. Art is a jewelled bird on a golden bough. This isn't a manufactured illusion, this is real."

"The box or the book?"

"The box, the book. Bacon."

"Who is dead."

"Who had the courage to declare, '*I do not believe that any man fears to be dead, but only the stroke of death.*' The transition from something to nothing is frightening. To help you through, while alive, you connect with the dead. *Only connect*, that is a dictum to live by. Then you die, and time is irrelevant. Because you connected."

Whether or not her listeners understood seemed irrelevant. The three of them stood close over the cabinet, gazing through the glass, only vaguely aware their vision had to penetrate their own reflections to see the book splayed open in its own small world, within an aura of infinite loneliness.

The likeness of Francis Bacon opposite the title page in an elaborate ruffled collar was juxtaposed to an etching of a globe labelled *Mundus Intellectualis*. The globe lay poised between two pillars extending to heaven, where a sun identified by Hebrew script radiated downwards, illuminating the known world and casting the unknown in deep shadow.

Jennifer Pluck began explaining the symbolism, slipping unpretentiously into a scholarly mode, then said abruptly, "You know, if I were to have killed him, I would have done it exactly the way it was done."

"And how do you know how it was done."

"It's headline news, the *Sun* at noon. They've labelled Professor Kurtz 'the ghost of Philosophers Walk.'"

"Ghost! The only place he's haunting right now is the morgue."

"Give him time," said Jennifer Pluck.

"Too late," Miranda responded enigmatically, with the lunch conversation still in mind. "Time is of no consequence to the dead." There was a brief shuffling, then she addressed Jennifer. "And would you have wanted to kill him? And why?"

"He deserved it. His life was a testament to the

necessity of murder, it just took a long while coming."

"Care to elaborate," said Miranda.

"No," she responded. "If I'm not under arrest, I'd like to go now." She edged towards the door and looked up at them through a tumble of hair that had fallen in front of her eyes. "I will be at Lord Webb's tonight, if you change your minds—about arresting me. I'll bring a toothbrush, just in case."

Miranda and Morgan shared a look of bemused exasperation as Jennifer Pluck slipped away.

Her disguise just might be who she was.

chapter nine
The Unusual Suspects

Miranda dropped by Police Headquarters on College Street to requisition a car. Her own was a 1959 British racing green Jaguar XK 150. There wouldn't be room for the three of them. Then she went back to her place to change. Parking out front, she entered the squat yellow-brick building on Isabella Street where she had lived since second year university, before the apartments became condos. She rang her own buzzer, a reaffirming ritual, knowing the sound would resonate in her empty apartment, and trudged up the stairs. She had a couple of hours before she was scheduled to pick up Morgan. She needed a nap.

Lying naked under the top sheet—covered because when it was this hot currents of air passing over exposed flesh prickled as the moisture on her skin evaporated—her mind raced. It was running simultaneously in two events, a frenetic marathon in which she rehearsed her long list of unsatisfactory relationships, former lovers, boyfriends, paramours, bobbing along beside her, just outside her field of vision, and a protracted dash in which the names on Jane Latimer's list peeled off and scooted ahead, just out of reach, some distinct and some a blur.

Morgan would be having a nap, too. Dreaming, perhaps, of past conquests. Of challenges ahead. *Damnit*, she thought. *Failed relationships for a male are conquests. He's probably fantasizing about running, too, but it'll be about Jane Latimer, hot and sweating, hard-bodied and slippery. Damnit.* She stretched her legs out full length, then drew them up and rolled onto her side. It was too hot. She got up and showered, dressed for the occasion, sexy but subtly severe, her Armani look, and then changed into a light summer dress, knowing Morgan would present in a more relaxed mode, and headed off to Morgan's. If she couldn't rest, why should he?

His door was unlocked so she walked right in and started talking to where she assumed he was, lying down upstairs in the darkness of the loft.

"Morgan, do you ever miss being married?" There was no answer. "Morgan, are you asleep."

"Yes," came a muffled reply.

"Deeply?"

"No, I don't"

"Don't what?"

"Miss being married."

"A little?"

"It was a romantic arrangement, not a condition of being." He moved into view and sat with his bare legs dangling through the balustrade, leaning forward against the railing. "Sometimes I almost forget her name. Do you miss being married?"

"I never was, not even close."

"Yeah, but sometimes we miss most what we've never had. Do you wish you'd been married?"

"Present tense, yes," she said, looking up at him from the living room glare, trying to find his eyes in the shadows. "Sometimes I think it would be nice."

"The guy last night?"

"He was a lawyer. Youngest senior partner in his firm. Bryan spelled with a 'y.' You coming down?"

"Oh, yeah, sure." He came down the stairs gingerly, taking one at a time, dressed in a T-shirt and boxers."

"Thought you never wore boxers," she said.

"Not as underwear," he said. "They're warm-weather pajamas. It's too hot to sleep naked."

"Sit down," she said. "I'll bring you a beer."

"Just water, please. No wonder marathon runners walk down stairs backwards after a race. The walking wounded. Some of them were backing down into the subway, last year. I'm rethinking my marathon ambitions."

"So you said." Miranda handed him a glass of water.

"Her name was Lucy."

"Who?"

"My former wife."

"I knew that. Now, then, what do you think of our Baconites?"

"Thus far, a motley crew. There's much to suspect, little to sustain a conviction."

"Yeah, well let's consider. Felix Swan. Exudes motives. Blackmail; sexual improprieties. Professional conflict between the Rector and a Professor Emeritus; rivalry as Bacon specialists."

"And he's a Freemason, there may be some arcane connection with Bacon that manifests itself in murder."

"Morgan, Red Skelton was a Mason."

"You're dating yourself! And what's the point?"

"I don't think you can equate membership in the Masonic Lodge with a predilection for killing people."

"No, but when intelligent men subvert their rational natures playing with the occult, you've got to wonder."

"Playing?"

"Play can be deadly," said Morgan. "They're sparring with the supernatural."

"There was a time when alchemy was considered a science."

"And there was a time when a quick execution was considered merciful. Again, what's your point?"

"Bacon as a Mason in the seventeenth century—it was a world where magic and wonder illuminated the darkness of the ages preceding."

"Miranda, you're beginning to sound like me."

"I'm remembering a course I took on the history of ideas. You know, it might have been Kurtz who gave a guest lecture. I think he spoke on the Renaissance in England, I think possibly he spoke about Francis Bacon. It all slipped through at the time—coloured water through a sieve. I didn't realize when I dozed through his lecture I'd eventually meet him as a corpse."

"Did you know slow burning at the stake was more humane than fast?"

"Really?"

"Yeah it allowed you to choke on the smoke and not suffer the flames?"

"Very poetic. You get my point, though, Morgan. Felix Swan being a Mason now, in the twenty-first century, has more to do with a facile imagination than wonderstruck awe."

"Not really," he said. "But what about Jennifer Pluck? What was she doing in Kurtz's house? Finding something, hiding something, changing the evidence? I mean, we could have charged her. And she casually shows us around, then leaves with a bit of a wisecrack. And she clearly wants us to know the extent of her bitterness towards Kurtz."

"The extent, yes, but not the source. There's something sinister about her indifference to the old man's death."

"Relief," said Morgan. "I would say relief at his death, not indifference. Disturbing, not sinister."

"And Bacon for her, familiarity with Bacon, offers a refuge from the brutality of the human condition." Miranda tried to reconstruct the young woman's existential sermon in her mind.

"From loneliness."

"That *is* the human condition. Conditional immortality; it's better than nothing."

"Then there's Professor Li Po," said Morgan.

"Li Po, I liked him."
"Yeah, I know."
"He's sexy."
"Sexy!"
"Yeah, what's your point?"
"He's old."
"I like older men."
"How much older."
"It's all relative."
"To what? Yeah, well. Bacon gives the old man a lens to examine the world. Why would he want to kill the man who kept the glass polished."

"Morgan, the Bacon Society also represents an insuperable barrier between Li Po's background as a scholar in China and his acceptance in the West. Perhaps an intolerable situation for a man whose whole career was devoted to knowing the Other."

"Did you say Other with a capital O? Oh my goodness, you've been reading Cultural Theory."

"An occasional article in *The Atlantic Monthly*, a couple of stories in *Granta*."

"Do we know anything about his background in China, do we know why he was called back from his scholarly travels just when he was about to spend a year studying in Rome? That would have been when, late 1940s?"

"According to Jane Latimer, Li Po was with Mao Zedong on the Long March."

"That was 1935, my goodness how old is the man?" said Morgan.

"He would have been barely a child. Then when the Communists came to power after the War he must have returned to his homeland."

"Perhaps for the battle, but not the rewards. He ended up with a nondescript university post in Lanchou."

"Don't you think that *was* the reward, Morgan."

"Yeah. So let's say he's well into his eighties, and long ago he marched with an army of the dead across the breadth of China, retreating from the nationalist forces, and after years as a student-scholar he is carried on a wave of blood to revolutionary victory, and for nearly two generations he is content."

"Except for the era of the Red Guards—he worked as a farm labourer during the Cultural Revolution."

"Maybe he was content with that, too."

"Maybe."

"So here is a man who has lived through a great deal of history."

"We all live through history, Morgan."

"No, that's just it, we don't. History is what's written down. The big events. We just live through time. And what happens to a man who has been a witness to historical events, and yet lived most of his life in scholarly contemplation, what happens when he turns up in the back rooms of an ethnic restaurant in downtown Toronto. He has moved so far onto the margins the centre is only a blur."

"He joins the Bacon Society."

"Precisely, my dear Watson. He joins the Bacon Society. And why?"

"You tell me," said Miranda.

"He joins the Bacon Society because, there, he is at the centre, the heart, the vortex of a world which all his life he has observed from outside. In Toronto, among his cadre of Baconites, he has truly come home!"

"If you're right. And if his belonging among them were threatened, then ..."

"He would murder. We know from experience it is often the contemplative person who rises to violence if sufficiently provoked. Through his life he has witnessed a necessary correlation between ideology and death—the execution of a tyrant might seem the most natural event in the world."

"But could he do it?" asked Miranda.

"Physically? We don't know exactly how Kurtz died. Asphyxia? Probably, but by what method? He was an old man, too. He didn't struggle. He was murdered close to where we found him. Commitment more than strength was what killed him. It could have been a man or a woman, young or old, even very old but in good shape."

"And that leaves us with Jane Latimer."

"Well, and a bunch of others on the list we haven't met yet."

"So what about Jane?" said Miranda.

"She's certainly in good shape.'

"You noticed."

"I bear the battle scars."

"Poor Morgan. Maybe you should have a hot shower or a cold shower or whatever it is you athletes do. As for Jane Latimer, she's on my A-list. No one so casually tries to orchestrate a police investigation without a vested interest."

"Everyone in her Bacon club has a vested interest. Late in a long hot summer we're the only game in town. She's amused; we provide entertainment."

"Morgan. Cleanse yourself, run hot water over your aching muscles, suck ice cubes, stop talking, let's move."

chapter ten

Lionel Webb, Sir David, Rafe And Porrig

When they drove through the gates of Lionel Webb's city residence on the Bridle Path, the two detectives felt momentarily disoriented, then Morgan chuckled from the back seat and said, enigmatically, "It's amazing what money can do." They had been in comparable mansions a number of times, always to investigate murder. Tonight, murder was secondary, at least on the surface.

Morgan was wearing a rumpled linen jacket with a black T-shirt underneath, and khaki chinos. He had brushed his hair. Miranda was comfortable in her light summer dress and black pearl earrings. They knew instinctively that the way into this group would not be through professional detachment. The lack of urgency surrounding Kurtz's death made sociability a necessity.

Standing outside the front door between soaring Corinthian columns Miranda for the first time noticed Jane Latimer's outfit. When they picked her up, she had been waiting at the curb and Miranda was focused on driving, while Morgan, in the back seat, might have been oblivious. He wasn't now. Her neckline was scooped so low he could see the lower curve of her breasts each time she exhaled. If she bent forward, Miranda thought, they'd tumble out like sentient melons. Her white skirt was disconcertingly tight. No panty-line, not even the Y of a thong. Loose boobs, tight ass. Cheap by design. A worldly virgin's rendition of 'slut.'

Morgan was staring. Why not? That was the point, to compromise men who know better. Still, it made Miranda uncomfortable that he was so obviously trying to be covert, rubbing a finger along the bridge of his nose with his head tilted forward, as if to distract from where his eyes were focused. He glanced up and saw Miranda watching him, stifled a small cough and, briefly rubbing his chin, looked away.

The door opened and a handsome young man greeted them with a proprietorial air, as if answering doors and telephones were his function, but not as a servant, more as a friend of the family.

"Jane!" he exclaimed, his enthusiasm suggesting he was surprised by her appearance. "You look simply stunning." Cambridge, not Oxford, Morgan noticed, and quite genuine.

"Sir David," she muttered in a lusty whisper as they

embraced.

"Please, Dr. Latimer, it's David. And these are the detectives. A pleasure to meet you. Do come in and make yourselves at ease." He did not say, 'at home.'

The young man ushered them through the foyer into a vaulted two story chamber embraced by parenthetical staircases sweeping around on either side, with doors and hallways leading like opulent promises in several directions. He turned to Miranda and smiled winsomely. Shaking hands with him, she felt a twinge of regret for the gap in their ages. To Morgan he offered the firm handshake of a gentleman, and a more collegial smile, suggesting that despite his youth they had much in common as men of the world.

"Sir David," said Morgan, paused, then added: "My condolences."

Miranda and Jane Latimer looked puzzled, but the young man nodded cheerfully in affirmation.

"Thank you," he said.

"Morgan?" said Miranda, confused by the expression of sympathy.

"He's too young to have earned a knighthood and he's not a rock star, so I assume the title is hereditary."

"Do go on," said the young man who was the object of Morgan's discourse.

Pleased to oblige, Morgan continued: "He uses the title, but finds it awkward, so he has come into it recently. His father died only a short time ago."

"He did, indeed," said the young man, "While I was at Cambridge. Of course, I don't use it in Canada, except at our meetings. It seems appropriate, when dealing with Viscount Bacon. He was a Cambridge man, himself. Cambridge boy, actually. Sir Francis graduated at fifteen. Americans find the title quite titillating but it makes Canadians nervous. And Australians aggressive. It was my inheritance. That, and enough cash to get through university in comfortable circs. Well, here you go, then," he gestured towards the library. "Please mingle, I'll find Lionel."

Miranda held him back, gently grasping his arm. "I'm sorry about your father," she said.

"Not to worry," he responded in a confidential tone. "Sir Nigel was a lovely man and he died too young, but one deals with such things and moves on. It's really not all that bad, is it? For the living, I mean. Moving on. A more extreme situation for the dead."

"You called your father Sir Nigel?"

"One always said his name with affectionate contempt. He was quite embarrassed, having no estate commensurate with his caste. The landless gentry, a twentieth century phenomenon, the wars, the Empire in a muddle, socialism, the contagion of middle class values. It confused him. Myself, I enjoy working for a living, and I find being a baronet occasionally useful. Can't sit in the Lords, though. Not like Lionel, not that he does."

"And your mother?"

"Mummy was just mummy," he said ingenuously. "I would never have dreamed of calling her Susan. She enjoyed social chaos, the collapse of privilege."

"She's dead, then, as well?

"Oh no, she's very much alive. Being over here, I have developed a nasty habit of referring to everything English, including my friends and relatives, in the past tense. An expression of difference, perhaps, or of their inaccessibility. I really must find Lionel for you. Excuse me."

Morgan was distracted. From somewhere in the depths of his mind, he dredged out an image of twin stairways as the Masonic symbol for movement from darkness into transcendent illumination. Since he hardly knew anything of the Masons, the origin of his insight puzzled him. He turned fully around, surveying his surroundings without embarrassment that he might appear gauche.

Through the arched window extending high over the front door above the foyer, he could see the upper reaches of two of the white columns of the portico that extended across the front of the ante-bellum mansion. These, he thought, are the pillars of Hercules, the symbol of the limits of knowledge and imagination for Renaissance thinkers like Bacon. He remembered seeing them in the frontispiece of the open book at Dieter Kurtz's house. Jennifer Pluck had explained their significance.

Miranda watched Sir David as he walked across the black and white marble in front of the stairs and tapped lightly on a large door. All the doors were large. He disappeared into the muted light of what appeared in its brief exposure to be a private study.

Morgan observed Miranda, following her line of vision, curious about the instant connection she had made with the young man. Clearly he had a gift for intimacy, making whoever he talked to feel special. The diametric opposite of Felix Swan.

Morgan could hear Swan's ingratiating sincerity competing in the welter of voices emerging from the library behind him. He cringed slightly before turning around and joining Miranda to enter the din.

Miranda found the room difficult to assimilate in her mind. It was vast and yet intimate, cold but inviting, and teeming with books of every sort, ancient leather-bound books, contemporary coffee-table books, books behind glass and books in the open. Like a mausoleum, a repository for the words of mostly dead writers. The hubbub of infinite conversations glanced off walls. Austere and intimate, animated with the presence of the surviving members of the Francis Bacon Society.

Felix Swan was the first to greet them. He bustled over with both arms outstretched, prepared for either a hug or a clasping of hands. Since Miranda could not avoid being first in order of reception, she enduring a sweaty embrace without returning it and quickly stepped to the side. Morgan sidled behind her, leaving Jane Latimer in Swan's direct line of attack. Huge limbs aflutter, as if he were preparing to take off like an obese pink flamingo, he suddenly stopped in front of her, flapped his great arms and proclaimed extravagantly, "Oh my, my dear Jane, you look ravishing, absolutely breathtaking, just gorgeous, oh my, you are every man's dream come true."

Miranda was unsure whether Felix Swan was being

exposed as a closet heterosexual, or just had very bad taste. Swan reached to the side and shook Morgan's hand, but did not take his eyes off the breasts of the interim president of the Bacon Society.

"Well," said Morgan, embarrassed by the unbridled vulgarity of the Rector's effusions, "do you suppose you could introduce us around?"

"No need for that," said a resonant voice from behind them as Lionel Webb stepped into the library. The entire company fell momentarily still as the focal axis of the room shifted, then conversations resumed in small clusters, but none turned their backs to the host. Morgan surveyed the group. He could identify everyone by name from Jane Latimer's prepared list. He caught sight of Professor Li Po, who was looking directly at him from behind a massive antique globe, and they exchanged nodding acknowledgement of each.

"I'm sure everyone knows who you are, Detective," said Lionel Webb, moving close beside Jane Latimer. "Felix, please bring our guests a drink. No, just flutes. We'll start with Dom Perignon. David, if you will gently pop a cork or two and see to the charging of glasses."

Morgan looked around for the champagne. Then he realized the young man from Cambridge shared his first name. I don't usually think of myself as David, he thought, I seldom think of myself by name and when I do, it's not David. David's too intimate. Whimsy lines at the corners of his eyes crinkled slightly. Miranda noticed, but had no idea what was amusing him. Perhaps it was in anticipation of the Dom Perignon.

As Jane Latimer receded, leaving a small region of inviolable space around their host, Webb shook hands with both detectives, lingering with Miranda's in his just a little too long, making her uncomfortable without being sure why. Somehow, it gave him the advantage.

"Excuse the presumption," said Lionel Webb with the slight melony inflection of the Toronto elite, "I thought it would be more advantageous for you to wander among us and introduce yourselves, since your identities and purpose are not in doubt. You can assess each of us in turn and sustain the illusion that we are simply a congenial gathering of eccentrics. Much more productive, I think, than a mass confrontation."

"Thank you," said Morgan, "that would be fine."

Webb had the aura of a celebrity. He was familiar without being known, like a movie star, a high-profile recluse whose achievements and peccadilloes were monitored by the popular press for mass entertainment. In his case, despite his best efforts at anonymity, fame was a function of fortune. He was widely known for collecting cultural artifacts the public admired and museums coveted, the icons of nations which he spirited off to private galleries for his solitary pleasure and that of a few chosen associates.

Young Sir David, perhaps, was a curator on hire to facilitate his lordship's acquisitive desires. The young man moved about the room, pouring champagne, having removed the corks without ostentation. Morgan admired his capacity to serve without appearing to be in service. He identified with the young Englishman, in spite of the vast discrepancies between them. Morgan had grown up in Cabbagetown, reputed not long before to have been the largest Anglo-Saxon slum in the world outside of Great Britain. He had been a scholarship student, he was a generation older, he was a cop. And even dressed up, he was slightly dishevelled. Miranda had assured him that linen was meant to be wrinkled, that's why he originally bought the jacket. It was easier than mounting a defense for being rumpled and disorderly.

Looking around the room, he recognized a more likely parallel to himself in a casual man with glittering eyes who must be Simon Sparrow. He knew this by a process of elimination, since the only other two men he had not met were obviously a couple. They must be Rafe and Porrig, which as Jane had explained, was how Ralph and Padraig preferred to be addressed. He walked over to them.

"It's an honour." said the tall thin one, "I'm Rafe." He nodded in the direction of his shorter heavier partner. "He is Porrig."

"Oh-oh," said Porrig. "I think Lionel is about to propose a toast. Good, mustn't let the bubbles fizzle to nothing. I do love Dom Perignon. The only time we get to drink it is here at his lordship's. It's always so nice when it's his turn to play host. And it usually is, it seems, his turn."

"Ladies and gentlemen," said Lionel Webb quietly and the room fell silent. "Welcome to you all, and a special welcome to our friends, Detectives Morgan and Quin. If your glasses are charged, then, ladies and gentlemen, the Queen!"

Morgan choked, stifling a burst of involuntary laughter. Miranda sidled closer to him, biting her lower lip to hold off a giggle, and issued a modest nasal snort which she covered with a cough. They did not dare look at each other, but he nudged her arm and she glowered without turning.

"The Queen!" The toast rang out in unison. Each member of the Bacon Society took a modest sip, holding back enough for the inevitable tribute to their departed past president.

"Ladies and Gentlemen," said Lionel Webb, obviously enjoying his role as host, "I believe we should drink to Dieter Kurtz, who could not be with us this evening. To Dieter Kurtz!"

There was a restrained smile on his face as there was on most of the others. It could have been mistaken for an expression of fondness for someone unavoidably absent, or of modest pleasure that an irritant had been removed from their midst, or possibly restrained approbation that a scoundrel was dead.

Another toast was proposed, after an inconspicuous servant had moved through the crowded room refilling the glasses with more Dom Perignon, this time to Jane Latimer as incoming president. There had been no discussion as far as Miranda could tell, and certainly no vote. Yet it was clear that Lionel Webb spoke for them all in celebrating her ascendancy. This was about the assumption of power, not its sharing. Democracy among neo-Renaissance Baconites was tenuous at best.

Miranda leaned over to speak with Morgan privately, her sober expression to all appearances suggesting an exchange of police information.

"I've never seen more than one bottle of Dom Perignon opened on the same occasion," she whispered.

"No," he responded with a confidential sigh. "Neither have I. It's a lovely incentive to toast the world."

Unfortunately, with the salute to Jane Latimer the toasts came to an end, but at Lionel Webb's behest the socializing was to continue while more drinks and *hors d'oeuvres* were served by his unobtrusive staff under the watchful supervision of Sir David. Their host slipped easily from the centre of attention and the focus of the room shifted to Jane Latimer, with everyone now positioned relative to her, like iron filings to a magnet.

Her outfit no longer seemed reckless. It's strange, Miranda thought, it now looks like a costume designed for the occasion. Perhaps it's the way she carries herself, her perfect athletic figure defiant of stereotyped epithets. Where another woman might appear sleazy, the president of the Bacon Society looked like she was having fun. Flashing flesh out of joy, not tawdry desperation.

Morgan was in a conversation with Ralph and Padraig. She turned to listen.

"You see," the tall, rather elegant one was saying, "We neither of us think much of marriage as an institution—have you been married, Detective? Yes, probably you have, well, you understand my point, but we wanted to affirm our alliance in a public statement of some sort."

"So what we did," said his shorter heavier partner,

"We adopted a common surname."

"We spent days going through the telephone book, reading the society columns."

"Combing *Vanity Fair*, sifting through the works of our divine Jane Austen."

"And that's when we decided on D'Arcy, you know, as in Mister."

"How fitting, we thought. Gay is all about pride, and it's all about prejudice."

"Not to mention sense, within reason, and a great deal of sensibility. So we both went through legal name changes, we are the Misters D'Arcy."

"Of course we spell it with an apostrophe. Jane spells it as one word, d-a-r-c-y. We like the Continental flair, the implication of roots in the Norman conquest."

"1066 and all that. When you give yourself a new name you have to invent a history to go with it."

"Lovely," Miranda exclaimed.

Morgan had said nothing during Ralph and Padraig's discourse. He was conventional enough to be impressed whenever he met a married woman who kept her own name. But this was a twist he had not encountered before. Naming was important—it was about power. Cult leaders re-named their followers, bullies gave cohorts nicknames, called their victims abusive names—why not a name by consensus. *Beautiful*, he thought.

"Interesting," he said. "Was it your idea, Ralph?"

"Rafe."

"I'm sorry, I thought it was Ralph."

"We say Rafe, it's spelled Ralph."

"I see," he said, amused by the unpretentiousness of their affectation. "And Padraig?"

"Is Porrig," said the stockier of the two. "We pronounce Padraig in the Irish way, as Porrig."

"Are you Irish?" asked Miranda.

"No, not at all," he replied. "Not me. Rafe is old Irish stock. I'm English, I suppose, if you go back far enough. British. My grandmother used to say we're all British, whatever we are. She mourned for the Empire as it slipped away, she died of grief. At one hundred and three. She actually remembered Queen Victoria."

"Then how did you end up with the name Padraig, or Porrig? It's a variant of Patrick, isn't it?"

"Well, I didn't actually. We traded first names."

"Pardon?"

"It's all part of the big adventure."

Morgan was fascinated. Miranda was perplexed. Realizing he was expected to clarify, the shorter heavier man continued. "I was Ralph Robertshaw."

"And I was Padraig O'Suillibahn."

"But really, you know, when Ralph is called Rafe—"

"—and Padraig is Porrig—"

"—our names seemed inappropriate. I mean, look, isn't he gorgeous, he's slender and dashing and I'm squat and homely. So he became Rafe and I became Porrig. We traded. It seemed the right thing to do."

"We had our names legally changed: Ralph Robertshaw became Porrig D'Arcy and Padraig O'Suillibahn became Rafe D'Arcy."

"I hope you never break up," said Morgan. "I can see

the custody of names being very messy."

"Oh we won't," said Porrig.

"No," said Rafe. "We have a murder-suicide pact. If one of us should fall out of love, well, you know—"

"—he is honour-bound to do away with the both of us."

"That's quite an incentive for a prolonged and enduring relationship," said Miranda with a whimsical absence of irony.

"Murder, then, doesn't disturb you?" said Morgan.

"Not when it is appropriate," said Ralph.

"Sometimes it's the only way," said Padraig.

"The obvious next question," said Miranda, "is where were you two last night when Dieter Kurtz met his ignominious end."

"Together, my dear," said Ralph.

"'The young in one another's arms,'" said Padraig, putting his words in oral quotation marks.

"In other words, you have no alibi."

"Yes, of course we do, I'm his," said Ralph.

"And Rafe is mine," said Padraig. "We were at home. You don't doubt our veracity, my dears, simply because our domestic situation is unusual."

"I suppose you will need to come up with our motive, Detective, to offset the alibi," said Ralph. "Kurtz was such a dreadful man, to know him was to wish for his expiration. You are in a room surrounded by a cacophony of motives, Detectives. Just listen, listen, they're swarming through the air like wraiths in a maelstrom."

"As for us," said Rafe, "we can save you some time.

He despised us. For being gay, me for being Irish and a nominal Catholic, Porrig for having a Jewish mother. He loathed us and threatened us repeatedly with expulsion."

"On what grounds?" said Miranda.

"Moral turpitude, intellectual ineptitude, genetic deviance," Padraig responded quite cheerfully, "excessive sensitivity, insufficient gravity, poor colour sense. Who knows? But we have a first edition more valuable than his."

"Of course," Ralph conceded, "we each own half of it, so only by combining our shares did we own more than him."

"Whatever else he felt about us, he would never have challenged our commitment to the cause."

"The cause?"

"Bacon, my dears. If ever there was a cause it were Bacon."

"How medieval. If ever there *were* a cause, it *was* Bacon."

"If ever there is, Bacon is. Final word."

"Final."

Miranda found herself losing track of which of them said what, or if it mattered.

"Now," said Padraig, "let us introduce you to the most fervid Baconian of them all, Miss Hermione M."

"MacGregor."

"No, that's Hermione Mac, she's the spy. Mac the Spy. Did you know Bacon founded the British Secret Service. He invented ciphers to encode state secrets, he and his brother. This one's McCloud." He leaned over and whispered: "Think M for murder, she's the one who got rid of her mother. You know all about that, I expect."

chapter eleven

The Two Hermiones, Simon Sparrow, And Marie Lachine

The two elderly women were standing side by side, both sipping champagne, almost close enough for their clothing to touch. By their stiff posture it was evident they were studiously ignoring each other's presence, yet they were drawing support from each other, the way some people will by standing near an open doorway or a wall.

The one nearest to them as they approached was Hermione McCloud. She was handsome, as no doubt she had been when she was younger. She stood a head taller than the other Hermione, who in her late seventies was sinuously pretty with a quickness to her manner that hinted of a renegade youth.

During the introductions the shorter Hermione gazed into the upper shelves opposite, perhaps looking for bugging devices in the crenellated shadows above the rows of leather-bound books. She did not acknowledge the social activity at her elbow until Miranda moved directly in front of her. Then she took a half step away, severely indicating she would conduct her own audience with the police when she could expect their undivided attention. Miranda shifted her focus back to Hermione M, catching her in mid sentence.

"— after Mummy died, yes, it was fun," the woman was explaining. "The whole house was a treasure hunt. I would open books and find money stuffed inside. *Great Expectations* had hundred dollar bills between each set of pages. Of course, she chose an edition with small print so there was not as much as you might suppose. *Crime and Punishment* had a map showing where stocks and bonds were buried in the old coal cellar."

Morgan had asked her, right off, what her interest was in Francis Bacon. She was in the process of explaining the source of her devotion, that in some oblique way it connected to the death of her mother.

"I had never heard of Bacon; women of my generation seldom knew about such things. We were busy busy busy, being virginal spinsters, you know, or wives and widows. Yes, and I left home in Dundas, near Hamilton, and worked in Toronto, and Mommy did not like that at all. I was not a wife and not a widow, not even a spinster, and only the Lord knows whether I was virginal."

The other Hermione snorted and mumbled: "The

Lord and half the PPCLI."

"Oh no, dear. The Princess Pat's were from the west. I preferred the Van Doos." Hermione M paused to enjoy her own risqué wit, then explained to Miranda, "Vingt-Deux, the royal Twenty-Second Regiment. The PPCLI are an infantry battalion."

She was obviously pleased to have an interested audience, but decided to curb her discourse on military affairs: "My mother and I were reconciled shortly before she died."

"More likely after," said the other Hermione, addressing the top shelves on the farthest wall.

"Yes, dear. I'm sure the detectives know all about that. I was barely charged and never convicted."

She twisted slightly to address her adversary's bosom, then turned back to the little cluster awaiting the denouement of her peculiar narrative. "Before she died, Mommy had rather a lot of fun. She dispersed the entire remains of our family fortune, the modest residue of a nineteenth century manufacturing enterprise—my family made cast-iron stoves—all about the house. It was her little joke."

"And you were away when she did this?" said Miranda.

"Well yes, of course dear, or else I would have known what she was doing."

"Of course."

"I did not move back until the evening she died. You see, that was the source of the confusion. The police could not understand how I knew to come home at precisely the right moment."

The Dead Scholar

"That, and the empty box of rat poison," interjected the other Hermione, who had given up the pretense of ignoring the little group to which she was, she made it clear, unavoidably attached by an accident of proximity.

"Of course, the Warfarin in Mother's blood stream, that confused them, the poor dears."

Miranda had never heard the police addressed as 'poor dears' before. She took a step back to broaden their circle, drawing Hermione Mac closer into its reach. Professor Li Po and Simon Sparrow had joined their group, making the rest of the large room appear sparsely populated.

"Well, Mummy had laid out the most elaborate treasure hunt, and—"

"The poison?" said Morgan. He, like Miranda, was caught up in the story and asked out of curiosity rather than as a detective.

"Oh Mommy! She was getting long in the tooth, the poor thing. It seems likely a mouse not a rat, we prefer to think it was a very large mouse, squirrelled the poison away in her oatmeal bin—they're little green pellets you know—and Mommy likely thought they were raisins, her eyesight had become rather vague. And she served up her own fate with brown sugar and cream."

"My goodness," said Morgan, as much interested in her manner of telling the tale as in the account she related.

"Yes," said Hermione M. "The clincher was mouse poop they found in the oatmeal. It was sufficient to convince the police."

"Anyone could put rat turds in the oatmeal," muttered

the other Hermione. The spy.

"But it would be very difficult to prove," said Hermione M with a beatific smile.

"Actually, I understood your mother died from electrocution. In the bathtub," said Miranda.

"Did you, dear?" said Hermione M.

"Uh, well yes."

"I suppose she might have," said Hermione M.

"But she didn't," said the other Hermione. "It was rat poison in the oatmeal, tell them, old thing."

"Well, it might have been either. I used to say it was an electrical accident."

"And was it?" asked Miranda.

"It is so much easier to live with death by electrocution, don't you think?" She smiled. "I may have raised the possibility."

"Which was ridiculous, of course," said the other Hermione, "since we all knew how her mother died. It was in the papers."

"Not a big case, though," said Hermione M with modesty.

"The treasure hunt," said Padraig, "you must tell them about the treasure hunt."

"I already have, dear Porridge, but if you want more, let me think. Well, she was quite ingenious, she kept loose diamonds in a crystal decanter, Waterford, deeply etched and filled with schnapps of all things. The diamonds eventually accumulated a sugar coating and revealed themselves, the little darlings, they did. And she devised an elaborate paper chase before I found the deeds to the house and the cottage. It started in the wall safe, but I had to guess the combination, third guess and it opened—last two digits of her widowhood year, year of her birth-date, and then her wedding date—and from there she led me through every single room in the house, notes scrawled on the backs of bathroom mirrors, codes sewn into cushions, scraps of paper tucked up inside closets, and each led to another with cute little rhymes. "If you should find this, you're still aloof. Now try looking under the roof." That was the attic where I used to hide as a child. She was not a great poet. The penultimate message read, "You're almost there my dearest daughter, the treasure is yours, so much for slaughter."

"Enigmatic, but rather accusative," said Miranda.

"Or reaching for a rhyme," Morgan observed aloud, to himself.

"Well actually, she was quite precise," said Hermione M. "Out in the old summer kitchen we had a stove that had once been used to render fat for tallow after butchering an Easter lamb each spring; there was an old tea canister inside the stove—I got that one right away, my grandmother used to talk about rendering when I was a girl. Light from the slaughter, she would say. They'd take the old stove out into the yard and fire it up and boil down the fat. They were the most prosperous family in town but she made her own soap and candles. Of course, they were the first to have gas, and then the electricity."

"As your mother said, you got *so much* for slaughter, my dear" said the other Hermione. She had obviously delivered the same line innumerable times in the past, for although it was brutal, everyone laughed except Miranda and Morgan.

"What did the final note say," Morgan asked?

"The final note. Oh, yes, the final note—there was nothing but a key in the tea canister—the final note was in the security box at the bank, along with the property deeds. I believe it said, 'Be as happy as you can be, There's not much rhymes with Hermione.'"

"And?" said Padraig.

"There was a book, and another couplet," said Ralph, urging her on.

"Ah, Porridge and Rake, you've heard this before. 'By my demise don't be undone, Find solace in Sir Francis Bacon.' And indeed I did, in that very book. He explained the world and everything that's in it."

"Yes," said Padraig, hardly able to contain his excitement. "In the pages of *The World* you found wisdom and a lottery ticket."

"*The World?*"

"His *Essays*," said Hermione.

"Worth how much?" Miranda asked.

"The book?"

"The lottery ticket."

"Nothing at all, my dear," said the old woman, smiling. "That was the point. My mother was telling me, don't waste your life investing in silly dreams. As far as I know it was worthless. I never checked. I had all I needed—enough to last me, and I had my beloved Francis Bacon to share my solitude in small-town opulence, what more could I want?"

"Friends, family, society?" suggested Miranda.

"My dear, you have only to read Bacon to find a response to that. *'She that hath husband and children is hostage to fortune.'* It is so well stated—the wisdom and brevity alone could be evidence that Bacon wrote Shakespeare."

"Don't be ridiculous," muttered Hermione Mac. "Shakespeare wrote Shakespeare. And Bacon wrote Bacon, and he was talking about a man taking a wife, not a woman a husband, and producing children who would grow up at fortune's mercy. She's got the genders confused. No surprise there. And she's got the sentiment wrong."

"I know women from men, and Shakespeare from Bacon," Hermione M responded, addressing Miranda as if the other Hermione were not there.

"And the damn fool reads her book like it was a paperback," the other Hermione continued. "She flips through the pages, she gets fingerprint marks on the paper, she devours the damn thing."

Still speaking directly to Miranda, Hermione M countered with a sweet smile and another quotation, this one apparently more accurate: "*'Some books are to be tasted, others to be swallowed, and some few to be chewed and digested.'* I consume the book, it is my sustenance and when I die, it shall perhaps go with me."

"Over my dead body," said the other Hermione.

"Then perhaps we shall go together," rejoined Hermione M. "We'll share crematorium fees and mingle our ashes, along with the remains of my book."

"It might be worth it, just to see you gone," said Hermione Mac, with cheerful vehemence that belied her quite frail appearance. Simon Sparrow reached between the two women, taking a judicious opportunity to introduce himself. The Hermiones immediately drifted towards opposite sides of the room.

"I'm Simon Sparrow," he said. "You know Professor Li Po, and this is Mademoiselle Marie Lachine. Is there anyone else you haven't met?" He gestured across the room where Jennifer Pluck was chatting with Jane Latimer, the two of them looking like improbable guests in what was certainly the most extensive and opulent private library Miranda had ever seen. "Have you met our Jennifer?"

Jennifer cocked an eyebrow when she heard her name, but did not even glance in their direction. Miranda noticed that she had changed her entire outfit, yet still managed to look like she dressed in leftovers from a rummage sale, however expensive they might originally have been. With Jane wearing such a strange outfit as well, they both appeared to be in costume. That's it, she thought, they're not in disguise. They don't dress, they dress up. They're in costume. Like transvestites and high fashion models and hookers and bohemian wannabes.

Near the door, Lionel Webb and Sir David were standing side by side, and Felix Swan was endeavoring without much success to capture their attention. Hermione M was listening to Swan intently, but the Rector seemed unaware of her presence and several times bumped against her as he gesticulated and shuffled, the rhetoric of his body betraying the self-consciousness of a man on a losing mission.

The other Hermione was on her own with her back to the room, surveying a random shelf of leather-bound books. Lionel Webb walked over to her and said something and she turned and took his arm and joined their little group. Felix Swan's eyes had followed Webb's progress across the library and brightened significantly when he returned.

Ralph drifted away and came to rest beside the two women in costume and Miranda realized, in his own way he too was dressed up in play clothes. The outfit exactly suited him, but the wide shirt lapels and his high-waisted pants made him look like a cross between Errol Flynn and Fred Astaire, neither of whom in fact had come into her consciousness until years after they were dead. He looks dated, she thought. Dashing and dated.

Her attention shifted to Simon Sparrow. He was explaining to Morgan and Mlle. Lachine the intricacies of consuming water from a crushed paper cup while on the run. Apparently Jane Latimer had announced that Morgan was an aspiring runner. Since she had arrived with them, she must have been talking to Sparrow on the phone. It wasn't the kind of thing you dropped into an e-mail. Somehow, with a fanfare of modesty, Simon Sparrow had conveyed the information that he had run Boston eleven times.

"There's no other marathon like it in the world," he said. "Everyone has to qualify. New York is bigger, the Venice Marathon is more exotic—you know, the canals and all those little bridges—but for Boston, only qualifying runners get in."

"A dozen times," Morgan declared.

"No, eleven."

"Maybe next year," said Morgan in a consoling tone. Miranda could not tell if her partner was being bitchy, or just amusing. She suspected he was being bitchy. She knew he still hurt from his inaugural run that morning.

"What's your connection with the Bacon Society?" asked Miranda.

"The Arctic," said Simon Sparrow cryptically.

"Simon has trekked across Baffin Island by himself," said Padraig, quite proud of his fellow Baconite.

"Seven times," said Sparrow, modestly. "Not across, though, Porrig. And not lengthwise, either, that's been done but it's a major expedition. I just go back to Baffin now and then to do what the Australians describe as a 'walkabout.' I've crossed several peninsulas, hiked over the Meta Incognita to Lake Harbour, it's called Kimiruit now, and across the Auyuittuq divide from Broughton to Pangnirtung. Boats at either end. You can't walk town to town."

Miranda was fascinated. There was something tentative about his manner, a slight quaver in his voice that undermined the significance of his vaunted achievements. This man seemed able to make what should be exciting seem ordinary. He was a nice man, that was obvious. Almost too obvious. Polite, pleasant, the kind of man her sister in Vancouver would have liked; in fact the kind of man her sister in Vancouver had married. This was not true, of course, her sister's husband played golf.

Sparrow, capable of murder? Almost guaranteed. People like him invent themselves as they go along. With nothing to fall back on, they have to keep doing unusual things just to maintain a sense of their own identity. *I've met variations of this guy before,* she thought. *Defines himself by what he's done, lives for what he'll do next.*

People like him are essentially pathological, they don't live in real time. The present is only a gathering point between their personal past and the future. They only have a conscience for convenience, it makes their lives easier.

"Miranda." Morgan was intruding on her private discourse. "Miranda, you do that too!"

"Yes, sure, what?"

"I was saying how much I like scuba diving, Ms. Quin. I understand you dive."

"Yeah, Morgan and I went for a good one near Tobermoray last spring. Down among the freshwater wrecks." She was referring to a case where they had both nearly drowned.

"I've never been under in freshwater, it must be fascinating, but very cold, I love saltwater diving, not the garishness of the Caymans, but say the Galapagos, that was astonishing, the animals were astonishing, no wonder Darwin invented evolution, I'd have come up with the origin of species myself if he hadn't beat me to it."

Why would he want to kill Dieter Kurtz, she wondered? Could it have simply been something to do? But if you wanted to know what it felt like to murder, who better to murder than a man no one liked.

"Actually, I enjoyed the Caymans, especially Cayman Brac," she said. "It's some of the best diving in our part of the world. Someday, I'd like to try the Great Barrier Reef."

"It's superb," he said. "Be sure to go from Cairns, pronounced Cans by the locals, that's the main dive centre."

Morgan seemed intrigued by the man. Miranda found him irritating.

Morgan was listening carefully. This was a man, he thought, for whom murder would be an adventure. Motive: curiosity, with nothing to connect him to the victim apart from the intricacies of circumstance. Motive: no motive.

He felt paradoxically reassured about his own life as he listened to Simon Sparrow. *I think an average day on the job, with coffee and a muffin at Starbucks, is as exciting as this guy's combined adventures. Poor bugger, he's struggling just to make himself real.*

While Simon kept talking, his attention drifted and Morgan followed his line of vision until his own eyes focused on Jane Latimer's décolletage, or, rather, on the converging contours drawing the interest of both men down into the deep shadows between her breasts.

Peremptorily shifting his attention to Mlle. Lachine, Morgan asked her where she was from, and Simon Sparrow's voice trailed off, although he seemed not at all concerned that the centre of focus was shifting. It was almost a relief, thought Miranda. *He can go back to his interior monologue, telling himself the story of his life. We didn't find out his connection to the others, though. How does his interest in the Arctic relate to membership in the Bacon Society?*

At first Marie Lachine looked startled by Morgan's question, and almost offended. She had sleek black hair highlighted with strands of grey and a slight cast to her eyes that suggested something exotic. Clearly she had been asked before where she was from. It was a way of placing her as an outsider.

"I am from Toronto," she said in cadenced English that suggested her Montreal origins. "I was not born here." Her enunciation and syntax were precise. "I have made Toronto my home. There is more opportunity for a *separatiste* in Toronto these days than in Québec, and in France it is *passé*."

"A Toronto separatist?"

"A separatist in Toronto. I do commentary on radio and television, providing the *Québéçoise* perspective, and I am frequently invited to social gatherings among the corporate elite to provide a *soupçon* of the *Francophonie*, suitably feminine, mildly threatening, with Gallic charm. And you want to know why I am here? I am here because I studied Francis Bacon at the Sorbonne. D.Litt, 1981. You wonder if I had a motive sufficient to murder? Quite possibly."

She stopped, waiting for Morgan to indicate further interest. Instead, it was Miranda who spoke up.

"What motive would that be, Dr. Lachine?"

"Why, the same as virtually everyone in this room, Mademoiselle Detective." Her tone was patronizing. She had that peculiar habit of some women who find it necessary to position other women they think are beneath them through sly twists of condescension that allow no rebuttal. "Whatever you could imagine, that would be motive to murder. What you might conjure as possible, that would be real."

"Very enigmatic," said Morgan, and, rising to Miranda's defence where she would have appeared petty to do so herself, he added, "Mademoiselle."

"I never use 'doctor,'" she answered back, deflating his rejoinder. "For us, it is, how would you say, pretentious."

"Motives?" said Miranda, steering the conversation back on course. "Would you clarify, please, Mademoiselle."

The woman smiled; she looked around their little group which still included Professor Li Po, also an alumnus of the Sorbonne, and Padraig, and the self-absorbed Simon Sparrow. She then looked across at the cadre gathered around Lionel Webb (although it was Felix Swan who was doing the talking, gesticulating and sweating profusely, despite the perfect air-conditioned ambiance). She looked at Jennifer Pluck and Jane Latimer and at Hermione M, who had joined the others, a neat little coven of three generations. She looked back at Miranda, then at Morgan, still holding her strained Gallic smile.

Slowly, in a loud clear voice, she began to speak. The derision in the words that came out was in disconcerting contradistinction to the horror of the sentiments expressed. "Monsieur Dieter Kurtz was a sexual predator, and worse, an intellectual predator, a warlock on the prowl to the end of his life, swooping without mercy on wary and unwary alike. He was a vampire, Count Dracula of

Scarborough, sucking the lifeblood from everyone here; he knew secrets, he knew scandals, he had a demonic understanding of the weaknesses in others and he knew how to exploit them. Do you honestly think we are a band of comrades? We are counter-apostles in thrall to the Antichrist. Any one of us could be the murdering Judas, *bien oui*?"

The entire room came to attention. No one spoke. Feet shuffled. Morgan noticed the main carpet on the floor, an antique Heriz, hand-knotted with vegetal dyes. Why would she declaim such virulent sentiments? Miranda glanced from person to person, reading in the responses to Mlle. Lachine's statement nothing more than shared discomfort at the social awkwardness. Except perhaps for Lionel Webb; his eyes revealed contempt. Was it contempt for her violation of the group's confidence, or for the man being denigrated in such dramatic terms, or for something more personal?

"Well, well," said Felix Swan, interjecting much needed diversion into the silence and addressing the entire company, "We do seem to be a ship of fools, don't we? Have you read that, has anyone read that? Katherine Anne Porter's novel."

"I know the song by *The Grateful Dead*," said Padraig.

"There's a painting by Hieronymus Bosch called 'The Ship of Fools,' said Ralph. "*Das Narrenschiff*, it's in the Louvre."

"And who do you suppose Judas is, if Kurtz was the Antichrist?" said Jane Latimer ignoring them as the group slowly gathered into the centre of the room, some sitting down on the leather sofas, some standing or leaning. "It could be any one of us, even me."

"Judas as Peter," said Ralph. "The role is yours."

"As Peter?" Padraig seemed puzzled.

"Jane has ascended to the presidency."

"You see, Porridge," said Hermione M. "In the inversion of the world that Mademoiselle has constructed for us, Judas is Peter, the rock on which to rebuild—oh my, this is more amusing than when Dieter was alive."

chapter twelve
A Goodly Huge Cabinet

Apparently, their meeting was about to begin in earnest. Two servants quietly removed the various dishes, wine glasses and champagne flutes, soiled napkins, food-trays and left-over *hors d'oeuvres*. All eyes shifted from the new leader to Lionel Webb. He was a man of few words, it seemed, but with the charisma endowed by great wealth that placed him always at the centre of a gathering, no matter how peripheral his actual position.

As everyone settled in, Miranda catalogued their common characteristics: they were all devoted one way or another to a long-dead philosopher-mystic; they were mostly elderly, with young Sir David and the peculiar Jennifer Pluck the exceptions. No, Mademoiselle Marie Lachine was at most in her early fifties, and the redoubtable Simon Sparrow was Miranda's own age, give or take a few years, as was Jane Latimer, and the perspiring Buddha, Felix Swan, was only a decade older, the same age as the D'Arcys. Their ages spanned the decades, it just seemed they were old.

Lord Beavermarsh or whatever his name was, Lionel Webb, was surely still in his fifties, and very fit for his age. Some people, she thought, take wealth as a license to let themselves go and others consider it an obligation to look gorgeous, or as close to gorgeous as they can approximate with personal trainers, clothing designers, and a conscientious staff in the kitchen.

They were all of western European stock, with the exception of Professor Li Po, who probably knew Europe better than any of them. They were all childless, apparently. That struck her as odd. Li Po had a nephew, they must have relatives, but none of them is married. *None of us,* she amended, *including Morgan and me. Each of us is isolated in our own brief time in the world.*

Lionel Webb, she remembered from tabloid headlines years ago, had been married. His wife died in a boating accident. He was a widower. She had been very ill at the time of her death.

It bothered Miranda that she found herself identifying with such a peculiar conclave—whose strongest bond seemed to be a profound dislike for the man whose death brought them together. Interestingly enough, she found herself disliking him as well. She looked over at Morgan who appeared to be enjoying himself. He was examining smaller carpets around the perimeters of the room which were poised colourfully beneath the soaring shelves of leather-bound volumes. He would be cataloguing the carpets in his mind, assembling their identifying characteristics into patterns of memory to be checked out in his books later on.

In fact, Morgan, while admiring the rugs, was simultaneously contemplating the collective nature of the people around him, drifting towards a determination of their group personality as impossibly elusive. How could you sum up a gathering that included a cranky spy of ancient vintage and a woman who inherited a treasure hunt, a venerable Chinese scholar and a titled young Englishman, a sweating Buddha and a misanthropic *Québéçoise* opportunist, a disenchanted flower-child, an infinitely acquisitive and charming tycoon, a stunning and brilliant fitness buff, a man who explored the world in search of himself, and of course Porrig and Rafe.

Miranda and I hardly seem like outsiders in such a motley crew, he thought—*she with her beautiful mind, me with gaping spaces in mine that cry to be filled.*

It was the death of Dieter Kurtz that held them all together: for Miranda and himself, how it happened, who did it; for the others, as a fortuitous act; for one among them, a necessity. And perhaps that one is Judas, for good or ill.

Morgan looked up and caught Miranda's eye. She smiled. She seemed to be enjoying herself.

Miranda admired the huge door beside the fireplace, so solid and ornate it seemed daunting. Opposite, there were French doors opening into a conservatory that had the opposite effect. They seemed to welcome entry with the promise of orchids and the scent of the countryside. It was a room lit with the subtlety of evening, with skylights open to admit bees, even butterflies.

Nature by design.

Lionel Webb cleared his throat and began to speak in a quiet but resonant voice.

"Ladies and gentlemen," he said. "I think we all know who killed Dieter Kurtz."

Miranda cleared her throat.

"And while not meaning to show the police disrespect," he continued, "I put it to our president to call for a vote of solidarity. Let us, the members of the Bacon Society, stand together as one." He smiled benignly, like any chairman of the board who has just called on his CEO to underwrite his demands.

"In favour?" said Jane Latimer. "We hang together."

"So to speak," said Padraig.

"Porridge!" said Hermione M, "We'll do no such thing."

There was a show of hands. The declaration of mutual support was unanimous, except for Morgan and Miranda, who were both wondering if such a vote qualified as obstruction, and how they would go about laying charges.

Miranda leaned over and whispered to Morgan. "He might only mean that Kurtz brought death upon himself."

"He might."

"Now, before we forget," said Lionel Webb. "The Labour Day weekend is still on, despite the absence of Professor Kurtz. I expect to see you all on the government wharf in Port Carling next Friday evening, 8 o'clock sharp. The Lake Rosseau side by the old launch works. The boat will leave at 8:05. A late dinner will be served on Briar Hill Island. You, of course, are included, Detectives. This is our annual Muskoka jaunt. You will be honoured as our guests—or is that ambiguous? We would like to honour you, the honour is ours. Bring swim suits, tennis rackets, and warm clothes. Cottage country can be unpredictable this time of year."

There were murmurs of encouragement. They would have a lovely time and it might prove rich grounds for their investigation. It was fun. Under the circumstances, it was unavoidable.

"Now," said Lionel Webb, "For those who wish, the *Wunderkammern!* Sir David, if you would lead the way."

The massive door leading off to the side, with a bust of Pallas perched ironically on top of the lintel, drew the entire company forward as young David stood before it with a large antique key in his hand. He waited dramatically for a few moments, then inserted the key in the lock with a rattling flourish and swung the door open. Morgan was startled when an inner door made of thick glass was revealed, obviously impervious to ambient temperatures and humidity, but more importantly, a major obstacle to unauthorized entry. Beside this door was an elaborate key-pad on which the young man tapped out a code before applying his thumb to a screen to affirm his identity. Above the key-pad was a brass plaque, incongruous in the high-tech context, etched with the aphorism, *'Wonder Is The Seed Of Knowledge.'*

The glass against a blackened background reflected the assembled crowd. Their dark image, reminiscent of the damned being gathered on the shores of the River Styx, disappeared instantaneously when the interior lights were switched on from beside the key-pad. Suddenly revealed was a dazzling array of display cabinets and shelves and sealed cupboards in a large windowless chamber. The room was brilliantly illuminated, and yet some displays were discreetly in shadow, lit selectively in a soft blue glow.

"Welcome to my Cabinet of Curiosities," said Lionel Webb from the rear.

"Ms. Quin," said Sir David, addressing Miranda while unobtrusively barring access to the room, "I'm assuming you are not wearing perfume. Thank you. Deodorant is acceptable." He turned to Morgan, "As is after-shave, except Old Spice which for some reason lingers interminably. But I noticed, you are not wearing Old Spice."

"Go ahead, David, lead the way," said Lionel Webb, adding, as they all filed in: "Detectives this is my *sanctum sanctorum*."

"It is 'a goodly huge cabinet,'" said Felix Swan. "You honour us, Lion. You honour our mentor."

"Dear God!" said Lionel Webb, "not Kurtz?"

"No, no. I meant Bacon." Swan let his voice trail off in a brief indication of his embarrassment for being misunderstood.

"A *wunderkammern?*" said Morgan, speaking to Lionel Webb. "Your personal cabinet of wonders."

"Essential for the true Baconian, Detective Morgan. And I have been blessed by good fortune with the resources to assemble the best. Not an indulgence, I assure you. A necessity for the cultivated mind." At this point, he turned to Felix Swan who was standing in damp anticipation, awaiting his summons. "Rector," he said, and added as an aside, "You can always count on the Rector." Then, in a request that repetition had turned into a ritual, he intoned, "Rector, would you recite for us Bacon's admonition of 1594 that every man who would be truly informed should cultivate a garden, assemble a library, employ a laboratory to his purpose, and be possessed of a goodly huge cabinet. Rector, please."

"'...*wherein*'" said the Rector, beginning to recite with that curious plumy resonance that some people affect, through which language is transformed to indicate the words coming out of their mouth originated in another's mind, "'*wherein whatsoever the hand of man by exquisite art or engine has made rare in stuff, form or motion; whatsoever singularity, chance and the shuffle of things has produced...*'"

Was he trying to sound like an Elizabethan, Miranda wondered? She had seldom heard ordinary words given so pompous a representation, except perhaps when her grade ten Latin teacher, Miss Collip, would declaim passages from Virgil.

"'...*whatsoever Nature has wrought...*'"

Good grief, thought Morgan, *the others are laughing under their breath. Lionel Webb, simply by asking him to recite, has made him a figure of ridicule.*

"'...*in things that want life...*'"

The poor man, thought Miranda. *He's speaking with the self-importance of a small child reciting 'In Flanders Fields' on Remembrance Day.*

"'...shall be assorted and included—'"

"Thank you," said Lionel Webb in a clear voice, indicating the occasion for quotation had expired.

While the others wandered the passageways between display cases, clearly familiar with the labyrinthine complexity of their layout, some flicking on dull blue lights to get a better look at one thing or another, some craning to see onto the upper shelves along the windowless walls, Lionel Webb turned to Miranda and Morgan, corralling them to the side.

"My people tell me, Detectives, both of you graduated from the University of Toronto and either one of you might have gone on to an academic career. You have solved many cases of murder, resolved many mysteries. You, Detective Quin, are somewhat of an Aristotelian in your approach, and you, Detective Morgan, are decidedly Baconian. Deductive, inductive, a nice combination."

"You had us investigated?" exclaimed Miranda, interrupting his discourse even though she found it engaging and, for the moment, complimentary.

"Yes, of course. Otherwise you would not be here," he gestured around them to take in the entire confines of his *sanctum sanctorum.* "At least, not without a warrant."

"And we checked out okay?" said Morgan, amused. *Wonder may indeed be the seed of knowledge but knowledge is the seed of power, and certain kinds of knowledge can be bought, even if wisdom cannot.* He was in no hurry to bring their conversation around to the curious death of Dieter Kurtz. He wanted to explore Webb's Cabinet of Curiosities, impelled by being described as Baconian, even if he was too much of an adult to request clarification.

Miranda had no such compunction. Rather than asking about her own designation, however, she inquired ingenuously about her partner.

"Why," she asked Webb, "does Morgan, according to your *people* (she said people in italics), fit the Baconian profile?"

"Profile? Hmm. Bacon preached the benefits of inductive reasoning. Anything worth knowing is founded in the observable world. The trick is in seeing, in knowing what to observe. So you observe everything, and as the mind sifts through its discoveries, knowledge becomes evident. Exactly the opposite to speculative deduction, your specialty, I believe. You and Aristotle. You construct theorems about nature from a single bloom. Your partner, builds gardens."

"And revels among the profusion of flowers!" said Miranda, not disappointed with this estimation of either Morgan or herself, and pleased to pick up on his metaphor.

"And in the end," said Morgan, "I get to know a lot about individual blossoms, but not much about metaphysics and ultimate ends. Is that what we're saying? Details and not the big picture."

"*Au contraire*," said Lionel Webb. "For Francis Bacon, the big picture was *in* the details. The ideal mind, I suppose, would harness the intuitive and deductive modes together, but that might be like setting draft horses to pull in opposing directions. Tremendous power, no movement."

Miranda smiled. "It could also mean the person harnessing them had limited imagination. Turn your horses in the same direction, they might pull the earth right out from under him."

"*Touché*," said Lionel Webb. "You do bring out the French in me, Detective Quin. Shall we join Mlle. Lachine?"

chapter thirteen
The Annex

After they dropped Jane Latimer off, Miranda suggested they go out for drinks to recap the evening's events and revelations. It was too late, so they went back to Morgan's postmodern nineteenth century condo in the Annex, a time-warped monstrosity with cantilevered stairs and balcony entrances superimposed over the medley of cut-stone and red brick that marks the high Victorian style in Toronto, with two-story windows cut into the venerable walls and gingerbread trim in retreat among shadows. He poured them each a glass of chilled Ontario riesling from an open bottle with the distinctive Henry of Pelham blue label. They settled facing each other on the sofa, Miranda with her legs tucked up underneath her and her dress drawn taunt across her knees, and Morgan with legs outstretched, twisted comfortably to the side.

"So, tell me?" she said.

"What?"

"Who killed Dieter Kurtz?"

"Don't know."

"I think we've narrowed it down to one or more of twelve," she said with a tired smile. "What did you think of Webb's treasury of artifacts—drawn, as Felix described it, *from Nature and History*."

"David Jenness called it that."

"Morgan, how did you know?"

"What?"

"That his name is Jenness. On the list he's only 'Sir David.' You weren't introduced to him formally. No one said his name was Jenness."

"Yeah, I don't know. I thought he said it, or maybe Jane Latimer did."

"I don't think so."

"Well, maybe I ran across it somewhere, reading about Webb. I've never met him before. It just seemed to be there in my head from the moment I met him, that was his name."

"Have you ever known anyone called Jenness."

"I don't think so. There was a famous anthropologist who worked in the Arctic called Diamond Jenness."

"Here," said Miranda, handing him her glass which was still full. "Take this away, I don't want to diminish the effect of the Dom Perignon. My head's spinning, Morgan. Nothing holds up after champagne. Is your head spinning?"

"No."

"Well, you're bigger, it wouldn't."

"That's why you had me drive. I thought you were just tired."

"Tell me about the Chamber of Curiosities. The *Wunderkammern!* What do you think of the whole idea? What did you like the most?"

"I'm not sure," said Morgan. "It felt invasive, like being exposed to the inside of someone's head. You know, same as going into an office papered with kid's pictures and vacation posters and newspaper clippings. The more that's revealed, the more unsettling it is."

"Yeah, like witnessing the residue of an orderly explosion."

"I liked the skulls."

"How do you mean, *liked?*"

"I don't know where else you would see cranial fragments, jawbones, whole skulls representing the last several million years in human evolution, all in private possession."

"But Morgan, is that what it's all about—they're privately owned? To be shared as an expression of power?"

Morgan shrugged, he wasn't so uncomfortable with *noblesse oblige.*

"I could have spent hours searching for patterns in the arrangement of things. I mean, in a single case he had a Neanderthal knuckle-bone, letters from Wordsworth to his sister Dorothy, a Spanish doubloon, and three feathers from Napoleon's pillow on St. Helena. In the next cabinet were core drillings from the Coppermine region in the Arctic and a piece of the one true cross purchased at Canterbury Cathedral the day Thomas à Becket was assassinated.. Next to that, an astrolabe, a sextant, a wind-up doll of the Kaiser made of pressed metal and an original Barbie Doll. You tell me—if we were inside someone's brain-case, he would have to be a madman, right, or obsessive-compulsive."

"Maybe the random order of things is a code, it's not random at all," said Miranda. "A code that even he can't decipher. Like a lunatic's diary? And what about the desiccated body in the chair, he claimed it was the actual authentic remains of Jeremy Bentham."

"Poor old Bentham. The great utilitarian, he ended up under the stairs at University College London where they bring him out to attend the occasional meeting. They declare him present, but not voting. If Lionel Webb has the real Jeremy Bentham, then the College has an imposter."

"Good thing he can't vote, then. That's where Rowling got the idea for Harry Potter."

"What, pardon?"

"Harry's Muggle family keep him under the stairs."

"But he's not dead. That's very macabre."

"So is keeping a philosopher's body for strategic display."

"Bentham would be pleased to be in Webb's *Wunderkammern*; the ultimate end of a good life, I suppose, providing somebody pleasure, even if it's not himself. Did you notice how quick Webb was to show us papers authorizing the possession of a corpse '*for scientific or cultural purposes*?"

"I was surprised there were no paintings or sculptures," said Miranda.

"They're in another sealed gallery, according to, I think it was Simon Sparrow who said that. They're not accessible to the Bacon Society."

"What did you make of him?"

"Sparrow? The most likely among them to be the killer, and the least likely."

"Sometimes, Morgan, being enigmatic is just an excuse for having no answers."

"There were actually a lot of artifacts from the Arctic in there, and Simon Sparrow has travelled a good deal in the far North, or so we were told. Maybe he brought them back."

"Did you notice the dolls dressed in caribou with ivory heads from Clyde River, they were exquisite? And that beautiful piece of scrimshaw etched with images of whaling vessels."

"The scrimshaw was probably bought at a southern auction. They were mostly done by the whalers and ended up in back corners of New England seaports."

"Yeah, but there were lots of tiny stone carvings and an ivory swan and a stone lamp that had obviously been used to light and heat generations of igloos."

"Okay, so maybe Sparrow was buying for Webb in the Arctic. That explains their connection, and maybe connects Sparrow to Bacon."

"We're a long way from Kurtz, here."

"Nothing with this group is a long way from Kurtz,"

said Morgan. "We can't leave out the possibility of an arbitrary crime, death not by misadventure but literally *for* adventure. Motive: no motive."

"That notion seems more likely to implicate Webb than poor Simon Sparrow. Webb accumulates 'everything,' as he said. That's the point of his limitless collection. So, commit murder—add that to your goodly huge cabinet! It's Webb."

"Maybe not," said Morgan.

"Okay, maybe not."

"Why *poor* Simon, why poor?"

"Because he tries too hard. You've got to feel sorry for anyone who tries so hard to prove to himself he's alive. I don't think he'd bother with murder; not this one, it's too public. For him, audience is secondary. If Simon Sparrow killed anyone, it would be himself. And he wouldn't do that, because he'd need to hang around to see if he's really dead."

"Interesting. Not completely convincing, but interesting."

"Jennifer Pluck was quiet," said Miranda.

"Yeah, I noticed. So was Hermione Mac."

"The spy?"

"Yeah."

"She had a few caustic remarks to vent from her system, all related to Hermione M. Did you hear the claim for Francis Bacon as the founder of the British Secret Service?"

"Yeah. Based on his facility with codes, transferring messages across the Channel for Queen and country."

"He was better off when King James came to power, apparently." Miranda smiled sleepily. "Someone said that."

"Well, someone also said he was Elizabeth's bastard son, the eldest of several."

"Yeah, well someone else claimed he was Shakespeare."

"Wrote Shakespeare, was Bacon."

"Yeah, well…" She fought to stay awake. She was enjoying herself.

"Well…"

"What did you think of Jane's get-up?"

"I didn't notice."

"Morgan, you liar."

"She wears sleaze like a costume. It takes class to do that?"

"We'll leave that as a point to be argued. You know Webb was married, once?"

"Yeah, he's a widower," said Morgan.

"His wife died in a boating accident."

"I thought it was cancer. Or was she dying of cancer when she was knocked overboard? He made a huge donation to the Princess Margaret Hospital Foundation."

"Her death wasn't big news. Except in the *Sun*. Competition papers played it down. Professional courtesy, I guess." It had slipped Morgan's mind that Webb's fortune originated in the newspaper trade. "God, Morgan, I'm tired. We'd better call it a night."

"You wanna stay here."

"Sure, I get the couch."

"No way. The guest gets the bed. The couch is mine.

Host's prerogative."

"Are the sheets clean?"

"Fairly."

"!"

"I'll get you clean ones."

He walked through into the bathroom and returned with clean sheets and trudged up the stairs. A few moments later he tossed a singlet over the railing which landed on Miranda's outstretched body, where she had squirmed around on the sofa into a comfortable reclining position.

"Mmmpff," she said.

"You're welcome," he called down. "Wash up or whatever you do, there's a toothbrush in the cabinet, and get yourself up here. You can shower in the morning."

He came down the stairs wearing the same boxers she had seen him in earlier in the day. He had on another singlet and as she sat up the small tattoo on his right shoulder caught her eye.

"Bird-man," she said.

"What? Yeah, my constant companion."

"Morgan, why in God's name did you get a tattoo, you of all people.'

"That's why, so you'd ask. Go to bed."

She was sitting upright, now, tugging her dress down to her knees.

"Come on Morgan, let me touch it."

"You cannot touch my *tangata manu*. You've had too much Dom Perignon. Touching my bird-man gets me stirred up, and I am not prepared to take advantage of you in your compromised state, and I'm still sore from running. My goodness, that was only this morning."

"I am not incapacitated. I am curious."

"You are a veritable cabinet of curiosities."

"I just want to touch your tattoo. I've never touched a tattoo. In the area of tattoo touching, I am a virgin."

"Miranda, go to bed. You haven't slept in two days. You had a bad date last night, remember?"

"Was that only last night! I forgot. Morgan, why did you go to Easter island?"

"To get a tattoo."

"Me too."

"You don't have one."

"Or maybe I do."

He helped her to her feet and walked her to the bathroom. One minute they had been having a reasonable conversation, the next she was semi-coherent. He held her close as they walked. There was no one in the world he was more fond of, not that he could think of, or wanted to think of.

"Come on, old girl. You go in there and brush your teeth and do what you have to do. I'll just wait out here."

"You didn't go to Easter Island to get away from me, did you?"

"No, did you go there to get away from me?"

"Possibly. Except you'd already been there so I was dogging your footsteps, walking in your shadow, repeating the feat. Not much of a getaway. Bet I had more excitement."

"Miranda, I went on a holiday. I wanted to see the

moai, the giant statues, before they disintegrate. You sometimes go on holidays. I went somewhere that interested me, you go places that interest you. You go to the Caymans to get laid."

"I do not!" she declared through the open bathroom door. "And I did not. And if I went for a sexual adventure, it would be for sex and adventure, not to get laid. I am not a receptacle! Where's the damn toothbrush. Found it! Mmmpff."

She came out wearing only the oversize singlet. She had left her clothes, with uncharacteristic abandon, in a clump on the floor, her panties on top.

"And don't think you're going to follow me up the stairs."

She paused, then she declared, "I need help. You will have to walk up with me— side by side. That's the only way. Nobody's compromised, we go up together." She giggled. "Do you have a double bed? I've never been in your bedroom, your *sanctum sanctorum* (she adopted the voice of a basso profundo for '*sanctum sanctorum*'). I intend not to have sex with you tonight, Morgan." With that she raised an arm so that a breast nearly popped through the singlet sleeve as she draped her weight over his lowered shoulder. "Come on, old sport, let's get me to bed."

Morgan tucked her in under a clean sheet, kissed her on the forehead—she was already asleep, she didn't notice the pillow slip was unchanged—and descended to the living-room where he stretched out on the sofa, and even before he shut his eyes he could feel himself falling, and when they were closed he looked around the spreading space in his mind for Saint Augustine, whom he knew would be waiting.

Miranda stood, poised in the bright morning light that was streaming through the two-story living room window. The lower part of the vertical blinds were jammed open although in the upper reaches they were permanently closed, leaving the bedroom loft in perpetual shadow. She was dressed and held a mug of coffee in each hand.

The festive look of the night before was a little worn at the edges but she herself felt fresh and attractive. She had slept soundly in spite of the unfamiliar bed, having fallen asleep giddy with champagne and high spirits. Walking almost naked by Morgan on the way to the shower she had been surprised he didn't stir. He was splayed on the sofa with arms and legs outstretched for maximum air. The night had been almost as hot as the previous day and while he paid shares for a central cooling system it was painfully ineffective.

Looking down at him now, she wondered just what it would take to arouse him. He was wearing a Lone Ranger sleeping mask like the ones they give you on overnight flights, and he had ear plugs jammed in, probably from the same flight. Arouse might not be the right word, she thought. He looks comically vulnerable and like he could sleep forever.

He twitched, she set one of the coffees down, and sat

on the floor beside him, sipping from her own cup in muted slurps to avoid burning her lips. *There is something beautiful about watching another person sleep, something comforting in being able to touch their vulnerability with unmediated affection.* She wanted to reach out to him and yet waking him would destroy the illusion.

She had felt this kind of benevolent affection several times when her daughter had slept over, drawing the covers up around her shoulders in the cold of the night. She thought of Jill as her daughter. The girl had been her ward for only a couple of years and they had never lived together. Jill was abused by the same man who years before had abused Miranda. The man had been Jill's father. He was dead. Jill's mother was dead. The man's name had been Griffin and he had owned a vintage Jaguar XK 150. Now Miranda was the administrator of monies he had left to charity, she owned the Jag, and she was the girl's official guardian. *Whatever meaning there is to our life,* she thought, *comes from the order we impose on its infinite complexity.*

Morgan's bare legs twitched. The fly of his boxer shorts gaped open and she glanced away demurely, then in spite of herself she gave in to curiosity and looked back with a quizzical expression on her face, impishly ducking her head sideways to see if an altered line of vision could penetrate the shadows, but the diminutive stature of his sleeping penis eluded her vision. Strangely, however, when she sat up, took a sip of her coffee, and watched him, the shadows of his boxers shifted configuration as the hidden flesh rose slowly to awesome tumescence.

She wondered if he was free-falling with a saint, or had something more exciting entered his sleep? She would have to find out more about Augustine. She had vague memories that he had been instrumental in devising a notion of heaven from the abstruse symbolism of the Book of Revelation. He had not figured large in her life. Was Morgan unconsciously aroused, or conscious in his dreams of an unknown lover? Was it her?

She had never witnessed anything like this; she had seen men's private parts at ease and at full attention, she had felt men rise against her own body. But she had never observed the procedure, watched the metamorphosis from the pathos of small to a state of alarming potency. Even though it all happened behind a thin layer of his shorts, it was exhilarating, daunting, and funny to watch.

Meanwhile, Morgan soared through air that was filled with the buoyant smell of fresh-brewed coffee.

She reached over almost to touch him, slowly stroking his imagined aura, several inches above the bare flesh of his thighs.

Morgan's eyes opened to the darkness behind his mask but he could see in the slits of light at their lower edges a curious smudge of flesh-coloured activity.

Miranda's hand hovered over him.

Suddenly, his legs flared upwards with a life of their own and clenched around her outstretched hand. She let out a small scream and tried to withdrawn her hand. His thighs held it fast. With the other hand she tried to push away and was astonished at the power of his grip.

"Morgan!"

"Miranda."

She reached with her free hand and pulled his sleeping-mask down over his nose to his chin.

"You look ridiculous," she laughed.

"Me! You're the one caught with her hand in the cookie jar. Oh my goodness, I have to pee."

"Is that what it is?"

"What?"

"That! You just have to pee."

"Yeah, and it's painful. Let go."

"Me let go! You're the one holding on."

"Miranda." She looked down. He had released his grasp and she was clinging to his closest inner thigh with her nails dug into the flesh almost deeply enough to draw blood.

"Instinctive reaction," she said, releasing her grip, patting his tumescence through the material of his shorts with dismissive condescension, barely touching. "There, there, you take it off to the bathroom with you and do what you need to do."

He got up, and drawing his hands close around to the front he walked off to the bathroom, mumbling.

Miranda pivoted on the floor and leaned against the sofa, stretching her legs out across the bright-coloured Gabbeh rug. She drew the skirt of her summer dress up and flexed her thighs, admiring the strength revealed by the definition of her quads. She modestly rearranged her skirt. She sipped at her coffee and smiled to herself.

When Morgan came back in the room, still in boxer shorts and a singlet but with everything tucked into place, she handed him his coffee and he sat down beside her on the floor.

"I know how Kurtz died," she said.

chapter fourteen
The Office

Their colleagues were surprised to see them at Police Headquarters at the same time. Alex Rufalo, the Superintendent of Homicide, looked out from his office and observing them sitting face to face at opposing desks thought it must be the air conditioning that brought them in. It was a mercifully slow time in the department and they were on one of those cases not fraught with urgency that would eventually be resolved, perhaps be written up in a forensics journal for criminologists to savour, but was already yesterday's news.

Miranda had not yet told Morgan how the murder had been accomplished. She wanted to check out a couple of details. For his part, he found her secretive behavior amusing, endearing, irritating, frustrating.

They were turned out well, with appropriate grooming.

Miranda looked crisp and fresh and Morgan, as usual, looked clean and comfortably dishevelled.

Morgan was pouring through a sheaf of records. Miranda, who was on the telephone, stared at the facsimile copy of Bacon's book that she had pried from the dead man's clutch. It was lying on her desktop.

"Well," she said triumphantly after hanging up, "we're getting somewhere."

Morgan ignored her.

"You wanna know? You curious?"

"Yeah, I want to know more about Kurtz. Turns out his accent is authentic. You know how everyone thought it was an affectation—"

"Morgan! I know how he died."

"And I know how he lived. He claimed to be from Scarborough. Everyone knew he was from Scarborough. Well, he wasn't. He was born in Berlin. Grew up in Germany."

"Seriously?"

"Arrived in Canada, 1959, via Oxford. With a couple of degrees from Freiberg. Landed-immigrant status granted immediately. Settled in Montreal, did a brief stint at McGill, active with the Goethe Institute. Citizenship in '67. Came to UofT, no more Goethe Institute, now he was from Scarborough. The accent was teased into an inflection, his English was better than most native-born Anglophones."

"You're reading all that?"

"Reading, and from memory. Remember, I took a course with the guy."

"Twenty years ago."

"Twenty-two. But you don't forget a man like Kurtz."

"I did. I think he gave a guest lecture in that course I told you about. I told you that, didn't I?"

"You're not sure?"

"If I told you? Oh, if I heard him? Yeah, pretty sure. Our minds didn't connect. I don't remember the face. I recall the accent, it was like nothing I've heard before or since. Morgan, for goodness sake, don't you want to know how he died? It's very exotic!"

"Yeah, I do.'

"Okay, I was just talking to the crime lab."

"And?"

"You know that stray hair I found at the scene, I sent it off for analysis. Morgan, it's a pubic hair."

"That's what you said it looked like."

"Yes, well but it actually is. Now, remember, this morning," she lowered her voice to a conspiratorial whisper and leaned forward across her desk. "You had me in a mighty grip, uh, there." She nodded over their desks towards his lap.

"On your hand." He squirmed and looked sheepish.

"Morgan, don't you get it," she hissed in a voice loud enough to draw attention. Both of them sat back and let the conversation dangle in the air until they were ignored, then both leaned forward again.

"Morgan, oral sex."

"What!"

"Good grief, Morgan, do you need diagrams."

"That's disgusting," he said.

"Oral sex?"

"Dying from it!"

"With a woman, it had to be a woman. Old Dieter was smothered to death between a woman's thighs."

Morgan gazed into her eyes, wondering how to read the light reflected from the luminescence of the room.

"Why didn't you tell me?"

"What? I wasn't being coy, Morgan. I wanted to be sure."

"Coy wasn't the word that came to mind."

"Shhh!"

From the Superintendent's perspective it appeared they were flirting and he found their behavior annoying. They could at least keep it out of the office. Then he looked again. Miranda's face was flushed with triumph and Morgan's suggested complicity. This wasn't sexual. They were doing their jobs. Such acumen is what got him into this office, he understood people.

Morgan looked up as Jennifer Pluck approached their desks. She was carrying a large leather-bound book and was accompanied by a uniformed officer from Kurtz's house. After they discovered her yesterday afternoon, security had been tightened.

"Nice book," Morgan said, reaching out and taking it from her. "How'd she get in?" He addressed the officer. "You charging her?"

The police officer seemed confused. Jennifer Pluck did not appear either intimidated or contrite.

Morgan and Miranda exchanged looks, both wondering if DNA tests on the pubic hair would implicate this young woman, and in spite of himself Morgan surreptitiously glanced at her thighs, which were hardly visible through the voluminous material of her skirt. He felt a little embarrassed, then noticed Miranda was doing the same thing.

"I thought you should see this," she said.

"Is this Kurtz's book," asked Miranda.

"It was in his cabinet, if that's what you're asking."

"And you were trying to walk off with it?" said Morgan. "That's almost dumb enough to convince me you're innocent."

"Of murder?"

"Among other things."

"Well, I probably am," she responded, with uncharacteristic cheerfulness.

"I gave her a ride," said the officer. "I'm just off shift and she said she needed to see you guys right away."

"No B&E charges?" said Morgan, a little disappointed.

"Break and Enter?" said Jennifer Pluck, translating into English and finding the notion amusing. "P&B; prowling and burglary. What about S&M; snooping and messing about. No, Detective Morgan. I was there with a mission."

The officer excused herself and wandered off, still confused.

"Would you like to explain?" said Miranda.

"I got a call this morning from Lionel Webb. Personally. Usually he has someone else do the calling. He arranged for a bench warrant, I think that's what it is, from a judge, a friend of his, they're all friends when you're as rich as Lionel—anyway, it was a signed paper for the release of Kurtz's *Sylva Sylvarum* into Lionel's custody for safekeeping."

"No one told us about this," Morgan said with a scowl.

"Perhaps they didn't feel the need," the young woman responded.

"Why send you?" said Miranda. "If the book is so valuable, why not one of his security people?"

"Because I knew where it was, I knew what it was, I knew how to open the cabinet. I'm sure Lionel trusted me to bring it safely home."

"Home?"

"To his place, to his Cabinet of Curiosities."

"Well then there now," said Morgan. "What is it doing here?"

He turned the book over several times in his hands. It was heavy, the size of an encyclopaedia volume or a bound collection of law journals. The leather was worn, the page edges were feathered and brittle. Tiny bits of detritus fell away into the air as he handled it. Seldom had he held something that felt so venerable, ancient, and vulnerable.

"It's a fake," said Jennifer Pluck as he set it down carefully on his desk.

"What?" said Miranda.

"A fraud."

"You're kidding."

"I wouldn't be here if I was. It's a beautiful fake."

Miranda turned to Morgan. "Like the one Kurtz was holding?"

"Professor Kurtz was holding a facsimile," said Jennifer Pluck. "That's a very different thing."

Morgan looked down at his desk. The fake sat beside the facsimile bagged in plastic. The only thing to distinguish them to the untrained eye was that one was wrapped, the other exposed.

"Would you explain?" asked Miranda, picking up the book Jennifer Pluck had just brought in and flipping through the dusty pages.

"Intent, for one thing."

"Sorry?"

"A facsimile wants to be known for what it is, a copy, and to be admired for being a copy of good quality. A fake is just the opposite. It pretends to be the original, and fails if it is found out."

"Well, that's succinct," said Miranda.

"You were meant to know the copy you've got wrapped up there isn't real, the one Professor Kurtz was clutching when he died."

"After he died."

"*After* he died. I'm just going by what the papers say."

"That part wasn't in the papers," said Miranda.

"Gossip, then. Bacon Society gossip. Jane was there, wasn't she?"

"Yes, she was."

"You were meant to know right off, that book wasn't the real thing. That was the whole point."

"Whose whole point?" Morgan inquired.

"Whoever did the old man in. It could have been any of us."

"Including yourself?" Miranda asserted. "You certainly seem to appreciate the joke, which must be about the most esoteric joke ever devised."

"For the amusement of an exceptionally limited audience," Morgan added.

"Depends how you measure *limited*," said Jennifer Pluck. "Now look at this book." She reached over and took the copy she had brought in. "This pretends to be Professor Kurtz's trophy but it isn't, although it is a beautiful work of art in its own right."

"Explain?" asked Morgan.

"Well, the first edition is finely crafted to serve a function; paper bound up in leather to contain words. It is what it does, it's a delivery system, beautifully rendered to serve its purpose. This," she said, returning the book to Miranda, "is an illusion. It is created specifically to deceive, to trick the eye, to command the mind and the senses in the manner it chooses."

"It sounds like you admire this one as much as the original," said Morgan.

"Only as a bibliophile. This one is art. But it does not connect directly to Bacon. The artist who made it is a brilliant mediator. But as a devoted Baconian I want access directly to the creator himself, the man who uttered and muttered the words and set them in writing. Only the original can give me that."

"You make it sound like a religious experience," said Morgan.

"For me, it is the only religion that doesn't seem ludicrous. This has nothing to do with souls or God, I've never seen a soul or much liked the notion of God."

"If it's the words that connect you with Bacon, then the book doesn't matter. Isn't that how it should work, you don't need the tablets to honour the ten commandments."

"Which I don't. But it would be a kick to hold the stone plates in your hands and cast your eyes on the handwriting of God."

"Especially since you deny his existence," said Miranda. "It is amazing how Bacon leads away from the matters at hand."

"Eschatology," said Morgan, as if he were summing up their exchange.

"What?"

"The study of final things, last judgment, the disposition of souls. I was trying to think of that word yesterday when we first started talking about Bacon. Eschatology. That's the business we're in, Miranda. Homicide detectives, we're eschatologists. I like that."

"Sorry, Jennifer," said Miranda. "My partner has recently been troubled by saints." She grimaced, knowing her observation might seem equally obscure. "Let's get back to the book. You had a court order to rescue Kurtz's copy of *Silva Sylvarum* for safekeeping in Lionel Webb's vault. But you're saying there's been a switch."

"I guarantee it. This book is a fraud."

"Is this the one we saw yesterday?" asked Miranda.

"I'm not sure. It never crossed my mind we weren't looking at the real McCoy. Without actually holding it in hand it would be nearly impossible to tell." She picked the book up again and turned it over several times. "It's

The Dead Scholar

brilliantly done. The leather is old, I'd say authentic, but it was taken from another book. See how it's been worked on the spine to eliminate markings that were probably a title or author's name. See the gold in the letters, how it's been pushed in, the leather's too smooth underneath it, it's been recently tooled. Open the book, the paper is a genuine blend of old fibres, but they've been pressed by machine. Again, too smooth. Then they've been aged, repeatedly dampened and dried, air blown. And the ink, the depth of the letter imprint is too even. Squint at the page, all the letters are the same intensity. They have been applied electronically. The same computer system used by big-time counterfeiters. This book is made to look like it came off the press with others in the same edition, most of which have been lost. In fact, books of this era each have their own character, each one is slightly different to the trained eye. This book has no personality."

"Thank you, Jennifer," said Miranda. "Do you have any idea who could have made the exchange? Or where the fake might have been made? That would be a start, to find out who made it."

"When you find the missing book, Detective, you will find someone who wanted Kurtz dead; but that doesn't mean you'll have the killer." She paused. "I don't know that much about fakes." Miranda waited, but when the young woman continued, she merely announced, "I have to go, now. I have to give a lecture in an hour. On Bacon. You're both welcome to drop in, if you'd like." She said this with the flicker of a smile, suggesting that they might have more productive things to be doing. "If you wouldn't mind contacting Lionel, could you let him know about the book. I imagine he'll be furious."

Jennifer Pluck turned and walked away, leaving Morgan and Miranda sitting at their opposing desks with back to back computer monitors. Morgan's desk was cluttered with strategic piles of paper and Miranda's was clear except for an open file. The two large books lay like a challenge between them, one a facsimile and one a fake, although both contained virtually the same contents that were indisputably by Francis Bacon.

"Did you notice her thighs?" said Miranda.

"It was difficult with that outfit she was wearing."

"You don't see many women dressed like Jennifer Pluck."

"We'd better run a DNA test on the lone strand of pubic hair? I'd bet it was hers."

"Yeah. But Morgan, even if it is, there's a real anomaly, here. Let's suppose Kurtz died *in flagrante delicto*, with his face buried deep between someone's thighs, where's the evidence? One hair? Come on! It could be a plant. Let me call the M.E."

She dialed and after a couple of annoying delays with the automatic answering system connected to Ellen Ravenscroft.

"Sorry to bother you," she said.

"No bother, love. I'm up to my ears in blood and gore. Motorcycle and an eighteen wheeler. Head-on. Guess who lost. Talking to you is just the break I need. What can I do."

"Dieter Kurtz ."

"The dead scholar, yeah, what about him."
"He suffocated, right?"
"He did indeed."
"Did you check his face thoroughly?"
"Yes, that's what I do. I mean, no, I was careless. Yes, what about his face?"
"Anything unusual?"
"No, yes."
"And."
"It was exceptionally clean. His beard was, if there's such a word, kempt. It's very short but it was brushed; and his face was scrubbed—"
"*Post mortem?*"
"Couldn't say. I took his cleanliness to be the expression of a fastidious nature. Germanic, I suppose. Why, what're you looking for?"
"Vaginal fluids. Flecks of skin. Pubic hairs."
"On his face? Aha! No. He had a few of his own where they're supposed to be. Sparse, of course. Vaginal fluids? No, love, nothing at all except maybe a bit of after-shave. Old Spice, it lingers, and possibly a lightly perfumed cleaner-upper like you'd find in Baby-Wipes. I see where you're going with this, but sorry, no vaginal souvenirs, nothing even vaguely titillating."
"Thanks, Ellen. Talk to you soon."
Miranda turned to Morgan. "She didn't even ask about you," she said.
"Your pubic hair is meaningless."
"I do beg your pardon?"
He shrugged. "It wasn't an existential pronouncement."

"I don't think DNA tests will tell us much, really. With this motley crew it could mean anything. Let's suppose it belongs to Jennifer Pluck. Like, who had access? Who put it in the old man's beard? I realize now it was meant to be found. There was only one. So, perhaps it was planted by a former lover."

"Not necessarily. The whole bunch of them go up to Webb's cottage for their annual sleep-over. Anyone could have scoured the bedclothes for an incriminating hair or two."

"Yuck."

"Squeamish?"

"It just seems the opposite of cool," said Miranda. "Searching through someone's sheets for pubic hair. If it was done last summer, then Kurtz's murder has been a long-term project."

"Unless, as you say, it was a naughty keepsake."

"We're assuming it's a female hair," said Miranda.

"Only if we accept the plausibility of death by genital asphyxiation. It's your theory. There must be worse ways of dying."

"We could take this one step further. Someone truly dedicated to gamesmanship could plant her own hair so we'd find it, but clean the old boy up so it would be inconclusive. I think we should check out the DNA, anyway. I imagine they'll all relish giving samples, it's all part of the game."

"I'd like to ask for it when they're together in a group. I'd like to see the responses."

"You've lost me."

"Human nature. If there's any sort of conspiracy, each one alone may reveal nothing, but when they're together, they might check to see if the others are hanging tough, you know what I mean?"

Alex Rufalo sat back from his desk and gazed out through the open door, watching Miranda and Morgan at work. The strange-looking young woman had left. He might have been wondering how she fit into their current assignment. She looked like a university-type; he had known women like her when he studied criminology in Michigan, before dropping out to become a cop on the beat. He had worked his way up, married a lawyer, enjoyed authority, and appreciated an organization in which everyone had a place in the pyramid. Everyone except these two.

Morgan and Miranda somehow worked outside the system. They didn't flout authority, they ignored it. He could deal with their idiosyncrasies, their clumsy paperwork and negligent attention to protocol. They would never be a threat, there was no place for them to advance in the hierarchy. They made the people around them look good, especially their immediate superior.

Miranda worked her computer keyboard in sporadic flurries, obviously searching the net. Morgan was reading through files. He got up and went to a machine for coffee, bringing back two, one of which he set down beside Miranda.

"Thanks, Morgan," she said, then looked up. "I've got something here."

"What."

"I've tracked down Marie Lachine's doctoral thesis from the Sorbonne."

"Yeah, what's it on?"

"Like she said, on Bacon. Something pretty esoteric. It's in French, but I think it's about the work he did with his brother as a spy."

"The cipher business."

"I guess. I think they carried state secrets back and forth across the channel. That's what Jane Latimer told us. Mlle. Lachine seems to have done her dissertation on that end of things. No, there's more. Her interest isn't in spying, it's genealogical. Actually, as far as I can make out, it's both. She obviously has things to say about misplaced parents and cast-off children. I think there's an existential argument, here, connecting Bacon's position as outsider—if Queen Elizabeth was his mother and denied him legitimacy—with being the ultimate insider, as Elizabeth's spy in the royal courts of her various cousins on the Continent. I wish my French were better."

"Playing the illusions of questionable parentage against the illusions of espionage, neat. Wonder why she didn't go into an academic career? You'd think with a doctorate from the Sorbonne she'd have the credentials."

"You've met her, Morgan. She doesn't strike me as the professor type."

"Whatever that is."

"It's not her. But listen. There's a copy of her title page and an abstract, and at the bottom of the abstract there's a short list of acknowledgements, and…"

"And?"

"Guess who she thanks, first off?"

"Jean Paul Sartre."

"She thanks one Professor Li Po from Lanchou University in China."

"You're kidding."

"No, she does. So Mlle. Marie Lachine and the charming Professor Li Po are intimately connected."

"Intimately?"

"A figure of speech, Morgan. He's old enough to be her father."

Morgan looked at her to see if what she called a figure of speech was the revelation of reasoning she wasn't yet prepared to share. Miranda stared enigmatically at her computer screen, the twitch in her brow suggesting she was trying to decipher the French text in front of her. He glanced over at the Superintendent and saw that they were being watched. He shrugged and went back to his files, almost immediately coming up with a revelation to match Miranda's.

"So, guess what," he said.

"*Bien oui*," she said, "What, what?"

"I have summoned on *my* computer the official academic file of one Jennifer Pluck."

"How did you get in? That's a closed system."

He shrugged, pleased with himself.

"Who says you're not an outlaw? Anything of interest?"

"Yeah. Top marks all the way. Did her doctoral work at the University of London."

"I assumed Toronto, I suppose because she's got the

post-doc here. Where'd she do her undergraduate work?"

"Trent. She's from small town Ontario—Lakebridge, out near Peterborough. Queen's for an M.A., then London. What's interesting is she went the whole way through on a single bursary. No grants or scholarships in spite of marks that would certainly have qualified her. You'll never guess in a million years who put up the money for the bursary."

"The Webb Foundation."

"Come on! How did you know that?"

"Your tone of voice. I didn't even know there was a Webb Foundation. But when you started talking about putting up money, it seemed likely. And anyway, his grandfather started their newspaper empire in Lakebridge with a weekly, the *Clarion*, the *Bugle*, or something."

"Yeah. I don't need to raid files. In future, I'll just ask you. So, do you think they knew each other?"

"What, when she was graduating from high school and he was sitting in the House of Lords. They probably met for crumpets and tea from time to time, or a round of cricket and cucumber sandwiches. No, I don't think he knew her. Their families might have been aware of each other, though. Lakebridge is small enough, the local publisher probably knew everyone, even the Plucks."

"Even?"

"It's not a name that exactly rings like struck crystal."

"If her grandfather had made a fortune instead of his, we'd be admiring the name for its apposite sonority."

"Apposite, hmm."

"Thank you."

"Strange, though."

"What?"

"Well, you said she didn't receive any other scholarships or fellowships. You say her marks were stellar. That means she didn't apply. Most universities insist their graduate students try for maximum support. So, if she tried, she didn't try very hard. She had all the resources she needed. Enough to survive at the University of London, apparently with no student loans."

"No loans. Maybe that's why she learned to dress like a thrift shop blowout."

"Morgan, you don't dress like that from the Sally Ann, not these days. Those are designer clothes, I thought you realized."

"No, but I noticed they were clean."

"Good for you. Do a search for the Webb Foundation Scholarship Fund."

"That's what I've been doing. I'm coming up blank."

"Now that's interesting. Do you think she's the only recipient?"

"Possibly. It needs explaining. The more we know about this bunch, the more they connect. And paradoxically, the more elusive they become."

"You talk about 'they' as if we were dealing with a single entity."

"Don't you feel in some ways we are?" said Morgan.

"A monster with its rump in the sixteenth century and its head in the twenty-first."

"Or vice versa. An Egyptian sphinx. The body of a

lion and the head of a woman."

"I always thought it was a man's," said Miranda.

"In Greek mythology, the sphinx is a woman."

"Thank you," said Miranda, her voice slightly scratchy. "With Bacon's Freemason link, Egypt is not out of the question."

"But Bacon was also enthralled with the Athenian philosophers. The Greek sphinx strangled victims who couldn't solve her riddle, and when Oedipus did, she killed herself."

"Can a riddle arrange its own murder?"

They looked at each other and laughed, swallowed up in their runaway metaphor and enjoying the intimacy such nonsense disguised.

chapter fifteen
Muskoka

Miranda wheeled the green Jaguar across the old swing-bridge in Port Carling and around the corner onto a side street that plunged at a perilous angle to the government wharf on the Lake Rosseau side of the locks. Half way down the slope she sidled the car into a diminutive space where it came to an abrupt halt with its front wheels canted against the curb.

Morgan was not a driver. He did not get his license until he was an adult and he found such feats unnerving since he could not be sure whether the driver's accomplishment was an act of skill or of luck. Since he could never have parked in a small space on a steep hill without ricocheting between bumpers and cement, he admired Miranda's accomplishment but preferred to think it was luck.

They were early. The drive north had been pleasant. Talk was limited because the aerodynamics of the XK 150, while among the most aesthetically pleasing in the history of automotive design, were not conducive to conversation, especially with the top down. Morgan was content to sit back, let the wind rake his hair, and watch the scenery as it transformed from cityscape to suburban, suburban to rural, and rural to cottage country as they moved into the rugged granite and bush of the Canadian Shield.

Miranda loved driving, the feeling of connection by superb engineering to the landscape itself, more so in the car than when walking, or even in a canoe, which she had been taught as a girl at camp was the perfected union of design and desire.

Miranda had daydreamed as she drove about her summers working at camp. It seemed another world now, a world of innocence and fun. Perhaps it was all an illusion, the re-invention of youth as an idyllic adventure. *But such illusions are necessary. They sustain us through lives filled with villainy and violence. Or is that only my life*, she wondered. *Surely most lives are untouched so direrctly by death. Or is that, too, an illusion?*

She had kept the car when the estate of Jill's parents was resolved. She was the girl's guardian and the executor of her father's very large estate. It was not a souvenir. The malevolence of Robert Griffin was not something she wished to remember. He was a predatory voyeur who had inflicted gruesome suffering on others, young women including herself and her ward. They had survived.

Most of his victims died. Through a quirk of fate and the perverse machinations of the dead man, and of the girl's dead mother, they had been brought together. The car, to Miranda, was a symbol of their survival, a thing of beauty arising out of the ashes of evil. As her love for Jill was defined by the horrors each held secret deep within, this car was a phoenix, defiant of death and its terrible origin.

Miranda sat with her hands still splayed on the steering wheel and tilted her head against the back of the bucket seat which rose up behind her with a reassuring grasp on her body that made her even now, at their destination, want to remain in the car. She had taken off her sun glasses. Her eyes were closed. Morgan looked over at her. Her hair, like ridges of shale in the evening light, was swept back in thick waves. The creases at the edge of her eyes radiated with exquisite subtlety, showing the exhilaration and the strain of the drive.

There was sadness there, too, an elusive sadness in the rich character of her face that sometimes confused him. His response to the sadness confused him, not the sadness itself. He nearly reached over to touch the back of his fingers against her cheek, but instead let his hand fall to her knee which he cupped with a congenial squeeze, rousing her from her peaceful reverie.

She looked over at him lazily and smiled, as if she had just awakened beside her lover after a long and satisfied sleep.

"Good morning, Morgan."

"Hi," he said. He looked at his watch. "It's barely past seven. In the evening."

She looked at her watch. "It'll be dark soon. Why don't we put the top up and walk back for a coffee. That hamburger at Dunnes' made me hungry. I should have had fries."

In the Robertshaw Café, perched by the bridge above the locks so that customers could peer up the Muskoka River if they looked one way, or across the Bay and down the Rosseau River, if they looked the other, they shared a plate of fries and each had a coffee. Morgan ordered double-double, just so Miranda could amend his order, explaining to the waitress he'd have milk only, no sugar. He liked putting her in a position where she could fuss, although he pretended to resent it. She liked fussing, but veiled her pleasure in exasperation.

"Do you think this is crazy, Morgan."

"Coming here? Sure."

"I could have been packing up heirlooms in Waldron."

"You sure you want to sell the family estate."

"An estate, it's not. It's an ordinary village house, brick with a front porch, roadside view. You'll have to see it some time."

"Maybe you should rent it out."

"Anyone in Waldron who could afford it has enough money to leave."

"It's commuting distance from Toronto."

"Only in desperation."

"So keep it for your retirement."

"I can think of no better way to turn into a spinster!"

"So, sell."

"I don't want to."

"So, don't sell."

"Maybe I won't. Sometimes I drive out with the intention of crating everything up, sorting and disposing and packing, but I never do. Mostly when I'm there, I sleep. And here we are in Port Carling. So why are we here again?"

"Rufalo thinks we're crazy."

"That's his job, he's supposed to think that."

"Yeah, well, he's good at his job. But he's surprisingly nervous about this case. He's afraid of Lionel Webb."

"I don't think Webb's putting pressure on him, Morgan."

"No, I think Lionel Webb is enjoying the game. We're the players, but only he knows the rules."

"He's the one with conventional power," said Miranda. "He's not necessarily the brains, though. I think the game master could as easily be someone unlikely, like Simon Sparrow or Hermione M."

"The spy?"

"No dear, the other one."

"The matricidal nymphomaniac."

"Where on earth did you get that?"

"Hermione the spy called her a slut."

Miranda turned away. Some words aren't retroactive. You don't call an old woman a slut, even if that's what she was in the past.

"Look who's here," said a familiar voice.

Miranda swung around on the bench seat and saw Simon Sparrow approaching.

"Hello," said Sparrow. "Not bothering you, am I?

Could I join you?"

"Yes, of course," said Miranda. "We were just talking about you."

"Good things, I hope."

"Given that we're in the middle of a murder investigation," said Morgan, "the likelihood is limited."

"Of course, of course. Would you like to be on your own?"

Morgan shrugged.

"Are you running, still?" said Sparrow, not knowing what else to say.

"I'm thinking of retiring. There's not enough time."

"You can always make time," said Sparrow. "I think you will enjoy this weekend. It's a lovely cottage. Why would I want Professor Kurtz dead?"

"It must be very grand," said Miranda. "We don't know why you would want him dead more so than the others. That is a possibility we intend to explore."

"Nobody makes time," said Morgan.

"Pardon?" said Sparrow.

"Morgan's being metaphysical."

"Tell me," said Morgan, "I'm not quite sure, what is your interest in Francis Bacon?"

"Do you mean, how many early editions do I own? None. And if you gave me one, I'd sell it in a New York minute."

"What's that?" said Miranda.

"A New York minute? I don't know, just an expression. A New York minute," he repeated the phrase as if he had coined a spectacular aphorism and wished to bask in the credit that was surely his due.

Miranda remembered that she had found this man excruciatingly boring.

Morgan persisted. "What is your interest in the Bacon Society?"

"I collect things for Lionel. And I suppose Lionel has collected me. I am part of his human collection of odd sods and eccentrics."

"What makes you odd?" Miranda asked.

"I really don't know," Sparrow responded, misunderstanding her question. "I suppose it has something to do with an uncomplicated childhood."

""Not quite what I meant," she said. "From Lionel Webb's perspective, why would you be collectable?"

"Oh. I suppose because I live a life others only dream of. I travel, I have adventures. I like to think of myself as a Renaissance man, not of the intellect but of sensibility. I will try anything. For instance—"

"I get your drift," said Miranda.

"Where did you meet him?" asked Morgan.

"Lionel? In the high Arctic, actually. I was trekking across Ellesmere Island. On my own, a solo trip. Ellesmere is as big as Great Britain and hasn't had people living there in a thousand years, except for a re-located village of hapless Inuit in Grise Fiord. I discovered an ancient camp. I found Viking artifacts, explorers from Greenland, from the time of Leif Eriksson. I found evidence of earlier native habitation. And relics from Elizabethan explorers. It was all very exciting. It took me twenty-eight days backpacking before I stumbled onto this astonishing place and I had just enough supplies to get me back to my pick-up point. When you travel in the Arctic you have to carry everything on your back, even your fuel."

Morgan and Miranda were both intrigued. Simon Sparrow no longer seemed quite so tedious and self-absorbed.

"And then, out of the blue, Lionel Webb dropped in. Literally out of the blue. He was touring Ellesmere Island by helicopter from a base camp near Lake Hazen. He had spotted me there at the site and came down to offer supplies, that's what people do in the north, they share and look after each other. Before we even shook hands, though, he could see something of what I had discovered. That was the beginning of our friendship and collaboration."

"Just where is this place?" asked Morgan.

"Ah," said Simon Sparrow. "It is still a secret. Government agencies have a way of taking control of archeological finds."

"For a reason," said Miranda.

"You can be sure we are being responsible," Simon Sparrow responded. "We have removed nothing. Our only work has been to assure preservation."

"You have artifacts there from Elizabethan times, from a Viking settlement, and from pre-Dorset Inuit culture, and you've removed nothing."

"No, in fact, we have secured the area."

"How so?"

"The site is no longer a fly-over zone."

"How did you manage that?" said Morgan.

Simon Sparrow hesitated, then responded evasively, "I'm not sure. Lionel has influence. I'm not exactly sure."

"Have you been back?" said Miranda.

"Yes, of course we have. Well actually, no. When I say 'we,' I mean Lionel. He goes there periodically with appropriate experts sworn to secrecy. He would deny the site even exists, if you ask him."

"So he has commandeered an important archeological site as his own private preserve," said Morgan.

"Gives a whole new meaning to collecting curiosities, doesn't it?" Miranda offered. "He's cordoned off a small portion of the world as a private museum."

"Yes, I suppose he has."

"Unless everything has been removed, and you just don't know about it," said Morgan.

"Oh no, I don't think so, he wouldn't do that. Not without telling me."

"Why bother?" said Morgan, unable to suppress his contempt for a man able to relinquish such a discovery to a single acquisitive individual, especially so it could be sequestered away from the public domain.

"He trusts me," said Sparrow. "I pick things up for him here and there in my travels. Old things, odd things. He has never refused to reimburse me, and always with a decent commission. Mind you, I don't work for him, I'm an independent adventurer, that's how I like to think of myself."

He likes to think of himself, period, thought Miranda.

I wonder if there really is such a site on Ellesmere,

thought Morgan? *Or is this guy fabricating a mysterious bond between himself and Lionel Webb? Or trying to shift suspicion towards Webb's insatiable propensities. I wonder,* Morgan thought, *if he really did run the Boston Marathon?*

On the way out, Morgan remarked on the name of the café.

"We've heard the name before," Miranda agreed, looking back up at the sign. "Recently…where?"

"Well, it could be Porrig," said Simon Sparrow. "He's from here, you know. Port Carling, born and bred."

"Ah, Porrig's family," said Miranda, as they crossed the swing-bridge, three abreast. "Before the convoluted name changes where they turned themselves into characters from a Jane Austin novel, he was Ralph Robertshaw and Rafe was Patrick O'Sullivan."

"Padraig O'Suillibahn," said Morgan. "And I doubt Jane Austen ever encountered quite such a twosome as them."

"Undoubtedly she did, Morgan, but in her day they would have been unmarried uncles—there's no want of unmarried uncles in Austen."

"It just seems like that. I can't think of one, not one, but it's been a long time."

They cut away from the steep side street and descended a staircase cut into the embankment. Padraig and Ralph were standing on a catwalk that ran across one end of the locks. They were apparently comparing the water depths on either side. They looked up simultaneously and, walking over the narrow catwalk, greeted the three figures approaching them in the late evening light with effusive declarations of welcome. Simon Sparrow wandered away to wait in the shadows.

"You're from Port Carling?" said Miranda.

"Yes, dear, he is. Can't you tell," said Ralph.

"Rafe thinks it's quaint to have roots in such a storybook place. Isn't it a sweetheart of a town. We were the only Jews, of course."

"How was that?" said Miranda.

"How, oh what was it like? It wasn't always easy. Mind you, just my mother was Jewish. If it had been my father, I would probably have been bullied at school and become a rabbi or a comedian. As it is, I was only tormented for being awkward and indifferent to hockey. I therefore became an interior decorator with an exotic background."

"Your father was in the restaurant business?" said Morgan.

"No, he did boat things. He ran the Launch Works, it's closed now. The diner is my brother's place, my brother and sister run it together. She married and the rascal ran off with a waitress. My brother owns it, he shares the profits, fifty-fifty, and helps with her children. He never married.'

"A kindly uncle," Miranda observed.

"No," said Porrig. "I'm Uncle with a capital U. My brother is Sam."

Miranda looked at the squat little man. He grinned sadly, as if he had taken her into his confidence and shared intimate family secrets.

Their small party walked along the wharf towards a

large steam boat glittering with lights, picking up Simon along the way. Miranda leaned close to Padraig.

"You knew Lionel Webb when you were a boy, did you?" she said.

He clasped her arm with both hands.

"Yes," he said. "It was hard not to. We weren't friends. No, we were not at all friends."

The others walked ahead, but he held Miranda back. It was, she thought, not like he wanted to elicit sympathy or confess a crime. Instead, he needed to clarify his childhood relationship with Lionel Webb. It apparently mattered.

"You see her," he said, nodding towards the lake steamer. "My father restored that boat for Lionel. After the Launch Works closed down, Webb hired him. The boat was hauled up on the shore down by Beaumoris and my dad trucked it back to Port and worked on it with his crew from the Works until the day he died, it was his crowning achievement. I owe that to Lionel. Dad lost his business when outboards took over the Lakes and Lionel not only bailed him out financially, he gave him a purpose in life, something to be proud of. You see the name, it's called the *Lady Ruth*. That was my mother. Lionel insisted on calling the boat after my mother. She died just before the Works closed down."

"But you say you weren't friends."

"No, it doesn't work that way. He was summer money and I was local. I'm younger. He was dashing and knew how to water-ski. I delivered groceries. Sometimes I'd work on the launches at the Works. I saw him around.

By the time the *Lady Ruth* project got under way I was off at university. I'd see him on holidays, I worked for my father. By then he was only coming north on the occasional weekend. He was in business with his own father, working in England, mostly."

Miranda found it touching to be taken into his confidence, but wasn't sure why.

"He took a liking to me. Decided I reminded him of his childhood, which was absurd, of course. But once I was in the nostalgia niche, I was sort of co-opted into his life, and that's fine with me, we have interests in common."

"Bacon?"

"Among other things."

They caught up to the rest of their party standing close by the *Lady Ruth*, peering in through her open sides at the immaculate brightwork within. The boat was an old steam-driven laker, about sixty feet long with three decks above water and a bridge on top, broad in the beam, wood-hulled, white with green trim, and grand beyond anything still plying the Muskoka Lakes, except the old *Seguin* which had been restored by public subscription and was used as a tour boat.

Despite the carnivalesque lights and looming presence, the *Lady Ruth* was regal. She seemed both formidable and inviting to the gathering cluster of Baconites who waited patiently on the wharf until the captain appeared from within and invited them aboard. Crossing the gangplank, Miranda had the feeling she was entering another time, another world. As the huge ropes were cast off the dockside capstans, she shared her impression with Morgan, who was leaning against the off-side rail, looking out across the Bay at the lights of grand old summer residences glittering through the trees.

"The boathouses, alone, are as big as most cottages," was his oblique response.

"It is another world, isn't it?" she reiterated.

"Old money," he said. "They can keep what they want of the past and discard the rest. I suppose they can afford to avoid what they want of the present, as well."

"Well, Morgan, if it's any consolation, I don't imagine the future is any more certain for them than for the rest of us."

"Perhaps they have more to lose."

"I've never known you to buy into the illusions of wealth."

"See that white cottage over there with the rambling verandah, the two-story boathouse. What's it say, 'Claremont,' it's been in the same family for generations, that's no illusion."

"Unless of course you're wrong and it was recently bought by a twenty-six year old micro-chip magnate."

"No. It wasn't. Look at these cottages. They're all shabbily elegant—new money doesn't have the confidence. There's a gentility here that the *nouveau riche* can't fathom."

The *Lady Ruth* emitted a reverberating blast from her steam whistle and rounded the corner out of the Bay into the short river leading to Lake Rosseau. "They can't buy what they can't see." A few people sitting on their boathouse docks waved as they went by, thrilled by the memories the *Lady Ruth* evoked of earlier times, when launches cut through the Muskoka waters with rakish elegance and steamers plied the lakes with jocular majesty. "It's not my heritage, you know, but it is, it is."

Morgan was confused because he was not one to be impressed with the trappings of wealth or of class, and yet the old-fashioned display of affluence and restrained good taste intrigued him.

As the boat rounded into Lake Rosseau and he looked out on the broad expanse of water, with cottage lights twinkling on the farthest shores, he marvelled that this world was so close to Toronto yet he had never known what it was like. He grew up in old Cabbagetown, among the remnants of slums before gentrification took over completely. He had travelled the world after graduation from university. But here, just beyond his doorstep, was a magical realm of dark waters and dancing illumination and muted opulence that thrilled him, quelling his natural impulse to be cynical about the link between privilege and beauty.

"What did our friend Porrig have to say," he asked, emerging from his thoughtful silence.

"He has a connection with Lionel Webb. He declared they were not exactly friends, but also revealed that Webb was a family benefactor and Porrig was in his debt."

"Sounds straightforward enough."

"Somewhere between them falls a shadow. There's something sinister connecting those two, and it is either contained or concealed by their common interest in

Bacon. He said nothing overt, maybe it was in what he withheld. You know—eternally indebted, but not friends. I'm thinking Kurtz."

"Kurtz what? You're thinking in circles."

"I am. Did anyone do a head count? Is everyone here."

"Yeah, I think so. Except our host. I assume he's at his cottage, waiting for us."

"Did you see *Mlle Le Docteur*, Marie Lachine."

"She came on board with Hermione M. From the looks of it, I'd say they drove up together, along with Professor Li Po."

"That's quite a threesome," said Miranda.

"Well what about our friend Jane Latimer, she appeared on the wharf with Felix Swan."

"What about David, did you see Sir David?"

"David Jenness, he was already on board. Sort of the unofficial purser. I saw him conferring with the Captain. We walked right by him."

"The D'Arcys arrived with us," said Miranda.

"The who? Oh, Porrig and Rafe. Yes."

"Hermione MacGregor simply appeared out of the shadows at the last minute. I have no idea how she got here."

"What about Jennifer Pluck?"

"I didn't see her come aboard. Maybe she's already at Briar Hill."

"I can't imagine Jennifer missing things. And there's Simon Sparrow, he must have driven up on his own. So, that's the lot," said Morgan.

"If Jennifer's already there, then it is. And you and me,

we're part of this strange mélange."

"Inextricably, it seems. We'd better be careful not to have a good time."

chapter sixteen
Briar Hill Island

They stood on the upper deck leaning into the breeze as the old steamer churned through the dark waters towards a distant row of lights illuminating a large dock and a boathouse the size of a barn. As they got closer, the lanterns on the dock cast highlights upwards through clusters of ancient pines soaring to a separate horizon, indicating this was an island set proud from the dark shoreline behind.

Briar Hill Island, of course.

Rising in gothic splendour from a cliff with a vantage through the tops of the trees was a cottage larger than either Morgan or Miranda could have imagined. It had verandahs and turrets and gables and a profusion of rooflines, with walls of board-and-batten, clapboard, shipslap, and cedar-shakes, all unified by somber green paint on the woodwork which in the darkness looked black, except where lanterns cast emerald spheres in a random display. There were railings and French doors and chimney columns of fieldstone and panes of glass shimmering against the gloom. It was a grand place, a castle of wood made even more sumptuous by the absence of architectural coherence as it merged with the shadows of trees and rocks and the darkness of night.

Instead of sharing Morgan's fascination with the approaching scene Miranda drew him away towards the stern.

"Look," she whispered. Below them on the stern deck were three figures. Their words were muffled by the sounds of the steam turbines, but their body language in the festive light emanating from the boat's interior showed them to be in animated discussion.

Hermione M had her hand on Professor Li Po's arm. She was saying something urgently that made him smile. He put his arm around her. Together they drew Marie Lachine into their embrace. They had apparently been quarrelling. As the boat's engines revved in reverse, sideslipping her stern towards the dock, their intimacy dissolved as each withdrew to assume a solitary posture against the rail, watching the deckhands maneuver the huge ropes as the *Lady Ruth* settled into a position of rest and the turbines were cut. For a moment there was an eerie quietness.

Miranda looked knowingly at Morgan.

He shrugged.

"Maybe it doesn't mean anything," she said.

"Every time we see people talking, if we don't hear their words, do we suspect a conspiracy?"

"Yeah, that's what we're here for."

"Okay," said Morgan. "What I saw was anger giving way to intimacy."

"Exactly."

"And why do we find that worthy of interest?"

"Because they would seem to have the least in common of any three people here—oh, there's Jennifer Pluck on the dock, hauling the gangplank into position. She's right at home, isn't she? Look, Sir David is stepping ashore, they're kissing. Is that a romantic kiss, Morgan? Or just kissing air?"

"Now that," said Morgan, "would be an unlikely pairing. You want strange, that's strange. They're holding hands. No, they've let go. They were. They're lovers. The aristocrat and the waif. Lovely. Only in Canada," he said, quoting an old Red Rose tea commercial. "Pity."

"I think they're sweet together," said Miranda. "But they're hiding it. That's suspicious. Look, the way they're standing close, but turned away from each other, helping people down the gangplank."

"My goodness," said Morgan. "Have you seen Jane Latimer's outfit? Look at her!"

"What? It's her northern safari costume. Tilley hat, Tilley vest over a sheer tank top, Roots boots, hiking shorts. Long lean legs, her own design. She's set for the wilderness, or a serious tryst. Wonder what she'll wear for dinner?"

"She's having a good time," said Morgan, appreciatively.

"Maybe at our expense."

Morgan was puzzled. "How so?"

"I think she dresses for an audience, and we're it. She wants us to think about her. She's like, look at me, I dress with passion, I'm an eccentric. Maybe I'm the killer."

"Miranda, I don't think she cares what we think."

"Oh, she cares, Morgan. She cares."

They were the last to file off the boat. The captain was assisting the crew to heave baggage and supplies onto the dock, where another man was organizing it into separate piles, tagging each piece of luggage as members of the party identified their own, and assuring them it would be delivered to their rooms.

Jane Latimer was standing in a separate pool of light, Felix Swan was at her elbow. She was gazing into the slick black water lapping between the ship's side and the pilings under the dock. Morgan could see the sheen of sweat on Swan's forehead, even though the evening breeze across the lake was cool enough to merit sweaters and jackets. He nudged Miranda in their direction.

"You look amazing," said Miranda.

"Thank you," said Jane, assuming the remark was meant to be complimentary. "Beautiful boat ride, wasn't it?"

"It's such a privilege to ride on the *Lady Ruth*," gushed Felix Swan. "It is one of the greatest of Lion's collectibles. Did you bring plenty of warm clothes? You're city people," he said, implying that he was Indiana Jones. "You have to dress for the wilderness, you know. It can get very cool at night."

Morgan slowly rolled his eyes, taking in the entire dock scene and the vast rambling cottage looming above them. He looked at Felix Swan's outfit and realized the Rector was attired in his own version of his colleague's costume, including the Tilly hat with one side folded up, Australian style. Morgan supposed they both bought new outfits every year for their Labour Day weekend on Briar Hill Island.

"I hope we're not too late for a swim," said Miranda, trying to be amusing.

"Oh, no," said Felix Swan. "There's a sauna just down there at the end of the dock. Everyone goes skinny dipping after dinner."

Miranda looked at him with restrained animosity. *I would rather die than go skinny dipping with Felix Swan*, she thought.

"We turn the boathouse lights out, of course," said Swan, sensing her resistance, if not her revulsion.

"Felix has never actually removed himself from the Madeira and cigars in time for a postprandial swim. Some of us go in. Wait and see how you feel. And yes, we turn out the lights so Felix can't watch from the verandah."

"Jane! You know that's not true." Felix Swan sputtered as Miranda and Morgan walked off, joining the others for the long climb up the cliff-side stairs. Behind them, they could hear the sweating Buddha conferring with Jane Latimer with strange urgency.

"Now that is an odd alliance," she whispered to Morgan as they proceeded up the stairs. "She couldn't stand him last week."

"Did you know we were going to be served dinner? It's nearly ten."

"I think the big dinner is tomorrow night. Tonight it'll be a few snacks. I wonder where Lionel is? There's young David on the verandah still acting as purser; I guess now we're ashore he's *concierge*."

"And if we dine, he'll be *maître d'*."

"You don't like him," she hissed into his ear.

He stopped dead in his tracks, or at least poised between one step and the next. "I do. That's the strange part. I do like him." Morgan looked up at David Jenness and resumed the climb. As they got closer and the young man's illuminated face fell into perspective, Morgan whispered: "He looks familiar."

He does, she thought. He looks like Morgan.

Morgan, meanwhile, was scouring the back corners of his mind, trying to come up with features and a manner to match David Jenness. Suddenly, he understood. He knew who David looked like, and it wasn't him.

"Detective Morgan," said the young man. "You and Detective Quin are in Philip's Folly. Just go off to the side and follow the lighted path over the hill."

"No," said Morgan, primly. "We need separate quarters."

"Yes, of course," said David Jenness. "You may stay in the main cottage, by all means. But I assure you, I have assigned you each a room of your own. Philip's Folly has places for four."

"We're here on business." Miranda spoke with exaggerated righteousness, to indicate she found Morgan's propriety amusing.

Morgan grimaced, then laughed. "We have a working relationship."

"That is," said Miranda, "we only have a relationship when we're working."

The worldly young man blushed in the light of electric lanterns hung from the verandah rafters. And in his discomfiture she could see Morgan's features in his face, as surely as if time had collapsed.

"Dinner will be in twenty minutes. You just have time to check that your bags were delivered appropriately and have a quick wash-up. Now Felix, there you are. Bringing up the rear…" His voice trailled off as Miranda took Morgan's arm and the two of them walked off the side of the verandah into the tunnel of light through the trees.

They emerged around a corner in the open, high on a rocky cliff with the sky a deep blue overhead. The guest cabin was well illuminated but Miranda stopped their progress and stepped off the path into the natural light of the moon.

"Morgan," she said in a soft voice. "What was the name of the girl you lived with in London when you were a student."

"I'd graduated. I told you about her, the woman I should have married instead of what's-her-name."

"What was her name, the non-wife?"

"Susan."

"Morgan?"

"Yes?"

"Are you thinking what I'm thinking?"

"Yes."

"It's a very small world, Morgan."

"It can be."

"And?"

"The odds aren't as astronomical as they might seem."

"Given her life, given your life?"

"Given our ages, that we both lived in London, that we had common interests, that her son has an affinity for Canada."

"That you lived together."

"Susan and I didn't live together. We had adjoining rooms in a bedsitter. In Knightsbridge, of all places, just down from Harrods."

"Morgan…"

"Yes?"

"Could he be your son?"

"Susan had a friend called Nigel. Her boss, I think."

"Sir Nigel?"

"She never said. She wouldn't have. Only that he was much older. I think he had a thing for her."

"A thing?"

"A thing. He was in love with her."

"And Susan?"

"She was in love with me; she thought she was."

"And you?"

"I was in love with me, too. It wasn't until years later, I fell in love with her retroactively. We would have been terrible for each other. She was lovely and serene. I was on fire."

"On fire?"

"Burning. Driven by hormones and fear, dread and desire. I wanted adventure. I needed, as we used to say, to find myself."

"Were you missing."

"Yeah, a lot."

"Like Simon Sparrow?"

"Yeah, except I grew out of it."

"What?"

"Looking."

"Is he your son?"

"Yes."

"Did you suspect."

"Not until coming up the stairs."

"Seeing yourself, waiting at the top."

"Seeing my past."

"How do you feel."

"I'll tell you when I do."

"What?"

"Feel. Right now I'm numb."

"Are you going to tell him?"

"Maybe he knows."

"He doesn't know, Morgan."

"Maybe I will, probably I won't."

"Maybe you should."

Morgan turned her to him and gazed into the twin moons in her eyes. He shuddered and drew her close and held her so that he could feel the length of her body against his and he shuddered again. Someone was coming along the pathway. They pulled apart. And as he turned to look out over the water, she could see his face was shining with tears.

"This was built for Prince Philip, you know," said a disembodied voice that unmistakably issued from the corpulent body of Felix Swan who was struggling along the path towards them. "Hello, you two, you're not lost, are you?" he demanded, addressing their silhouettes against the shimmering waters of Lake Rosseau. "Hermione and I are bunking in with you." Then, with a lascivious sneer, he added, "Hope you don't mind."

Miranda and Morgan ignored the innuendo, more for its inept delivery than its impertinence. The four of them walked across the verandah of Philip's Folly and entered a large room with a huge stone fireplace that filled the far wall. Only when they were inside did Morgan realize it was a log house. From outside in the darkness it had the shape and roofline of a classic Muskoka cottage.

"This is one of the smaller outbuildings," said Felix Swan. "Can you believe it was built especially for the Duke of Edinburgh in his capacity as patron of World Wildlife? He stayed here in my room." He spread his arms expansively to take in the entire building. Miranda noticed the perspiration stains in the moonlight that had leeched through his shirt and jacket, lending his posturing an air of pathetic absurdity. She glanced at Hermione, the shorter, pretty one, the spy. Both women toured the room with their eyes, taking in the large framed photograph of Prince Philip in front of a WW banner, and an astonishing collection of disembodied animal heads with lolling tongues, dust-riddled fur, racks of antlers, ivory horns, bared teeth, all staring glassily into the dead centre of the room.

"Well," said Morgan, knowing what they were thinking, "Ducks Unlimited saves the wetlands, and the members kill mallards for sport. So there you are."

"And there you are," said Felix, missing the irony of their surroundings. "I sleep downstairs off to the side in Prince Philip's room and Hermione takes the other side. That leaves you two upstairs on your own." He paused. "Good luck."

Morgan picked up his battered black leather bag— he had bought it in the leather market in Florence two decades earlier—and resisting the urge to kick Felix Swan in the groin trundled upstairs. Miranda, also resisting the impulse to kick Swan in the groin or otherwise maim him with maximum pain, picked up her own bag, Roots, chocolate-brown elk-skin, deliciously in and out of place, and followed her partner up the stairs.

Miranda looked down from the balcony that ran, tucked under a cathedral ceiling, around three sides of the room. Hermione the Spy was standing alone, staring through a screen into the crackling fire. She seemed like a lost soul, somehow disengaged from the frail body held proud in the light of the flames. She was a woman with a past and Miranda wanted to know more, not to implicate her in murder but because her memories seemed to give her such a formidable presence, in spite of her diminutive size and her age.

Suddenly, Hermione turned and looked upwards, straight into Miranda's eyes. For an instant, the old woman's eyes were predators, then they softened and she appeared vulnerable, and, as so often happens with the old, all that she had been through in her life was swallowed up in a look of benign resignation. But Miranda could not let go of the life that appeared in the flash of Hermione's glance. She nodded, and without checking her room or washing up, she turned and descended the stairs.

"We haven't really talked," she said, reaching out and taking the old woman's hand, which felt like chamois. "I just wanted to tell you how lovely you look in the firelight."

"Thank you, Miranda. All women look lovely by firelight, and all men look sinister. We're lucky, aren't we?"

"It must be something in their eyes," said Miranda.

"Fear," said Hermione M. "Watch when Felix comes out, he'll glisten with fear, and he will until the day he dies. You don't think I killed Dieter, do you, for heaven's sake?"

"Dieter?"

"Dieter Kurtz."

"Yes, I know, but you called him Dieter. No one else has used his first name like that. Were you fond of him?"

"Yes," said the old woman and turned her head so that fire gleamed from the depths of her eyes. "I, of course, despised him, as well. How could you not. He was quite despicable, you know. I'm sure you have gathered that. But yes, Dieter and I go back a long way."

"Really," said Miranda, surprised that Hermione seemed almost eager to reveal her relationship with the murdered man.

"We met during the war."

"World War Two."

"How young you are, dear Miranda. For people of my age there was only one war. The wars, that's how my parents referred to The First World War. So-and-so went off to *the wars*. And so many died in the trenches. My future husbands. My older brother. Two uncles. But *the war*, that was the *Nazi war*."

She elongated the word 'Nazi' to resonate with 'nausea,' filling the ululant sound with illimitable venom. She added,

"They were both with the Germans, of course."

She mouthed the word 'German' with gentle condescension, almost affection.

"Dieter and I met in Paris, we knew each other for only a short time. We were so young; the world was much too real. I met him again forty years later in Canada."

"You remembered each other?"

"Some people you never forget." She looked up from the fire, then back into the flames. "You want to know more?"

"Yes."

"Perhaps I shall tell you more. Not now, your partner and Felix the Swan are about to converge."

Miranda wondered how the old woman knew, then realized it must be the sound of water, the sound of it no longer running through pipes strapped against the log walls.

Felix Swan emerged and walked into the firelight, glistening, as if he had not dried himself after washing.

Morgan appeared above them, leaned over the railing and surveyed the room. The mounted animal heads from this perspective seemed life-like, as if they were poking through the walls. They no longer glared with the fire in their eyes, whispering of death. They seemed quite cheerful and strangely proud from his perspective above them.

"Damn," Miranda whispered to Morgan as they walked through the tunnel of light towards the main cottage a couple of paces behind Hermione M, who had taken Felix Swan's arm to help her negotiate the menace of roots twisting through the gravel shadows of the path.

"What?" Morgan whispered back to her.

"Never mind," she said, aware their muffled voices were drawing attention. "Isn't it beautiful?" she said as they reached the small set of steps at the side of the vast verandah. "Hermione, this is so beautiful, no wonder you come back year after year."

"My dear, " said the old woman, "only death could keep me away."

The dining room was actually a closed-off portion of the verandah. There was a more formal dining room within, but at this time of year, with a glass wall overlooking the lake, the casual setting was appropriate. The guests milled around the table set casually for a light dinner. All that was missing was their host.

At first there was only a faint tremor. Then the panes began to rattle against the window mullions and a whup-whupping resounded as the crystal jangled and the flatware clattered, and somewhere a door crashed shut, and everyone smiled. All but Morgan and Miranda, who had no way of knowing the helicopter, that seemed from the roar like it would land in their midst, was bringing Lionel Webb from the city to preside over their festivities.

Jennifer Pluck and young David slipped away from the gathered company to meet their host at the helipad just up the hill between the cottage and tennis courts. Soon they were back; David looked like he had been relieved of onerous responsibilities and Jennifer's furrowed brow suggested a kind of nervous defiance.

Lionel Webb apppeared fresh and robust. Although they were Kurtz's strange entourage and Jane Latimer was their new president, Webb came across with the casual authority and congenial grace of a person clearly in charge.

If there is a conspiracy here, thought Morgan, *he is at the centre of it. And yet, he's so obviously relishing his role at the centre, it almost suggests that he is simply naïve and really quite marginal. Is it possible to run an empire, to be worth hundreds of millions, to be on chatting terms with the House of Windsor, and to be so unabashedly innocent you flaunt your complicity in murder. He must be complicit,* Morgan thought, *one way or another.*

They could all be guilty of killing Kurtz, or possibly none of them, or some weird combination, perhaps one or two acting by proxy for the rest. Not a single one had a substantive alibi. All of them had a motive, if loathing were a motive. And, of course, Morgan knew it was not. There had to be reasons for killing beyond the desire to see someone dead.

He glanced at Miranda. She was staring at Jennifer Pluck, letting her eyes range back and forth to examine the animated features of Lionel Webb. Was she looking for a resemblance between them? He looked at David Jenness. He could see his friend Susan, and for an flash, Susan was there, aged twenty-two, and he felt a terrible grief that he had not loved her in time.

"Well well well," exclaimed Lionel Webb as he took his place at the head of the table, signalling the others to be seated. Miranda and Morgan were disappointed when no toast was made to the Queen.

"Detectives," he said. "You sit there if you don't mind, at the other end."

They exchanged amused looks as they sat down. The table could easily have seated twenty, and they were only fourteen. But there was ample room for them at the end, side by side, and both suspected it was Webb's not too subtle way of setting them apart. The others seemed to know where their places were.

"That was where Professor Kurtz used to sit," said Felix Swan, leaning over to address them as a single bead of sweat rolled across one eyebrow and dropped to the table. "I always sat here, to his right. Didn't want him out of my sight, the old curmudgeon."

That's one of those words you see in print, thought Morgan, who had never actually heard one person call another a 'curmudgeon' out loud.

Miranda was struck by what a limp epithet it was, calling a man everyone at the table despised a curmudgeon. *Maybe Hermione the spy has a certain residual affection for*

Kurtz. I don't think anyone else has. Without even knowing the man, she had come to dislike him immensely.

"You were close to him, then?" said Morgan to Felix Swan.

"Oh no, not at all. Our interests converged, but no, I did not like him. One certainly did not trust him, if you know what I mean."

"No," said Morgan. "How so?"

"With your emotions," Swan explained in a confessional tone, as if no one else at the table could hear. "You could not relax, if you did, you were skewered. With a few *bons mots* or a smile. Do you know he would comment on my weight. Not directly, of course. He'd say things like 'Felix will not have more pie.' When clearly I wanted more pie. He would hand me his napkin and make a motion to wipe my brow, as if sweating was something I did to be rude. I am a big man and he resented my presence."

Miranda, leaning across Morgan to address Felix Swan, said in a conspiratorial tone: "You have a great deal of presence."

"Thank you," said Felix Swan. "You are the nicest person in the room."

"Thank you," said Miranda.

The door behind Lionel Webb leading from the kitchen opened and the cook, a large florid woman dressed in immaculate whites, with two helpers also in white, filed into the room, each carrying several large precariously balanced platters, heaped with cold delicacies. There were plates of chicken, prosciutto, thick slices of ham and beef, along with bowls of potato salad, caesar salad, cole slaw, and patchwork bean salad. It was all cottage food, but prepared with such finesse and presented with such opulence, the entire company murmured sighs of delight.

Lionel urged them to help themselves. There were bottles of the best Ontario wines, cabernets from Chateau des Charmes and chilled Henry of Pelham Rieslings. There were pitchers of ice water, and lemonade for the tea-totallers. The napkins were linen, while the table covering was old-fashioned oilcloth, polished immaculate and rent with innumerable fine creases from years of use. *A nice touch*, thought Morgan.

To the surprise of both Morgan and Miranda, who were eating without talking in order to pick up on the table conversation, the earnest chatter as well as the jovial repartee was all about Francis Bacon. No one was talking about the Muskoka weather, no one was talking about murder. Apart from occasional riffs on the food and hospitality, each of the Society members was focused in his or her own way on the long dead figure who had brought them together.

Miranda heard the word *Rosicrucian* popping about, and *Masonic Order* slipped in here and there, along with words like 'ancient' and 'mystical.' Mostly, it was gossip, not ideas. The Virgin Queen, was she his mother? Who else could have written *MacBeth*? Was he framed or did he really take the bribe? Was he covering for someone? It would have to be no less than a king. What about the German text? Bacon wrote it! Wrote what, Miranda wondered? *Fama Fraternitatis*. Supposedly by Christian

Rosenkreuz. He brought Rosicrucian doctrines into the modern era. Kurtz's principal thesis. The buzz seemed to focus. Did you know a 1624 copy of *The New Atlantis* is rumoured to have turned up in Oxfordshire? No, really! The earliest version (until now!) appeared as an addendum in the posthumous edition of *Sylva Sylvarum*. My goodness! *The New Atlantis!* If there really is an authentic copy, it'll go for a whopping sum! If it exists.

"It exists," said Lionel Webb and the room fell silent.

It was as if the others had been waiting for an announcement. The room throbbed with anticipation. Even the serving staff came to a stand-still.

"Negotiations are in progress. The English of course do not want it removed from the U.K." There was conspiratorial laughter.

Jane Latimer leaned over and whispered to Miranda. "He's a peer of the realm. They're hardly going to prevent him from buying what he wants. You wait, he'll bring it over, tucked in with his shirts, the next time he makes a jaunt across the pond."

As the chatter diffused and the food was devoured, Miranda observed Lionel Webb playing the gregarious host. He was a Canadian businessman and a titled Brit, comfortable in either world, although they seemed mutually exclusive. And yet, she was aware he was only at the head of the table by default. If Dieter Kurtz had been there, the order of precedence would be reversed. Where Miranda and Morgan were now sitting, this would have been the head of the table. Webb as the principle acolyte would have been at the foot.

The Dead Scholar 233

In fact, she thought, he only creates the illusion of being gregarious. On either side of him, insulating him from the general conversation, sat Jennifer Pluck and Sir David Jenness. My God, young Jenness looked like Morgan, she thought. Talk about degrees of separation. Yet the odds were not all that bizarre, they couldn't be or it wouldn't have happened, they wouldn't have met. She glanced sideways and saw that her partner was staring at his son, lost in thoughts she could not begin to imagine. *From his eyes, I'd say it was more about loss than recovery.* Sometimes Morgan hurt in strange ways.

Periodically, one of the young people would lean over to Webb and say something. He would smile a brief private smile, then smile openly as host. At one point he reached out and placed a hand over Jennifer Pluck's, which was resting on the antique oilcloth. The curious thing, thought Miranda, despite his gesture it was she who appeared proprietorial.

And what about David Jenness? They suspected his relationship to Morgan, but that was poignant, not relevant. What was Sir David's relationship to Lionel Webb? Was he, too, in Kurtz's thrall? Or was he the one true innocent here, with no vested interest in the dead man's demise?

When they rose from the table, Morgan walked straight over to the young man and put his hand on his shoulder, turning him close to look in his eyes.

"Yes?" said David Jenness, curiously relaxed, given the close encounter.

"Yes," said Morgan. He hesitated, then in a neutral

voice, he asked: "You said your mother's name is Susan?"

"Yes."

"Susan Croydon? Did she ever live in Knightsbridge."

"Croydon before she was married, yes. She lives there now, in Knightsbridge. We have a flat in Beaufort Gardens."

Morgan grimaced at the irony. Their adjoining bedsitters had been in Beaufort Gardens, back in the days when sometimes they would go out and share a pint because it was cheaper by tuppence than two half pints, and nurse it through an entire evening. Mostly, they sat close by the gas fire, in his room because it was smaller and cheaper to heat than hers, and shared endless details of their young lives. Susan: so emotionally generous it hurt him to remember.

He knew Knightsbridge was an elegant address, as it was when they lived there as an impoverished minority.

"It's been in the family for generations—the flat, it's been ours since before Albert died."

"Albert?"

"Victoria's Albert."

Morgan felt a surge of something like nostalgia for a country where time could be measured by the death of a dead queen's spouse.

"And Lady Susan lives in Beaufort Gardens," he reiterated.

"Lady Jenness, actually. One would only use the first name if she were a baronetess in her own right, and then it would be Dame Susan, not Lady."

"B*aronetess*! But as a baronet's widow she is *baroness*."

"Precisely," said Sir David with a sympathetic smile.

Morgan's wistfulness for England evaporated and was displaced with melencholia for the young woman he had known. He scrambled for facts to ground his emotions.

When they had lived side by side, Susan's friend Nigel had a flat in the same *cul de sac,* perhaps across the tree-lined boulevard. She never mentioned it. Nigel was her boss. Morgan had been on the Continent during the last six months of her pregnancy, running with the bulls in Pamplona, touring art galleries and ruins, making love with girls and women, desperately searching. He had not known she was pregnant. When he came back, she told him her baby's name was Nigel, but he knew it was David. He had returned to Canada knowing the baby's name was the same as his.

"I, ah, I think I knew her."

"Really! How splendid. I must let her know. She will be pleased, I'm sure."

"Yes, do let her know."

Morgan remembered distinctly the first evening after he moved in…there were only two rooms on the fifth floor of the house…he could sense a woman's presence…at that age, hormones rampant, he could pick up the scent of a woman his own age in the corridor, in the shared bathroom…he knocked on her door, asked if he could borrow a cup, he already had sugar…she didn't get the joke…said her name wasn't Sue, it was Susan, and they went out for a drink…and were together with casual intensity through the seasons to follow until he took off to find himself or lose himself on the Continent.

"Did you know her well?" asked David Jenness.

"Yes I did." Morgan's mind racing, confronted by the image of Susan in the young man's features, rounded on itself quite abruptly. He felt an ambivalent urgency to flee and to embrace, to disengage and to connect, to deny and to explain. But all he added was, "No, I don't suppose I really did." Then he said: "She came to Canada once, I saw her just before I got married." *I wanted her to save me, but it was too late.*

"She always had a soft spot for Canada. Actually I didn't know she had been here. Perhaps it was before she was married, herself. I'm hoping she'll come over for a visit. Maybe we can get you together."

Morgan looked at the young man. *My goodness,* he thought, *I hope he has nothing to do with Kurtz's murder.*

Morgan smiled. He was happy Susan had made a good life for herself. He was hurting so deep he felt like his heart was bleeding, longing for the life and the family he had never had, that was gathered in this graceful and handsome young man. He reached out and squeezed his son on the shoulder and turned away, looking through a misty glaze for Miranda.

She was at his side almost instantly, having monitored his encounter with David Jenness while talking to Simon Sparrow. She squeezed his arm and drew him against her so that his arm pressed into her breast, and he smiled at her. Simon Sparrow stayed close.

"Simon was just illuminating me about Easter Island. He's never actually been there, but it is on his agenda."

Both of them had been, though not together.

"Really," said Morgan. "Tell us about it."

Walking back to the guest cottage arm in arm, Miranda and Morgan stopped on the bald rock hanging high over the water. They were out of sight of the main cottage where things were still going strong, although no one apparently was game for a skinny dip. With their backs to Philip's Folly, they stared out over Lake Rosseau. The moon was behind clouds, the lights of the hotel at Windermere twinkled like a constellation caught on the tangled horizon. They pressed comfortably against each other.

She knew he was thinking of David's mother.

"David," she said, calling Morgan by his rarely used first name. "Was she beautiful?'

"Yes."

"What colour hair did she have?"

"Auburn, why?"

"Just wondered. Was it long?"

"Yes."

"Did you love her?"

"That was a lifetime ago."

"If you love someone, time doesn't matter."

"I didn't love her when she loved me; and then it was too late. Time matters."

"It's never—"

"—too late? It is."

"He is a very nice young man. You should be proud."

"I am. And deeply ashamed."

"Of what."

"I don't know."

"Of leaving?"

"Yes."

"Sounds like she came out of it all right."

"I guess."

"Old Sir Nigel must have acknowledged the boy as his own."

"He must have, it's a hereditary title."

"Adopted his own son. Or so they must have made it seem. Sounds like a decent sort. You've nothing to be ashamed of, David."

"Yeah."

Morgan nestled his head against hers. He was just enough taller his jaw-line rested against her temple. Miranda felt tears on her cheeks and was startled they were cold; it took her a moment to realize they were his. She stayed very still.

"I need to tell you, Miranda…"

"What…"

"You know…"

"Yeah, Morgan. I know. Same here…"

chapter seventeen
Suicide Virgins

Miranda rapped on Morgan's door, cocked her head sideways to listen, then rapped again more imperiously, and when she heard nothing, pushed the door open. He was asleep with a huge down pillow drawn over his head to shield him from the sun streaming through his open window. She jiggled his leg through the covers to rouse him, then backed out of the room. She shut the door and started to walk away, then turned and spoke through the wood.

"Morgan, they rang the first bell! Breakfast in half an hour. It's just like camp."

"Mmphpt."

"Time to come in for a landing. Leave Saint Augustine to his own devices. Rise and shine."

Felix Swan had come out of his room and stood

watching her speaking to Morgan's closed door.

"My, my, Miranda, your friend must have had a hard night—all by himself."

She turned and looked at the Rector, who seemed to be shuffling even though he was standing perfectly still.

"Your fly is down," she said.

His hand darted to the front of his pants and he ran his fingers up the zipper. It seemed secure but he was disconcerted.

"Excuse me," he said. "I will see you at breakfast." Hiking his pants higher, he lumbered out the door, across the verandah, and out of sight.

Miranda settled into one of the Muskoka chairs on the verandah to wait for Morgan. Almost immediately she felt a bony hand on her shoulder. She had not heard the screen door open behind her but she knew who it was. No one else moved with such stealth, like a cat.

"Lost in thought?" said Hermione the spy.

"Thinking, but not lost," Miranda replied. "Good morning. I was thinking about you."

The old woman sat down in the chair beside her and sighed in pleasure as she gazed at the splendid panorama spread out before them. She seemed not at all curious about Miranda's thoughts, or perhaps just patient after years of waiting for the world to reveal itself as it would.

Rising up sparsely from over the granite shoulder in front of them, sumacs held gaunt fingers of crimson against the dazzling blue water, and to one side the stand of great pines surrounding the main cottage poked their tops above the rock while low on the other side the maples amidst giant beech trees betrayed flamboyant signs of an early autumn, flashing gold and scarlet in the morning glare.

The two women sat like old friends, soaking up the beauties of morning.

Finally, Miranda broke the silence.

"I was thinking about you and Dieter."

"Were you? I expect you were."

"We know he was German."

"Well, of course."

"He claimed to be from Scarborough."

"Oh, no one believed him. It was pure affectation."

"To be from Scarborough!"

"Dieter had a strange sense of humour."

"Hermione, I need to know…"

"Yes, dear." The old woman twisted in her chair and smiled a rare smile; it was benevolent rather than jovial, a beautiful smile.

"Were you?"

"Lovers? Yes we were. A long time ago."

"In Paris?"

"Yes, in Paris. We were both very young. I was younger of course."

"And in Canada?"

"No, never."

Miranda paused, not sure where to go next. The old woman would reveal more of her story, if she were asked the right questions. And if she were not, she would not be likely to volunteer anything.

"During the war?"

"Yes, during the war."

"I don't understand," said Miranda. "You were in Paris during the war? You're English aren't you?"

"Scottish. But I grew up in Chelsea, a stone's-throw from the Thames."

Hermione gazed out over Lake Rosseau at the colours of morning or perhaps at scenes from earlier lives, Miranda could not be sure.

"I have heard you were in, involved in, espionage."

"Have you? Do they call me 'Hermione the spy'?"

"Sometimes."

"I was very young."

"And?"

"And, dear Miranda, I was very young. There was a war going on. War defined everything. I was thirteen during the Battle of Britain. We watched men die above London. Germans and our own boys, their bodies, their machines, rained from the skies. Jousting to the death. And during the Blitz people died all around us. My family died when I was away at school. Why they bombed Chelsea I really don't know. Probably it was a mistake, or they were after the Tate Gallery. And when I was seventeen, and war was all I knew, I was recruited, I joined up, and I was given special training."

"At seventeen!"

"It was the war. Have you ever heard of a project, very hush-hush, dubbed 'the suicide virgins'? I don't suppose you have."

"The suicide virgins? No." Miranda felt her own voice rising in excitement but the old woman's remained curiously unexpressive.

"There was a book, mid-eighties, that was the title, *The Suicide Virgins*. It received quite a lot of publicity. The man who did it, I can't remember his name, was highly reputable. Did a book on that Mitford girl, the one who married Churchill's nephew, Esmond Romily. He was shot down in '44, the season I signed on. Everything was much too real back then, so that nothing was real."

"Were you one of them?" asked Miranda, leaning closer over the large arm of her Muskoka chair. She hoped Morgan wouldn't appear too soon.

"We were recruited from car pools mostly. That's where they put well-spoken girls with impeccable manners. Drivers, chauffeuring officers about. Upper class girls who knew how to drive, public school girls who had summered on the Côte d'Azur and were fluent in French. We were not all virgins, my dear. Virtue is no match for the seductive combination of urgency and opportunity. Nor were we suicidal. With death all around, we thought we could live forever.

"Can you imagine us, handsome in khaki, wearing stockings, no one had stockings, driving through blackouts with warriors resplendent in their dress uniforms in the back, counting on us to get them through, sharing their scotch and their cigarettes, testing their virility with gallant flirtation. It was enough to make a girl hope the war would never end.

"I joined up because I wanted to work in Bomber Command. I knew a girl who was a plotter in Bomber Ops. It sounded exciting. Instead, they made me a driver.

Then, suddenly, because I spoke French, I was volunteered, I was whisked off to a camp in the Yorkshire Dales for special training."

"For what?" asked Miranda, unable to listen passively, anxious to participate in the unfolding narrative.

Hermione turned her head to the side and looked at Miranda with obvious affection.

She seemed to be sharing her story because Miranda wanted to hear. It was the old woman's response to her inquisitor's sympathetic intelligence and not because she needed to tell it or because she felt that the investigation would bring it to light.

"Well, there were six of us trained at a time. All public school girls, all of us fluent in French or German."

"What kind of training?"

"Weaponry. Yes, but mostly to make us tough. Three months. Stripping Bren guns blindfolded, marching, running, climbing. I learned to love the smell of machine oil. Sten guns and revolvers. Grenades. Parachuting. And taking orders—that's what they taught us, unquestioning obedience. No more messing about in the back seats of cars, no more dinners at Claridges, no more naughty evenings at the Windmill. We learned how to kill. We learned how to die. As I said, it was unreal, it was too too real to resist. And then, one by one we were sent away. I was the last, and the day I left, six new recruits came in. All pretty, we were all pretty. I think that was a requisite. At seventeen it is easy to be pretty.

"I was dropped out of cloud cover on a moonless night over France, near Reims. One of those absurd bits of coincidence that shape our lives—it was my eighteenth birthday. Maybe they knew that, maybe it made it all seem more noble, that I was of age. I jumped. After all that training, I was unarmed. I knew how to use a stocking to garrote my enemy, my thumbs to strangle, my teeth to rip out carotid arteries from an enemy's neck."

"In 1944? France was still under Nazi control. You were alone?"

"Yes, each of us was alone. The war was turning. We carried messages to the Maquis. The Germans were efficient in their desperation, they could break codes, catch radio transmitter-receivers, we had to get word through. Sometimes it was the only way. Schoolgirls might not be noticed. We were pretty enough to pass for being younger than we were. No one met us when we landed. No one knew exactly when or where we would arrive. It was safer that way. I came down in a pasture. A few sheep scurried away. A dog barked in the distance. I buried my chute and made my way to the outskirts of Reims. When dawn broke I moved with the flow of morning traffic into the centre of the city. It is a lovely place. Have you been there?"

"No," said Miranda. "You had a contact, you knew where to find him?"

"A Maquisard, he found me. It was safer that way."

"How did he find you."

"That first morning I went to a particular church. I went to confession. The priest told me of a room for rent over a café. After several days a man came to my room. I told him what I had to tell him. It was over, as simple as that. I did not understand my message. I do not know if it made a difference. My work was done."

"And then?" said Miranda, breathing deeply, "what happened?" She could envision rainy night scenes and railway yards, steam engines, soldiers, the clattering of boots on cobbled streets, safety in a stranger's arms.

"I went to confession regularly. I am not a Catholic, I had no friends."

"But what happened, how did you get away?"

"You don't understand, my dear. My war was over. I was expected to fend for myself. When the allies landed, I might be liberated. There were no contingency plans, no plans for escape."

"You were sacrificed."

"I was a soldier."

Miranda looked over at the old woman; she was staring out across Lake Rosseau, and Miranda could tell that her memories were vivid and disturbing after all these years.

"Hermione," she said. "How did you meet Dieter Kurtz."

Without hesitation, the old woman responded. "He took me prisoner. We became lovers."

My goodness, thought Miranda. Those few words conceal a huge story. She waited, and Hermione continued.

"I did not blend in to the small section of Reims that was to be my home for the duration. Imagine. A British schoolgirl living on her own in Vichy France. I would have seemed grotesque; a young woman with English manners speaking French too perfectly, with no apparent purpose in life but to wait, and with only one set of clothes and little money. We were expected to fend for ourselves. The truth is, we were not expected to live long enough to need money; we were as expendable as empty artillery casings. And most of us didn't live long. The suicide virgins, we embraced death out of ignorance, we died miserably, tortured and by summary execution."

She talked about her comrades as if they were a unified being, as if she too had been tortured and died.

"The priests gave me a few francs. The café owners refused to charge rent. I worked in the kitchen for food. But I was British, you know, and when German soldiers would come into the café, they knew I did not belong there. They didn't care. I was young and pretty and did not appear to be dangerous. They thought perhaps I was a runaway aristocrat from Slovenia or a renegade Dane from Schleswig. Their French was not good enough to know mine was too refined, too textbook. They were foreigners too."

Miranda wasn't sure just when, but she had become aware of Morgan standing on the other side of the screen door, quietly listening.

"Dieter came to my room one night. It was late. He was alone. He knocked and when I refused to let him in he went away. The next day he came back with another soldier, both of them were SS, and they arrested me."

"I thought you were lovers," Miranda exclaimed.

"They took me to the basement under the Hôtel de Ville for interrogation."

"Were you tortured."

"And raped. After a week, Dieter escorted me to Paris."

"Did Dieter Kurtz?" Miranda reached over and placed her hand on the old woman's, but Hermione drew hers away, leaving Miranda's hand strangely empty.

"Yes."

She paused.

"Once in Paris, I was interrogated for another week, it seemed endless, with no sleep, little food, time stopped, but the pain did not, and I told them everything."

Miranda was surprised. She wanted to console the old woman but she realized no consolation was possible.

"I knew nothing. I told them everything. I was little more than a child. What could I tell them? I did not know the Maquisard who took my message. There was nothing to indicate the owners of the café or the priests were not acting out of kindness, with no intent to sabotage the Vichy regime or their Nazi confederates. I told nothing about them. I confessed to driving cars in England, I confessed to being trained as a special agent, a spy. I was condemned to death. It was Dieter Kurtz's responsibility."

"What?"

"To kill me. Death was commonplace. Execution was a trivial thing, it was war. But Paris was falling. He was young. He was brutal, but not a psychopath. And he was not a coward. I believe I had fallen in love with my captor, *mon violeur*. I adored my executioner as he walked me to the wall, I felt sorry for him. I could see where bullets had gouged the stone. I could feel the earth at my feet thick with the blood of executed partisans. Outside the compound, we could hear the roar of Allied tanks. It was absurd, I was to be shot against the very wall separating me from liberation. Dieter placed his Luger against my temple. He looked me straight in the eyes, I admired him for that even then, he took a deep breath. Tears filled my eyes but I did not cry or cry out.

"Over the rumble of tanks, I could hear the flesh of his finger bend. The firing mechanism in the Luger clicked as it slid into place, I could feel the cold steel of the barrel against my skin, and the quick surge as the firing pin released. But nothing happened. The gun misfired. Lugers are remarkable examples of German engineering. They never misfire, but this time a Luger misfired.

"When we both understood what had happened, we looked around; everyone had fled. No more SS, no more guards, no more tortured prisoners awaiting execution. Only the blood-soaked earth of a residential compound in central Paris. Dieter dropped his Luger to the ground, he untied my hands, and then he walked towards the gateway leading out of the courtyard. He would never surrender. He turned back, picked up his useless weapon, smiled at me, he smiled at me, and turned again to meet death in the street outside."

"But you were lovers?" Miranda interjected. She started suddenly as a bell tolled from the main cottage. Morgan shuffled a little in the shadows and then opened the door and stepped out onto the verandah.

"And what do you think happened next, Detective

Morgan?" So, she knew he had been there, listening. Of course, she knew.

Morgan took her arm to help her rise out of the deep comfort of her Muskoka chair. Miranda took her other arm. The three of them stood with the morning sun in their eyes, looking out over the water, all three of them seeing in their minds a Paris scene, as terrifyingly real and as unreal as anything in their lives.

"I stopped him from martyrdom, I suppose. I held him back. I provided an alternative. We escaped. We lived easily in the backstreets of Paris for several weeks. Vichy had fallen but France was ambiguous about liberation. Many resented the Allied invasion. It was a strangely bohemian interlude."

"But for yourself, didn't you want to reveal yourself to the Allies? Was it to protect Dieter?"

"I had betrayed my country."

"You were tortured," said Miranda.

"You told them nothing they could use," said Morgan.

"But I did not die, we were supposed to die."

The three of them walked closely together. On the bare rock high above the water, Hermione stopped.

"Dieter needed to go home, I helped him get to Germany. We walked across Luxembourg. Even that early in the spring the gardens were lovely. It doesn't take long to walk across Luxembourg. We walked into Germany. Then we travelled by train. Even though he was very young, in his early twenties, because he was SS he had privileges, and my French proved useful all the way to Berlin."

"I don't understand," said Miranda. "How did you use your French?"

"In the chaos resisting the Allied advance, it was difficult to travel without papers. The Germans were bogged down in procedural obsessions, trying desperately to effect a strategic retreat with appropriate records. Travelling without documentation was virtually sabotage. But Dieter was imperious, he proclaimed me his prisoner, a French partisan scavenged during the withdrawal from Paris, with knowledge invaluable to the Reich. If I was British, I would have been shot. When we stepped off the train in Berlin, since we had no papers, Dieter changed his story. I was now his French mistress, brought to Berlin to work as a whore. No one much cared. We lived together. He was busy. I got by. Then the Soviets came. Dieter was taken prisoner."

"By the Russians?"

"He bargained for his life by turning me over as a spy."

"He betrayed you!"

"For his life; it was war."

"Hermione."

"The Reich was putrescent, Berlin was in ruins. In the Empire of Death, the laws of survival are absolute, morality was an indulgence no one could afford."

"But you were lovers," Miranda protested. "You were in love."

"Love, in 1945 Berlin, was the cruelest joke. When the Soviets came, the women of Berlin were raped. Most of the surviving population was female, girls, old women, widows, housewives, whores, almost all of the women were raped. It was Soviet policy, the penis as weapon. Vengeance; contempt. And I was not raped, not then. I was beaten to such a bloodied mass by the Russians that no one would have wanted to touch me, no one could find their way in through the gore. Soviet torture was not so refined as the Nazi methods. They used brute force, it was easier to embrace death as the best possible outcome. But I did not die. I was turned over to the Americans in exchange for Soviet defectors who were executed. The Americans turned me over to the French, currying favour. The French, when they realized I was British, turned me over to her Majesty's troops for evacuation and trial as a traitor."

"But you weren't!" Miranda declared.

"No, when they got me back to London and cleaned me up, they realized I was an accidental hero and an embarrassment—and they had enough of those, with stories less conflicted than mine. I was honourably discharged from service and left to my own devices. My family was dead. After a few years I came to Canada. End of my story."

"But your life here?" said Miranda as they started walking again in response to the bell that was tolling imperiously, clearly a summons directed at the three of them for being so tardy.

"It has been uneventful, my dear."

The diminutive Hermione Mac looked up at Miranda and smiled, somehow forgiving the world for being what it was.

"And you met Kurtz again?"

"In Toronto. In the early eighties. On an escalator in Eaton's. He was going the opposite way. He waited for me to reverse my journey and catch up."

"Did you want to kill him?" said Morgan, not thinking at all about the murder under investigation.

"No, Detective. No more than he wanted me dead when he turned me over to the Russians. I think I even still loved him, or loved within myself the unconditional love I had once felt. But, I confess, there was strange satisfaction is seeing him old, in watching him grow older and older, even if it meant I was getting old as well."

"Love is perverse," said Morgan, as if he had discovered something original.

chapter eighteen
Buffet Breakfast

Morgan, Miranda, and Hermione Mac picked up their pace and soon entered the closed-in portion of the verandah where breakfast was laid out in a magnificent buffet, and after serving themselves each drifted into solitary corners of the immense room, hoping to eat quietly and digest all that they had shared.

Inevitably, others took their isolation as an invitation to socialize. Padraig and Ralph settled down on chairs beside Miranda and chatted amiably about the weather. Lionel Webb leaned over from where he was seated to engage Hermione Mac in solemn conversation. Young David Jenness positioned himself beside Morgan and while he remained standing he assumed the casual posture of someone prepared to discuss any topic deemed of interest.

Morgan looked up from his plate heaped with French toast, melon slices, and crisp slabs of Canadian bacon, all swimming in dark maple syrup.

"The darkest is best," he said to David Jenness. "They market the light stuff for quality, but the dark has more flavour."

"Really," said the young man. "I haven't quite acquired a taste for maple syrup. I mean, I like it, but I'm not a connoisseur."

"It tastes like trees," said Simon, leaning towards them.

"But not like wood," David offered, apparently feeling he should defend a product on which national pride seemed to depend, almost as much as 'ice' hockey.

"Burnt wood," said Simon.

"And Simon should know," Jane Latimer chimed in. "He grew up on a sugar farm, didn't you Simon."

"Honey and maple syrup and sugar beets," Simon acknowledged. To every season there is a sweet. In winter we hibernated."

"Lovely," said David Jenness, who had yet to feel the icy blast of a true Ontario winter. "Was there no school?" he asked, taking Simon's observation literally.

"We got through the winters on whiskey and hot chocolate, same as in England, I suppose."

"My father kept bees," said Miranda. "He wasn't very good at over-wintering, though. He had to keep replenishing the hives with packages sent up from Florida. A queen surrounded by a half-pound of workers. The post-office lady—"

"Mrs. Pannabaker," said Morgan. Their conversation made the room seem smaller, more intimate.

"Mrs. Pannabaker did not like it at all. She complained to Ottawa, but they told her it was part of the job. Handle bees or lose the business. She ran the post office out of her house, with a drop-down counter separating the foyer from her living room."

"Same with us," said Simon. "Renfrew Country. Our post-lady gave us cocoa and cookies when we picked up the mail. The maple syrup capital of Ontario."

"Really?" said David Jenness. "And both your families kept bees."

"We tapped the big trees by the driveway, " said Miranda. "But I don't even think they were sugar maples. I think they were silver. As kids, we'd boil down the sap on the barbeque outside. We did it once in the kitchen and it peeled off the wallpaper."

"Really?" said David once again. The conversation was for his benefit and to play his part he was obliged to project interested naiveté, yet to avoid seeming ignorant. "You can get syrup from silver maples, can you?"

"From just about any hardwood," said Simon.

"And honey from mosquitoes," Porrig piped up.

"But you have to be very delicate milking them," said Ralph. "Their tiny little teats will fall off in your fingers."

"Oh I know that," said David Jenness. "In England, we use tiny wee milking machines imported from Japan."

"Pass the syrup," said Morgan as they all chortled at their own wit and tucked into the food. "David, have some more. It's good for you. Lots of nutriments, zero calories."

"Really?"

"No."

"I know."

David Jenness sat down and turned in his chair to speak directly to Morgan, hiving the two of them off from the others.

"I was on the telephone to my mother this morning," he said. "I told her about you and Detective Quin."

"My goodness," said Morgan. "Did you mention my name?"

"Yes, she was fascinated to hear about the murder. I wrote her last week but the letter hadn't reached her yet. We don't e-mail."

"How is she?"

"I told her you used to know her."

"And?"

"She said to say, well, I don't know what she said, exactly. We had a bad connection, bad reception or whatever, we seemed to be cut off for a few minutes. She said something about giving you her very best."

"Thank you," said Morgan. He regarded the young man's handsome features, wondering if he had any idea what a decent sort Sir Nigel must have been, how devoted to his mother and to him.

"What's on the agenda for today?" Morgan asked.

"Well this is my first time, too."

This surprised Morgan. The young man seemed so comfortably at home; no, not quite at home. At ease.

"I would think you could do anything you want," he

said. "Swimming, it's warmed up beautifully. There's tennis, you can go for a walk, the island is apparently riddled with forest paths and breath-taking vistas. You can go for a paddle or a rowboat ride. I'm not sure of the difference. You can read, or snooze on the verandah, or you can just observe the rest of us." He turned his head to the side and gave Morgan a boyish grin. "I think that is perhaps what you came for and I'm sure we will each in our own way oblige."

"As much is revealed by people who know they are being watched as by people who don't." Morgan spoke quietly, as if taking the young man into his confidence.

"Yes, I can see that. The guilty, especially, would want to shape your impressions of how they appear." He looked around the room. "It is strange to think one of these people could be a killer."

"Very revealing."

"What? That I am trying to shape your impression of me? Or that I think one of them did it? Or, or that I excluded myself? Well, I would exclude myself, wouldn't I? If I did the crime, I most certainly would. And if I am not the guilty party, then it would not be to my advantage to include myself among the possible culprits."

"Sir David, you don't mind, do you, I rather like calling you Sir David, well, Sir David, you have an elliptical way of getting at the truth."

"I've been told that before. By my mother, actually. You really must get together next week."

"Next week?"

"She's on her way over from London. She'll be here

in a few days. Excuse me, I must speak to Felix and Jane." He nodded congenially and drifted across the verandah in a perpendicular direction, closing in on his quarry with a social directness that Morgan admired, an ability to connect that he knew he was lacking himself.

The news of Susan's impending arrival hit him hard. He was not at all sure he wanted to see her.

In his mind she was twenty-two. His own age seemed for a moment uncertain. Each of them had lived entire lives since they had last been together. So long as she was young in his mind, there was a part of him that was young as well. Not that he was sentimental about the past, but sometimes for all its awkward absurdities, the past was more real than the present.

He glanced across at Miranda. She kept him sane. He sometimes feared he would slip into self-absorbed melancholia, were it not for her. He would often lose himself in books about wine and tribal carpets and old Canadian furniture and exotic fish that he could never afford to collect, and he sometimes worried that without his bulwark of facts and enthusiasms, there would be no one there.

He sipped his coffee.

He would have to read more about Rosicrucians and the Masonic Lodge. And especially about Francis Bacon. He had been too busy with the details of the case to pursue this strange man from the irretrievable past who held such a motley crew in thrall.

Miranda looked past Ralph at Morgan sitting alone. She offered an invitation with a flash of her eyes for him to join them, which he acknowledged but ignored. She shortened her gaze to focus again on Ralph, who was explaining something about the facilities in the boathouse, that the toilet upstairs over the launch slip once flushed with hot water.

"It was a lovely screw up with the pipes. The plumber from Port got it all wrong. It was rather lovely on a cool morning to flush a couple of times before using. I do hate a cold bum."

"Well so do I," said Padraig. "Nudge wink."

"You've been coming here for a long time, then?" said Miranda to Ralph.

"Oh yes, for a very long time."

"We met here," said Padraig.

"Porrig," exclaimed Ralph in a cautionary tone.

"Well, we did."

"I know we did, but never mind."

"When was that," Miranda asked.

"Oh very long ago," said Ralph. "Porrig was only a boy."

"Rafe, I was not! You'll give Miranda the wrong impression. It goes without saying, Detective, neither of us is interested in boys."

"Well speak for yourself!" said Ralph.

"I was quite mature, I assure you. Rafe is much older than me, by three and a half years, and he was not so mature."

"Porrig!"

"Yes, Rafe."

"You are a bitch."

"Thank you, Ralph."

Miranda was fascinated: proper pronunciation, an insult.

"Well thank you, Padraig."

Mispronunciation as insult.

"Ralph!"

"Patrick!"

Miranda suspected that even they must get confused about who was who.

"Porrig D'Arcy né Ralph Robertshaw!"

"Yes, Padraig O'Suillibahn?"

"You sometimes have a big mouth."

"Well thank you my dear for noticing."

Nodding towards Miranda, he added, "She's going to know, anyway, dear, if she doesn't already. She's a detective, that's what she does, she detects things about people like you and me."

"And what is it I am about to detect?" asked Miranda.

"Rafe was an habitué of Briar Hill Island when we met."

"Habitué," Miranda said, "exactly what does that mean?"

"Just what it sounds like, dear. He was a bit of a tart—before I got my hands on him."

"And then what did I become?" said Ralph, sulking with pleasure at being the centrepiece of the unfolding story.

"He was what we now call 'eye candy.' His job was to loll."

"To loll?" Miranda found the presentation of their

revelations amusing, and yet the direction they were going quite disturbing.

"Lionel's father, the second Lord Ottermead of Duoro and Smith, he liked to have young bodies around. They were brought up from Toronto in clusters and their purpose was to *loll* about."

"Both men and women?"

"Boys and girls, Miranda. He liked them young. He paid them, he paid my beloved Rafe, who was P. O'Suillibahn at the time, to be decoration. They lived upstairs in the boathouse, boys and girls together. Sometimes, it is rumoured, there was much debauchery. My earnest lover will neither confirm nor deny."

"Porrig, that's enough."

"Is it ever enough, dear Rafe? Don't you just long for those days before I rescued you from a wasted life?"

Ralph rose to his feet, he had tears in his eyes, he reached down and squeezed Miranda on the shoulder, then, inexplicably, he gave Porrig an affectionate squeeze as well, and walked off down the broad main steps towards the boathouse.

Miranda observed Padraig, expecting to see an indication of remorse. His expression was cold. "I can never quite come to terms with his past. He was a slut, that's hard to forget."

"I'm sure it would be better for both of you if you did."

"And I'm sure you're right, but the past has a habit of sneaking up on you and slamming you down."

"Especially when you make yourself vulnerable. He

seems a very nice man."

"He is, and Errol-Flynn handsome, I know. So did old man Webb, and I can't forgive him for that."

"Forgive who, the old man or your partner? My goodness, it's all over a long time ago."

"The past is never over, Miranda. Don't you know that."

"Poor Porrig," she said.

Their conversation dwindled into an awkward silence which suited them both.

Miranda joined Morgan down on the boathouse dock after breakfast. The *Lady Ruth* was no-where in sight. Several people were already sunning themselves on a wing of the dock that extended along the shore past the boathouse, where a cluster of Muskoka chairs sat empty and a diving tower loomed over the scene, its skeletal frame connecting water, land, and sky. Despite a mild onshore breeze, it was all quite idyllic.

A sculptural array of brightly coloured canvases suspended from poles fluttered in sinuous contrast to the rigidity of the tower, casting a weird panoply of dancing shadows.

"Let's take a peek upstairs," Miranda suggested, drawing Morgan inside the boathouse. They ascended a wooden staircase into a large room with windows across one end that offered a stunning view of the lake. There was a modular fireplace in the centre, suspended from the cathedral ceiling, surrounded by sofas and loose cushions strewn casually on the floor. Along either side were doors leading off to small rooms that gave the impression of an austere dormitory, in spite of the party atmosphere of the common space. Everything was immaculately clean but a smell of mildew permeated the air, tempered by the scent of gasoline rising from the launch and several outboards in the slips below.

Miranda told Morgan Rafe's story. Morgan's immediate response was anger, that kids were exploited by power and money. This gave way to dismay, as he realized they had not been children but were young men and women enamoured by a world they were only allowed to observe as voyeurs, and to be used in their turn.

"Do you think it got pretty sordid, or do you think they were just part of the décor?"

"Yes, and yes," Miranda answered. "My impression is that the old man wanted the whole Lake to know that he was having grand times. I certainly don't think Lionel was part of it! As scion of the family he was too busy building his fortune to pay much attention to his father's pathetic diversions."

"And?"

"And I think the old man sometimes got involved with favourites, and I think Rafe was a special favourite. Otherwise, Porrig might accuse him of bad taste, but not with such vehemence and so little forgiveness."

"Do you think there's room for blackmail, here?"

"By whom, and for what? The old man apparently flaunted his proclivities. The kids, daydreaming actors and models, most of them probably live middle-class lives by now, nurturing memories from back when life was green and golden. Who, to blackmail whom?"

"I love when you say *whom*," said Morgan. "You're the last holdout in Canada. No-body says 'whom.'"

"I can't see blackmail."

"Suppose no-one actually blackmailed anyone; what if there was only the threat of blackmail. That might be enough to enforce."

"Morgan, that's what blackmail is, it's a threat. If it goes beyond that, it's extortion."

"Let's suppose Dieter Kurtz, remember him, let's suppose he didn't exactly threaten exposure, but simply lorded what he knew over the D'Arcys, his knowledge an instrument of power."

"To do what?"

"Nothing. That's what we're learning about Kurtz. It isn't what he did, it's what he knew. The Baconians couldn't afford *not* to be his friends. His knowing was like an adhesive binding them to him."

Miranda walked to the glass wall at the front of the boathouse loft and stared out. Looking to the side, she could see Hermione Mac, the spy, sitting with Hermione M. Perhaps Kurtz knew enough about both of them— the compromised loyalty of his erstwhile lover, the fact that she broke under torture, and that she helped him escape to Berlin; the matricidal depravity, perhaps, beneath the other woman's cheerfully righteous pretensions. Miranda was familiar with cases where battered wives feared more to be on their own than to remain with their husbands. Co-dependency. A variation of the Stockholm Syndrome. Willful victimization. *How complex we are*, she thought, including herself.

Morgan stood beside her. Their two reflections were dim spectres in the glass, like ghosts hovering against the late summer vista that stretched across the morning to the lakeshore horizon.

"It's a puzzle," he said.

"We've known it's a puzzle from day one in Philosophers Walk. It's a picture puzzle, and we've picked out all the blue pieces, Morgan, but we don't know yet whether they're sky or reflections in water. We don't know what the picture is, that's the problem, maybe the sky is a wall, maybe the water is silk."

"You sound like Li Po."

"How do you think he fits in?"

"To the puzzle."

"Yeah, the thing about puzzles, Morgan, is that everything connects. There are no extra pieces."

"What about Jane Latimer?"

"I have a feeling about Jane," said Miranda. "I can't quite explain it."

"Try me."

"I think she and Felix are keys to the overall design."

"Felix?"

"Jane suggested pedophilia. Rumours. But substantial enough he might lose his position as Rector. Predilections that date back to his days as Kurtz's protégé, before he went south to the Ivy League. Maybe we should question him on this?"

"You want to do it? It might work better, coming from a woman. We checked for a rap sheet. No charges, no convictions. You'll have to be very diplomatic."

"Yeah, maybe we won't go there just yet."

"So, what about Jane? You think she was a victim of Kurtz's notorious predatory maneuvers?"

"Possibly, yes."

"You think she's been abused?"

"If she was eighteen or nineteen, or twenty or twenty-one—and he was, what, in his fifties, yeah, I think it's possible. Abuse is about breaking boundaries, about sex and power. Rape is brutalizing, but so is seduction if the power differential is extreme—say between a rich man and a boy, between a Professor like Kurtz and an undergraduate like…"

Her own story was intruding. She lapsed into silence.

Because he said nothing in response, she knew he understood.

chapter nineteen

Getting Together

Miranda slid the glass doors open and stepped out onto the balcony so she could survey the entire swimming dock.

"Everyone's there, except," she paused, doing an inventory, "except Professor Li Po and Mlle. Lachine and Jane Latimer. I wonder what those three are up to?"

"Come on," said Morgan, turning back into the room. "Let's go down and do some detecting."

The people on the dock were broken into two groups, the sun worshippers and those who shrank from its carcinogenic rays.

Morgan and Miranda retrieved bathing suits from Philip's Folly and changed in the boathouse, but after a brief swim joined the group under the intricate concatenation of shadow sails, wedges of red, yellow, and blue canvas tied to poles in overhead planes to catch the sun but let the breeze flow through.

"Like a Calder mobile," Miranda observed as she sat down.

"Yes," said Lionel. "One of a kind. I had it designed for right here."

"It's lovely," she said.

The D'Arcys had clearly reconciled and were out in the bright morning sun, stretched side by side on beach towels. Simon Sparrow had sprawled into one of the Muskoka chairs in the sun, incongruously clothed in bathing trunks and a huge battered Stetson or one of those Australian Acubra's with a rolled rim. David Jenness and Jennifer Pluck were a little off from the others, lying with heads crooked on arms, talking quietly. When they got up and walked over to the diving tower, the eyes of everyone in the shade followed them.

They were beautiful and lithe. David was muscular (*like his father*, Miranda thought, *but without Morgan's mature solidity*), and he moved with the fluid grace of an athlete (which struck Morgan as fortuitous, since neither he nor Susan were conventionally athletic). Both wore the briefest of swimwear. David was young and supple enough to get away with a tiny black Speedo and Jennifer wore a string bikini that accentuated her nakedness as it looped around the sinuous contours of her body, so limited in fabric and inseparable from flesh it was hard to tell what colour it was, maybe taupe or beige.

Then all eyes shifted as Jane Latimer strutted across the cedar planks of the dock from the direction of the boathouse. She was wearing a shimmering sun-blouse, a wide-brimmed hat, and wedged sandals that stretched her legs sensuously as she walked. She looked as if she had stepped out of a fashion spread in a high-end magazine, but one of indeterminate vintage. *Stunning,* thought Miranda, *but not quite 'now.'*

With everyone watching her, like a command performance in which she got to be in command, Jane chose her place in the sun between the group in the shade and the others, then spread out her towel, sat down languorously, took off her blouse, her skin was already glistening with oil, and stretching provocatively so that her whole sleek and perfectly turned body was on display she reached behind and unclasped her bikini top, whisked it to the side, casually applied sun-block to her breasts, holding each in turn like a favourite pet, and slowly reclined on her back, with one knee cocked in the air to catch smooth planes of sunlight on the curve of her flexed quadricep.

"Now that," said Miranda to Morgan under her breath, but not concerned if she was overheard, "that is a costume."

Hermione, her friend, leaned over and said, "Whatever else, my dear, she is a perfect advertisement for maturity, there isn't a girlish body that could touch that figure, not even young Jennifer's. Oh my, she makes me feel good about being a woman."

The taller handsome Hermione mumbled in a choked exclamation as she rose to her feet, "I'm glad something does. But this is Muskoka not the French Riviera."

The others laughed and she walked off towards the main cottage.

"Is she forty?" the remaining Hermione asked Miranda.

"Yes," said Felix, who has sitting quite erect in his chair. "She is."

"How do you know," said Hermione.

"Her files," he said. "As Rector I get to see everything. So to speak."

The others laughed and Felix Swan sank back in his chair.

Simon meanwhile had cocked his hat back sufficiently: Jane fell into his line of vision without moving his head.

Lionel lifted a hand into the air and flicked an imperious forefinger, as if summoning an unseen aid. Sure enough, within moments a young man from the kitchen appeared to take orders for snacks and drinks. He must have been watching from the main verandah. That was his job. Miranda admired how detached he appeared when he walked over to Jane Latimer, squatted down beside her, casting a shadow over her exposed breasts, and asked if she wanted anything. Only when he stood up did she observe a crease in his slacks that implied he had been more interested than he appeared.

She leaned over to speak privately to Morgan but chose her words carefully in case she was overheard.

"You know what I said about her," she nodded in Jane Latimer's direction. "I was right. I'm sure of it. Really. When she's with these people," she lowered her voice to an incomprehensible whisper and mouthed the words, "she acts out roles, and they mostly have to do with—"

she mouthed the word— "sex."

"What about the Abercrombie and Fitch outfit she came up in? Stylish, but not exactly erotic." He spoke in a private voice, meant for her only.

"I'll bet she was wearing Victoria's Secret underneath, the most outrageous! Count on it, Morgan."

"Okay. Were you?"

"What?"

"Wearing Victoria's Secret?"

"You'll never know. Look at her, Morgan. That's what a good running bra does for you. She has an amazing body, even on her back, and they're real."

Morgan smiled, and she was not sure if he knew what she was talking about, but he did.

After lunch it was nap time. That seemed like a good idea to Morgan and he wandered back to Philip's Folly. Miranda decided to go for a walk. The pathways leading back from the main cottage invited exploration and she wanted time on her own to let the information and impressions of the last day to fall into place. That was what Morgan would be doing, unless he was actually asleep. It was how his mind worked. She was more likely to glean from acute observation a single pertinent fact, a flaw in the narrative, and through it struggle towards illumination and closure. It was like entering a darkened room with a penlight, and from the small glare as she shone it about, putting together an account of the room's entire inventory. Morgan's way was more fun: in the same room, random flashbulbs exploded with light, blinding and illuminating at the same time. Through the discursive accumulation of possibilities he could stumble on the resolution of a plot while daydreaming, or thinking of carpets.

Sometimes, it is necessary to focus on the warp and the weft to appreciate the effect of the weave.

Briar Hill Island lived up to its name, but by staying on the well-marked trails Miranda avoided snags in her sundress or snarls on her legs as landscape that reached out with barbed fingers gave way to deep beds of dried pine needles, then to the euphoric smell of last year's maple and beech leaves, and mounds of rich green moss yielded in the open sunlight to the brittle softness of lichen. She realized as she walked she was never actually far from the main cottage. The island was no more than a dozen acres, but it was private, and it was rugged granite, overgrown with every possible type of flora, as if Lionel had been collecting Muskoka landscape for ten thousand years, since the last ice age retreated. She even came upon a small sandy beach tucked away on the west side, sheltered by a poplar grove flashing silver from the leaves tipped upright by an onshore breeze.

She was tempted to strip off her dress and run naked in the sand, although in fact the beach was no more than a sprint in length and barely wide enough for two people to walk abreast. It proclaimed its own sense of privacy, as if no one else had ever been there before. Looking out over the water she could not see a single cottage on the islands in the distance or on the far shore. Perhaps it was because of her low vantage, but this beach seemed an absolute sanctuary.

So, she was startled to stumble over Simon Sparrow. He was reclined against an impression in the embankment where the sand turned to earth and the poplars were clenching the soil with roots running haphazardly over the surface. He had his battered broad-brimmed hat pulled down over his face. He had not heard her approach. She thought of walking around him or turning away, so as not to disturb his solitude, then remembered why she was there. This was a good opportunity to catch him at ease.

Miranda feigned a small cough by way of a salutation.

"Hello, Miranda," he said without looking up.

"Hi, Simon Sparrow. How did you know it was me?"

He tilted his hat back and patted the sand, inviting her to join him. "We all know why you're here. Don't think for a minute any of us forget it, no matter how casual we seem."

"Is that an Australian Acubra?"

"No, it's a Stetson I picked it up in Laredo a few years ago on my way through from Mexico. I have an Acubra at home with an opal in the rim band. Bought it in Alice Springs. I collect hats the way Lionel collects—well, the way Lionel collects whatever Lionel wants to collect."

"What're you doing on your own."

"I could ask you the same thing."

"What would your answer be," said Miranda. "Then I'll tell you mine."

"I'm regrouping, I suppose. Getting myself together."

"Were you falling apart."

He did not take her quip as a joke.

"No," he said. "Sometimes when I'm around other people I end up feeling I've given away too much of myself. I've got to check and see what's left and rebuild. Sounds weird, I suppose."

"I think most people feel that way sometimes. But apart from my partner and I, these are your friends."

"Do you think it's possible for an adult to have friends?"

She flinched, she gazed at the wavelets lapping silently against the wet sandy shore. It was the kind of question people don't really ask other people, but one everyone asks herself.

"I don't know, Simon. I think it's different for men. I see men bonding around a particular activity, but I don't know if they just hang out and share time, the way women sometimes do. I don't know whether watching a hockey game with someone or doing your toenails together is friendship. I don't know."

He picked up a dead poplar twig and inscribed his initials in the sand between them.

"Do you have friends?" he asked.

"Do you?"

"I don't think so," he said inconclusively but without hesitation.

"Were you friends with Dieter Kurtz?"

"Yes, I suppose I was."

"Yet you aren't stricken by grief that he's dead?" she said, letting her voice rise into a question?

He said nothing. They were sitting close enough, she reached out to touch a small silver locket hanging on a thin chain from his neck, but he flinched and she withdrew her hand.

"What's that," she said, feeling awkward for the implied intimacy of her gesture.

"Nothing," he said. "A souvenir. It sterling." Unexpectedly, he took it off and handed it to her. "Very old, a pre-Columbian talisman. Peruvian."

"Does it open?"

"Yes. It's only the top part that's old. It was made into a locket by Spanish silversmiths in the eighteenth century. Destroys its value as an artifact."

"In direct proportion to increasing its usefulness, I suppose."

"Yes, although it's empty," said Simon rather sadly, and Miranda knew there was an untold story there, perhaps one of many in Simon's life.

"How well did you know Dieter Kurtz?" she asked. "You're more of an adventurer than a scholar."

"They're not mutually exclusive. We met through Lionel. Years ago. Dieter had just retired. He helped me with my book."

He spoke as if it were common knowledge that he had authored a book. Miranda looked quizzical, waiting for an explanation.

"*The Many Lives of Simon Sparrow.* That was the subtitle, actually. It's called *Confessions of an Adventurous Soul: The Many Lives of Simon Sparrow.* You don't know it?"

"Sorry."

"The epigraph—

Some touch things and they collapse into dust. Others from a handful of dust build worlds.

"Nicely evasive. Who wrote it?"

"I did."

"Oh. Well, it's nice. The first part's sad. Good recovery, though: Others from a handful of dust breathe words."

"Build worlds, not breathe. Worlds, not words."

"And where are you in that equation?"

"That's just it, I don't know. My life doesn't seem as real as everyone else's. Stories and dust. But from the stories I build who I am."

"We make worlds of words. We're each our own creation," said Miranda, then, trying to lighten things up, she added, "It's better than the alternative."

"What?"

"Not being here at all."

"Is it?"

"Simon, what's bothering you."

"He actually encouraged me to write it."

"Kurtz?"

"Yes."

"That's the first generous thing I've heard about him."

"Generosity can be treacherous. He gave Jennifer access to his copy of *Sylva Sylvarum*. That was generous. And once it was published…"

"Your book, the *Confessions*?"

"Yes, after it was published, he made me aware of certain discrepancies that he'd known about all along."

"Maybe you were both confused."

"Dieter Kurtz was *never* confused." He paused

reflectively, captivated by his newest role as a character analyst. "He let the book go to press with errors."

"Such as?"

"You know, errors."

"Such as?"

"I said I swam the Hellespont from Abydos to Sestos, I wrote about crossing the Dardanelles doing the breast stroke. I didn't. I only swam the Bosphorus. Down the other side of the Sea of Marmara near Istanbul. Pierre Trudeau did it, too. From Europe to Asia. But not like Byron, not the actual Hellespont."

"Well, how on earth did he know that? And so what?"

"Research. He found a small article in a Turkish newspaper."

"He found it?"

"Yes. In the *Cannakale Espress*."

"And?"

"In 1982 I crossed the Sahara by camel."

"Yes?"

"In 1982 I was in bed with rheumatic fever. I crossed the Australian Outback in '84. By camel. I never crossed the Sahara. He knew that."

"Simon, so he knew, so what? It's your life, you can invent yourself any way you choose. You can't blame him for your imagination. I mean who cares, I've never heard of the book."

Miranda nearly choked when she heard the words come out of her mouth. She tried to recover: "My goodness, I mean, no one expects memoirs to be truthful, so long as they're honest, if you know what I mean. Have you never read Farley Mowat? The most honest writer around, and a consummate liar."

"Our relationship for a dozen years was based on the fact that my life was made up and we both knew it."

"Not all of it, Simon!"

"If parts are lies, the whole is a lie."

"In your eyes."

"Exactly! What else matters in the end."

"!"

"It was a good thing my book sank like a stone. A literary *Lusitania*."

"You disliked Dieter Kurtz in direct proportion to how much you dislike yourself."

"I loathed him."

"I suppose you're not the first person to loathe a friend."

Simon Sparrow pushed his broad-brimmed hat back on his head and an opal gleamed in the sun. He must be wearing his Acubra, she thought. He's confused. He left his Stetson from Laredo at home.

"That doesn't mean I killed him."

"No, and it doesn't mean you didn't. I'm going to walk back to the cottage, maybe go for another swim. Want to come?"

"No, I'll wait here a bit. See if my various parts come together."

They both laughed at his forced humour and Miranda rose, brushed sand from the skirt of her dress and walked off along the beach, feeling sorry for the man who wasn't quite there.

Simon Sparrow called after her just before she disappeared into the foliage.

"What were you doing out here, you promised you'd tell me."

"Looking for you!" she responded as she slipped into the shadows.

Miranda ambled. She was in no hurry to get back. She had found the company of Simon Sparrow both intriguing and oppressive. Being with him made her want to be on her own; his introspective self-absorbed manner was mawkish, and yet it made her want to follow the same unhealthy pattern and look for herself in the world.

Climbing the path that led around a granite shoulder, she was lost in thought, wondering about friendship. Suddenly, sliding down through a narrow cleft in the rock from above, a figure nearly tumbled her over the edge. They grasped at each other for support and fell tangled together on the path. Miranda pushed away at the light material of her sundress that seemed to envelope them both, and saw almost immediately that Jennifer Pluck was heaving with anxiety rooted in something more sinister than a narrow escape from their mutual death off the side of a cliff.

The young woman's face was contorted, her features frozen in a silent shriek. She left it to Miranda to disengage and rose to her feet when Miranda helped her. She was wearing only her minimalist bikini with a thin cotton shirt that had been pulled askew so that it hung from her shoulders like the remnant of a violent act.

"Jennifer, what happened, are you all right?" Miranda

was struggling to bring light to the young woman's eyes. "Jennifer, did you fall, what happened, speak to me, what happened?" She wished she had something to wrap around the young woman to make her less vulnerable. She reached out and straightened Jennifer's shirt.

Why would she be out here, walking through forest still swarming with summer insects, through brambles and briars and rocky crevasses, dressed like this? Her legs were scratched and her hands seemed bruised. Miranda remembered she had come in for lunch in her bikini, with only the thin cotton shirt thrown over her shoulders. She glanced down. Jennifer was bare-foot. She looked up through the cleft. Sure enough, she could see a sandal wedged among rocks and another, further up.

Both women started at the sounds of someone coming down the main path. When Lionel Webb appeared, Jennifer shrank away, but not towards Miranda. She was not looking for comfort but escape.

"Are you—is she—alright?" said Webb, his voice quavering.

"I think so," said Miranda. "I think perhaps you should go back to the cottage. I'll bring Jennifer."

The man appeared angry, bewildered, embarrassed. Such a variety of emotions struck Miranda in dramatic contrast to the inscrutable expression frozen on Jennifer's face.

Webb hesitated, took a step towards them, then turned and began to make his way back up the path.

When he was out of sight, Jennifer Pluck sank to the stony ground. Miranda squatted beside her, but when she tried to put an arm around her, the young woman leaned away and twisted so that she could look into Miranda's eyes.

"How could he?" she mumbled, barely above a whisper.

"What? What did he do?"

"He put his hands on my breasts, he touched me," she gazed into the depths of Miranda's eyes, and with more horror than she had ever before heard invested in such a seemingly innocuous word, Jennifer whispered, "*inappropriately!*"

Miranda regarded her with puzzled concern. The young woman's bikini top was precarious, but apparently secure.

"Exactly what did he do, Jennifer?"

"It's not what…"

Miranda waited.

The young woman's eyes flashed, then, with a shudder of contempt, she said in a clear voice, "It's not about what, it's who. Lionel Webb is my father."

chapter twenty

Lionel's Story

"I don't think it was sexual assault, it depends," Miranda was saying to Morgan as they walked from Philip's Folly to the main cottage. She had gone to find him after convincing Jennifer Pluck she needed to meet with Lionel Webb and resolve what might have been a simple misunderstanding. If he did touch her breasts, if he was her father, *inappropriate* would be putting it mildly. But a confrontation could be illuminating. Anything to shed light on relationships among the intimate associates of Herr Doctor Professor Dieter Kurtz, even acting as mediators and witnesses in dealing with the fallout of possible incest.

"It depends, it usually does," said Morgan. He had been in a deep sleep, induced by the oxygen-drenched Muskoka air. He was still groggy and a little confused. He understood there had been an impropriety. *But if it wasn't assault, then wasn't it just bad manners.*

"She says the man is her father, for God's sake," Miranda declared.

Ah, thought Morgan. *Inappropriate*, absolutely!

They walked through the main doors off the verandah, across the large entryway and past the drawing room, up the stairs to Webb's second-floor study. They had not really been inside the main cottage before. It wasn't off limits, but there had been no need. It was wonderfully rich and casual; the walls and ceilings were unpainted wood, narrow strips bevelled at the edges, mellowed golden after a century exposed to the air. On the walls were Canadian landscape paintings, a few by notables but mixed randomly with journeyman work by local artists or family. The floors were strewn with antique tribal carpets, possibly bought new in the bazaars of Persia when the building first went up, chosen with an impeccable eye for quality, and now, Morgan thought, unspeakably rare.

Both found it difficult to resist exchanging expressions of their appreciation for the casual opulence of their surroundings. They did not want to appear gauche, even to each other. At the top of the stairs they were surprised by the number of corridors leading off in a variety of directions to the various wings where the guest suites were tucked away beneath turrets and gables. It was not difficult to recognize Lionel Webb's quarters, however. There was a large door opposite the head of the stairs which, although it was closed, would obviously lead to the rooms directly above the main veranda, with a magnificent view looking out over Lake Rosseau.

The Dead Scholar

Neither wanted to go in until Jennifer appeared. They were sure she was not there yet; she would not be inside with the door closed. Leaning side by side over the balustrade, watching for her entrance, they were startled when she appeared at their side. Of course, her room would be along one of these corridors, on the same level as Lionel Webb.

"Okay," said Miranda, "are you ready? We're with you, this isn't an official inquiry, we just want to clear up what happened."

"You know what happened."

"Don't you want to go in?" said Morgan. "You don't have to."

"I do," said Jennifer. "I need to get this out in the open. I owe him a lot, I know it. Indirectly. It's complicated."

"The Fellowship?" said Miranda. "We know about that."

"And more. He's been good to me. But he's never admitted to being my father. You'd think with enough money and power, you could confess to anything. I mean, it isn't such a big deal—but even after his wife drowned, he didn't own up, so he wasn't protecting her." She gazed down into the foyer below, then looked up again. "I think I'm partly disgusted with myself, maybe I was flirting with incest."

"Let's get in there and sort this out," said Morgan.

Miranda knocked on the door and it opened immediately. Webb led them to a pair of wicker sofas, cushioned in frayed chintz. He had drinks on a tray on the table and without asking handed them each a tall gin and tonic, garnished with twists of fresh lime.

He could see how bitterly distraught Jennifer was.

"I don't think I've ever seen you in jeans," he said, trying to ease the tension. It was true, Miranda realized Jennifer Pluck was not in costume. Low slung jeans and a T-shirt; she looked like any other woman of her age. She was wearing make-up, applied delicately but with deliberation, her only concession to a disguise.

Since Jennifer did not respond, and the detectives seemed disinclined to lead the conversation, Webb rose to his feet and walked to the French door leading onto a balcony. He stared out as if looking for something in particular. Then he turned and addressed the young woman in a clear direct voice.

"Jennifer, I sincerely regret our misunderstanding. I would not hurt you for the world."

"You have," she snapped back.

"Apparently I have. But you must realize I am a little confused." He looked to Morgan and Miranda. Neither offered anything as they returned his gaze. "Jennifer, I am a reasonably worldly man."

"For God's sake! Is that an excuse."

"No, not at all. But it is an attempt at explanation. You are an attractive young woman, far more interesting than my sort tends to encounter."

"That explains exactly what?" Jennifer snarled. Despite the fury, there were tremulations in her voice, as if anger were suppressing a deeper sorrow.

He seemed shaken by her rage.

"Is it so offensive, a man of my age being attracted to

a woman of such wonderfully dramatic intensity."

"Have you no shame?" she demanded, and in spite of herself had to stifle the giggle evoked by her righteous cliché.

"You think I can buy anything?" he said. "I can't. If I could, I would buy peace between us, I would collect all the happiness of your life and offer it to you now as a gift."

"Do you realize how stupid that sounds?" said Jennifer Pluck. She looked to Miranda and then to Morgan, then back at Lionel Webb. She was smiling and tears rolled unchecked down her cheeks, as if her small body could not contain any more emotion.

Lionel Webb gazed at her with confused affection. The way he leaned forward, he clearly wanted to go to her but was afraid of the outcome.

"I'm sorry I touched you, Jennifer. I hope the detectives know it wasn't more than that."

"Touched me! You copped a feel," she said, with another stifled giggle. "You felt me up."

Lionel Webb looked horrified.

Articulating each word with precision, he said, "I have not 'felt up' any person since I was a very young man." Then he realized how pompous that sounded. "Anyway, that's below the waist, and I only touched your…" he paused, realizing he was about to incriminate himself, then he mumbled the word, "breasts."

"That's copping a feel," she responded. "Above the waist is copping a feel. You did that."

"With subtlety, dear Jennifer. I barely touched your

skin, nothing that wasn't showing already."

"So, you're saying I brought it on by the way I was dressed?"

"No, not at all. I—"

Suddenly, she drew herself up and turned on him venomously. "You are charming, Lionel Webb. But you are a depraved pervert."

"For touching the rise of your breasts with the back of my hand."

"You're my father, for God's sake."

The room thrummed with sudden silence. The air grew instantly so thick it was difficult to breath. In a tired display of pathetic fallacy, the sun passed behind a small cloud over the lake and the room was filled briefly with shadows.

Then Lionel Webb spoke, and as he did so he moved closer to Jennifer.

"Is that what you think?"

"Yes."

"I'm your father?"

"I know."

"No, Jennifer. I'm asking, is that what you think? That I am your father?"

"Yes," she said and her voice quavered. It seemed to Miranda that for the first time seeping into Jennifer's mind was the possibility this was not true.

"I am so sorry, Jennifer."

In spite of a situation with all the elements of a Greek tragedy playing out before them, Morgan could not help but find the miscommunication between protagonists amusing. He was seated beside Jennifer. He glanced over at Miranda. She avoided eye contact.

"You're sorry?" Jennifer exclaimed. "Really, Daddy? May I call you Daddy."

"Dear dear Jennifer, you may call me anything you like," he smiled at her with deep affection, "but I am not your father. I have never been your father. I do not expect ever to become your father, unless I adopt you. And given the current state of our affairs, I do not expect to be the father of your children."

"Oh," said Jennifer Pluck.

Again there was silence so palpable one could reach out and catch hold of it in the air, Morgan thought. He shifted his weight on the cushion and the wicker creaked ominously. "I hope this thing will take the weight," he said.

"Oh yes," said Lionel Webb. "It's as old as the cottage, but it carries its ancestry with pride. It won't let you down."

"You should never have re-painted it," Morgan offered. "It would be worth a lot more with the original paint."

"Thank you, Detective. I appreciate the financial advice."

"Would you like us to leave?" Miranda asked.

"You believe him?" said Jennifer in bewilderment.

"Yes I do," she answered.

"Do you?" Jennifer asked Morgan.

"Why would he lie? We'll be requesting voluntary DNA samples, it would come out then anyway. So, we don't really have sexual assault, do we? More like, genetic misappropriation. And a middle-aged man not quite so worldly in his maneuvers as he might have thought."

"Would you like to discuss things alone."

"Yes," said Lionel Webb.

"No," said Jennifer Pluck. "Please stay."

Lionel Webb was already moving towards the door in a gesture of showing them out. A man in his position did not want to expose more of his private affairs than he had to. Jennifer, on the other hand, wanted allies, witnesses to share whatever revelation might come that would change how she fit inside her own life.

Miranda settled back on the sofa, making it clear she intended to stay. Morgan, who was already on his feet, shrugged and moved back to a wicker armchair. Webb remained standing.

Since neither of the principal players seemed inclined to speak, Miranda decided to play interlocutor.

"Would one of you explain what the Webb Foundation is?" she asked, being careful to avoid sounding like this was an interrogation.

Jennifer responded: "It's how my 'father' supported me through my B.A., M.A., M.Phil., and Ph.D. And for all I know, he's paying for the post-doc as well."

"What's an M.Phil.?" Morgan asked.

"It's just another degree," Jennifer answered. "For those of us with confidence problems. It gives credentials short of the doctorate, for course work and comps."

"Comprehensive exams?"

"Yeah. But it's meaningless. If you're successful, you

go on for the doctorate, which trumps an M.Phil. And if you fail out, well, then it obviously has no meaning at all. It isn't enough to get you a job"

Miranda turned to Lionel Webb.

"Are we agreed on that? You paid for her university education, M.Phil. included."

"We are, although obviously it was not to assuage guilt—don't you think if the girl, this woman, had been my daughter I would have proudly stood up and proclaimed it to the world."

"Not when your wife was alive."

"I am not so meek as you might think, Miss Quin."

"Why, then. There must have been many young people in Lakebridge who would have benefitted from your family's largesse."

"It was something I owed to her mother. I would rather not go there just now."

"I think it is a little too late for proprieties, Mr. Webb."

"Poor Mr. Pluck!" exclaimed Jennifer.

"Who?" said Miranda. "Oh, Jennifer's mother's husband, her putative father."

"Putative, be damned," exclaimed Lionel Webb. "Pluck *was* her father."

"Then why the Webb Foundation?" Morgan interjected from his place off to the side.

"I owed it to Jennifer's mother. Can't we leave it at that. It's not relevant. The post-doc has nothing to do with me. She's on her own now and doing very well. What's past is past."

"Or prologue," said Morgan.

"How could you let me think—"

"I didn't. It never crossed my mind. You had a father."

"Who was an incestuous old bastard!"

"Who was what?" exclaimed Miranda.

"Nothing! He didn't get very far. I fought him off through high school. He was inept even at incest. When he died, I got drunk for three days. Missed the funeral."

"But that explains your extreme reaction to Lionel's, ah, advances."

"My God," said Lionel Webb, "I hardly touched her. I really am not as awkward in these matters as you three seem to think."

"Indeed,' said Miranda. "So, what was your connection with Jennifer's mother? Whatever, it's going to come out. Acknowledged or not, we're in the middle of a murder investigation."

"Spill the beans, old chap," said Morgan.

"This is serious, Morgan," said Miranda, and immediately regretted passing public judgment on her partner. He blinked and she turned again to Lionel Webb.

"Was she blackmailing you?"

"What on earth would make you say that?" he snapped.

"The arms-length generosity. The fact you don't call her by her first name, your hesitation to clarify your relationship; a hunch, intuition, forensic deduction, take your pick."

"Yes."

"Yes what?" Jennifer demanded.

"Jennifer, your mother knew something she should

not have known. She never asked for money. But I knew she knew what she knew. That was enough."

"So not only do I lose a father, today, I lose the kindness of a benefactor's intentions as well. And my mother's reputation for decency, to boot. I should have gone off with David."

"What!!!" exclaimed the other three simultaneously.

"He wanted to go and snog about in the woods. He doesn't know there are voracious mosquitoes and blackflies out there. No way, I told him. Anyway, he's too young."

"Look," said Miranda, "let's get this sorted out. What did Jennifer's mother know, what would she possibly know that could not be squelched by the power and wealth of a family like yours?"

"The source." said Webb.

"The source?"

"Of my family's power and wealth. I assure you the story is not relevant to the case."

From off to the side, Morgan interjected, "Did Dieter Kurtz know about this?"

There was a long and awkward pause, then Lionel Webb said in a quiet voice, "Yes. He did."

"Then it's relevant," said Morgan.

Webb sat down on the sofa beside Jennifer. He looked pained. They clearly wanted to reach out and comfort each other, but whatever was about to be said stood between them like an insuperable wall.

"Jennifer's mother, Miriam, was a good woman. She did not threaten me. But when you are vulnerable, then even the most discrete knowledge can be treacherous." He glanced up at Jennifer but she was looking determinedly at the indigo pattern in the carpet between the two sofas. "She worked for my family, for the *Clarion*, which was the original pearl, the clasp, perhaps, in the necklace of papers my grandfather accumulated and small though it was it remained his favourite. After he retired, he kept up appearances in the House of Lords until he was in his eighties. Then he came back to Canada. After driving himself into the heart of British society like a wooden spike and securing an hereditary peerage for his efforts, he left all that behind and returned to the family home in Lakebridge. He died at ninety-six."

"And?" said Miranda.

"I was close to my grandfather, closer than my father, who was like an outsider caught between us. The old man would have passed on his title directly to me if he could. As it was, my father only lived another few years and I took up the mantle."

"And?" Miranda said again, out of interest more than impatience.

"After his return, Miriam became the old man's private secretary. She worked for *The Clarion*, but she was there, in the old house, every day, until he died. He dictated his memoirs to her hour after hour, hours on end..

"He rambled and she wrote. He told her it wasn't for publication. Put it away for a hundred years. He told me that, too. Literally. Lock it away until we've all turned to dust. A man needs to know the truth will out, he would say. And it will, he would say, but not in my lifetime or yours. I will not deny history, but in a century our good name will be either unassailable or it will be gone. Either way, honour will be served."

"Sounds ominous," said Miranda.

"Very," said Lionel. "But I didn't pay much attention. Dictating his memories kept the old man amused. When I would listen in, he was lucid and wonderfully succinct. From years in the newspaper business, I suppose. He would write the occasional editorial for *The Clarion* right up to the end. Always published them unsigned. Always remarkably in keeping with the values espoused by the current editorial board."

"And?" said Miranda

"Miriam was his best friend for the last years of his life. My grandmother died before he returned from England, and my father and I were busy, draining the Atlantic."

"Pardon?"

"Trying to bring our British and American enterprises together. So, Miriam Pluck was his friend. When he died, he was buried as he wished in a family plot outside of Lakebridge. But my father got a court order and had him disinterred and shipped to the U.K. for burial in keeping with his status. But that is another story, isn't it? Back at the house, after the service, Miriam took me aside. She asked me what I wanted to do with the reams of notes she had taken from dictation. Several thousand pages. We both knew what the my grandfather wanted.

"I asked her if there were any ghosts in the family closets, the old man had implied there were swarms of them."

"'Yes,' she said. 'I think they should be exorcised. Destroy the notes.' I was surprised. 'Why?' I asked her. She at first refused to say, then indicated she wanted me to follow her into the library. I shut the door and she turned to me. 'I suppose you are going to find out. You have a right to see what we've written.' It was touching how she said, *we*. 'I would rather your father doesn't know about this.' She was quite insistent."

"'Lionel,' she said. It was the only occasion in all the years I knew her when she called me by my first name. 'Lionel, it would be better if you let me destroy all this,' she said. 'He was an old man.'

"Inevitably, I was curious. The notes or unedited manuscript or whatever you would call the transcribed memories of a man taking the measure of himself in death's antechamber, it was all in two boxes on the desk. I started to reach for them. She stepped between me and the desk. 'No,' she said. 'Let me burn them.'"

"She was trying to protect you," said Jennifer. "My mother was on your side."

"Yes, she was. And she was trying to protect the old man from himself."

"Then why do you hate her?"

"I don't hate her, Jennifer. I fear her. I do still. You fear your best friends if they know something that could destroy you."

"And did she?" asked Miranda.

"Yes."

"Are you going to explain."

"No."

"You don't need to," said Jennifer.

"I think he does," said Miranda with a certain authority in her voice, making it clear she was asking as a police officer, and not only as an acquaintance or friend.

"No, what I meant is, I know what he's going to say," said Jennifer. "The funny thing is, it's something my mother vehemently denied. Lakebridge is a small town, a community of rumours like any other small town. Do you want me to tell them, Lionel?" She reached over and took his hand.

"No," he said, clasping his other hand over hers. "When my grandfather arrived in Lakebridge in the eighteen-nineties, there was a newspaper, a daily, called *The Bugle*. My grandfather had apprenticed in Fleet Street, he was very young but he knew the business. He had a falling out with the publisher of *The Bugle* in his third or fourth year. He was fired. He claimed all his life that was the best thing that ever happened to him. He was fired because he couldn't spell. I think today he would be described as dyslexic. Back then, it meant you were slow. He's on record as saying in the Lords, if he had been able to spell 'bullshit' as well as he shovelled it, he'd still be assistant editor at the Lakebridge *Bugle*."

"Yes?" said Miranda.

"I guess the rumour Jennifer is referring to, well, the old man started his own paper."

"And?"

"And burned out the competition."

"What!"

"Burned *The Bugle* to the ground. So some people said. Burned them out, and the publisher left town. And *The Clarion* prospered. Was that it, Jennifer?"

"No, but it's almost as sordid as the story I actually heard."

"Oh, my God," said Lionel Webb. "Tell me?"

She laughed with uncharacteristic ease. "No, that's about it. Did you read your grandpa's notes?"

"Your mother's notes. No, she told me about the fire. Then she turned the manuscript over to me, then and there, and she resigned."

Lionel Webb looked curiously like a small boy, thought Miranda, and very old, all at the same time.

"I heard she married Pluck," he continued. "I heard about you, Jennifer. I followed your progress through school. I knew your father didn't add up to much. I went to your mother and offered help. She refused but she said, would I look out for you. She was not asking for a favour. It was negotiation. Help my daughter; I've helped you. And I did. I tried. I have a special file, you know. It's marked 'Jennifer Pluck.'"

"Come on, Morgan," said Miranda. "Let's give these two some privacy." She stopped at the door and turning to Lionel Webb she asked, "How did Dieter Kurtz know about this?"

"Research. Assiduous research in small-town archives. And guesswork. He was good at putting things together in the worst possible light."

"I gather that."

"My grandfather established philanthropic projects

and gave away millions. Driven by guilt, I suppose."

"Most generosity is," said Morgan.

"I hope he did something for the man he destroyed," said Miranda.

"He did," said Lionel.

"And the manuscript," said Morgan. "Did you destroy it?"

"I am a collector, my dear Morgan. What do you think?"

chapter twenty-one

A Secluded Beach, Afternoon Tea

Downstairs, Morgan and Miranda lingered, both of them aware how sinister or how splendid the cottage interior could be, depending on lighting, on who was there, on whether or not there had been a murder or incest or eccentric good fellowship. Looking up at the gallery, it seemed like generations of eyes peered down at them from the shadows. The smell of dry wood, old leather, and faded lavender permeated the scene. A slight breeze flickered, coming through from other rooms with their French doors opening onto the verandah.

As they stepped outside, Miranda said: "Did you see off to the right, that must be the formal dining room. We're having dinner there tonight."

"I think it doubled as a ballroom," said Morgan.

"A ballroom?"

"Felix Swan was telling me about it when I went back for my nap. He said the first Lord Ottermead, otherwise known as Lionel Webb, senior—since Lionel Webb's father was also Lionel Webb, Lionel Webb, junior, does that make our Lionel the second or the third? He's the third Lord Ottermead."

"Morgan."

"Yes.

"The ballroom?"

"The original Lionel Webb, the first Lord Ottermead, used to hold fancy balls here before World War I. Apparently it was an annual event. All the best people on the Lakes would show up in their magnificent launches and they would dance to an orchestra until dawn."

"Sounds idyllic, doesn't it?"

"If you weren't the launch mechanic or a lady's maid, yeah."

"Sometimes, I think, even if you were just part of the support system, Morgan, it must have been grand to witness the lives of the very rich."

"Unless you were sick and couldn't buy medicine, or unemployed and had no place to live. Or dead, and couldn't afford to be buried. You're a Tory."

"And you're a Whig. If I am, I'm a Red Tory."

"That's an oxymoron."

"And so are you."

"You're in a good mood."

"Well, yes, the secret worlds of the Bacon Society are slowly coming to light."

"Peeling away like layers of an onion? No, let's go for

an artichoke. At least when you peel an artichoke, there's something inside."

"A delicate savoury encased in prickles. You want to go for a swim?"

"Sure, if there's time before dinner."

"I know a secluded beach. You game for it."

"Okay," said Morgan. "Our bathing suits are in the boathouse."

"Do you need a bathing suit, Morgan. I told you it was secluded."

He looked at her through narrowed eyes. He did not want to make a fool of himself by seeming either too quick on the uptake or too slow.

"Come on," she said. "We need time on our own." She realized she was flirting. She appreciated the intimacy of their relationship, that she could, if not flaunt her sexuality, at least give it a modest airing. She could trust Morgan to read her with casual affection and not take advantage.

She thought about sex as they walked. In spite of the vast range in ages of the company assembled, the atmosphere was strangely charged, it wasn't just her. There were sexual tensions and cross-currents, some more overt than others, some of ancient vintage and some, like young David Jenness's raunchy designs on Jennifer, not fully matured.

Out loud, she said: "You know, I think I'm beginning to understand the alliance between the Rector and Jane Latimer. If what we suspect is true, that she was, let's say, compromised by Kurtz when she was a student, she needs Felix."

"How so?"

"Let's say Kurtz extorted sex from her in return for being an academic mentor, then her achievement as a scholar has shaky foundations, not intellectually, but in terms of moral surrender. The greater her success, the more confused her sexuality."

"And you figure Felix Swan, who has built a very successful career to mask his depravities, would be her natural ally."

"Even if she hated him. Especially if she hated him. The greater her contempt, the more he fills a niche in her life. And they have Dieter Kurtz as an enemy in common."

They had reached a high rise in the granite landscape and could look back beyond the tops of the soaring pines close to the cottage, or down over the grove of poplars flagging their white-bellied leaves in the breeze.

"Li Po," Miranda said.

"What about him?"

"What's his connection with Hermione M. They're spending a lot of time together, always off to the side. If they were fifty years younger, I'd think they were lovers."

"Fifty years ago, maybe they were."

"Watch your step. This is where Jennifer Pluck burst through the rock and nearly sent us both to our doom. Do you really think they were an item?"

"An item? Probably not. Lovers, quite possibly."

"How are we going to find out?"

"Ask them," said Morgan.

"You ask them."

"Okay, I will. If I get a chance. Maybe."

"Do you think there's a connection between Hermione M and Mlle Lachine? We know there is between Ms. Lachine and Li Po. They knew each other at the Sorbonne. But she's a cosmopolitan *Québéçoise* and Hermione is small-town all the way, whether she eliminated her mother or not."

"Or had bedroom adventures like the other Hermione implied."

"Implied, hell. She stated outright. I think the old girls know a lot about each other and kind of get off on being abrasive at the other's expense."

"Well," said Morgan, as they began to skirt along the edge of the beach, walking on the loamy embankment held in place by gnarled roots of generations of poplars. "So this is it?"

"This is it," said Miranda. She reached up with both hands and undid a button on the bib front of her sundress as she stepped down onto the narrow strip of sand. She swirled around and squinted up at her partner. "You coming?"

"No, maybe I'll watch."

"In your dreams, Morgan. We're in this together."

"Okay," he said, looking up and down the length of the beach and around through the stand of poplars. He kicked off his loafers, sat down on the embankment and took off his socks, and stood up barefoot in the sand.

Miranda undid the other button. Morgan lifted his T-shirt slowly over his head. He took a deep breath.

When he suddenly realized while his eyes were covered that she had dropped her sundress around her ankles and stepped out of it into her own shadow, he rapidly exhaled and took in a deeper breath that seemed to remain clogged in his lungs, which were distended by the self-conscious clenching of his gut.

Forcing himself to exhale, he said in a low voice, "Victoria's Secret."

"Yes."

"You are a goddess, Miranda, you are beautiful."

"Thank you."

He dropped his pants and stepped out of them.

"Blue."

"Yes, Morgan. Blue."

Blue lingerie. He struggled for another breath and then relaxed and his breathing came more naturally, in deep drafts through his nostrils. He had never seen her like this, exposed nearly naked in the open light. They had, on a few occasions, changed in each other's presence, they had shared rooms at night, even beds several times. They had one night been lovers, a long time ago, but in the morning both knew it was a mistake, that they were friends who counted on each other, sometimes literally, for survival. Their relationship depended on conflict where lovers would be compliant, and compliance where lovers might be conflicted. They each had their reasons why the affair lasted only one night. Neither of them let it intrude on the intimacy they continued to share.

He had never been in a position to stand back and simply look at her, not quite like this, with no clothes to tease the imagination. It occurred to Morgan she was doing the same thing, her own eyes sweeping the contours and textures of his exposed body.

Damn, he thought, I wish I'd worn boxer shorts. Bunched up jockeys are only attractive on manikins.

Miranda smiled to herself in appreciation of his remaining article of clothing. Jockeys show the man. *Damn, he looks good.*

"Is that a flashlight or—"

"Forget it!"

"Sorry. Poor taste."

Miranda reached around to unhook her strapless blue bra, but instead of shrugging out of it when the clasp was released she held it against her breasts with her hands in what Morgan perceived as a provocative pose. He stuck his thumbs in the sides of his jockeys, then waited.

"You first," she said.

"No, you," he responded.

"You."

"No, you."

"I think we're at an impasse," she said.

"You started this, it was your idea."

"Yeah, well now I feel silly."

"Me too," he said. "Tell you what. We'll go in in our underwear."

"Sure, and like that won't show when we go back to the cottage."

"Okay. Here's the plan. Stay still, turn around, now, I'm going to stand beside you, okay, we're too close to look at each other. Off with the clothes and in we go.

Skinny dipping is no big thing, we just pretend not to look at each other."

"Okay," she said. "We pretend. Don't you feel ridiculous. I mean, this isn't titillating."

"Not until you said *titillating*."

"*Titillating, titillating.*"

"Okay, one-two-three go." Morgan slipped his jockeys off and before they touched the sand she had dropped her bra and wiggled out of her panties. They stood side by side, both very still.

Without turning her head, through gritted teeth she said, "Morgan, this is one of our dumber ideas. If anyone's watching we must look like a pair of fools."

"Feels that way, doesn't it."

"What?"

"Foolish."

Suddenly the bell on top of the kitchen wing of the cottage tolled its resonant command, summoning the company for afternoon tea.

They both shuddered. Miranda turned her head sideways towards Morgan with an exaggerated twist of her neck to prevent her from glancing downwards. He crossed his arms over his chest and with his feet planted squarely in the sand turned his own head until their eyes met. Miranda started to giggle. He glanced down at himself. What in her Mae West voice she had suggested might be a flashlight was down to manageable size; not much more than a battery.

"Okay," he said abruptly, "it's teatime," and he exploded in motion, thrashing through the shallows and lunging into a dive when the water reached his knees. Miranda was almost as quick off the mark and they swam out side by side, settling into easy strokes that were not in unison because his were more awkward but powerful and hers were faster. At what might have seemed a predetermined point, they reversed direction and switching to the breast stoke swam lazily back toward shore. When they lost depth, brushing their knees against the sandy bottom, they rose to their feet and walked side by side without any self-consciousness at all, not playfully like kids, but casually. Her breasts were bigger than he had imagined and set very high. His body was lean and more muscled than she had thought. They retrieved their underwear, shook out the sand, shimmied their wet bodies into the skimpy dry cloth, and then put on the rest of their clothes unceremoniously and proceeded along the beach, grooming their wet hair with their fingers as they went.

During tea, Morgan talked with Lionel Webb about the missing Kurtz volume that had been replaced with a fake. Their host seemed relaxed, even though he had been the one to suggest the original be placed in his care for safekeeping.

"It will turn up," said Webb. "We have to be patient. It is not the kind of treasure to remain buried for long. Its worth depends on the appreciation of others—as does the worth of most things, I suppose."

"But a first edition of Bacon," said Morgan. "Wouldn't you say it has an intrinsic value?"

"Value, yes. Worth. No."

"A common sentiment, but in this case confusing."

"May I explain. It is a rare thing in itself, not for its content, which is reprinted in a dozen more recent editions, but for its authenticity as an artifact of its time, for the directness of its connection to the author, himself. That makes it valuable. What gives it worth is people like me, like those of us gathered here. Worth is the measure of how much something is covetted; the highest bidder determines the greatest worth."

The practical cynicism of an inveterate collector with illimitable resources intrigued Morgan. He was the polar opposite, himself. He spent time, not money, on acquiring information about things that attracted his interest. He read volumes on oriental carpets, focusing on tribal rugs from Persia, or Iran as the historical present insists, and on early Canadian furniture, for instance, but accepted with equanimity that these things were out of his reach. He had no particular desire to own an antique Qashq'ai or an Ile d'Orleans sideboard with original paint. It was enough to know they had been made, that they existed. Admittedly, as a seasoned reader about fine wines, there were a few classic bordeaux he would dearly love to taste, for the gustatory pleasure, the aesthetic delight of an actual experience beyond the capacity of words to describe.

He was about to say something when he noticed a distracted look spread over Webb's face, as if he were listening for something. Gradually conversation in the entire room fell away and they could hear a low thrum that rose rapidly to a throbbing immediately overhead as a helicopter hovered briefly above them and then receded towards the landing pad.

David Jenness got up and excused himself. He walked around the verandah and disappeared up the side of the hill. Conversation picked up again.

Lionel Webb had turned to talk with Jennifer Pluck, leaning close to keep their exchange private. *Glad to see they've worked out their differences,* Morgan thought. Miranda noticed the same intimate chat and was more wary. She felt Jennifer was especially vulnerable now, and found the way the young woman's natural edginess had subsided to be awkward and vaguely ominous.

Miranda looked around for Li Po. He was sitting off by himself, with his eyes lightly closed. He seemed to be feeling the warm breeze coming through the screen as it bathed his face, as if he were deeply at peace and Muskoka was the most natural setting for him in all the world. She liked him, she liked how self-contained he seemed without being isolated from his surroundings.

Marie Lachine and Hermione M sat side by side on a cushioned settee, quietly sipping their tea. Miranda looked from one to the other, expecting them to resume an interrupted conversation, but they appeared to be happy enough with silence.

Marie had an exotic quality about her, a deep complexion framed with hair that was jet black, with a touch of grey, mostly at the temples, and with almond piercing-grey eyes. Hermione, beside her, was equally handsome and although a full generation older had the kind of ageless features that bespeak a life of relative ease and good fortune, more so than her younger companion.

Padraig and Ralph sat one on either side of Hermione Mac, with their wicker chairs pulled close to hem her in, although she did not seem intent on escape. The D'Arcys were either reconciled or were using the old lady as a buffer. Ralph seemed cheerful enough but the strain of their disagreeable exchange earlier in the day showed on Padraig's face, even though he was smiling. For some reason Miranda found it easier to picture Padraig, much younger, working in his father's boatworks, up to his chubby ears in varnish and grease, than to see Ralph, for all his sleek good looks and charming manner, as dockside decoration.

She tried to imagine what it must have been like on Briar Hill Island in distinct eras of the past. Before the First World War, a convergence of fine launches carrying belles in ball gowns and their beaux, many of whom would die short months away in the blood-soaked trenches of Europe. She could see this in her mind, the horror itself and the beauty that drowned in its wake. And fifty years later, a cluster of young hustlers and hangers-on, lithesome male models and television starlets, disporting themselves on a free and lavish holiday in the Muskoka Lakes, all by strutting and lolling for an old man's prurient pleasure, she could see this with even more clarity, where beauty and horror had merged.

Gazing about, Miranda could not help but think how benign their present gathering might appear. Were it not for the murder of Dieter Kurtz, they could have been among the most charmingly eccentric and harmless company this grand cottage had ever hosted. The Bacon

Society, what could be more pleasant than teatime on a verandah overlooking Lake Rosseau at the turn of the summer with this strange array of intellectual and social misfits, pariahs and renegades, characters and oddballs. *Ah, but for the corpse and the fact that among them is a killer with a droll sense of humour, they are such good company.*

When David Jenness returned around the end of the verandah while the helicopter could be heard thwapping the air on its departure, he walked straight to Lionel Webb and said something in his ear. The other nodded, smiling, and sat back in his chair, apparently content. David leaned over and spoke to Jennifer Pluck. She glanced around with a peculiarly self-conscious look on her face, then rose and joined him, and the two of them sauntered together down the main steps to the boathouse.

After a few minutes the pungent smell of burning cedar wafted up from the shore. This was gradually displaced by the dry sweet smell of a maple fire.

"They're stoking up the sauna," Felix announced, as if he were sharing an observation that might have missed everyone else.

Miranda shifted around in her chair and gazed across a table teeming with teatime delectables at the Rector, who had been sitting quietly, thumbing through a magazine. If the rumours were true and he was being released from his duties at Jesus College because of indiscretions with juveniles, then she would have to revise her estimation of their collective benignity. Since Lionel Webb was Chair of the Board of Governors, Swan's presence was viciously ironic. And, of course, Hermione M, she might have done-in her mother. And Hermione the spy, whatever else, had not lived passively through the tumultuous mid-century era. Nor Li Po, she suspected. And Lionel, how often had he sold his soul to add to his collections of everything.

She swivelled to see who else she could draw into the snare of her shifting judgments. Jane, who was sitting quietly, sipping her tea and enjoying the panoramic view of the lake, Jane Latimer did not seem benign at all, but she did not seem malevolent, either. Simon, she thought, Simon Sparrow was missing. But she twisted around the other way and saw him in conversation with Morgan, and when she focused, she could hear them talking about Easter Island. She wondered if poor Simon was even aware that Morgan had been there. Surely yes. Quite possibly not.

Her attention shifted back to Marie Lachine.

Miranda rose from her chair and sauntered over to the pair on the settee as casually as she could. "Do you mind if I join you?" she said, sitting down on a bench in front of them.

"Of course," said Marie Lachine. "You may sit there. You may sit wherever you wish."

The woman's curt response made Miranda address the old woman beside her with more directness than she had intended. "Hermione, how did you meet Lionel?" she asked.

"Oh, through Professor Kurtz. He was the one who authenticated my copy of Bacon and sponsored me in the Society."

"Do you drive in from Hamilton for the meetings."

"Dundas, it's near Hamilton. No, I take a taxi to the train and another taxi from Union Station. I do drive, but I prefer not to."

"And how do you know Hermione MacGregor?"

"The same way, dear. Through the Society. Professor Kurtz brought us together."

"He's had quite an influence on your life, hasn't he?"

"Yes, I suppose he has. Which does not mean I liked him. I did not," she assured Miranda.

"*And we only kill the ones we love*," Marie Lachine chimed in, delivering her words in oral italics.

"My experience suggests otherwise," said Miranda.

"It was not to be taken seriously, Detective."

"You knew Professor Li Po at the Sorbonne." Miranda observed, shifting her attention to the younger woman.

Marie Lachine tilted her head and stared at Miranda through narrowed eyes.

"Yes, perhaps," she said.

"It's there in your dissertation," said Miranda. "In your acknowledgements."

"Well, then I must have been in his debt."

"Apparently."

"Yes?"

"Were you lovers?"

"I beg your pardon, Detective? That is an impertinent question. What gives you the right to ask such a thing? It is vulgar and it is not your business."

"It may be impolite, Mademoiselle, but in a murder investigation, no question is inappropriate. Vulgar seems an odd word to describe your relationship."

The woman blanched, then as she looked away she glowered.

Hermione reached over and placed a hand squarely on top of Marie Lachine's intertwined fingers.

"Detective Quin is a policewoman, my dear. You must be cooperative with the police. You may answer her question, you know. It will not hurt anyone to be honest."

"No," said Marie Lachine. "Emphatically not. We were not lovers."

"I'm glad," said the old woman in a soft voice. "Because … *we* were."

"Who?" said Miranda.

"*Ce qui!*" exclaimed Marie Lachine. "*Maudit, qu'est que tu dit?*"

Hermione M leaned forward on the settee.

"Help me up, the two of you. Both of you come with me."

Together, the three women walked inside the cottage and found a secluded corner near the large fieldstone fireplace. Hermione and Mlle Lachine settled side by side on a worn leather sofa. Miranda sat on the matching ottoman which deflated beneath her weight until she discovered a precarious balance which allowed her a semblance of comfort.

Both Marie Lachine and Miranda waited for the old woman to begin, allied in their anticipation.

Marie offered an elliptical incentive for revelation. "Your French," she said, addressing Hermione. "It is Parisian, not *Québéçois*. It is not very good, but it is continental."

"I lived in Paris after the War, Marie."

"You never told me that."

"And you knew Li Po?" Miranda asked.

"I was not always old, my dear. Nor was he."

Miranda had no difficulty comprehending, but Marie Lachine seemed to be struggling with the idea of her mentor and this eccentric elderly woman being intimate.

Unable to think of anything else to say, Miranda asked, "How long were you lovers?"

"Nearly a year. He was studying, I learned about Francis Bacon from him. He would read to me passages in English, it was love poetry between us. And then he went away to study in Rome. I was to join him there. We had to be very discreet. You must know, inter-racial relationships were widely considered immoral. People went to jail for breaching the boundaries. Women in Canada were imprisoned in the thirties, there is a woman right now who is suing the government, she spent ten months locked up and they took her baby away."

"Who, who took her baby?" Marie demanded, as if the entire story were in doubt.

"The authorities, the Canadian government. The case is before the courts, but no one wants to know about it. It gets almost no coverage. Seven pages on hockey, seven lines on a woman jailed for loving a man of colour, as they say. He was Chinese. What colour do you suppose the Chinese are? I do not think of myself as white. Beige, perhaps, with streaks of blue and green. Pink, here and there. Blotches of red and brown."

Marie persisted: "If we took her baby, remember, we were at war."

"No, this was before the War. And he was Chinese, not Japanese. And Li Po and I, we were only a few years after the war. Rome, then, would not have been a good place for us. The Church was powerful and everywhere, everywhere. There was no safety, no privacy. But, it did not matter. Li Po was summoned back to China. When I got to Rome, he was gone."

"So, you came back to Canada?"

"Yes, the Church paid my boat passage to Montreal. The Sisters of Mercy. And I'm not a Catholic."

"Did you live in Montreal?" Miranda asked, sensing there were complexities in the tale yet to be revealed.

"Yes."

"I did not know that," said Marie Lachine, as if it were in her purview to know everything about the other woman.

"I did, I stayed for some time, then I went back to Dundas. Actually to Toronto. I was not welcome in my mother's home until the end."

"Her end?" asked Marie Lachine.

"Yes, but that is very much another story, as you know." Her voice trailed off.

Miranda looked at the younger of the two women. Marie Lachine was fiercely *pûr laines*, pure *Québéçoise*, even though she lived outside the province and made her living mediating between cultures. She was not an apologist. She was someone who explained *différance* from a fixed perspective.

"Hermione?" Miranda asked, trying to figure how to frame an awkward and invasive question. "Hermione?" she repeated, leaving the question open.

"No dear, not now. I'm tired. Mlle Lachine would you help me to my room. Just give me your arm." She said this as they rose from the leather sofa. "I think there's time for a nap before dinner."

Miranda extricated herself from the ottoman and stood by the stone fireplace as she watched the other two women cross the room and ascend the staircase, leaning on each other for mutual support. She turned and walked out onto the verandah and was embraced by the innumerable summer sounds of water lapping against boathouse pilings from far below, and plush pines combing the onshore breeze overhead, and the rustling of dry grasses on the hillside, and the murmuring of voices from the the shadows all around her.

chapter twenty-two

Cottage Life

Morgan dressed for dinner in his linen suit, which was *supposed* to look crushed and wrinkled. With a black designer T-shirt under the jacket he felt quite natty. Miranda had bought him the T-shirt and explained that the close fit, the high neck, and, of course, the label, justified the price. Since it was a gift, she did not actually tell him how much she had paid for it, but left the receipt in the bag.

He waited for her in the main room of Philip's Folly, gazing up at the dead animal heads arrayed in a random pattern on the walls to make them seem natural. When she came out of her room and descended the stairs into the light, he looked at her and looked away and looked again. She was stunning in a dark pencil-thin ankle-length skirt and a white blouse that draped sensuously, revealing and concealing at the same time, sleeves folded back for a muted dramatic effect, with a bold brown belt declaring simple elegance, and with earrings made of silver loops that reached down to her jaw-line and framed her face in a shimmering radiance. She was wearing evening makeup, more than he was used to, but subtly applied so that, paradoxically, he thought, her red lips, lightly flushed cheeks, and luminous hazel eyes seemed more natural than ever.

"You look lovely," Miranda said. "You're wearing my T-shirt, it goes with the suit."

"You told me if I didn't wear it with anything else it might last forever."

"You look good, Morgan. Congratulations."

"Yeah," he shuffled in exaggerated diffidence, then lifted his head and pronounced: "You look lovely." Then he broke the magic by adding: "Really."

"Really? Thanks partner. Shall we go."

A door in the shadows under the balcony clicked open and there was a startled intake of breath, as if they had forgotten they were not alone in the cottage. Hermione Mac walked out into the room, their breathing relaxed, then picked up tempo when they saw what she was wearing.

What might have been taken for frailty now seemed sinuously attractive, her figure at nearly eighty was as perky and lithe as a girl's. And yet her outfit was not a young woman's, nor really of any particular era. Miranda smiled as the old woman's black sequined dress shimmered when she moved, and her double strand of pearls swayed easily in counterpoint rhythm. Was this how she might have appeared in the forties, when her life was bursting with terrible adventures, or was this how a woman dressed sixty years later, who had lived very little in the interim?

Morgan offered Hermione his arm. Miranda stepped after them through the door, and then took his other arm, and they descended the steps and started their walk as a threesome to the main cottage.

When they reached the high shoulder of rock before the path wheeled away through a brief grove of hemlocks into the stand of pines, they could hear a wheezing and thumping behind them and stopped to admire the evening view while they waited for Felix Swan to catch up.

Dinner was a sumptuous Elizabethan affair, preceded by a formal toast to the current Elizabeth. Except for the wines, everything was as authentic to the period as money could buy. The helicopter had brought in a brace of suckling pigs and great slabs of mutton and beef. Salvers heaped with braised parsnips and buttered brussels sprouts, dishes of dumplings and bowls of squash, all this vied for the gourmands' delight with bounteous trays of smoked salmon, a salver of squab, a platter of glazed pheasant and a larger platter of cold venison, plates of savoury tarts, plates of cheeses and plates of both fresh and dried fruit, all served together rather than in a sequence of courses.

The wine, Lionel Webb explained to Morgan before they sat down, was chosen to complement the period fare but was in no way intended to emulate the rough vintages of Elizabethan times. Morgan surveyed the best array of the vintners' art that he had ever seen except in the pages of wine magazines. The whites were impressive. He settled on an '86 Hugel gewirtztraminer to start. But he had his eye on the reds. There on the table before him were open bottles of Chateau Margaux and Chateau Lafite, both 1966, a very good year. One would be round and fulsome, and the other, austere but with infinite depth. And then he noticed, sitting in the middle of the table without fanfare, a 1961 Pétrus. It was unopened. He looked down the length of the table and saw Lionel Webb watching him, following the line of his vision. Their eyes met, and Morgan signaled his appreciation with a wry smile. Lionel Webb motioned to a person serving and whispered something in her ear. She walked along the side of the table and leaned over to retrieve the Pétrus from its obscure spot at the centre of the feast, and then she disappeared.

In a few minutes she came out from the kitchen area with two crystal tulips, each filled a little past half way with deep brick-coloured wine. She served one to her employer and the other she delivered into the hands of David Morgan, who took the glass by the stem, careful not to touch the bowl which would warm the contents beyond room temperature, and swirling it briefly held the lip to the base of his nose and drew in a deep breath, letting the rich and complex aroma flood his senses. Morgan raised his glass in a gesture of appreciation to Lionel Webb, and then carefully set the glass down to let the wine open more fully. Webb smiled and, nodding to his appreciative guest, did the same.

The others tucked into the food and for the most part helped themselves to buttery chardonnays and sociable beaujolais *villages*, ignoring the Hugel gewirtz, the Lafite and Margaux. Morgan was trying to decide whether it would be a violation of privilege to share his good fortune with Miranda. He unobtrusively slid the large glass of Pétrus over until it was within her reach, then indicated for her to take a sip, even though he had not actually tasted it yet, himself. She did and smiled, at first searching his expression for an indication of what he was expecting her response to be, then grinning as the realization took hold that this was the most astonishing wine she had ever tasted.

She set the glass down and slid it back in front of Morgan. He took a small sip and swirled it in his mouth before swallowing. He decided to let it breathe for another twenty minutes. The woman who decanted and served the wine appeared at Miranda's shoulder and unobtrusively leaned over and set a crystal tulip of the same wine in front of Miranda. Morgan put his hand over his glass, to indicate she should wait for awhile before drinking hers. He looked down the long table at Webb, who was apparently engrossed in conversation with Jane Latimer.

A din of laughter and raucous chatter filled the room, which seemed to resonate with voices and music of the past. In the deep lustre of the wood paneling, Morgan caught glimpses of ball gowns swirling by the flicker of innumerable candles. In this one room, especially, it seemed the furnishings were just as they must have been, and as he gazed down the long table he had no trouble imagining the thronging dead who had chattered and dined in this same space, laughed and danced, and left only a few black and white photographs behind, and a country shaped in their image.

Miranda leaned closer and said in a clear voice, "There's enough food here for a small army, you'd better eat up."

"I am," he responded. "It's amazing, I don't know whether to be thrilled and accept it all with good grace, or appalled, and eat anyway."

"The job does have its perks, doesn't it."

"What?"

"The job, solving murders."

An explosive quiet filled the room, detonated by Miranda's use of a single word: *murders*. Gradually, conversation resumed but the laughter for a time was subdued.

"Sorry," she whispered to Morgan. "So tell me about the wine?"

"Chateau Pétrus. Pomerol from Bordeaux, the best of the best. And '61 was a very great year. That bottle would cost the price of a wedding ring."

"You mean engagement ring. Wedding rings are usually just bands."

"Whatever."

"It's an odd analogy. Do you have marriage on your mind, Morgan?"

Ignoring her, although his glance down the table

at Sir David was not unrelated, he declared, "This has been unlike any meal I've ever had. I can't say 'devoured' because there's still enough food left—"

"To feed a small army."

"Yeah, nice original turn of phrase."

"Thank you."

Miranda scanned the company at the table, puzzled and disturbed that so much food should be offered up for only fourteen people. Discreetly, she had been monitoring how much each person was eating and what choices they made. Padraig, for instance, had served himself huge portions of suckling pig and savoury tarts, while Simon Sparrow had rather anxiously filled his plate with samples of virtually everything, and Jane Latimer had divided her plate into quadrants and each was the context for modest servings of fish, fowl, mutton, and pork. Felix in contrast was eating sizeable portions of various things in sequence, one dish at a time, so that it was difficult to keep track of what or how much he devoured.

She glanced sideways at Morgan's plate. Squab, with a side portion of suckling pig. On her own plate, slices of cold pheasant. She looked down to see what their host was eating. Roast beef, the fillet, blood rare.

Felix Swan got to his feet. Perhaps he needed to stretch upright to elongate his digestive tract before taking another run at the food, beginning the whole sequence all over again. He picked up the magnum of beaujolais and began to move around the table, helpfully topping up glasses.

Both Miranda and Morgan reached out and raised

their own glasses, sipped, savouring the smooth aroma of the Pétrus before swirling a taste in their mouths of cassis and plums, and swallowing with deep satisfaction. Miranda set her glass down.

"That is exquisite, Morgan. It's probably the best wine I've ever tasted."

"You can be sure it is," he said. "Wine doesn't come any better than this. I've never tasted Pétrus before, never mind the best vintage of the last century."

"Where would he get a bottle like this?"

"Probably at auction. Christies or Sothebys in London, an estate sale—some poor buggar cellaring it, waiting for perfection, suddenly dies. Lionel probably bought it by the case."

In a conditioned reflex, they leaned apart when Felix Swan pressed forward between them, then both let out a squawk as he prepared to pour beaujolais into Miranda's Pétrus. Her hand shot out to stop him by covering the top of her glass. Beaujolais splashed across the back of her hand and splattered crimson over the white folded-back sleeve of her tailored silk crêpe blouse.

Miranda sprang to her feet, jamming her chair against the Rector's legs. He staggered back, then got control of his shifting weight and stood solidly in place, looking desperately for some way to disappear. Morgan instinctively rose to his feet as well, to back up his partner in crisis. Miranda, however, said nothing, ignored Swan, and strode from the room. Felix Swan resumed his job topping up glasses, but steered clear of Morgan who sat down with one hand firmly over the top of his own glass.

In a bathroom upstairs, Miranda removed her blouse and ran the stained sleeve under cold water, rubbing the material gently on itself. The door opened and Hermione M came in, carrying a sterling salt shaker.

"Salt," she said. "It stops the colour from setting. Works with blood and wine. Here." She unscrewed the silver top and poured salt out onto her palm.

"That's very thoughtful," Miranda said in appreciation. She held out the soiled blouse and remarked that the beaujolais did look very much like a blood splatter.

"Felix can be such an oaf," Hermione said.

"It was an accident. I put my hand over the glass. He couldn't help it."

"Only an oaf would add last year's beaujolais to an incomparable Pétrus."

"So you knew what we were drinking."

"Yes, of course. I'm sure several of us did. But it is Lionel's prerogative to share whatever he wants with whomsoever he chooses. It is not as if his generosity is in doubt. I'm quite sure you appreciate fine wines more than I."

"Actually, I was lucky. He was sharing with my partner. I just happened to be in the right place at right time. It is a great wine, what I tried of it."

"I'm sure there will be more when you go back down."

"Hermione."

"Yes."

"You didn't come up here to bring me salt, much as I appreciate it."

"No."

"You needed to speak privately?" The sleeve of her white blouse now seemed clean, and Miranda began waving it back and forth to dry.

"Yes, I thought we might have a very quick chat."

"About Marie Lachine?"

"About Professor Li Po. Yes, and about Marie, as well."

"You said the Sisters of Mercy arranged for your return to Canada."

"Yes, they did."

"Isn't that a little unusual, unless the circumstances—"

"Yes, the circumstances."

"Were you pregnant?"

"Yes, I was."

"With Li Po's child?"

"What an old-fashioned way of saying it, Detective. She was my child. Li Po was the father."

"Yes, of course," said Miranda, a little embarrassed. "And you had your baby in Montreal. A girl?"

"A girl. When she was born she had oriental features. Many babies seem to, from the trauma of birth. But after a few weeks, she looked exotically European."

"And you gave her up for adoption."

"I was very much alone in the world. My lover had disappeared into the great imponderable we call China, my father was dead, my mother did not want me at home. I had no money, no job, no skills. In those days it was not easy for a single mother to support her child. The nuns in Montreal convinced me it would be better to give up my baby."

"And you did."

"It broke my heart." She said this without a trace of sentimentality.

"Marie?"

"Yes."

"She is your daughter?"

"She is."

"She seems *pûr laines*! She does not know."

"No. I do not want her to know."

"Professor Li Po, does he know she is your daughter?"

"No. Dieter arranged for us to get together in Toronto, he got us all together. Li Po already knew her, of course. He was an adviser for her disssertation at the Sorbonne."

"And she suspects nothing?"

"No, nothing."

"And Dieter Kurtz, he knew all this?"

"There was very little Dieter did not know."

"How did he find out?"

"Perhaps things I said, perhaps things Li Po told him; he researched records in Montreal after we met, he reconstructed my life from data-banks and archives. It was his hobby, to invade privacy. It's something that kept him going."

"He was a man who traded on secrets."

"Traded, not exactly. I was his friend because he would not let me be otherwise. That was true of us all."

"And he knew about your mother?"

"Everyone knows about my mother, and no one knows anything for sure, not even Dieter Kurtz."

"Did you kill her?"

"Ha! Nothing like a direct question." The old woman

flashed a cunning smile and Miranda felt foolish for asking.

"Is there a direct answer?" she said.

"No, my lovely Miranda, there is not. I would be a boring person, wouldn't I, if we resolved Mother's death either way? I mean, death by rat poison is commonplace, and someone who has to wear the mantle of murderer to make herself interesting is dreary beyond words."

"And being interesting, that's what is most important."

"Yes it is. That much I have learned about life from the incomparable Francis Bacon. *Be Interesting!* Shall we descend into the melee. They'll wonder what we're up to."

"She died from poison, not electrocution?"

"Apparently."

Miranda put on her blouse and with a quick check in the mirror she joined the tall and elegant Hermione. Together they walked down into the formal dining room, which on occasion had doubled as a ballroom and tonight was resplendent with food and drink sufficient to please Queen Bess herself, and with conversation that might have resembled the chatter at court—about Bacon and Bacon's ideas and intrigues, and the scandals to which he gave rise like mushrooms in the richest compost.

Hermione slipped back into her chair and Miranda into hers without attracting much notice, beyond a few raised eyebrows that might have suggested to be spilled upon, in some circles, was slightly *déclassé*. Two raised eyebrows, to be exact, both belonging to the Rector, who, by now had shifted the blame for the incident entirely to

Miranda and found himself blameless.

She noticed her crystal tulip had been replaced with another and was filled just past the break in its curve with brick-red wine, more Pétrus she was sure. She glanced down at Lionel to acknowledge his thoughtfulness, but he was deep in conversation with Jane Latimer and engrossed in the drape of dark grey silk across her breasts, although he tried gamely to look up every once in a while and engage with her eyes. Whenever he did so, Miranda noticed, Jane would gaze into the distance, so that he had no choice but to continue his perusal of the deep shadows and gleaming contours of her blouse.

Morgan, who had been trying to follow a story by Simon Sparrow about himself, broke free and leaned over to welcome her back just as Lionel extricated himself from his own particular bondage, tapping a spoon on his empty Pétrus glass, and asked for their attention. Morgan nudged her and winked.

"Ladies and gentlemen," said Lionel Webb in a curiously formal manner, "It is time for us now to move into the drawing room. There is coffee waiting, and a choice of liqueurs. First, if you would please take your dishes to the kitchen."

Miranda squeezed Morgan's arm. What was this! Bussing their own dishes after such a sumptuous feast? It seemed highly unlikely, yet everyone set to work without hesitation. Morgan leaned forward and picked up a platter still piled high with glazed pheasant, deboned and plumped out with a whole small goose stuffed inside, sliced cold, and from which only a few pieces had been removed for consumption. Miranda was holding the large platter of venison cut in wafer-thin slabs.

"No, no," said Ralph to Morgan. "Not the food, just your plates and cutlery, your own things."

"I don't understand," said Miranda in a covert voice to which Padraig responded, "It's for the staff."

"For the staff? Porrig?"

"It isn't like they're eating leftovers. The cook will clean up the plates and platters, and then the staff will sit down here and have their own feast. It's an annual event. Very egalitarian."

"I would have thought having us all eat together would be even more egalitarian," said Morgan as he picked up his dishes. "This seems a postcolonial variation on *noblesse oblige*."

"How many are there?" Miranda asked, intent on avoiding a political discussion. "It must take a lot to run this place."

"Half a dozen in the house, the crew of the *Lady Ruth*, another four or five for the boats and the grounds, and of course their families—the local people have been bringing their families all day, a few at a time. It all adds up. Maybe twenty-five or thirty altogether."

"That explains it," said Miranda. "There was of course far too much food for the Bacon Society and a brace of detectives no matter how hungry we were."

As they settled into the main room in the cottage Morgan whispered to Miranda, "It's strange how so many outsiders could gather on the island and we didn't notice."

"It's not cottage as retreat or sanctuary, Morgan. This place is an event in itself. Boats have been coming and going since we arrived, people scurry around doing their jobs and we hardly notice them." She looked at him, admiring his rumpled elegance. "The blindness of entitlement, my friend. It comes much too easily." She cast him a patronizing smile. "And saying, that, Morgan, I align myself, of course, with the serving class."

"And the Baconians align themselves with Lionel Webb. I think we're somewhere between. But the Pétrus was very good, wasn't it? Very very good." He looked at her and wondered about other lives, parallel worlds. "I think just being Lionel Webb must be an event."

As if on cue, their host called for everyone's attention. After surveying the room to see no one was missing, he nodded to David Jenness who was standing within the door-frame of a study off to one side. David stepped back into the shadows, then brought forward a wooden casket about the size and shape of a very large book. There was a collective intake of breath. Everyone knew what it was.

"Ladies and Gentlemen," said Lionel Webb with a flourish as David Jenness set the casket down on the coffee table in front of him, "May I present for your pleasure the most rare and astonishing edition of Francis Bacon extant in the world." He gestured for David to open the container. "Herewith, the only known copy of *The New Atlantis* to have been published before the author's death."

The entire Bacon Society craned forward over the table. The chatter was frenzied, with questions and possible answers, suppositions, and conjecture filling the air. "Is it authentic, for sure?" "Where was it found?" "Why was there no record of its publication?" "Oxfordshire…" "Printed in London…" "Yes, for W. Lee." "No, no, 1624…" "Never reached auction…" "…returned to England eventually." "Cost a fortune." "…by helicopter, today." "Priceless, just priceless."

Miranda and Morgan stood back patiently, trying to decipher the tidbits, eager to see the book but willing to wait for the tumult to subside.

"Do you suppose he's breaking the law by bringing it to Canada?" Miranda asked Morgan.

"Whose law?"

"Who knows?"

"I imagine he spirited it out of Great Britain before anyone thought to make it an issue. And when word gets around who bought it, even the most vigilant cultural nationalists will relax. They know it will eventually be given to an appropriate body in the U.K., probably the British Museum, to be housed in a new wing named for the beneficent donor and patron, Lord Ottermead the Third."

"You understand these things so well," she said with sufficient derision to mask her appreciation.

"Thank you," he responded with mock gravity. "Probably the benefit of my aristocratic connections." They both looked at David Jenness who was standing back so the others could see the book.

"Have you spoken to him yet?"

"David? No. And I won't. He did tell me his mother

will be in Toronto next week."

"Oh, really. Are you going to get together?"

"I don't know."

"You should."

"That's a complex imperative, 'should.' I'm not sure."

"I haven't told you what happened upstairs."

"With you and Hermione, the matricide?"

"Yes, Hermione M. She's sweet, Morgan, and handsome. When we first met her she seemed a bit silly, but she's not. She's led a very eventful life."

"And she has dark secrets. Everyone here has dark secrets."

"That's what brings them together. Dieter Kurtz was the catalyst."

"Magnet, perhaps. I wouldn't call him an agent of change."

"Well, sometimes he was! In the other Hermione's story, he was definitely a protagonist."

"Antagonist."

"Sometimes pedantry can be really annoying."

"Okay. But in the convoluted connections among these people, in every case, he's a sinister presence, whether he's the villain or merely malevolent. What did the unfortunately orphaned Hermione tell you?"

"That Marie Lachine is her daughter."

"I'm not really surprised," said Morgan, although he was.

"And Professor Li Po is her father."

"Now I'm surprised!" He lowered his voice to a nearly inaudible whisper. "I assumed they were lovers."

"They were."

"!!!"

"Not Marie, Morgan! Hermione McCloud. She and Li Po were lovers in the forties. In Paris."

"In Paris, well of course. And Marie?"

"Conception in France, gestation in Rome, born in Québec."

"And did the wily professor know his paramour was pregnant?"

"No, apparently not. And Hermione does not want him to know."

"And Marie Lachine, does she know."

"She thinks she's pûr *laines*."

"Her name, La-chine…"

"Yes, I thought of that."

"The nuns, amusing themselves."

"I suspect the Sisters of Mercy had no idea of the infant's paternity, they were simply responding to her post-natal complexion. And the name 'Marie,' of course, is wishful thinking. All nuns want to be either Mary Immaculate or Mary Redeemed, the Blessed Mother or the Saved Whore."

"You show a profound understanding of the mysteries of the Church."

"Thank you."

"Inevitably, Kurtz must have known all this."

"Inevitably."

chapter twenty-three
The New Atlantis

The entire Bacon Society was absorbed in *The New Atlantis*. Morgan and Miranda walked out onto the verandah and settled in a far corner where they could look out over Lake Rosseau in the moonlight. There were people splashing down at the boathouse and they figured it must be some of the diners, having finished their feast, now using the sauna.

"Okay," said Morgan. "We have a real rat's nest here of information revealed and information withheld. With Dieter Kurtz at the dead centre."

"So to speak."

"Let me get this straight, then. Hermione and Li Po were lovers. Yes? And they had a daughter, who is Marie Lachine. Yes? Who does not know she is their daughter. Right?"

"Probably not. And Li Po does not know he is her father."

"As you say, probably not. So there's information Kurtz could wield."

"Why would that be such a terrible secret?"

"We're assuming wherever Kurtz was, the secrets to be exploited were terrible, the confidences to be betrayed were cruel."

"All right, Morgan. Let's say there's more to Li Po being her father than we know, what then?"

"You say Marie Lachine doesn't know she's adopted?"

"She might, but she doesn't know her parentage. At least that's what Hermione thinks. Of course, if the data were available to Kurtz, so that he figured out her exotic paternity, why wouldn't it be available to her?"

"It might never have crossed her mind as a possibility."

"You're right. She seemed genuinely surprised to discover that Hermione had lived in Montreal. And Morgan! Morgan, she was really pissed off when I exposed the fact that Hermione and Li Po had been lovers."

"Pissed off?"

"She was outraged, Morgan, and I'll tell you why! Marie was Li Po's mistress too. I'll bet on it. Neither of them knew it was incest. We'll give them both credit for that. But I wonder if Hermione figured it out? They'd both be horrified to think they had shared a lover."

"Hermione, more so."

"For sure, if she's the only one of the three who knows about the Oedipal thing."

"Electra."

"The Electra thing. As for Li Po, he knows he was the lover of both women, one when he was a young scholar, one when he was back at the Sorbonne on a sabbatical from Lanchou, years later. No wonder he has that beatific smile! Each woman obviously knows she was his lover. It's doubtful Hermione knows about Marie."

"As her lover's mistress?"

"Or that Marie knows about Hermione," said Morgan.

"That she's her mother?"

"She suspects. And Hermione, as you said, knows Marie is her daughter."

"And Marie knows both women were Li Po's lover."

"Which Hermione does not."

"He would have been a generation older than Marie," said Morgan.

"Literally. But it happens."

"What?"

"Universities, they provide a context for the breakdown of barriers."

"Some, and the raising of others. It's the age difference, isn't it?"

"What?" said Miranda.

"We both described Hermione as Li Po's lover but Marie as his mistress."

"Yes, I suppose it is."

"Interesting."

"To you, Morgan. So if Dieter Kurtz had the various permutations figured out, he'd be a threat to all of them."

"How so, unless he tells them what he knows?"

"Good point. So, he does it shrewdly. Let's just say knowledge is power: he wields it like a rapier in one instance, a slow poison the next."

"Let's just say."

"So, assuming Li Po didn't already know his young mistress was his daughter—"

"That makes Kurtz a threat to Marie, who knew the old man would be mortified. Literally, *humiliated unto death*."

"Only if Kurtz had already told her Li Po was her father," said Miranda.

"And he could equally be a threat to Hermione."

"Who would be mortified on Li Po's behalf."

"But if Kurtz told Li Po?" said Morgan.

"He might be driven to kill. Any one of them might have been driven to kill."

"It would probably have taken some combination of all three," said Morgan. "It depends on who knew what. If we're right, there goes our explanation for how Kurtz died."

"How do you mean?"

"It's unlikely a culprit with killer thighs would want a witness, never mind two of them."

"Yeah, we still have to follow that one up. We haven't asked for DNA yet."

"Well, we know it's not going to prove much. We'll do it tomorrow when everyone's together."

"Lovely." Miranda was surprised to find herself squeamish, perhaps defensive. "We'll ask for DNA samples during brunch."

"And observe their reactions. It's important to have them together, to see if anyone flinches."

"Why wouldn't they flinch separately?"

"If there's a conspiracy, someone might just scan the others for reassurance."

"That wouldn't necessarily indicate guilt, just lack of confidence."

"But it would give us a point of entry," Morgan insisted. "Deconstruction always begins with a flaw, offering a way in."

"It might not be a conspiracy," said Miranda. "It might not even be a member of the Bacon Society."

"Kurtz's murder is inextricably linked to Francis Bacon, I guarantee it. Bacon is the social cement holding these people together—that, and Professor Kurtz's furtive knowledge about their hidden lives. Even if it's not a conspiracy, it *is* a conspiracy. They just don't know it yet."

"And we do?"

"We're leaning that way."

"We are, are we?"

"Yeah," said Morgan. "The point is, the killer is going to be confident the blame has been shifted. That hair could have been retrieved from any of the beds up here after previous get-togethers, and tucked away for future use. By itself, it means nothing. But if the killer is worried there were other DNA bits left behind, he or she might 'flinch.'"

"More so in public than in private. Back to Li Po, Morgan. It seems to me if Marie Lachine does know everything, she is in a position of terrible power. Her mother would be devastated if it were known Marie and Li Po had been lovers. Marie knows that. She could imagine her father would be devastated if it were known she was his daughter."

"So if she's figured things out, that makes her the most vulnerable."

"And also the most dangerous."

"You said she seems desperate to avoid acknowledging the truth," said Morgan.

"Or to having the truth come out. But desperate to the point of murder, I wonder?"

Morgan stood up and leaned against the rail, peering through the darkness into the pool of lighted water in front of the boathouse. Heads bobbed within shimmering garlands, splashing fans arced against the moonlit waves. He could hear singing and laughter, he could smell the flint-sweet smoke of burning maple.

"Want to go down?" he asked.

"Morgan, I think the line between them and us is nearly absolute. You would manage to offend both our host and his minions."

"Minions!"

"I said it ironically."

"Yeah, maybe we should go back in."

"Morgan. Doesn't it strike you as odd for a cultural nationalist to move into the heartland of the enemy. I wonder when did Marie Lachine move to Toronto?"

"I'd say about the same time she discovered the wool was dyed, and maybe it wasn't wool at all, but a blend of cotton and silk."

"Pardon? Oh, *pûr laines*. Authentic *Québéçoise*. Perhaps not so pure, not even wool."

"For someone so proud of her heritage, it would have been a mortal blow to find her ancestry thoroughly compromised."

"Serious enough to send her into exile, and yet cling to what she's lost. It explains a lot, doesn't it? A Toronto *independiste*. So, she does know Hermione is her mother, she's just not saying she knows. No wonder she's bitchy."

"She is?"

"Let's go in."

Miranda paused at the door and turned to her partner.

"How are we ever going to keep track of who knows how much about what. There is a great deal of alarming knowledge still holding these people together; I don't want to see anyone hurt unnecessarily."

Morgan drew her back into his own shadow. "We've got a dead scholar in a drawer at the morgue. Somebody's already been hurt."

"I know, but it's hard not to lose track of ourselves as the newest members of the coven. Which we're not, of course."

She pulled away from him and stepped through the French doors. Lionel Webb's latest acquisition was still the centre of attention, but the knot of people around it was beginning to unravel. Clusters were forming nearby, some to discuss the content of the book, comparing its utopian vision to that of Sir Thomas More. Others were confounded by the book's lack of a publishing history: in all empirical respects it was authentic, yet there was no provenance, no record of its existence. Its monetary value was therefore based on a metaphysical paradox. By buying it, Lionel proved it existed.

No one knew how much he had paid for it, except possibly Sir David Jenness. It would have been rude to ask.

Yet another group, gathered around the Rector of Jesus College, was constructing an elaborate conspiracy whereby the book was actually written by Shakespeare and its original publication under Bacon's name was suppressed by Bacon himself, having afterthoughts about allowing his name to be used by the proletarian playwright's executors. This, proclaimed the Rector, would explain why it was not received by the public until the second edition, when it was included posthumously as an addendum to Bacon's own *Sylva Sylvarum.*

Miranda softened a little towards Felix Swan. Anyone capable of such esoteric nonsense was not beyond redemption, she thought. She had noticed when they came in that Morgan had walked straight over to David Jenness, who was standing on his own and a little to one side, watching the frenzied reception of the book with an almost proprietorial air.

Having cautioned her about letting things get personal, Morgan had gone directly to the one character in the evolving drama who seemed outside the treacherous web of secrets and deceit, and the one to whom he had a personal attachment.

She wanted to speak with Li Po, to get a sense of how much he knew about the connection between his two lovers and his own Oedipal position between them. *Electrical,* she whimsically corrected herself, *Electra position. It's all very ancient Greek,* she thought. *Tragedy lies in the knowing, not in the action.* She wasn't at all sure this was true, despite Sophocles, Aristotle, and present experience. *Sometimes knowing and understanding turn tragedy into nothing more than bad memories.* Freud, she was sure, would agree.

Li Po was engaged in conversation with Lionel and the smaller Hermione. She would wait and catch him alone. She drifted away from Felix Swan's group over to where Morgan and his son were chatting about life in England. Then, and now. Morgan had been back only briefly since he lived there two decades previously, but London remained as vivid in his mind as if he had been there a week ago. She could see in his face something of what he must have been like in his early twenties, as he talked of walking the perimeter of Hyde Park, hanging about in Soho pubs and the bookstores along Charing Cross Rd., subsisting on curried beans and yoghurt. David was listening attentively, throwing in bits here and there as if to confirm the reality of Morgan's memories. He was not saying very much about his own life.

Miranda intruded. She had a hunch.

"Excuse me. David, did your father attend Cambridge as well?"

Morgan looked at her in surprise. The young man was guarded.

"No," he responded. "Why do you ask?"

"Your mother, did she go to university?"

"Not at all. After she finished school she went up to London and worked in an office."

"Your father's?"

"Sir Nigel's? Yes."

Morgan was puzzled by Miranda's line of questioning. She was only confirming what they already knew.

"David," she asked, with enough solemnity in her voice to alert Morgan she was not making small talk. "Did your father attend Oxford?"

"Yes, actually he did. That's why he sent me to Cambridge."

When neither Miranda nor Morgan laughed, he continued:

"Rivalry, you know. Very healthy antidote to excessive inbreeding. Cultural cross-fertilization. So off I went to Cambridge."

"What college?" asked Miranda.

"Cleese College."

"And did he know Dieter Kurtz."

"At Oxford? As a matter of fact, he did. Professor Kurtz was his tutor."

"At Oxford?" Morgan exclaimed.

"It was on his *curriculum vitae*, Morgan. He came to Toronto from Freiberg, via Oxford and McGill, with a brief stint at Princeton."

"Where he paved the way for Felix Swan," said Morgan. "Your father must have been much older than Susan."

"Who? Oh, yes," said David Jenness, a bit thrown by Morgan's familiarity with his mother's name. "Mother only recently entered her forties, relatively speaking. Sir Nigel would have been sixty-five in October—retirement age at his firm."

"Did your father and Professor Kurtz keep in touch," Miranda asked.

"Yes, when Dieter came to London he would visit us in Knightsbridge."

"He knew your mother," said Morgan. "How well?"

"I'm not certain why you want to know that." David Jenness appeared visibly uncomfortable. "She had known Professor Kurtz before they were married."

Miranda decided to force the line of questioning. "Before you were born?"

"Yes. No. Well, it's rather complicated."

"How so?" said Miranda.

"It doesn't matter," said Morgan, abruptly. "You knew Professor Kurtz before you came to Canada, then."

"Yes He introduced me to Lionel."

"What was so complicated, David?" Miranda persisted.

"It's just one of those things, Detective Quin. I'm not at all awkward with it."

"What?"

"They had me before they were married. Nigel officially adopted me afterwards. I was born out of wedlock but I am not a bastard; my parents did the right thing by me, so to speak."

"Thank you," said Miranda. "Just one more question. You say your mother does not like to talk about it."

"She is not in the least ashamed, if that's what you're

getting at. She was not vulnerable to Professor Kurtz. Nor am I. I'm rather proud of the old girl."

"Thank you, David. I'm sorry if I've upset you. We need to know everything we can."

"There is nothing to be upset about. But if you think Prof. Kurtz had access to skeletons in the family closet, I very much doubt it."

Morgan was perturbed. He needed to clear his mind to assimilate what he had just heard. In fact, he realized, Kurtz may easily have known things about young Sir David that might compromise his claim to the peerage. *What did David know?* That is the real question. *Were his irritation and defensiveness a disingenuous evasion?* Morgan doubted it. *Nigel was the only father his son ever knew.* Morgan excused himself, telling David he'd catch up with him later and they'd talk more about London.

Miranda, realizing she was left in an awkward social position, alone with the young man she had just interrogated, suggested they join one of the groups chatting about the *New Atlantis*. As it happened, they were closest to the group considering the relative social merits of Bacon's visionary text. The two D'Arcys were good-naturedly tossing back and forth ideas drawn from their intimate familiarity with the Baconian utopia, while Hermione M, Simon Sparrow, and Jennifer Pluck contributed occasional support for one side or the other. David Jenness was eager to join them and slipped into their midst close by Jennifer's side, leaving Miranda at the group's outer margin where she was happy enough to remain an observer.

After wandering around the drawing room for a bit, Morgan ventured down a wood-panelled hallway, looking for a downstairs toilet. Not that he needed one, but it was something to focus on until he could assimilate David's revised position in the moral chaos surrounding the death of Dieter Kurtz. As he pushed open a door he was thinking, *it only appears to be chaos, it's really a labyrinth, and if we keep our shoulders to the wall and move ahead, we'll eventually find the beast at the centre—and end up back on the outside, looking in. That's the way it is with a labyrinth: when you immerse yourself in the mysteries surrounding a murder, and discover their resolution, you're back where you started from, only everything's different.*

The door opened into a gallery that opened into a large kitchen. Morgan was surprised to see the cook there by herself.

"Hello," he said. "You've been deserted, have you?"

"No, Detective Morgan," was the weary rejoinder of the large woman who turned from attending her chores to look up at him. "I'm past having saunas. I'd prefer to clean up for tomorrow."

Morgan was surprised she knew his name, but realized that was perhaps part of her job, to know who the guests were and what were their needs. There was a housekeeper on the premises whom Morgan had observed as a fleeting shadow, but on Briar Hill Island he was sure the cook was of paramount authority.

The skin on the woman's face was florid and tight, but her eyes showed her age.

"You've worked for the Webbs for a long time, have

you? I'm sorry. You know my name but I don't know yours."

"Kate Nesbitt. Used to be Morgan, same as you. No relation, I'm sure. I've been with the Webbs since the nineteen-fifties. I was a girl when I started in this kitchen. It hasn't changed much. Still cooking on a propane range. After they put in electricity, they tore down the old ice-house. But gas is best for cooking—that's how Mr. Webb likes it."

"You call him Mr. Webb?"

"When he's in England, he's Lord Oatmeal. And he surely isn't Lionel around here." She chortled in a gesture of solidarity with something she saw in Morgan, as if his working-class origins were encoded in his voice or demeanour.

"How're those two doing out there, anyway?" she said.

He was puzzled, then gathered she must mean Ralph and Padraig, the only two who had crossed over from her world to her employer's.

"The D'Arcys?"

"Yes, Porrig and Rafe. I've known them since Rafe was Patrick and Porrig was Ralph. My oh my, but they live a strange life. They've done very well for themselves."

The woman's open face showed the strain of a long day, but her expression implied no malice. She might be younger than an initial impression led Morgan to believe. She must have been little indeed when she first came to the island, probably working alongside her mother. She would be about the same age as Lionel, maybe a few years older. They would have grown up within parallel lives that only converged in illusionary events like the annual Labour Day feast. For a village boy like Ralph Robertshaw to transcend the boundaries of class and privilege must have seemed a nearly impossible metamorphosis, and one that no doubt merited a change in name as well as behavior.

From her perspective, Morgan surmised, it would be less radical for Patrick Sullivan to make the leap, or Padraig O'Suillibahn as he chose to be called in his gigolo days. Morgan made a mental note to check out Ralph's birth-name. Miranda had implied the Gaelic twist was an affectation. He'd like to know, although it made little difference, apart from helping to define the man's character. The cook would have known him as Padraig, when he was between being Patrick and Ralph, pronounced Rafe—when he occupied that layer between worlds, the *demimonde* where class became merely the measure of one's failures and conquests.

"Do you remember Rafe, did he stand out? I've been told he was one of the young people brought up from the city by Lionel's father."

"My grandmother used to tell of earlier times, when even their decadence had style."

"Your grandmother?"

"My grandmother Morgan. She worked here when they used to have midsummer balls and gala events. That was before the Great War. Her husband, my grandfather Morgan, died at Ypres. My other grandfather, on my mother's side, died at the Somme. Two great uncles were gassed in Flanders: one came home blind and the other with his lungs scalded to bloody hell. Back just before then, they had fancy dress balls on Briar Hill Island. By the time I came along, it was trash and glitter."

"And Rafe, was he trash and glitter?"

She peeled her hairnet back and ran stubby fingers through her matted hair, as if stimulating the neurons to bring a particular image to mind. This woman who had worked her whole life in the kitchens of others was remarkably well-spoken and thoughtful. Immediately, cringing at the stereotyping his immersion in the world of privilege incited, Morgan disowned the generalization, as if it had been imposed from outside.

"He was," she said. "He was a dandy, but oh he was very beautiful. He and Mr. Webb were lovers one whole summer."

"Mr. Webb!"

"Not Lionel. His father."

"I thought the old man looked but didn't touch."

"Oh, he touched. The crowd of young beauties, it was his way of showing off, but they were camouflage for the one or two each year he would take to his bed. Sometimes a girl, sometimes a boy."

"Did Lionel know?"

"He tried not to. He was embarrassed by his father."

"Enough to be blackmailed?"

"By Rafe? No. By his friend, Professor Kurtz, not exactly."

"So you knew Dieter Kurtz?"

"You see that door leading to the dining room and that door leading to the verandah. They are like one-way mirrors, Detective. We look out without being seen. That's how it is when you're in service. Observers unobserved. Of course I knew Professor Kurtz." She paused. "And, of course, he would not have known me."

Morgan looked into the woman's eyes.

"But he did, didn't he?"

"What?"

"Know you? Kurtz did know you."

"Ah, yes. Yes." She paused, again. "I'm sorry, I can't think why I tried to hide that. It's because he's dead and his death is a story that doesn't concern me. We talked, we weren't involved in each other's lives. And a murder, my goodness."

"Kate, his death induces odd responses in a lot of people."

"We had some good old chats here in the kitchen. The heat didn't bother Mr. Kurtz. Every once in a while he needed to slip away from the others."

"He didn't want anyone to know?"

"That he was consorting with the help? No, it wasn't that, so much. It was, just, we talked about them, those out front, just between us, you know, it was private."

"And you think he might have blackmailed Lionel with the threat of exposing his father's decadence."

"No, the professor was more canny than that. It wasn't about threatening dark revelations. Not blackmail exactly. In the Webb circle, people already knew the worst, and pretended none of it happened. But Mr. Kurtz somehow reflected the evil of others back onto themselves."

A memorable line, thought Morgan. *He reflected their*

evil back onto themselves.

"And some of this power, this dark knowledge, was it from talking to you?"

"I would imagine, yes. What began in this room as gossip between friends became something else, perhaps. That wasn't my concern. He was a man who wanted to know everything, although I told him nothing that he couldn't have learned in other ways. Whatever use he put to the things we spoke about, well, as I say, Detective Morgan, it wasn't my concern."

"You liked the man."

"I didn't say that. It was not an option to like or dislike him. You don't decide to like or dislike friends, they just are your friends or they're not."

Morgan gazed at the woman's florid face without focusing on her features. In her own way she was quite beautiful.

"And you do describe Kurtz as a friend."

"Like you, Detective."

Morgan smiled.

She continued: "Some of my oldest friends, I don't like at all. Professor Kurtz and I, we were close, you might say, although we knew nothing about each other. Perhaps that was what drew him to my kitchen, and drew me to gossip. We were safe with each other."

"You've put a lot of thought into this."

"No, I haven't." She, in her turn, smiled. "It's just there in my head. You'd be surprised what takes form in your mind when you're scraping and cutting and stirring and straining. Now young Mr. Robertshaw." She smiled. "His story is a little more sinister."

"Than what?" said Morgan, but his question was ignored.

She reached into a cupboard and brought out a bottle of cooking sherry. She retrieved a pair of tumblers from another cupboard and poured each of them a liberal portion. Then she sat down at the long harvest table and motioned for Morgan to do the same.

"Here's to us Morgans, Detective."

"To us," said Morgan.

"The *Lady Ruth*," she began, then lapsed into contemplative silence. It was as if she were waiting for a story to catch up to her before she continued.

"Yes," said Morgan. "I understand she was named after Porrig's mother.'

"She was, and do you know why?"

"Porrig said Lionel was very generous with his father; a gesture of appreciation, I suppose, or respect."

"Or acknowledgment of an old crime."

"A crime?"

"Porrig's mother, Ruth, she worked here as a char. When she was younger. Most of the girls in the village did, at one time or another. The pay was the best on the Lakes. Mind, she wasn't from here. She was a Jewess from Toronto, no disrespect meant. Came north to work, met Robertshaw, stayed on for the rest of her life."

"And?"

"Lionel Webb seduced Ruth."

"Seduced? Ruth?"

"Raped."

"Raped. Which Lionel?"

"The middle one."

"Don't tell me! Was he Porrig's father?"

"No, but wouldn't that be one for the books! Porrig, a Webb. No, I don't think so, I don't think so at all."

"Then, the name of the boat?"

"There is no question that Lionel, this Lionel, was aware of a family obligation to the Robertshaws."

"Was Ruth married when the rape occurred?"

"Yes. They were getting the boatworks up and going, they needed the money. She worked at light housekeeping, just a few months a year. Then, suddenly, she stopped working here, and then the boatworks did very well for several decades. Then it collapsed and Ruth died, I'm not sure in which order, and our Mr. Webb hired Robertshaw to rebuild the old steamer."

"And he put money into the restaurant in Port?"

"Porrig's brother's and sister's place? I believe he might have."

"Blackmail?"

"Oh no, a debt of honour."

"Or dishonour."

"Perhaps it's the same."

Sometimes it is, thought Morgan. *It depends on perspective.*

"You've certainly added a twist," she continued, her voice conspiratorial. "It has never been part of the story around here that Porrig, who was Ralph when we knew him, might have Webb blood in him. A village has a way of closing ranks to protect its own. No one could have prevented the rape, but its aftermath was certainly controlled. It would not have done to think Ralph Robertshaw was family of the man who raped his mother. It would not have been an acceptable version."

"I thought villages and small towns were run on rumours and gossip."

"There are rules, Detective. Gossip defines community limits; draws people together, keeps others out. Maybe cities are different. I've never been to Toronto. I'm hoping to reach the end of my life without going. Looks like I'll make it."

"Well, I haven't spent much time away from the city."

"The city mouse and the country mouse. Same last name, different lives, both rodents. Let me top up your sherry, Detective."

"No," said Morgan, placing his hand over the top of the tumbler. "I'd better get back in there."

"You're all through here, then, are you?"

He didn't know what to say. She smiled at his awkwardness:

"Good talking to you, Detective."

"And you too, Kate Nesbitt."

Bracing against the harvest table, the cook hoisted her bulk from the chair and before Morgan had gone through the door she was back at work piling soiled dishes in the sink.

chapter twenty-four
Unusual Relations

Well before the warning bell for breakfast had tolled its mournful dirge, Morgan wandered out of his room to the verandah to enjoy the silver light spreading across Lake Rosseau as the sun rose above the horizon behind Briar Hill Island. He had slept restlessly, falling with Saint Augustine on their endless nocturnal descent. He was sure he dreamt about other things, but the substance of other dreams dissipated before he was fully awake.

He was surprised to find that Miranda already outside. She was wrapped in a coat over her pajamas, wearing wool socks but with her feet tucked up under her on a Muskoka chair.

"G'morning," he said. "You're up early."

"There's a lot to think about."

"Yeah."

"You still tumbling through the air with Saint Augustine?"

"Yeah."

"You know, Morgan, I think what it means is nothing at all."

"You're not the one falling."

"And neither are you. It's a dream. The mind gets stuck in a track, it replays the same piece over and over."

"This isn't a song. The imagery is real, even if the experience isn't."

"And you think it's a key to unlock your soul from the shackles of doubt?"

"No. I'm content with no soul. I'd be a poor atheist if I wasn't."

"Agnostic."

"Atheist. You're an agnostic. I'm a devout believer in the absence of God."

"But you believe there's a God to be absent!"

"Miranda, it's too early. You're the only proselytizing agnostic in the world. I'll go make us some coffee."

"I already did. It's all set to pour. Make them both black."

"Yeah." He disappeared into the lingering shadows of the cabin and emerged a few minutes later with two mugs of steaming black coffee.

"Where'd you get to last night?" he asked. "When I came out of the kitchen the party had broken up."

"You were in the kitchen?"

"Talking to Kate Nesbitt, the cook. Her maiden name was Morgan."

"Really?"

"And where were you?"

"Down at the boathouse. A few of us went for a sauna. The staff party had broken up."

"Did you go in?"

"Yes, with Lionel, and with Jane and Simon and Jennifer. Jennifer and Lionel didn't stay long, the rest of us went in and out a couple of times. You should have been there."

"Obviously. Instead, I made friends with the cook. Then I talked with the two Hermiones. They were on the verandah with Felix—ah, so that's why Felix was distracted, he was trying to hear the sounds of naked people. I thought it was the second wave of dinner guests down there. I should have known, since the dock lights were out. They wore bathing suits."

"They?"

"The 'minions.'"

"In quotation marks. Yes, I'm sure they did."

"And you didn't?"

"No."

"Oh."

"Poor Morgan. And there you were with the Rector for company."

"And the two Hermiones, who seemed to be getting along like old friends. We didn't see Lionel or Jennifer come up."

"They probably went around the side so they wouldn't track through."

"And where was David?"

"He must have gone to bed after he put the book away for safekeeping. He didn't come down with us. I think Li Po also went to bed. I know the D'Arcys turned in shortly after you disappeared."

"I didn't disappear."

"Tell me?"

Morgan related in detail the cook's revelations about Ralph and Padraig and the intricate relations between the Robertshaws and the Webbs.

Miranda took a deep sip from her coffee and regarded her partner with a mixture of fondness and exasperation. He looked like Gregory Peck in the morning light, the way Gregory Peck looked in *To Kill a Mockingbird*. Last night he looked like Cary Grant. It was less compromising to think in terms of yesterday's icons.

She had been up since well before sunrise. She had come out here to relax while the lake transformed from black under the endless night sky to the finite silvery blues of the day. She wanted to think about God or dreams or the aroma of coffee but not about murder.

She wanted to sit for a moment and let it seem there was nothing to think about.

"Well, so?" Morgan was saying. "The complexities expand exponentially. We should be eliminating suspects, and they just keep multiplying—their stories, not the suspects."

With her head lolling lazily against the back of her Muskoka chair, Miranda could see him past the corners of her eyes. He looked more like a blur than Gregory Peck. She turned her head to bring him into focus.

"Morgan," she said. "Do you wonder what's for breakfast?"

"No, but I wouldn't worry." He lounged back into the depths of his chair. "How be we don't talk for a while. We'll just drink in the morning."

"That would be lovely," she said.

"Okay," he said. "Let's do that. No more talking."

"Okay," she whispered, giggling because she knew they were both playing the childish game of trying to get in the last word.

"Okay, then" he said.

"Right."

"Alright."

"Yeah," she said, with definitive finality.

He grinned and said nothing.

They could hear sounds framed by the silence between them. Hermione must be stirring. Maybe even Felix was up. The bell rang, proclaiming breakfast in one half hour. Miranda groaned, slurped the remains of her coffee, and rose to her feet. Morgan sprawled lower in his chair.

"Come on, champ," she said. "We're on duty."

"Yeah," he said, without moving. "So, you were in the sauna with Simon."

"And Jane Latimer and Jennifer and Lionel."

"But Jennifer and Lionel left."

"And?"

"And there you were, you and Simon and Jane."

"Yes, Morgan. Naked. You'll get over it. Come on, let's move."

"Yeah," he mumbled and slowly gathered himself and

rose to his feet.

"Naked," she repeated. "Bare naked."

At breakfast, which despite the relatively early hour was actually a sumptuous brunch, Morgan announced a little awkwardly that they would like to take swabs for DNA testing. It was voluntary, of course, but their cooperation would be appreciated. No one flinched. They all thought it seemed rather fun. Later, one by one they came over to the corner of the verandah where Miranda chatted cheerfully as each submitted to the sampling procedure.

She had expected David Jenness to show apprehension at being tested, but of course, since they had no DNA from Nigel, and Morgan's DNA was not under consideration, even if he suspected his father was a cop, not a peer of the realm, he was in no danger of being exposed. Then she realized what a leap she had made in her line of reasoning: David Jenness might doubt Nigel was his sire but he had no reason at all to suspect it was Morgan.

Miranda also anticipated a wariness from Marie Lachine. Whatever she knows, why wouldn't she be apprehensive? Why wouldn't Hermione worry about being revealed as Marie's mother? About having Li Po exposed as her daughter's father? Whatever their secrets from each other, they all seemed indifferent to the revelations of DNA testing.

Li Po appeared especially at ease, as if there were nothing more pressing in his mind than the weight of the air on his fine handsome face. Miranda caught herself short—*is this how an elderly Chinese appears to an eye unfamiliar with the complexion and features of his race?* Did she read him with the same critical acumen she applied to caucasians like herself? Was her immediate affection for him a response to the grace of the Chinese people, to the serenity of a face that aged differently from any she knew? She would have to pay more attention to Li Po.

When Jennifer Pluck came forward, she winked at Miranda and with her innate nervousness under control opened her mouth wide in a curiously triumphal gesture. She had come around completely from the previous day, when she would have welcomed a test that might prove Lionel Webb was her father, to now cheerfully offering up proof that he was not. Lionel, who immediately followed her in the line, appeared similarly pleased to be giving evidence in confirmation of his innocence on that particular count.

Only Porrig, she thought, *remains vulnerable.* From what Morgan had told her, according to the cook his paternity might be ambiguous. *Would he want to be revealed as a Webb, would Lionel want him acknowledged as his half-brother? Neither of them appeared concerned.* Porrig treated it all as a joke, with macabre overtones, and dismissed the significance of the procedure the moment it was completed.

Of course, Porrig might not know.

When all the swabs had been taken, bagged, and labelled, the Bacon Society convened on the broad steps of the verandah to make plans for their next general meeting, the week before Christmas. Then everyone dispersed, some to their rooms but most down to the dock for a repeat of the previous day, basking in the last of the summer sun or enjoying the shadows from under the Calder-like canopies, with water lapping on the criblogs beneath them.

Morgan and Miranda sat down at a table on the dock strategically placed in the shade but giving them a panoramic view of Lake Rosseau all the way across to Windermere. Felix Swan joined them and then Hermione the spy pulled up a chair as well, so they were limited in what they could talk about concerning the investigation. Both were relieved.

Hermione seemed lost in her own thoughts and Felix was distracted, unabashedly observing contours of flesh in the rippling sunlight, Simon's as well as Jane's and Jennifer's. There was something unnervingly asexual about his leering, as if he were driven by greed or envy or another, more elusive, of the deadly sins. Miranda found his roving gaze annoying. Her own bathing suit was a smooth one-piece affair that draped across her body in a pleasing way. She knew it was flattering and she knew Felix periodically scanned her as well. She felt vaguely indignant. He wasn't daydreaming seduction. Perhaps hunger? He was a man who it seemed could not sort out his appetites.

Morgan sank back against his chair. He was deep in thought, thinking about the way minds differ, especially his and Miranda's, when he became aware of a slender figure standing between his chair and hers. He looked up. Li Po leaned down.

"Mr. Morgan, Miss Quin, I believe you should come with me right now," said Li Po.

Miranda tilted her head back to get a better view of the old man. In his silk robe he looked quite elegant, although his body appeared stiff, as if he had suddenly aged. She realized the kimono was not a makeshift beach-robe. He had come down from the cottage in bedroom attire.

"Professor Li Po," she said. "Are you all right?"

"Would you please come, Detectives. Right away." He wheeled awkwardly about and at a forced pace moved across the dock and was half way up the broad steps to the verandah before they caught up to him.

"Easy," said Morgan. "You're going to have an accident. Here, let me help."

To Morgan's surprise, the old man clutched hold of his arm, but then drew Morgan into a still faster pace. They did not slow down until they were outside his room on a wing of the second floor. Then he stopped and breathing deeply looked up at them, his eyes flicking from one to the other without focussing, suggesting panic, although when he reached to push the door open and took a deep breath, the panic dissipated and a great calm fell across his slight form as he led them into his room and over to the bed where Hermione McCloud lay dead, covered with a sheet drawn demurely to her neck, with her head resting on a pillow and her grey hair spread softly over the pristine white cotton, with her eyes gently closed.

For a moment, none of them spoke. Hermione M

looked quite beautiful, the way the old sometimes do when all the people they have been in their lives radiantly converge in easeful death. Both Miranda and Morgan had seen this in elderly relatives who had died in their sleep. It was a kind of peace, the cumulative face of a life ending naturally, that they never saw in their work. Murder leaves its own mask, to be confused sometimes with the masks of accident and illness and suicide, but never with the face of equanimity or grace.

Miranda was the first to speak.

"Did you arrange her like this?" Even as she asked, she realized how unusual it was that neither she nor Morgan had reached out to see if Hermione could be resuscitated. The old woman seemed so naturally the embodiment of death.

"Yes I did."

"Was she here, in your room, when she died?"

"Yes she was, that is so."

Miranda drew the sheet away from the body until she realized the woman was naked, then let it fall back into place. Li Po rearranged it over her shoulders, as if she might feel the draft seeping through the screened window, carrying the breeze from Lake Rosseau into the darkest corners of the room.

"Were you with her?" said Morgan.

"Yes, I was, we were together," said Li Po.

Morgan and Miranda exchanged glances.

"You were making love?" asked Miranda.

"Yes, that is so, we were making love." Li Po looked up at her and smiled.

He was in his eighties, Hermione was well into her seventies. Miranda felt a surge of warmth run through her entire system. Morgan felt a visceral surge as well. For a short while there was a pleasant aura pervading the room that seemed to hold all four of them in a strangely comfortable union, male and female, old and not so old, living and dead.

Morgan broke the mood.

"We'll have to call the county coroner."

Suddenly everything crashed as reality took hold. Examinations had to be made. Cause of death determined. The other guests would have to be informed.

This tranquil scene and the affections it revealed would collapse amidst emotional confusion and clinical expediency.

Miranda reached out and took Li Po's hand. "I think we had better leave her on her own until the coroner gets here," she said.

"Yes," he said. "I understand."

Morgan lingered for a moment, trying to inscribe the scene in his mind.

What he saw was a woman whose body had been prepared by a loving man to present death in the best possible light. It was curious. Li Po presented her as someone in a state of grace. It was a gesture of serene defiance He was making a statement, but Morgan could not decipher the language. Perhaps it was just an expression of solidarity, an old man embracing the immanence of death.

Morgan felt curiously relaxed, his mind teeming with words. He looked around and caught Miranda, from the doorway, watching him thinking. He smiled, first at her and then at Hermione M, naked under the tousled sheet.

By the time the helicopter landed with the coroner and his assistants, Lionel Webb had gathered his guests in the drawing room at the request of the Toronto detectives, who briefly explained that Hermione was dead but did not reveal the circumstances. Nevertheless, it soon became apparent that she had been in Li Po's room when she died, and that she had been naked. Miranda was fascinated by how the news had spread with a life of its own. Perhaps someone had walked by, just as the body was exposed for examination; perhaps someone overheard the coroner's conversation with Morgan when he showed them upstairs; perhaps a leap was made from seeing Li Po in a silk robe, summoning the police; perhaps one of the invisible members of the housekeeping staff saw something and passed it on. Possibly it was in the sounds of the vast cottage accommodating unusual activities, the nearly imperceptible creaks and groans of the wood that etched into everyone's mind in the quiet of the room the possibilities of sex and misadventure.

Only Marie Lachine seemed unduly distressed. Even Li Po appeared relaxed by the time they had all come together. The notion of a tryst between lovers in their old age astonished Simon, excited Felix, exhilarated Jane, puzzled Ralph, thrilled Padraig, confused Jennifer, irritated Lionel, amused David, and annoyed Hermione the spy. Miranda found it touching and Morgan, affirming.

When Marie Lachine cut herself away from the urgent chatter in the drawing room and withdrew to the verandah, Miranda realized their *pûr laines* from Toronto must have known Hermione M was her mother. She followed Marie out through the French doors, but Li Po had somehow preceded her and they were seated together on a wicker settee. Miranda was about to withdraw when the woman called to her in a low voice and asked her to stay. This gesture caught Miranda by surprise. She was used to Mlle Lachine's unconcealed hostility and had assumed it was because Marie felt vulnerable in Miranda's presence, afraid things might be revealed that she did not want to know, or already knew and wanted to ignore or deny.

"If you wish," said Miranda. "Professor Li Po, do you mind?"

"Yes, certainly," he said, as if relieved to have her there.

It occurred to Miranda she was meant to be a witness to coming revelations which neither of the other two quite understood. She sat down close to them.

Morgan came out, saw them huddled together, and withdrew. He suspected Miranda would learn more on her own. Miranda pulled her chair slightly back, indicating she might act as a mediator if necessary, but the discussion was essentially theirs.

Li Po turned to Marie Lachine and took one of her hands in his. In a very soft voice, he said, "I am so sorry, my friend."

She withdrew her hand and stared into his eyes which glistened with emotion.

He continued: "We were friends a long time ago, Marie."

"We were lovers."

"And love endures."

"*Bien, oui*," she said. "You told that to me in Paris, a quarter of a century ago. *Once loved, always loved, true love endures*. Oh yes, how you could talk about love."

"It should not surprise you that I have made love to others."

"It would surprise me if you had not. And it is shocking and it is wonderful, at your age—"

"Please." He smiled, forgiving her ignorance.

"She is my mother."

His smile collapsed. There was an explosion of silence. Li Po looked stricken.

"You are surprised that two women you have loved are related?"

Miranda felt the urgent need to intervene, yet there was nothing to say. She knew one revelation was sure to be followed by another, even more astonishing than the first.

"You are my daughter," said Li Po, gazing into her eyes. It was not a question.

Miranda flinched. Marie's response was a muffled shriek.

"It is true," said the old man, coming to terms with the notion himself. "We had a child."

"No, I, I am…" Her voice trailled off.

"I was in China, it was necessary. Our baby was taken away."

She said nothing.

"What might seem outrageous coincidence," he let

his voice trail off into a whisper, then continued: "It was not. Our friend Professor Kurtz was at the heart of the matter. Dieter introduced you to Hermione, yes? He brought you together. Of course, he said nothing about me, that I am your father? Nor to me about you. He must have known, but I did not know, my poor Marie. Not before, not since. I did not know."

"He always kept secrets in reserve," she said, trying to counter the betrayal of one old man by another. She reached out and touched his hand, held it resting open in the palm of her own in a gesture of mercy, perhaps of acceptance. "*Mon pauvre.*"

"I loved your mother for my whole life, from the day we met until I die."

"*Et moi?*"

"I loved you best in Paris for a season, and I will love you always for that."

"And in my heart that season in Paris remains alive forever, Papa."

She called him 'Papa' with an absence of irony that astonished Miranda. It crossed her mind this could be a macabre charade for her benefit, that they knew all along or had known for some time about their incestuous bond. But no, there was an awkwardness to their bewildering affection that seemed genuinely innocent. If Miranda had expected Li Po to shrivel in shame, she was wrong; or Marie to have been consumed by righteousness or rage, she was mistaken. They seemed like a family and somehow, strangely, they were a family of three.

Miranda stood up. "I think I'll go inside and leave you

two on your own. You will have much to discuss."

"Not so much," said Li Po. "But thank you, we would like to be alone now."

Marie raised her head with an odd beatific smile, as if she had made the connection she had been waiting for most of her life, but said nothing.

When Miranda returned to the drawing room, she took Morgan to one side.

"You won't believe what happened out there."

"What?"

"I think I left behind on the verandah the remnant of a happy family that never was."

"What on earth does that mean?"

"Well, I don't think Li Po knew his lovers were mother and daughter. I'm sure he had no idea Marie was his child."

"How'd he take it?"

"That's just it. He seemed almost relieved. I think the man is wonderfully intuitive, he carried the burden of not knowing and I think that might have been worse than knowing."

"Very metaphysical, Miranda. What about her?"

"She definitely had no idea he was her father, or that he and her mother were lovers. She did know she was adopted, she did know Hermione was her mother, that she wasn't *Québéçoise* pure wool."

"And she, how did she deal with it all?"

"Initial panic, then poise. They both assign their sexual relationship to a past out of reach, something to be cherished without shame or remorse. She seems to grieve the death of her mother but counters with the discovery of her father as a man she adores. Strange, isn't it?"

"Yeah, do you trust your reading?"

"My reading? Of their story. Yes, I think so, I do."

"Then I do too. But there's more to know about Li Po, there's another story. How did he connect with Dieter Kurtz? Somehow there's a link between those two, maybe something that ties Hermione, the surviving one, to Li Po as well."

"You know, Morgan," she said, surveying the room and inviting his eyes to follow hers, "I'm not sure that understanding these convoluted relationships is bringing us any closer to knowing who killed Dieter Kurtz."

"I disagree. Each time we make a connection, Kurtz is there. He's always there. Eventually we'll reach the limits of complexity and everything will fall into place."

"The limits of complexity? Is that like the law of averages? Don't count on them working in our favour, Morgan. If a person is standing in the middle of a giant mosaic, that person might not see the surrounding pattern. It's a matter of perspective. Coming here might not have been such a great idea."

"Yeah, I miss the city"

"Morgan?"

"Yes?"

"Do you think you'll be a good lover at eighty?"

"You tell me."

"Yeah," she said, looking at him through narrowed eyes, "probably. Me too. Of course, by then you'll be really very old."

"When you're eighty."
"Yeah."
"I'll be eighty-four and a half."
"Shall we make a date."
"For sure," he said. "You're on."

chapter twenty-five
The Boathouse Slip

The coroner came down the staircase followed by assistants carrying Hermione strapped onto a collapsed gurney and covered with a thin sheet. The entire Bacon Society looked out from the drawing room into the entryway, including Li Po and Marie Lachine who had come in from the verandah. Lionel walked over to the coroner and said something privately, then he went to Li Po and Marie and asked them if they'd like to walk up to the helicopter pad with Hermione.

So, Morgan thought, at least Lionel Webb understands something of their relationship. How much, he was uncertain, and he didn't think Lionel was likely to clarify.

As the remaining guests began to disperse, most of them down to the dock carrying fruit and rolls and drinks from the sideboard in the dining room, Miranda and Morgan intercepted Hermione Mac and asked if she'd join them on the verandah.

Once they were comfortably seated, she turned to them and said, "Well, now, then, what do you think? I suppose you want to grill me about Li Po."

"Grill you? I don't think so," said Miranda. "But we might ask a few questions."

"About Li Po?"

"Yes."

"Shoot. But I warn you, I am a trained liar. And I probably know less than you do."

"Let's see " said Morgan.

"Fire away."

Her feisty response seemed incongruous, coming from a diminutive old lady with a disarming smile.

"How did you come to know Hermione McCloud?" Miranda asked. "Who introduced you?"

"I'm not sure I remember, dear. Would it have been Dieter? I imagine that is the answer you expect. I think it was Dieter."

"Hermione," said Miranda in good humour, "are you being evasive?"

"No, dear. Just playful. For old time's sake. Yes, it was probably Dieter who introduced us."

"And Li Po, how did you know him?"

"Now that is more complex."

"Can you explain," Morgan asked.

"Oh yes. He came to visit me in London after the war."

Miranda was surprised.

"Then you didn't come directly to Canada? You said the Brits were embarrassed by what they did to you."

"And by what I did to myself, I suppose. I survived. But yes, I stayed in London for several years. Li Po turned up on my doorstep. He was studying at the Sorbonne. He had spent time at Oxford and tried to find me but I was His Majesty's guest for a rather lengthy time, being debriefed, as they described it. He had written from Freiberg at Dieter's urging—he studied there for only a short while. He had a message for me from my erstwhile lover."

"From Dieter!" Miranda exclaimed. "Where?"

"In Manchuria. They had met under peculiar circumstances."

"Peculiar?"

"Dieter was a Soviet prisoner in a gulag for German soldiers. He hid his affiliation with the SS but he was brutalized, of course. There was no expectation of ever getting out. That is what got him through, he told me. No expectations. Those who hoped, died. He accepted life as it was, vile beyond anything he could describe, living on the bodies of the deceased, living with the dead, and he accepted this was the best he could expect ever again, and he endured.

"Gangs of Soviet prisoners were shipped to Manchuria, Stalin's gift to the Maoists. Li Po was in charge of forcing a road through impossible terrain. Dieter was among the living dead at his disposal for the most treacherous labours. They had not met before the hostilities, as you might have thought. But they discovered each other, they talked. They had much in common. *In hell*, they say, *the banalities of intellectual discourse have a special currency.*"

"Meaning what?" said Morgan.

"I have no idea, dear."

Miranda and Morgan both looked into her eyes; she was seeing things they could not imagine.

"They talked," Hermione continued. "They did not become friends but Li Po occasionally gave him packets of food. Dieter had studied at Freiberg before the war. When Li Po left to study abroad in Freiburg, he said goodbye to his German cohort, expecting never to see him again. The life expectancy in a forced labour camp was measured in weeks. Dieter gave him an address where I could be reached in London. The message, there was no actual message. He just wanted me to know he had thought of me in the midst of chaos and death."

"So, did you and Li Po become friends?"

"He is a very attractive man, Miranda. He is lean and quick like a panther, and clever and courageous and very handsome. We both were handsome, you know. I was even what you might call beautiful."

"You had an affair?" said Miranda.

"Perhaps we did. You must think his life was a string of affairs."

"Perhaps it was."

"Perhaps. We became very close. I asked him, when he returned to China, would he look out for Dieter."

""I'm not sure why you cared?" said Morgan. "Surely there was more for you to hate than to love about Dieter

Kurtz."

"Perhaps. Perhaps hate and love are opposing aspects of intense emotion, two sides of the same coin. Li Po promised he would find Dieter if he were alive. When he left London I expected never to see him again. He went to Paris, to Rome, briefly, then disappeared into China and was swallowed up by the revolution."

Miranda glanced at Morgan. The redoubtable Li Po was a complex man.

"Hermione," she said. "I need to ask you again, did you have an affair with Li Po?"

"We were very close for a brief time, a season as he described it, a season in our lives."

"And did you have an affair?"

"Consummated?"

"Um, yes."

"No. He was in love with a woman in Paris. That did not mean we weren't in love, as well. His heart is very big."

"Did you know who the woman was?"

"No."

"Do you know who she is now?"

"That is a trick question, Detective. She is now dead. I discovered who she was long after I came to Canada."

"Hermione McCloud?"

"Hermione, yes."

"Did she know you knew?"

"Yes, I think she did. We never talked about it."

"And did you know about Marie?"

"Yes."

"That she was his mistress?"

"That they were lovers, yes."

"And that she was his daughter."

"Yes, I knew that but Li Po did not, and Hermione, of course, did not know Marie had been his lover."

"Kurtz told you."

"Yes, Dieter told me."

"Why?"

"Because he knew I would suffer from knowing."

"And you loved this man?"

"And hated him."

"What happened when Li Po returned to China?" asked Morgan.

"I think you should speak to him about that. He will tell you the truth."

"Did he help Kurtz escape?"

"I believe he did. I think you must talk to Li Po about that."

"He has quite a bit on his mind right now."

"I am going to Philip's Folly," said the old woman, rising to her feet. The other two rose as well. "I am tired. Do you realize it's mid-afternoon already. I need a nap."

"Do you want me to walk with you," Miranda asked.

"No thank you, dear. You two sit here and sort out your ideas. I'm sure that's the best part of your work, comparing notes."

Miranda smiled and, as Hermione the spy made her way along the verandah to the side steps, Miranda thought she moved more slowly, with more determination, than she had before. Morgan was already slumped back down in his chair, gazing pensively into the middle distance as if some revelation were hovering over Lake Rosseau, awaiting illumination.

Miranda stood watching as the old woman receded, wondering if she herself would ever be old. The two Hermiones, different as they were from each other, and their lives from hers, made the prospect intriguing.

"A penny," she said as she sat down again.

"Thoughts? Just words and images fluttering about. She's quite the old gal."

"She is. It was hard for her to admit she and Li Po had never been lovers."

"Why, I wonder."

"Because, Morgan, she wanted him desperately. Perhaps to obliterate the horrors of war. And the more he resisted, the more desirable he became. For the rest of her life, she has remained in love with the man who honoured her by his fidelity to someone else. Think about that. And she remained in emotional bondage to the man who defiled her."

"Sometimes I am in awe," said Morgan, meaning what he said. "Shall we go for a swim. We'll talk to Li Po after dinner."

"The beach?"

He met her gaze straight on.

"No," he said. "Down with the others."

Dinner was a quiet affair. Conversation was low-keyed but not somber. Hermione's death, an old woman at peace in her lover's arms, was disconcerting but did not strike the remaining members of the Bacon Society as tragic. Even Li Po and Marie joined in with the table conversation that centred, inevitably, on Bacon, this time as a diplomat for the court of Elizabeth, his putative mother.

Miranda contemplated parenthood. It seemed an attachment fraught with duplicity. Down the long table, David Jenness flashed a grin and despite the untroubled innocence of his features she saw in his expression her partner's face. And Jill, she thought, Jill has become my daughter; it's as if she has always been in my life. Strange how it can work that way.

Morgan was also thinking about the quirks of genealogy. How can the poised young man beside Lionel Webb be as well adjusted as he seems. Old Sir Nigel deserves credit, but then so does Susan. And so does David. So does everyone except Morgan, thought Morgan. *I seem to have screwed up. When she loved me, I was the feckless young man from the colonies, and when I loved her it was too late for us both. But damnit, she must be living a good life, it shows in her son. Perhaps the best thing for all concerned was my retreat from the scene.*

He glanced over at Padraig, who was already into the blueberry pie, although others were still eating pasta and salad. His paternity was problematic. And Jennifer, her story had shifted abruptly for the better. Marie Lachine and Li Po, their coming together at the expense of Hermione's passing, would enrich both their lives. He thought how lucky Miranda was to have Jill, even if the circumstances that brought them together were horrific. He did not think of Miranda as maternal. He wanted her to have babies, of course. That was the awkward measure of his affection for her, and of his limited imagination in such matters. He assumed she could have babies but stay exactly as she was.

After dinner, the entire company moved onto the verandah. Miranda cut Marie Lachine away from the crowd, giving Morgan a chance to corral Li Po. When Li Po was approached, however, he showed no inclination to leave the group. He sat down and motioned Morgan to sit in the chair beside him. Others gathered close. There was an air of expectancy that centred on the old man.

His sad eyes picked up highlights from the overhead lanterns, and Li Po began to speak in a voice so quiet everyone froze, trying not to muffle his words.

Morgan expected him to talk about Hermione and the love they had secretly nurtured for such a long time. He assumed the old man would want this circle of friends so far from Lanchou to understand that he had discovered his daughter among them. He thought perhaps Li Po needed to share his grief, to honour Hermione, and to redeem his love for Marie.

Instead, the old man spoke about other things. Gazing out into the night sky over Lake Rosseau, words began to flow, at first so quietly his audience could not be sure if he was speaking in English or Mandarin. Then, as the words became clear his narrative opened and they were enthralled by revelations from a man who never before talked about his own experience, but had been the best listener among them.

"Dieter was not my friend," he was saying. "In a labour camp there are no friends. But we needed each other." Hermione Mac, who was sitting on the other side of him took his hand. Looking out over the water, he articulated with precision, as if he were trying to understand something elusive.

"The prisoners, they endure horror with only the armour of suspended emotion. The guards, they cannot allow themselves feelings. Working in the jungle, building roads and bridges in intolerable conditions of heat and of rain and disease, each man is alone, captive or captor, slave or slave-driver, it is hard to tell them apart.

"When I met him, Dieter Kurtz was a man with no name, no country, no record of crime, he was a living corpse, enduring what must be endured until death. But he did not die. Each day he worked, and others died. The filth, the pain, weeping sores, broken bodies, these were his life. It was as if he had known nothing else. Sometimes he seemed almost happy.

"Occasionally we exchanged a few words. My rage or despair at being so infinitely far from serving the noble cause, and his indifference to suffering, they formed an equation of some sort, a connection between us. I gave him food from my own rations. We were starving as well, dying almost as rapidly as those others.

"To find in the fires of hell a reminder of what it is to be human, this was redemption. His refusal to die, to suffer, such redemption is rare. This man reached into me, sometimes talking of Francis Bacon, sometimes in German, sometimes English, mostly French. It was a shock to discover I was still alive. To believe I had the power, even there, to choose my own way.

"We kept very poor records in the camps. People died and were replaced. Personal identity was not of importance. It would be easy to disappear, one way or another. Before I deserted, he gave me the name of a woman in Europe, he said I might find her if I wished. Her name was a bond, a gift.

"I never expected to see him again. He was not sad to see me leave. He had not allowed himself to care about me. He did not allow himself to care about anything.

"I found the woman in London. There was no message, just that he was alive when I left him. That was enough for both of them."

Miranda became aware Hermione the spy was still holding his hand, not grasping it but letting it rest lightly under her fingers like a delicate object she wished to prevent from slipping away, perhaps falling and breaking.

"The woman told me he would survive. She did not ask me to help him but she was a witness to both our lives. She knew I would help, if it were possible.

"I returned to China. After three years away, I went back to build a revolutionary society, it was what I had dreamed about. In Manchuria, I found Dieter. He had endured so long in the camps, no prisoner nor guard remembered a time before he was there. Hardly a man, he was a golem, a figure of mud with no soul, and a mind bent only to endure each moment as it passed. When I found him, he knew me, but said nothing. There was nothing to say.

"After three days and two nights in the camp, I cleaned him and we escaped. It was not difficult. We simply walked out into the darkness.

"Several weeks later, he went out from the roadside house where we were hiding for the night, into a village for food. He was picked up. He told the revolutionary police where I was, he made a deal with them. They arrested me. They released him. They were sure he would die, a foreigner in China at that time. They did not know how well he spoke Chinese, that he could blend into chaos."

"And you?" said Hermione Mac.

"It turned out, my loyalty was not in doubt. I had been on The Long March with Mao. I was useful. I was sent to Lanchou, to teach European history and culture to ambitious young bureaucrats."

"He would have died," said Miranda.

"Without me? No, his story would not be the same, but he was not ready to die— perhaps death was not ready to face Dieter Kurtz."

"Not yet," said Morgan.

"Not until Philosophers Walk," said Miranda.

"And then it was time," said Professor Li Po.

"It was," said Hermione, the European woman who had known there was nothing that the man who had ravaged and loved her would not endure, if he wished.

Li Po's story was complete; this is what he had wanted to tell them. Morgan was uncertain whether it was because he wanted them to understand him better, or to understand Kurtz.

Marie Lachine helped her father from the deep embrace of the Muskoka chair and the two of them walked off into the shadows of the night, reappearing several times in the pools of light descending to the boathouse. The others sat together in the arc of chairs they had drawn up around the old man to hear his tale. It was as if they wanted to resist drifting apart, not wanting to acknowledge that their holiday gathering was drawing to a close. Yet no one really had anything to say. After a few awkward attempts at group conversation, people began talking to their nearest neighbour, but the effort to make small-talk withered the ambiance. Singly and in pairs they excused themselves and wandered off to their separate rooms.

Before long, only Morgan and Miranda remained on the verandah. Miranda moved her chair close to his.

"What did you think?" she asked.

"Of what?" In his account, the old man had revealed a life immersed in history beyond anything Morgan could imagine.

"I don't know. Of Li Po, of Dieter Kurtz. Who killed him, Morgan?"

He looked out across Lake Rosseau. The soft glare of the lanterns hanging from the verandah ceiling and the diffuse light of the moon drowned out the lights of the hotel at Windermere on the far shore. He was wary of being too comfortable, afraid they were missing the obvious from their distorted perspective inside the circle.

Miranda guessed what was on his mind. "Do you think we've been unprofessional, being here?"

"Uh-huh, maybe."

"I think it was necessary, Morgan."

"Me too."

Miranda reached over and gave his shoulder a friendly squeeze as she stood up.

"I'm off to bed. We're due out of here in the morning. I want to get a good start and beat the traffic."

"G'night Miranda."

"There's no sauna tonight. I would have liked another sauna. G'night Morgan."

She wandered off around the side of the verandah, feeling strangely nostalgic, as if the experience of the last few days were already an important part of her personal memory bank. Wistfully, she turned and looked back when she reached the high shoulder of rock on the way to her cabin. The lights of the main cottage glimmered through the trees like a magical apparition, then suddenly the lights went out. She could hear a low rumble as somewhere in a shed in the woods a generator throbbed back to life and the lights came on again. The brief stroke of darkness was enough to make her realize that her sense of personal belonging on Briar Hill Island was an illusion. She turned and walked on to Philip's Folly.

Early in the morning the low wail of the steam whistle wakened Miranda as the *Lady Ruth* sidled up to the boathouse dock. As she began to drift off again into a deep slumber, the steam whistle shook the air with a series of more urgent blasts. There was no question it was a summons. She dressed quickly and knocked on Morgan's door, which was opening as she approached it.

"Sounds like trouble," she said.

"Good morning," he said.

"What do you think," he asked her as they hurried along the path.

"The worst."

"Who?"

"Did you see Li Po and Marie come up from the dock last night?"

"No," he said and broke into a jogging pace, springing cautiously among the roots and stones along the path.

"Neither of them?" she asked, keeping up with his pace, still trying to get the buttons done up on her shirt.

"There's Marie," he said as they rounded the corner of the verandah and slowed to a rapid walk. "I don't see the old man."

When they reached the boathouse, they saw Ralph and Padraig were already on the dock, talking to the captain who was leaning down from the bridge. Several of the crew and Lionel Webb were standing in the gloom inside, over near one of the empty boat slips. They stepped out of the way for Morgan and Miranda, who peered into the water, trying to penetrate the planes of the rippling surface. There was silence except for the lapping of small waves trapped among the log cribs under the floor. At first they could see only a spectral image, and then a face came into focus as recognition allowed them to ignore the surface distortion, and they found themselves gazing into the expressionless eyes of Li Po.

"We didn't touch him," said Lionel Webb. "He's obviously been there all night. Thought we should wait for you."

Despite how elusive his image appeared, Li Po was lying in water too shallow for him to sink more than an arm's length below the surface. There was a thick length of white cotton rope tied around one of his wrists and around the base of a screw-winch used to raise launches above the ice in winter. Clearly, the rope was meant, not to hold him down but to keep his body from drifting away.

Morgan immediately lowered himself into the water and grasping the rope drew Li Po towards him. Miranda, kneeling on the boards at the side of the slip, grasped the dead man's collar and pulled him closer, then getting a better grip under his shoulders she lifted while Morgan heaved him forward. For such a small man, he seemed heavy. No one helped. The crew were clearly taking their lead from Webb, while the guests hung back, anxious not to display inappropriate curiosity or to interfere in police business.

As soon as the corpse was laid out on the boathouse deck, it became apparent why he was so difficult to move. His pockets were filled with pebbles from the shore. *This is how Virginia Woolf had died*, Morgan thought. The water in the slip was just deep enough, if the old man had sat up, his face would still be submerged, but if he had risen to his feet, he would easily have been able to avoid drowning. *Virginia Woolf had not left the option open; she had been more desperate. Or less determined.*

Lionel Webb was right. Li Po had been there for hours, possibly since late the previous evening. There were no outward signs of violence. Marie Lachine kneeled down beside him and ran the back of her hand over his cheek. Miranda asked her not to, then relented because it was so obviously suicide. Still, there would have to be a coroner's report, possibly an inquest. Miranda reached out again and gently drew Marie away.

Hermione Mac helped the distraught woman to her feet and the two of them stood side by side, staring down at the old man's glistening features. With his skin fleshed out from immersion he looked much younger, of an indeterminate age, of no age at all. *Each of them sees him,* Miranda thought, observing the distressed affection in their eyes, *as the man he had been when she knew him best. Each must be haunted by the possibility she did not know him at all.*

The others wandered off to busy themselves packing for home, somehow more isolated, it seemed, a little more alone in the world. Morgan stayed with the corpse while Miranda checked Li Po's room for a note and as she expected found nothing. She packed his few belongings, then walked over to pack up her own things and Morgan's and returned with their bags to the boathouse.

When the county coroner took off in Lionel Webb's helicopter with Li Po's body, the remains of the Bacon Society gathered at the dining table in the screened-in verandah where they had eaten most of their meals. Miranda and Morgan walked down from the heli-pad to join them. As soon as they came around the corner, the questions began. This was in stark contrast to the equanimity that met the passing of Hermione M, an event that seemed far less traumatic, perhaps because it had happened in bed.

"In all likelihood, it was suicide," said Morgan in response to a direct question from Felix Swan.

"There was no warning, isn't there usually a warning about such things?" asked Felix.

"I don't think that was Li Po's style," said Morgan. "I doubt he let anyone know, even Marie. His death wasn't a plea or a threat. It was closure."

All eyes turned to Marie Lachine, who had entirely regained her composure. It was as if the radically shifting perspectives on her personal history had collapsed and she was back to being herself as they knew her.

"When I left him," she said, "he told me he wanted to sit by the water and listen to the little waves under the dock. I had no idea, he seemed calm, very reflective, tranquil, I would say."

"The rope?" said Simon Sparrow. "What was that all about?"

"Consideration," Miranda responded. "He did not want to cause any trouble."

"Who found him," asked Jane Latimer?

"One of the crew. He went in for a pee."

"In the boathouse?"

"In the slip."

"How could he see? It's dark in there."

"—shadowy."

"—and the light on the surface, reflecting under the door—"

"—from the lake—"

"—dazzling. I mean if he wasn't looking—"

"—do you look when you pee?"

"—it would be a shock."

"— if the surface was still you could see him."

"—you think peeing stills the waters?"

"—he saw him, didn't he!"

"Is there any chance it was murder, Detective?" David Jenness addressed Morgan in the clear voice of someone who wanted to cut through the chatter.

"I don't think so," said Morgan. "I think Professor Li Po chose to die here, at this time, among friends."

"Slipping into the cold dark water on his own," said Felix Swan. "How very horrible."

Marie Lachine smiled to herself. She knew, as Miranda surmised, the old man saw the shape of his life was complete with the revelations of the last few days. The two women exchanged glances. *When there is nothing left of your story but postscripts and footnotes,* he might have said, *then it is time to bring it to a close.*

Suddenly a long shrill blast from the *Lady Ruth* filled the air, setting the flatware trembling. Everyone stood up, pleased to be on the way home. Lionel Webb nodded his head benignly as his eyes darted, making brief contact with each of his guests in a kind of fleeting farewell, then he left the room. Their baggage had already been picked up by the crew and deposited on board, all except Miranda's bag and Morgan's, which were already on the dock. Morgan slipped into the kitchen to say goodbye to Kate Nesbitt. When he came back out, Sir David Jenness had reassumed his role of purser and was shepherding everyone down to the boathouse and onto the boat. The *Lady Ruth* let out another ear-splitting shriek from her steam whistle and with her screws surging swung out and away from Briar Hill Island.

chapter twenty-six

Starbucks

"In January 1494, there was a heavy snowfall in Florence. The Medici family commissioned Michelangelo to sculpt a snowman." Morgan leaned back in his chair and smiled triumphantly. "There is no record of what it looked like." They were drinking coffee in Starbucks at College and Yonge, just over from Police Headquarters. He had fallen on this brief reference to the ephemerality of genius while scouring the web for information about Francis Bacon.

"Picasso once responded to an autograph hunter by signing his name on her arm," said Miranda, trying to trump him with what struck her as a brilliantly impish gesture.

"I think it was Claes Oldenburg who dug a hole in Central Park and then filled it in."

"That's different," said Miranda.

Morgan shifted in his chair and leaned forward over the table.

"That's what we're after," he said. "The buried hole. It's our job to dig it up."

"Morgan, if we dig up the hole, it's no longer there."

"Exactly."

"Actually, the buried hole would be gone, but there'd be a new hole in its place."

"No, no," he argued. "It was gone as soon as he filled it."

"Or not. If you believe art is in the mind of the beholder, it was there until we exposed that it wasn't."

"Or not. As a metaphor for solving a murder, it doesn't hold up."

"Whatever," she said. "Whatever."

They had been home for three days. Their Muskoka experience seemed to have occurred in a parallel reality. Back in familiar territory, any suggestion there was a vanishing point where the realities converged was an illusion.

The DNA reports had come in. No surprises. The D'Arcys were not related, not that anyone expected they were. Porrig and Lionel were not related. That was one less complication. Lionel and Jennifer were not related. Marie Lachine was related to both Li Po and Hermione McCloud, as anticipated. David Jenness was Morgan's son. The hair was Jane Latimer's, a pubic hair of indeterminate vintage.

"Morgan," said Miranda, "it's her hair, she's got

powerful thighs, we have a motive."

"So has everyone else."

"You don't *want* to think it was her."

"It's not that. It's just, given the wondrous complexity of the Baconian world, it's too neat. It doesn't ring true."

"How about Marie Lachine?" said Miranda.

"How about her?"

"What a weekend—her unlikely parentage revealed, incest discovered, and orphaned, all within twenty-four hours. She seems to take tragedy pretty much in her stride, though. She insisted on driving south on her own. Both her passengers coming up went back in body bags."

"Li Po's death, Hermione's death, they were sad, but they weren't tragic."

"For Marie? Come on, Morgan. How do you define tragic?"

"It might have been easier for her to deal with the complexities of her family with her parents both out of the way. Perhaps they knew that, that's why they went."

"Went?"

"Died."

"Maybe Kurtz knew what he was doing, bringing the three of them together."

"So they could be with each other, without knowing the Byzantine intricacies of their relationship. He was playing God with their lives."

"Playing God for their benefit or for his own amusement? Benevolent or malevolent, that is the question?"

"That's the first time I've heard anyone suggest he might have done something good," said Morgan. "Bad people can do good things."

"Yes, and vice versa, that's why we're searching for a killer among the Baconians."

"No, I mean, really. I've been reading about Francis Bacon. According to some, he's virtually the father of modern science and technology. He had the genius to argue that while matters of the spirit are comprehensible only through revelation, the wonders of the natural world are wholly accessible to the rational mind. Revolutionary at the time. And you know what else, he refutes my flying friend, Saint Augustine."

"That's a relief."

"Yeah, I checked it out. *Knowledge ... is available only through faith.* That's what Augustine says."

"Before or after he gave up debauchery?"

Morgan winked and continued.

"Bacon is a bit of an enigma, though. According to most accounts, he was a sleazy sycophant, a nasty self-aggrandizing hustler, a semi-educated intellectual charlatan."

"I thought he went to Cambridge."

"Yes?" He paused, wondering whether it was possible to make a condescending joke. Probably not. "He was twelve. He tagged along with his brother. And was back in London before he was sixteen. He was a barrister by twenty! No-body disputes his inquiring mind or his intellectual ambition: he made it his mission to wrestle Western thought away from Aristotle, to place knowledge within a new set of categories that would connect everything to everything and make all facts accessible to the open mind. But he was mean and devious and he ended up in disrepute for accepting a huge bribe while he was Lord Chancellor, a position he achieved by bluster, buggery, blackmail, and illimitable bullying."

"You don't like him?"

"I didn't know him. His wife is said to have died in the arms of her footman from, as my source exclaims so eloquently, *too much Venus!*"

"Well, good for her," said Miranda. "She knew how to compensate for being bound to a wretched husband."

"Too much Venus!"

"With all his bustling and hustling, he managed to write major stuff, though. Right?"

"Some say it was drivel or impossibly derivative, a lot of pretentious sophistry. Others, including major philosophers and scholars, especially in France, say it was truly inspired."

"They think Jerry Lewis is a comedic genius."

"Who?"

"The French."

"Miranda, my only point is, Bacon seems a strange figure to gather around in this day and age—but then so is Kurtz."

"So is Jerry Lewis."

"From what I've read about Bacon so far, you can't separate the good from the bad, the profound from the foolish—and he was foolish about a lot of things. He dismissed mathematics along with alchemy and astrology. He had contempt for the occult and yet allowed supremacy to religion. He was a rationalist but a Mason, a realist but a Rosicrucian."

"You don't want to talk about Jerry Lewis?"

"I liked his voice but he drank too much."

"That was Dean Martin."

"I wonder if Kurtz thought of Bacon as a soul-mate?"

"Morgan, I think we should talk to Jane Latimer."

"If you want."

"Yeah, I think we should." Instead of getting up, Miranda, who was facing the door, sat back in her chair. "Perhaps we could do it right now."

Jane Latimer waved and walked directly over to the counter to pick up a cappuccino, a sure indication she meant to join them. Miranda noticed she was neither in a costume nor tumbling out of one, although there was something about the way she was turned out that seemed unusual. What was it, Miranda puzzled? *How do I know she's an academic?* Then she realized it was the absence of makeup. A business woman dressed in skirt and a cashmere twin set, sporting heels, however low, would be wearing mascara, lipstick, possibly blush on her cheeks. Jane glowed with a radiance that proclaimed robust good health. Maybe there was a bit of lipstick, maybe a hint of eye-shadow. Not much, if any.

"Thought I'd find you two here," she said as she sat down.

"You were looking for us?" said Miranda.

"Of course," she responded cheerfully. "We didn't really get a chance to talk in Muskoka. I wanted to catch up on things."

"To catch up?" said Morgan, amused at her casual

re-entry into the investigation, as if she were once again their cohort and not a principal suspect.

"Well, at Lionel's place I had a role to play. As president and chairman of the board I was the subliminal co-host."

"Very subliminal," Miranda observed, not meaning to be unkind but to indicate she was aware Jane Latimer's presence had been largely passive on Briar Hill Island, for all her dock-side exposure: topless was inspiring when your breasts were perky, otherwise it was exhibitionism. Jane passed the test.

"Ah, but you see, there was a group dynamic that had to be maintained."

"Really? And how did you do that?"

"By behaving as if nothing had changed."

"It seemed like you were all doing that," said Miranda.

"These are not people who would naturally convene, Detective. Professor Kurtz brought us together. Symbiosis: we needed him and he needed us. Collectively we provided a context in which his own personality was most fully realized."

"Yes," said Morgan, with intentional ambiguity.

"We were a constructed alter ego. My job now is to prove that we are still a viable entity. We need each other. That was his legacy, I suppose. For good or ill, we need each other."

"To perpetuate Kurtz?" said Morgan.

"No," she responded without elaboration.

"You were looking for us, to tell us this?" said Miranda.

"I think we need you, the two of you, as well as each

other."

"Really." Miranda found the woman's candour amusing but a little unsettling. "That would make us thirteen, with the Antichrist gone."

"The precise number of an ideal coven," said Morgan.

"Oh, I mean after all this police business is over," said Jane Latimer, ignoring his shift from Christian allusion to Wiccan. "We'd like to have you as regulars."

"Well, it's not over yet," said Miranda. She paused, poising her next statement like an arrow. "We found a pubic hair belonging to you in the old man's beard."

Jane Latimer smiled. "I didn't know it was missing!"

Miranda choked on the dregs of her coffee and Morgan stifled laughter with a sequence of dry coughs. Jane Latimer chuckled confidently. People at other tables looked around and saw three friends sharing what might have been an outrageous joke or a deliciously sordid bit of gossip.

After a few minutes in which she regained her composure, Miranda explained, "We were on our way over to see you when you came in."

"Then I anticipated your intentions."

"How did you know we were here?"

"I didn't, actually. I was just on my way by to the Police station. Saw you through window."

"To catch up on things?" said Morgan.

"Actually, to fill you in on a few details that might be of interest."

"Great," said Morgan. "I'll get us more coffee. Either of you want anything to eat?" He had his back to them before they had a chance to answer. Miranda found his relaxed collegiality a little disconcerting. Jane Latimer seemed to take it for granted.

"Has he done any more running?"

"Morgan? No. He says he's going to wait until the weather gets cooler."

"We've still got Indian Summer, but now's the time, if he's serious. Is he serious?"

"You'll have to ask him. What do you have for us? You're not exactly bubbling with the effort of holding it back."

Morgan set two fresh black coffees and a cappuccino down on the table, shunting the empty cups to the side, and settled onto his chair.

"Shoot," he said. "What have you got for us?"

"Well, what about my pubic hair?"

Morgan glanced away.

"Good question," said Miranda. "What about it? How did a single hair end up in Dieter Kurtz's beard."

"Kinky," she responded. "Maybe he put it there, like an eighteenth century fop adding a beauty spot. It was part of his grooming strategy, he was always very well groomed; place a hair, just so, ah, divine. Perhaps he had a collection."

"And where would he have got them? Yours, in particular?"

"Miranda, you don't seriously expect me to answer that? How can I? I mean, here, look," she held out an imaginary strand of hair in her fingers. "Yours! Now where did this come from? Perhaps your bedroom on

Briar Hill Island. Perhaps we were lovers, it is a keepsake of love. Maybe I rummaged through your laundry basket. I mean, how would I know? He was a very strange man. But, ah, yes, I think I know where you're going with this."

"Do you?"

"Well, if I, um, parted company with it, there, at the crime scene…"

"Yes."

"No. You would have found others, there would have been more than one little errant fellow on deposit. No, that couldn't be it. An unusual idea, though. Talk about death by misadventure. Who did it come to first, you or your partner?" She turned to Morgan. "You're not saying much, Detective."

"No," said Morgan. His mood had shifted. "I'm listening."

"And what are you hearing."

"It's what I'm not hearing."

"And what are you *not* hearing?'

"Any concern on your part that you might be held responsible for Kurtz's murder."

"And what does that tell you?"

"That you know who did it."

"Really."

"Really."

"And who would that be?"

"I can't tell from your attitude whether you feel absolutely certain we won't solve this case, or if you're simply as indifferent to the outcome as you seem to be about the old man's death."

"Those are not mutually exclusive."

"No, but if we can prove you know who the killer is and you're not telling us, that is a chargeable offence."

"Conspiracy?"

"Accessory."

"Felonies and misdemeanours; in for a pound, in for a penny. Well, then, I hope you find me nothing more than a stone-hearted bystander. Meanwhile, are you up for some gossip? I have things to tell you."

She was irrepressible. They both nodded assent.

"The Rector has been fired! It's confirmed."

"And you came to share the news?" asked Miranda, knowing for certain it would take more than that to make Jane Latimer leave her academic sanctuary and walk over to find them here. *Whatever it is, it's something she wants to say in person,* she thought. *She needs to see our reactions or have us bear witness to something.*

"What will happen to him?" asked Morgan.

"Oh, he's very well established as a scholar. Impeccable credentials. The Board of Governors will write a diplomatic letter, suggesting there were differences in administrative policy but that Felix Swan is held in their highest esteem. Lionel will write the letter, he is adept at moral obfuscation as the lubricant of effective management. Felix will find a secure post at a smaller university desperate for the prestige of an international name on their roster."

"Has there been an announcement?" asked Miranda.

"No. Felix told me himself this morning."

"Was he upset?"

"Devastated. As soon as he walked into my office and closed the door behind him, I knew what had happened. He is a very big man and he shrank. By the time he sat down, he seemed as small and vulnerable as a hurt child."

"Did he say why he was being let go?"

"There is only one way you can dislodge someone from a tenured position. The Rector serves at the pleasure of the Board, but Felix was also given an academic appointment, and you don't get to fire an academic except for extreme moral turpitude."

"And what is considered extreme?" said Morgan.

"I suppose something depraved or deviant enough that it would interfere with teaching or compromise research."

"Or would reflect badly on the institution?"

"No, professors do that all the time! On the other hand, senior administrators are expected to radiate sweetness and light, that's how we bring in the bucks."

"How deviant? Pedophilia?" asked Morgan.

"Probably not on its own. Since university students are generally beyond the pedophile's range of interest, no. I can think of convicted pedophiles who still have tenure. Murder would do it, especially spousal murder, but spousal abuse would not, since that doesn't impact directly on research or teaching."

"What you're saying is there's no rhyme or reason."

"Exactly. Members of the Canadian professoriate have done hard time in jail without losing tenure. So, even murder in theory might be insufficient grounds to let someone go."

"Did Felix explain?" Miranda looked Jane Latimer straight in the eye. What was the extent of this woman's emotional commitment to Felix Swan?

"Indirectly. He wept. He insisted Dieter Kurtz was responsible. He said we are all still in the old man's thrall, death has not limited his influence. He blamed Professor Kurtz for Li Po's suicide and for Hermione's ignominious end."

"Ignominious!" Miranda interjected. "I thought it was quite romantic, dying in her life-long lover's arms."

"She had a bad heart. They had not been 'sexually active' for quite some long time."

"Really?"

"Hermione's death was erotic euthanasia. Although Kurtz's lingering malevolence was in polar contrast to Li Po's devotion, I think Li Po was the instrument of both their wishes. And Hermione's as well."

"That gives a whole new meaning to sex."

"Doesn't it. A lethal activity."

"And Li Po? What about him? Was he driven to drown himself by some mysterious power from beyond the grave?"

"He hasn't been buried yet," said Morgan.

"Nobody's dug the hole," said Miranda.

"We just haven't dug it up," said Morgan. "It's there."

"Yes he was," said Jane Latimer, a little bewildered by their allusion to holes.

"Li Po? Driven?" said Miranda. "You don't believe he died by his own hand?"

"By his own hand, yes, but not necessarily by his own

will."

"I would say everything about the way he died suggested a man in complete control of his actions," said Morgan. "Not only did he embrace death, he did so with consideration for his friends, drowning in shallow water, anchoring his body to the piling. He died with grace."

"Morgan, he drowned in a boathouse with stones in his pockets," said Miranda, then turning to Jane Latimer, she asked: " You feel Kurtz drove him to do it?"

"No. Not drove him. Dieter Kurtz shaped his life, particularly in his final years. Dieter knew more about him than any of us. It was the revelations through Dieter's death that filled out the contours of Li Po's life. I would say Dieter Kurtz released Li Po from *not* knowing. That is what Kurtz held over him, knowing things about his life that even Li Po, himself, did not know. In dying, Dieter Kurtz set Li Po on a course that led inevitably to death."

"That is one of the more convoluted exegeses of a relationship I've heard in some time," said Morgan. "And you completely leave out the fact that Kurtz himself did not die of his own choosing, he was murdered."

"Don't you think sometimes, Detective, a person anticipates his own murder, even plans for it, makes it virtually inevitable?"

Miranda and Morgan looked at each other. Morgan took a tentative sip of his coffee, although it was room temperature. Miranda downed the remains in her cup. This went beyond anything they had talked about before. It is commonplace in situations of domestic violence to find patterns of co-dependency. In less obvious ways, they had found victims of murder sometimes enact roles that facilitate their own deaths. Usually, it was a matter of pursuing dangerous behaviors. Occasionally, reconstruction of a crime revealed a victim who backed the killer to the wall, leaving no alternate. However, the idea that someone might intentionally construct events so that his premeditated murder was bound to occur, that was a novel suggestion.

"You think he knew he was going to die?" Miranda asked.

"Yes," said Jane Latimer.

"Because he was an old man." suggested Morgan.

"That too," said Jane Latimer. "I think Dieter Kurtz lived with the awareness of his own mortality. Knowing he would die made his life both authentic and of negligible importance. *Everything counts, nothing matters.* Applied existentialism, a philosophy of survival. Somewhere between Heidegger and Sartre, although he despised both, and Camus even more. Did he know he was going to be murdered? I don't think it would have surprised him. Did he literally bring it on? A good question."

"With no answer, apparently," said Miranda. "One could almost imagine, Jane, that you are thoroughly enjoying all this."

"Objectivity is an illusion, Miranda. I thought you would know that by now."

"Oh yes," said Miranda, "I do."

"What I see shapes how I see."

Miranda countered: "How you see shapes what you

see."

"As with you and Morgan in Muskoka."

There was a protracted pause. Miranda and Morgan exchanged glances; Jane Latimer drained the last of her cappuccino. Then Miranda picked up the conversation.

"What's your other news?"

"Other news?"

"You said you have things to tell us—things, plural."

"Well, let's see. Lionel and Jennifer Pluck are having an affair."

"What!" said Morgan. "That's unseemly."

"Unseemly!"

"Inappropriate."

"That's what she said," Miranda quipped.

"They're not father and daughter," said Jane Latimer, struggling to make sense of the joke.

"No, they're not," said Miranda. "And we can prove it."

"He's old enough to be her father," said Morgan. "She actually thought he was her father. It smacks of incest."

"Don't be absurd, Morgan. You're jealous on David's behalf."

"How so?" said Jane, puzzled by the connection. "Young Sir David? How does he fit in?"

"He doesn't," Miranda was quick to answer.

"He does," said Morgan, wishing to steer Jane Latimer away from the truth. "Didn't you see the way they were hanging out. Young David was clearly infatuated. It seemed like she was returning the affection. Obviously, she was humouring him. He's a very attractive young man. There seems to have been a radical shift on Jennifer's part."

"Very Greek, in reverse," said Miranda. "The father becomes lover; Jennifer's affections are nothing if not facile."

"That's harsh," said Morgan.

"I said facile, not fickle. And I'm not judging, I'm observing. So where does this leave young David?"

"Out of the loop," said Morgan with a hint of relief.

"His mother is in town? That's my other bit of news."

"That's interesting," said Miranda. "Isn't it, David?"

Morgan said nothing.

chapter twenty-seven
The Thief

Morgan settled in for an evening of reading. He had run, with walking intervals, for an hour through the intersecting ravines that connect disparate parts of the city and come back physically exhausted but alert. He had decided to keep up a running regimen without announcing it to anyone. Then if he quit it was no one's concern but his own.

He liked the mental process as he moved over the network of paths that allowed ideas and images to sift through his brain laterally, without regard for coherence or relevance. It was a new thing for Morgan, to have the body override thinking with its own urgency. It was liberating. Now, he looked forward to picking up in a book about ancient Persia where he had left off, almost a year ago. He wanted to understand more of the cultures that produced the exquisite antique tribal carpets he admired in books and on the net. Not being able to afford even the meanest among them did not mean he could not refine his appreciation.

The telephone rang. He contemplated letting the answering machine deal with it. The telephone continued to ring. Miranda had stayed late at the office. She was catching up on paperwork, trying to turn their Muskoka weekend into a police report. Perhaps Miranda was calling before she went home, anxious to talk about their afternoon encounter with Jane Latimer. Possibly more information had come through about Kurtz, confirming him as the agent of his own demise. Perhaps David Jenness had reconciled with Jennifer, and Miranda had to report how devastated Lionel Webb was, losing out to his young protégé.

The answering machine clicked on.

"Hello. Hello David?"

He picked up the receiver.

"Hello," he said.

"David?"

"Yes."

"It's Sue."

"Susan."

"Yes, Susan."

"How are you." He said this as a greeting, not a question.

"How are you?" she asked. What she meant was, how is your life?

"I'm fine," he said.

"Good."

"How are you?" he said.

"I'm well."

"Young David, he is very impressive. I like him."

"Yes," she said. "I knew you would."

"He's a very impressive young man."

"Yes, I hoped you would like him."

"He's not at all like me, is he?"

"You were impressive in your own way."

"And the rest is history."

"David, can we get together?"

"If you want."

"Don't you?"

"I'm not sure."

"We don't have to."

"What about tomorrow."

"It's your town, you tell me where."

"Where are you calling from?"

"Lionel Webb's, on something called with false modesty the Bridle Path."

"My goodness, you're staying with Webb?"

"David has an apartment. I'm staying with David. It's over the carriage house."

"There's a restaurant on the ground floor at Hazelton Lanes. It's in Yorkville, dead centre of Toronto. Twelve-thirty. How would that be?"

"Excellent, David. It will be good to see you."

"You too, Sue.

"Bye, then."

"Sue."

"Yes?"

"Maybe we should talk now, maybe when we see each other, face to face, it won't be the same."

"It won't be the same, David. We'll be fine."

"Yeah. It's good to hear your voice."

"And yours, David. See you tomorrow."

She hung up. Morgan hung up. He walked upstairs to the loft, then back down and into the bathroom, then into the kitchen, as if he were looking for something. He sat down on the blue sofa and turned on the television. As soon as it warmed up, he switched it off. He went into the kitchen and got himself a beer which he brought back out to the living room, drinking from the bottle. He ran the cool bottle over his forehead. He turned off the lights and watched the evening sky expand over the city in a great luminescent canopy. He wanted to weep but no tears would come. He set the beer down and lay back on the sofa. He hoped she would turn up at the restaurant alone.

Morgan's telephone rang, shattering his dream. He was plummeting through luminescent air, then suddenly he was fully clothed on the sofa, grasping a telephone to his ear in the dark.

"Hello," he said, expecting Susan's voice.

"Morgan?"

"Miranda. You okay?"

"Yes, I'm okay, not exactly. I'm in a bit of trouble."

"Trouble? It's the middle of the night, of course, you're in trouble. What's wrong."

"I'm in jail."

"You're what?"

"Jail."

"Metaphorically speaking?"

"Really."

"Really? What time is it? Where are you? With *whom?*"

"Whom! It's not funny, Morgan. I'm a guest of the OPP, Cambridge detachment."

"You're actually in jail?"

"They're requesting my cooperation."

"At three in the morning?"

"It's almost three-thirty. Cooperation means they're holding me, pending clarification."

"Without laying charges. They can't."

"I am being voluntarily detained."

"There's an oxymoron. It'll take me an hour. Damn, I'll have to pick up a car. I should be there before five. You need anything? Pajamas?"

"I came without my purse."

"Where, why?"

"Waldron. I got a call. I was in a hurry, frazzled. There was a B&E at my mother's house. I rushed off without my purse."

"No identification?"

"Nothing that says I'm a cop. I don't want to get Rufalo involved. This is a private affair."

"Much damage?"

"To the house? Not really."

"Why on earth are they holding you?"

"Morgan, I'm waiting. My Glock was in the glove

compartment. They found it."

"It's police issue."

"Apparently not if you don't have papers to prove it. It's a gun, I'm driving a vintage Jag. I'm disturbingly beautiful. And they've recovered stolen property."

"What!"

"Yeah."

"Gotcha. Sit tight."

Morgan hung up, rose from the sofa still dressed in yesterday's clothes. His initial alarm had turned to amusement. He took the time to shave and change. What had she got herself into? This should be worth a long drive in the dead of night, or at least, he revised, an hour's drive in the very early morning.

He picked up a car at headquarters. He had never owned one and hated driving. There was almost no car traffic on the 401. Transports rolled along like trains, piercing the darkness with their oncoming lights, and leading ahead in an undulating ribbon of red dots. Morgan settled in at the speed of his endless entourage; he was not comfortable going faster than the trucks and they would not tolerate him going slower, riding his bumper if he did not keep up.

Stolen property?

Knowing there was a mix-up, Morgan was not concerned. This would get straightened out in short order. Miranda was many things, but she was not a thief.

His mind drifted. Thoughts of his partner dissipated and re-formed around an elusive image of Susan Croydon. He tried to envision her as a woman of forty-two. At first in his mind she looked like Miranda. Then she looked like someone else, stunningly attractive with copper-red hair, in her early twenties. He could not quite see her directly amidst the crowded memories of their time together but he knew exactly how she would be. It was not her appearance that haunted him but her sweet forbearance of his earlier selves, as he had tried on one personality after another in his cavalier search for someone to be.

It was not that he had no personality back then; it was that he did not trust the personality he had. He had graduated from university, moved on from his Cabbagetown roots, extricated himself from an undramatically dysfunctional family, always a loner with no one to affirm or deny his progress as a human being. Then he had discovered Susan—on a fifth floor in Knightsbridge, a house converted into a warren of bedsitters, and by now undoubtedly transformed into a stack of luxury flats.

One night, months after they had been together, she came to the pub where he was working; it was nearly closing time. She had to work the next day, so this was unusual. The woman working the bar with him exclaimed on her beauty. Morgan still remembered the woman's name, Shimkovitz, Mrs. Shim. He couldn't remember her first name. She was married to a Polish flyer, he was a tout at a race track. Pimlico? Morgan never met him. Susan waited until Morgan was finished and had cleaned up. They walked back towards Beaufort Gardens together, holding hands. This too was unusual.

It was early spring.

"You want to walk down by the Thames?" she had asked.

They were on Brompton Road. The Embankment was more than a mile away. The air was mildly acrid but the damp illuminated darkness of London at night was infinitely inviting.

"Sure," he said.

They walked quietly, passing a few other couples. When they got to the river, they leaned over the stone railing and stared down into the dark moving water.

"David?"

"Yes."

"You know how there are moments that you know you'll remember the rest of your life? There's nothing special about them, they're just moments."

"Yeah."

"Sitting on the front steps when you were four. Looking out a train window when you were seven. The teacher catching your eye with a smile. Crying, and you don't remember what for. A billboard in the tube, a pattern of sky, a stranger's stare."

"Yeah," said Morgan. "I know what you mean."

"Just for an instant, you're not watching yourself. You're inside, one-hundred percent, the sole occupant."

He did know exactly what she meant. It frightened him that this was how people defined their lives. Not by the dramatic events, the tumultuous or triumphant events, the soul-shaping events. But by ordinary moments.

"I want this to be like that," she said.

They walked with the current.

"David, do you realize how far we've come?"

"?"

"There's Boadicea's statue. We'd better turn back."

The warrior queen gleamed in the lights of the city rising from the depths of the Thames.

"Okay."

"Should we get a cab?"

"No," he said. "Let's walk. I'd like to walk."

"Me too."

"It's already tomorrow," said Morgan. "You're going to be tired."

"*Frankly, dear David,*" she said in a throaty Clark Gable voice, with an English public-school twist, "*I don't give a damn.*"

Morgan shuddered in the gloom of the car. He wondered if Susan still remembered that moment they shared along the Thames Embankment that was somehow more precious than all their evenings huddled in front of the gas fire in his room or hers, exchanging secrets. It was precious because time changed everything as they both got older, but not that moment, it stayed the same. For him. Did it for her? What would she be like at forty-two? A widowed baroness, the mother of a handsome son who was the same age they had been when he was conceived. Morgan had fallen in love with her after they parted and was still in love with the young woman she was, and perhaps with the young man he had been.

Miranda was sitting with her feet up on a desk in the OPP office, chatting amiably when Morgan walked in. At a glance, he knew the book by her knees must be the missing *Sylva Sylvarum* from Kurtz's house. Not the facsimile, not the fake. The real thing.

"Hi, Morgan. Glad you could make it. This is Bill, this is Sharon. And this," she said, nudging the book towards him with her leg, "This is what's causing all the trouble."

"And the Glock in the glove compartment," added the officer Morgan presumed to be Sharon. She was chirpy and attractive. Bill had a paunch and looked tired.

Morgan nodded at the two OPP officers and carefully picked up the book. "What's the charge?"

"Possession of stolen property," said Sharon. "We haven't written it up yet, we were waiting for you."

He turned to Miranda:

"You realize we're going to have to drive home in two cars."

"You drove!"

"How else. Auggie and I plummet, we don't do lateral flights."

"I'm glad you and your saint could spare us some time."

"So what happened?"

"What happened is, I got a call just after I got home around midnight. Someone had broken into my mom's place. I became inordinately flustered."

"Inordinately?"

"Violated."

"Violated?

"For Christ's sake, Morgan, my childhood had been invaded."

He hadn't expected such an extreme reaction. He knew her version of Waldron was fraught with a tangle of memories, some good and some of them dreadful. Frantic with confusion, she would have jumped into her car, a macabre souvenir of the horrors she'd endured, and come straightaway. Like a moth to a burnt out candle.

"Why didn't you call me?" he said.

"I should have."

For a moment it seemed like the OPP weren't there, like they were in a well-lit room on their own. Then reality intruded.

Sharon coughed. Bill swivelled in his squeaking chair and returned to his original position. Miranda glanced at them and smiled, but addressed Morgan:

"When I got to the house, the place was a mess, but this wasn't a professional job. Nothing was missing except the colour TV."

"Aren't they all, these days."

"Yeah, well it was gone, like a token theft to establish a motive. But vandals usually vent anger at the world, smear excrement, pee on the beds, you know, leave obscene graffiti, tear up family pictures, and apart from a broken window in the door, there wasn't much damage. Whoever did it just littered books all over the floor."

"So, it was an attack against literacy."

Morgan glanced at the leather bound copy of *Sylva Sylvarum*.

"That was on the mantel, lying on its side. It was meant to be seen. I assume it's the one we posted as missing after Jennifer brought in the bogus copy."

"Ask her about the gun," said Sharon to Morgan.

"I already told you," said Miranda. "I rushed out without my purse, I never go anywhere without my purse but I did. And the Glock just happened to be in the glove compartment."

"Isn't that against regulations?" said Bill.

"Yes, it is," said Morgan. "Don't worry, I'll see that she answers for that."

"And do you in fact have credentials yourself?" said Sharon.

Morgan showed her his credentials. She passed them to Bill. He scrutinized them, then handed them back.

"So you can vouch for her," he said.

Morgan shrugged.

"Who noticed the missing book?" Morgan asked.

"I did," said Miranda.

"Does that sound like guilty behavior to you?" said Morgan, addressing the room.

"Yes, actually, it might," said Sharon. "She knew we'd figure out it was stolen, she's a cop, so she feigned surprise to cover herself."

"Sounds convincing to me," said Morgan.

Bill nodded in solemn affirmation. He liked the way the interrogation was going. Sharon was relaxed, Miranda was tired and wanted to go home.

"Look," said Morgan. "Somehow this book got here on its own."

"Not likely," said Bill, who took him literally.

"No," said Morgan. "But consider what you have. A book that was reported missing by the same person you are now holding for possession. Who called it in, anyway, the burglary in progress?"

"Mrs. Tilt," said Miranda. "By the time I got there, it wasn't in progress. The cops were there. I walked in, they arrested me."

"Who's Mrs. Tilt?"

"Next door," said Miranda. "She called the OPP, she gave them my number in Toronto."

"So there's no doubt who you are?"

"Not in my mind. No, apparently not. Is there?" Miranda said, turning to Sharon, who smiled, and Bill, who rolled his eyes.

"Okay," said Morgan. "The scene was clearly set for the book to be discovered. Who were the investigating officers?"

"They're back out on the road," said Sharon.

"Did they know the book was stolen?"

"No," said Miranda, sheepishly. "I told them."

"Well done," he responded.

"Or she was trying to deke us out," said Bill.

"There you go," said Morgan. He was smiling at Sharon.

Miranda became aware that Morgan was flirting with the OPP officer, who was young and quite pretty, in spite of a figure so slender the uniform looked borrowed.

"Morgan, I want to go home," Miranda said.

"Okay," Morgan said. "Tell you what, how about professional courtesy. You let us go, I mean you can't hold one of us without the other, we're partners to the end. You let us go, we'll sign for the book. It's material evidence in a criminal investigation. Should you wish to press charges at a later date, okay, but we'll be really pissed off. I'm sure that won't happen."

"Not if you can explain why someone would go to all this trouble to implicate your friend."

"The crime we're dealing with is murder. Someone wants her compromised; not seriously, just enough to catch our attention."

"How much is it worth?"

"The book?"

"The book."

"Maybe ten, maybe twenty thousand."

"Morgan, you blew it!" exclaimed Miranda. "Now they'll never let me go."

"No kidding," said Bill. "Hey, take it away. If it's material evidence, you'd better get it out of here."

"Twenty thousand," exclaimed Sharon. "Wow, you city police play in the big leagues. And we thought it was overdue from the library."

She spoke in such a soft and insinuating voice that Morgan nearly missed the sarcasm. Miranda did not. She knew from the beginning that Sharon was amusing herself on a slow night. Bill was sufficiently humourless to go along with it, but he was becoming bored. When they realized the stakes were higher than they'd thought, the game lost its appeal. Sharon slid the Glock across the table to Miranda. She carefully placed the book inside a plastic bag and handed it to Morgan. He signed for the book and together he and Miranda walked out into the early morning.

Driving towards the rising sun, Morgan leading in the police car and Miranda following in her British racing green Jag, they each struggled to stay alert. Miranda was exhausted. She had played along; there was nothing mean-spirited about what had happened. Still, she could not help wondering, if she had not had the right answers, the right credentials, what would it be like, caught up in a web of incriminating circumstances, at the mercy of whim and indifference?

Morgan wondered why she always referred to the Waldron house as her mother's. It was hers. Her mother was dead; her father had died when she was a teenager. Her sister in Vancouver wasn't interested in the family home and had signed over her share—Miranda suspected this was a gesture of disapproval, since her sister was a professional, married to a professional, with children, and Miranda was a cop, single, no children, with a modest income and no prospects apart from rising to an administrative post, the thought of which appalled her. Actually, she had Jill, but Jill was not her real child, as her sister had pointed out in a tone that somehow suggested Jill herself was not real.

Morgan periodically checked for Miranda in his rearview mirror. The sun in his eyes made it difficult to keep track, as traffic thickened in the morning rush towards gridlock.

They turned down the Allen Expressway and went their separate ways at Eglinton. There was to be a funeral service in Hamilton that evening for Hermione McLeod. They had agreed to drive down together. Their motives were mixed. It was difficult to say whether they were going professionally or in genuine tribute to a woman they liked. Or both. They were not aware of a service for Li Po. They expected his obsequies would be a private affair.

A reception was to be held back in Toronto following the funeral.

"At Marie Lachine's?"

"No, at Jane Latimer's."

"She's in charge."

"She is, and she isn't."

chapter twenty-eight
Hazelton Lanes

Morgan arrived early at the restaurant in Hazelton Lanes. He ordered a Perrier and waited. He had gone home for a couple of hours sleep but he felt strangely anxious. He worried that somehow they would have nothing to say to each other. She might be disappointed, and relieved that she had made a life for herself without him. He might find her matronly. The person she would have to be, to be Sir David's mother, did not coincide in his mind with the girl with the auburn-red hair and dark hazel eyes.

He was sitting at a courtyard table and when she approached from the side he jumped to his feet and thwapped his head against the parasol. He grinned foolishly and held out his hand. She stepped beyond the proffered hand and embraced him in a long and affectionate hug, then held him at arms' length and surveyed his face, while suppressing on her own face an expression somewhere between tears and laughter. He leaned forward and gently kissed her on the lips. He had forgotten to make an evaluation of her appearance; she simply looked like Susan, only older.

"Did you order already?" she asked, making it clear they could dispense with conversational initiatives and settle right in.

"No," he said. "Do you want to start with a nice Ontario wine, Henry of Pelham riesling. Chilled, it's a genuine treat."

"Let's. Do we have time, do you have to go back to work?"

"I've got a funeral this evening."

"A funeral?"

"One of the Bacon Society. She died at Lionel's cottage."

"Oh, of course. I gather she died suddenly. It was quite lovely, the old in one another's arms. She was nearly eighty."

"That's what death is. It's always sudden."

She looked at him quizzically.

Thinking she wanted clarification, he went on: "Dying may be brief or protracted; but death, well, you're either alive or you're dead. It's sudden, one way or another."

"David," she said. "I do understand. But I was just thinking how strange it is that your life's work is, for want of a better word, 'murder.' The rest of us speak of death as if it were a rare orchid, and for you, it's a wildflower.

Sorry, that's silly. I've been thinking about you. Using flower imagery, I suppose. It's safer that way."

Morgan could think of nothing to say.

She collapsed the brief moment of silence. "David told me all about Lionel's cottage; it sounds like a palace."

"More like a castle. With a lot of verandahs."

"Opening onto the great Canadian wilderness!"

"Muskoka's a far cry from wilderness; it is what you can do to nature with money."

"Like the gardens at Versailles."

"Not really." That seemed abrupt. "You're looking wonderful, Susan."

"Not Sue?"

"Sue, you look wonderful."

"You too, David. Or should I call you Morgan. It seems everyone here calls you Morgan."

"Everyone?"

"My David, Lionel. I've met Porrig and Rafe, they call you Morgan. And Dr. Latimer and the colossal Professor Swan, they dropped in for tea yesterday, and everyone speaks of you by your last name."

"They speak about me, do they?"

"You and your partner. They say she's very beautiful, not glamourous but very beautiful. One of those rare creatures, a beautiful woman who doesn't behave like she's beautiful. That was Dr. Latimer who said that, and she's rather beautiful herself, isn't she? And enjoys being beautiful. And you're investigating them all for murder."

"We're investigating a murder, and they are potential suspects."

"Isn't that redundant, David. Shall we order?"

They ordered salad plates.

"Not really," he said, picking up the conversation. "Since we haven't got enough to lay charges, they're still only suspects in potential."

"Including David?"

"He's the least likely."

"But possible?"

"Anything's possible. There's been a murder."

"Dieter Kurtz." She said this as if the victim might be in doubt.

"Did you know him?"

"Of course I knew him."

"He was your husband's friend."

"And mine."

"Yours? You were a friend of Dieter Kurtz?"

"Yes I was," she answered and as she looked deeply into his eyes he remembered his desperation, the last time they had been sitting together in a Toronto restaurant. It was two weeks before his marriage to Lucy. He had written, saying he was getting married. He needed to talk to her. Sue had flown over. He tried to tell her how much he loved Lucy. She had listened.

"David," she had said. "Do you want to *be* married?"

"I don't know," he had responded in a tone that he hoped conveyed tragedy and not just pathos.

"Getting married is an event," she said. "Like giving birth. Being married is a condition, like being a parent. I think perhaps you're wrapped up in the event."

"That," he said, "that's why I wrote you."

"Do you want to be married?"
"To you?"
"To anyone, David."
"Would you marry me?"
"Not at the moment."
"No?"
"Are you sure?"
"Given your anguish over your impending marriage to another woman, I'm quite sure."

She had reached across the table and held his hands in hers, and stared deeply into his eyes. They had gone back to her hotel and they made love the way they always had, as friends not as lovers. There was intimacy, there was affection, but there was retraint, and little passion. There was nothing dangerous about their relationship. They had fallen asleep together, both realizing Morgan's marriage to Lucy was as inevitable as was its eventual doom.

The next morning, after Morgan left to check in at Police Headquarters with his partner at the time, he couldn't even remember his name, Sue had telephoned Air Canada, changed her flight, and was high over the Atlantic by the time Morgan called her at the hotel, hoping to meet before dinner.

He looked at her now, her hazel eyes were enhanced by the crinkles at their edges, they had even more depth. He reached across and took her hands in his.

"Do you remember when I proposed to you?"
"I remember when you did not propose to me."
"Yeah."

"Yuh," she said, parodying his terse Canadian inflection. "Yuh, I do remember, eh. And how was your marriage?"

"Deadly. How was yours."

"Good."

"Nigel?"

"He was a lovely man and a very good father."

"Yeah."

"Yes he was."

"Tell me."

"He looked after me when I was pregnant."

"While I was running with the bulls in Pamplona."

"Yes, while you were running with the bulls in Pamplona, exploring yourself from one end of Europe to the other."

"Cynical?"

"Not at all, David. *Je ne regrette rien.* I loved you then. And I knew I would always love you."

"Do you?"

"I also knew we would be very bad for each other. I let you think too much, especially about you. You let me feel too much, especially about you. Does knowing that make me cynical, or simply a realist. Nigel was a good person, David. He was in his forties, one of those men you might have thought would never marry. He came down from Oxford fully formed. Then he surprised everyone by marrying someone young and pretty who had a baby and who was apparently drawn to his maturity and sexual equanimity."

Morgan was running through his mental thesaurus.

Did she mean evenness or indifference, was the old boy self-possessed or asexual? The *old boy* was Morgan's age now.

"He loved me. He had grace, not grace under pressure—nothing macho about him. He simply did not admit pressure into his life. And he was actually a charming lover and I stayed faithful to him. He was not very worldly, he was good-natured, and hopelessly innocent."

"Innocent."

"That kind of precarious innocence that comes from an inability to see bad in others. He was a good man, but he never would have married me, were it not for Dieter Kurtz. It simply would not have occurred to him. It would not have occurred to him that he could be loved, and for all our years together he was in a state of constant surprise that I did, I did love him."

Morgan felt a twinge of jealousy which he dismissed as absurd.

"Kurtz brought you together?"

"He used to drop by at the office. He had been Nigel's tutor at Oxford and whenever he came back to London, which he did almost every year, flying over from Canada, he and Nigel would go out on the town."

"Carousing!"

"Nigel would not have known how to carouse. They would dine at Simpson's on the Strand, *mutton and Mouton*, as they said. Or if they were in a cozier mood, it was the Cheshire Cheese off Fleet Street."

"Off the Strand," Morgan corrected her.

"No, I think it's off Fleet Street, down past Aldwych

and St. Clement's church, along a wee narrow walkway."

Perhaps she was right. He remembered sitting on the bench in the Cheshire Cheese where Dr. Johnson had sat with Boswell, and generations later where Charles Dickens had dined on his own, but he didn't remember for sure how he got there. He wasn't sure if he'd been with her at the time.

"And then they would go to Nigel's club for Port and cigars," she continued. "I met him at the office. He took a liking to me, the summer I was pregnant, three months after that memorable early spring night along the Embankment."

"The night we walked all the way to Boadicea's statue?"

"Yes."

"That's when you got pregnant."

"Yes, David, that is the night I got pregnant. Do you remember, by the dawn's early light we made love—in my room, not yours. Very passionately. We weren't good lovers before, we were so very young, but that night we were the greatest lovers whoever conceived."

It all seemed very real to Morgan; still happening.

"And that summer Dieter came into the office and he knew immediately I was pregnant. I didn't tell him and I wasn't showing, but he knew. When Nigel appeared, Dieter surprised him by suggesting they take me along to dinner. Dear Nigel could not think why *not*, so off we went. Dieter knew I was pregnant, he also knew I was on my own. Intuitively, it seemed. We went to Simpson's and all three of us had mutton served up on a huge silver salver. That's hard to say: *huge silver salver*. They dropped me at Beaufort Gardens before going off to Nigel's club. Nigel was astonished that I lived across from their family townhouse. Dieter was staying with him. I had known Nigel lived there. I never told you. I don't know why. He was my boss. And I never told Nigel we were neighbours, either.

"He watched out for me after that, in an avuncular way. Sometimes he would drive me home from work. When David was born, he would bring us presents, drop them off with Mrs. Shimkovitz, he never came in. You returned from the Continent. Do you remember, we met at Madame Tussaud's Wax Museum? The Chamber of Horrors. Of course you remember. I'm not sure whether that was your macabre sense of humour or my own. Probably mine. Then you left. The next summer two things happened. One, I came over to see you on the eve of your wedding. You had fallen in love with me, but it was too late."

"And the second thing that summer?"

"The second thing was, following an evening out in London with Dieter and Nigel, after they went on to Nigel's club and talked through the night, the next day Nigel asked me to come into his office.

"'Dieter,'" he said to me in a soothing voice, 'Dieter and I were talking.'

"'Yes,' I said.

"'We were wondering if you would marry me?'

"'Nigel! Don't be absurd.' I said.

"'That's what I anticipated, I told him you would find my proposal ridiculous.'

"'Oh Nigel,' I said to him. 'Not ridiculous, not at all. It is very sweet.'

"'I would adopt David, of course. For a silly moment I thought he meant you. He had never called the baby by name; always referring to him as 'the baby,' or 'the little gaffer.' And of course he knew nothing about you. Only that you had gone.

"Then he said, 'Dieter suggested I should try to arrange having my own name put on his papers as the natural father.'

"'I've already done that,' I confessed.

"You know, the strange thing is, he hardly seemed surprised that I had already named him the father.

"I told him I owed him an explanation and he insisted I did not. It never occurred to him that he was vulnerable. I told him he was the only male I knew in London whose signature I regularly forged.

"'Ah,' he said. 'Good girl, good girl.'"

"Why didn't you use my name?" said Morgan.

"You weren't around. And I was not about to put 'father in Canada, precise whereabouts unknown.'"

Morgan was confused by her presentation of Dieter Kurtz as a friend of the family.

"Kurtz," he said, "he knew a lot about you, things that could have ruined your husband's reputation."

"Not really, David. Nigel was a lesser aristocrat, that's how he described himself, and he was not in politics. Our arrangement was hardly the basis of scandal."

"He could have prevented David's succession to the title when Nigel died—I'm not really comfortable calling him Nigel, I never met the man."

"Sir Nigel Jenness. He had seven names, actually, but Nigel will do."

"You never said he was Sir Nigel when we were together."

"When we were together! How quaint, David. We were *living* together."

"With separate rooms."

"And a shared bed. David, impoverished as we were, we had a choice of beds, yours or mine, but we occupied only one at a time."

Morgan stared off into a patch of blue sky defined by the parasols in the courtyard fluttering like carousels in the gentle breeze. There was only one other couple outside, despite the brightness of the day. People were eating inside because it was early autumn. He looked back at Susan, who was watching him with gentle curiosity.

"Kurtz could have prevented David's succession," he repeated.

"But why would he do that? He was very fond of David. He was in many ways his mentor."

"Manipulating, to bring him into Nigel's family."

"Not *into* Nigel's family! He *was* Nigel's family."

"And you, where did you fit in?"

"Morgan. Nigel and I, and David, your biological son, we *were* a family. Do not think that Nigel was any less than a father for all that he knew and all that he chose not to know. And Morgan, David and I are still a family."

She paused. She clearly did not mean to hurt him, but she could not allow him to make assumptions. "Dieter

Kurtz doted on David. He was kind to me. And he was a devoted friend for Nigel, the only person who could make Nigel feel that his life, puttering away at business, was in any way significant."

Morgan was baffled. Didn't she see the power Kurtz wielded in the lives of her family?

"Sue, when you told me about David, about the baby, we were in Madame Tussaud's, it was very unreal, and you were aggressively self-reliant."

"No need to be defensive, David. I was very young and I was scared, afraid you might actually want to marry me, although I'm not sure the possibility crossed your mind."

"You didn't say outright the baby was mine."

"I left you an escape, and you took it." She smiled. "David, whose else would have been the father?"

"You implied it was Nigel's. I had never met Nigel, he was your boss; I had to assume he was better for you than I was."

"Why?"

"Well, as it turned out, he was."

"With a little prodding from Dieter."

"I didn't skip out."

"No, I sent you away. You're not to feel guilty, David. If anything, I should feel guilty for preventing you from knowing your son, but I don't. You and I needed Nigel, we both needed him. All three of us did. You and David and I."

The waiter had brought coffees in tall glass mugs. Morgan sat back in his chair, sipping carefully to avoid scalding his lips. *Glass mugs are an invention of the devil,* he thought. Susan blew across the top of hers but did not try to drink.

"Dieter Kurtz shaped the course of my life," Morgan said, with a caustic edge to his voice. "My goodness."

"In part, he did, yes. Perhaps more than you imagine."

"There's more?"

"Well, he brought you back into my life. Or me into yours, if you'd prefer."

Morgan waited, his face frozen; her features were relaxed.

"Kurtz knew about me?"

"Yes, of course."

"You told him?"

"One didn't have to tell Dieter anything."

She smiled again and her eyes had a darkness to them, depths that swallowed up the green and brown and golden colours. They here hazel, like Miranda's, but mellow, not radiant, not piercing, they were gentle, forgiving the world, showing forbearance for the human condition, forgiving even him by showing affection that made it seem there was nothing to forgive.

"It wasn't hard to figure out, David. We weren't at all secretive, we lived across the boulevard from his friend, we came and went places together. For all your concerns about working out your identity, you were hardly anonymous. You had been his student, one of a thousand, but among the more memorable. He knew you before I did, Morgan. He might have recognized you across the boulevard in Beaufort Gardens, although he would have stayed in the shadows. He preferred it that way. And when you returned to Toronto, he watched your career from the ivory tower. Occasionally, obliquely, he would mention you. Just to let me know."

"Why?"

"Just to let me know." A slight flutter of emotion crossed her face. "He introduced Lionel into our lives. He arranged for David to stay with him on the Bridle Path."

She said this as if David were a guest with private quarters over the carriage house, not a boarder or an employee.

"But it took his death to bring us together," he said.

"Perhaps it did."

"The world is small, but not that small. He couldn't possibly know—oh, for God's sake, even if he planned his own murder—he couldn't know I'd be the cop on the scene."

"Couldn't he?" She seemed to be suggesting the possibility of Kurtz engineering the particulars of his own death was not out of the question. "He had already lowered the odds of you meeting your son from one in seven billion to one in, what, a few hundred, and given my eventual presence in the mix, an odds-on favourite. And, as it turns out, you and your beautiful partner are the lead investigators of homicide among the more high profile and potentially litigious segment of the Toronto population."

"Litigious? He was a retired Renaissance scholar!"

"And Lionel's friend. Lord Ottermead. But perhaps

The Dead Scholar

he was counting on proximity."

"Proximity!" Morgan exclaimed. "Like: David and I might have bumped into each other in McNally's Bookstore. I can see that. Instant recognition, of course. Your eyes, my chin."

"Why is it so difficult to concede that he wanted David to meet you?"

"He didn't know me."

"Not well. But he knew me."

"Not as an exemplary judge of character."

"As a woman who liked him."

"Sue, if you knew about me, why didn't we get together after my divorce?"

"How strange you should ask. I'm sure it never crossed your mind—I had become an inaccessible part of the historical past you're always reading about. And it never crossed mine. You were enthralled, I was practical—I had married Nigel not long after I got back to England. I learned to love him, you learned love didn't suit your character. Not then, perhaps never."

"You did love me, once."

"You happened to be the object of my unruly affections, yes. And I eventually learned to subdue them. Nigel and David and I, we had a very good life together. And you, from the lines on your face I can see you lead an interesting life, not good, perhaps, but interesting. A life of adventure, and that's what you always wanted."

"Is it? I don't remember."

"Yes you do, David. You remember everything."

They talked for another hour, until the waiter asked

them to settle their bill so he could go off shift. They walked back to Morgan's condo in the Annex and made love through the afternoon; leisurely, affectionate love until Miranda honked from the curb. She was there to pick him up for Hermione's funeral. Susan Croydon, Lady Jenness, lay still in his bed while Morgan careened around his bedroom, trying to get ready.

He was struggling to tie his tie, the only one he owned, when the doorbell rang and then the door rattled against the lock.

"Here, let me tie it for you," said Sue as she bounced up onto her knees on the bed, completely comfortable being naked, and motioned him to back against her so she could lean around and tie his tie from the rear.

"Windsor knot?"

"I guess."

"I know you're in there, Morgan," said Miranda in a muffled voice through the door. "Let's get a move on."

"Oh," said Sue. "Can I meet her!"

She was half-way down the stairs from the loft, stark naked, when Morgan caught her arm.

"Maybe now wouldn't be such a good time," he said.

"Oh please, David," she said, moving against him with a languorous shudder that nearly sent him toppling.

"Morgan, what the hell are you doing in there?" said Miranda's voice through the door.

"Please, David! I've heard so much about her. Is she as beautiful as they say, is she clever?" Sue spoke in a throaty whisper as she stepped by him down into the living room, and the light from the late afternoon streamed through the window and highlighted her supple body that had hardly changed in twenty years, sunlight gleamed from the coppery curls of her pubic mound as she pivoted towards him but made no move to the door.

"Morgan, I have a key, I'm coming in!" shouted Miranda.

Morgan looked at Sue, she was smiling her demure smile, the one she picked up from Botticelli's 'Birth of Venus.' Insouciant innocence, wistfully foreboding, and the key was rasping in the door-lock. He turned and fled into the bathroom.

After an interminable wait while he brushed his teeth, flossed, had a pee, and combed his hair with rapid jerky movements that hurt, he ventured out into the living room. Miranda was sitting on the blue sofa.

"Hey, are you ready? You didn't hear me so I let myself in."

"Where's—"

"What?"

He glanced up into the gloom of the loft, directly over Miranda. The lights had been turned out but the blinds admitted sufficient illumination that the shadowy image of a nude woman standing in a casually wanton pose distinguished itself from the darkness. He nodded nearly imperceptibly in her direction, then reached his hand out to Miranda, helping her up from the sofa.

"Come on," he said. "Hermione's waiting."

chapter twenty-nine

The Funeral

As they drove along the Queen Elizabeth Way towards Hamilton, Miranda noticed that Morgan seemed distracted. Unaccountably, she felt a pang of jealousy. Morgan was her partner and friend.

"So how did it go with your old flame?" she asked.

"My old flame? That's quaint. Fine."

"Fine. That's it? Fine!"

"Yeah, well, she's nice."

"Nice! I hope you don't ever describe me as *nice*!"

"Okay, she is lovely, vivacious, genteel, and, well, you know how it is with some people, we just picked up where we'd left off." The cliché suggested sarcasm, even if his tone didn't.

"Like no time had passed." She countered with sarcasm of her own.

"Like we had moved through time at exactly the same rate."

"Despite your very different lives."

"Despite our very different lives."

"Li Po would have liked that."

"About time?"

"Yes."

"He would have, wouldn't he."

She glanced over at him in the passenger seat. "We don't travel through time at the same rate, you know. None of us do." She glanced over again. "So, she's *nice*."

"She's very nice, Miranda. Sometimes *nice* is a big word."

"She's put on weight?"

"Not an ounce! She doesn't drink to excess, she doesn't fly into rages, she doesn't sleep around, she doesn't talk in clichés, she is a very nice person. We had a very nice time."

"You sound like Hemingway."

"Yeah, I try."

"Passionate and terse, nice combination, Morgan. So how did it really go?"

"She told me something interesting about Kurtz. We've got to rethink a bit."

"Like what, how so?"

"She liked him."

"Liked him!"

"He was a close friend of the family."

"Morgan, if that's true, why hasn't young Sir David spoken up?"

"And said what? He's never commented on Kurtz, one way or another."

"Exactly!"

They drove in silence for a while, then as they veered onto the off ramp into Hamilton, she looked over at him. He seemed miles away, gazing into the light of early evening as if there were things in his mind's eye she could not begin to imagine. Was it seeing his girlfriend from a time when he was reckless for adventure and emotionally constrained, was that what he was thinking, thinking about what might have been? Or was he dreaming about the way it was, the way he remembered it, when he lived with her in Knightsbridge? Or was he thinking about Dieter Kurtz, was he trying to put together the improbable story of the dead man's life? Was he trying to solve a murder?

She didn't disturb him. She knew the way to the funeral home and said nothing until they pulled into the parking lot. The building itself was a rambling gothic mansion, Victorian colonial, tarted up with a chapel and garage and a portico meant to set the bereaved so much in awe they would find their dead suitably honoured at whatever the cost. Miranda drew in a deep breath before getting out. When she stood up, she exhaled slowly.

"Okay," she said. "Let's do it!"

She led the way through massive double doors into the cheerfully somber foyer where a chrome stand supported a notice board with removable letters that spelled out Hermione's name, and directed the reader to the Arcadian Room. The main chapel was apparently booked for someone with more friends.

Miranda recognized most of the people assembled in an arc of chairs facing Hermione's open casket.

"My God, Morgan," she whispered as they sat down. "I didn't know they did that any more."

"Yeah," Morgan grimaced, but when an elderly woman behind them leaned forward and said in a pleasant voice, "She looks so natural, you'd think she was sleeping," Morgan could not restrain a smile.

Out of the side of his mouth, he whispered in an even quieter voice, presuming only Miranda could hear: "Tarted her up, didn't they?"

Miranda leaned close. "Be quiet," she said.

"How can she look natural with her head on a cushion that looks like a souvenir from Niagara Falls, surrounded by crushed satin, and with too much rouge. She looks bloody dead."

Miranda suppressed a giggle. "She is, Morgan. Be quiet."

Miranda gazed around, catching an eye here and there. The remaining members of the Bacon Society were present, with the singular exception of Simon Sparrow. Even Lionel Webb was there, sitting discretely apart from Jennifer Pluck. Actually, Miranda noticed with surprise, he was sitting next to the Rector, and Felix looked quite relaxed, for Felix, even if Lionel seemed a bit crowded. The only other person she recognized was Yijun Sung, confirming in her mind that the obsequies for his uncle Li Po were over and done with.

Otherwise, there was the expected scattering of old

people who turned out for the funerals of other old people to confirm they were still alive. Miranda observed them with affection, these people who were no longer shy in the presence of death. Neither of her parents had reached old age. Her father died when she was in her teens, and she had never really forgiven him for leaving. Her mother was hardly past sixty. She liked old people, she liked knowing how full their minds were, and she wanted to grow old herself. Not yet, but eventually.

Driving back to the reception in Toronto, Morgan announced, "So help me God, if anyone puts me on display in a box like that, I'll come back and haunt them. Or I just won't die."

"So you want a plain pine box, none of the trimmings."

"Nothing I wouldn't have been comfortable with when I was alive."

"Sounds reasonable. That should be the rule. What about Simon Sparrow?"

"He wasn't there."

"That's my point. Why not?"

"Even members of the Bacon Society have lives," said Morgan. "He's probably off trying to find himself in the Barren Lands."

"You know how you said your friend Lady Susan liked Kurtz? Does she have a particular reason to like him or is it just a personality thing?"

"Lady Jenness, actually. Dame Susan if the title were inherited."

"What on earth are you talking about, Morgan?"

"Susan. I think she genuinely liked him but, yes, she

had reasons. Why?"

"I told you about talking to Simon on the beach at Webb's place, didn't I? Well, he claimed Dieter Kurtz had screwed him around but it wasn't convincing. He said Kurtz helped him get his memoirs published."

"Sounds like a positive move."

"Except, according to Simon, he played a little loose with the facts."

"Simon did, or Kurtz?"

"Simon, and Kurtz knew, but encouraged him to publish."

"And Simon resented what?" said Morgan. "He wrote a version of his life, that's all any of us have, a version, you know. I'm not sure the facts are relevant. We'd all re-write the past if we could—to make what we become seem inevitable."

"Interesting, Morgan. Then why would Simon Sparrow not be grateful? I mean, he's a guy who would fade to transparency if he didn't have stories to tell, especially to himself."

"Did he fear Kurtz knew about his alternate lives, or did he fear what Kurtz didn't know?"

"Hey, Morgan, if no-one is inside a house of mirrors, are there reflections? Maybe that's what it's like to be Simon Sparrow; endless empty mirrors."

"Or only reflections."

He liked the notion of reflections without mirrors. They became absorbed in their own private thoughts until Miranda pulled up to the curb in front of Jane Latimer's house on Parkhurst, near Bayview and Eglinton. They were not sure if anyone else was there yet. They had left the funeral immediately after the service. It seemed unaccountably graceless to chat in front of an open casket, like whispering in front of a deaf person or describing colours to the blind. Now they sat in the car, waiting.

Someone knocked on the window on the passenger side. He was standing too close for his face to be seen, but they both recognized Simon Sparrow from the tentative way he presented himself. Morgan started to roll down the window, then thought better of it and opened the door. Awkwardly, he unfolded himself from the confines of the low-slung car and rose to his full height beside Simon.

As Miranda joined them, Jane Latimer wheeled into the drive with Hermione Mac, followed by a limousine with Lionel Webb, Jennifer Pluck, and David Jenness. Another car with Ralph at the wheel pulled in behind the Jag and disengorged Felix Swan from the passenger seat, followed by Padraig clambering out from the back. Presently, another car showed up with Yijun Sung and Marie Lachine, the most unlikely of cousins. With Jane in the lead, they all went in together.

Food was served from the refrigerator and drinks were served from a makeshift bar and a toast was made to Hermione M, and a separate toast to Li Po. Felix then proposed a toast to Dieter Kurtz. There was an awkward silence.

"Well, he's dead," said the Rector defensively.

"Yes, of course," said Hermione Mac. "We must drink to Dieter."

"To Dieter Kurtz," said Lionel Webb, taking command. They replenished their glasses and drank.

"And what about Francis Bacon?" said Padraig. "He's dead too. There's not a time limit, is there?"

So they all drank to the various dead and were in great good cheer. As they hived off into separate conversations, Miranda turned to Yijun Sung.

"Mr. Sung—or is it Mr. Yijun, I'm never sure.

"Please, just Sung, or if you prefer, Yijun."

"Tell me about your uncle."

"Yes of course. What do you wish to know?"

"We heard many stories in Muskoka about his travels in Europe, but not very much about his life in China."

"Yes. He taught at Lanchou University. His life was very quiet."

"Perhaps, but he seems to have been involved in the great historical events of your country."

"My country is Canada."

"I'm sorry, of China."

"Yes."

"But he lived quietly in Lanchou. Did you live there, before coming to Canada."

"Yes."

"Your father was his brother."

"No."

"No? I thought he was your uncle."

"Yes."

"Then, oh, of course, your mother was his sister."

"No."

"Perhaps you could be more forthcoming."

"Forthcoming? About what."

"Li Po was your uncle?"

"Yes."

"Was it an honorary title, then?"

Yijun Sung smiled. "Yes," he said.

"You were not related?"

"Yes."

"Uncle was an honorary title?"

"Yes."

"Yijun Sung, you are being intentionally inscrutable."

"Yes."

"Okay. Perhaps you would explain."

"There is nothing to explain."

"It is a riddle, then. A koan?"

"Yes, life is a riddle." He smiled again.

Since Miranda could think of no good reason to continue, she turned away, and as she did so, her interlocutor bowed. Is he being condescending with mock courtesy, or courteous, and mocking himself? She turned back to address him.

"Mr. Yijun Sung, did you know Dieter Kurtz?"

"Yes. He was my uncle's friend. I did not know him well."

"But you would describe him as Professor Li Po's friend, would you?"

"Yes."

"Interesting. Thank you." She excused herself and walked across the narrow room to pour herself another half-glass of white wine. It seemed prudent to drink only half at a time. Jane Latimer took the bottle from her hands and topped up her own glass.

"Here's to Hermione," said Jane

Miranda took a sip and set her glass down.

As soon as they had come in the door, Jane Latimer had taken off her suede jacket, revealing a sheer blouse cut astonishingly low. Miranda stared unabashedly into Jane's cleavage, looking to see if she could spy her belly button past the wispy twist of her bra. Slowly, she let her eyes rise up and over the mounded flesh of her breasts and felt a strange stir of excitement. It was not lust, for she had flirted with loving another woman in the past and found it distracting. It was admiration for a woman's ability to show herself off with such casual authority. Not brazen but bold. Sensual, very, but not sexy, at least not from Miranda's perspective, although she suspected men were not so judicious in their appreciation of exposed female anatomy.

When her eyes met Jane's, Jane smiled.

"It's a long story," said Jane.

"What is?" said Miranda.

"Your partner has given up running, I gather."

"What's a long story, Jane? Not my partner's running career."

"Have you noticed, runner's have a particular flush of good health. It's the capillaries beneath the skin. I can always tell a runner."

Miranda gazed at the woman's alabaster complexion, and again lowered her eyes to her breasts, then back to her face. "Tell me, Jane?" she said.

To her absolute surprise, Jane's eyes flooded over,

tears gathered, hovered, and rolled down her cheeks. She smiled as tears streamed against the full curve of her upper lip and slid around and into the corners of her mouth. She smiled and more tears flowed.

"Jane, is it something I said?" She paused. She had not really said anything of consequence. "I was staring, was that it?"

She couldn't help herself, she let her eyes fall again to Jane Latimer's breasts, following her line of vision down towards the hard plane of her stomach. Jane cupped her hands under her breasts and hoisted them so that their upper curves shimmered with highlights.

She rolled her eyes with affected insouciance and in a Mae West drawl she mouthed the words, "Not bad, eh, for a country girl!"

Miranda was confused. Jane was doing a playful parody of the voluptuous slut, but there was something in her manner that suggested ironic detachment, as if putting on the act was itself an act. Somewhere behind the silly vulgarity there was a serious subtext, one that Miranda could not quite read.

"Jane," she said, preparing to cross the lines of propriety. "Did Dieter Kurtz… ?" She looked around. Only Morgan was paying them any attention and he was keeping his distance, tending to a conversation with Simon and the D'Arcys. "Did he, were you… ?" She couldn't find the right words. *Raped* was too abrupt, *harassed* seemed trivializing, *abused* implied a relationship. "Were you, did he assault you?"

"Sexually?"

"Yes, did he assault you?"

"No, Miranda, never."

"I'm sorry. I thought perhaps... ."

"I don't know why I should tell you this," said Jane, looking furtively around the room as if the glare of her eyes would guarantee privacy. She drew the neckline of her blouse a little higher and smoothed the material. Miranda waited, leaning closer in a conspiratorial posture. Jane leaned forward.

"Dieter Kurtz gave me a safe place to be free."

This statement struck Miranda as exceptionally enigmatic. She looked puzzled.

"I don't know, Miranda. Some women can relate to this, others can't."

Miranda's confusion showed on her face. She furrowed her brow, hoping that would be sufficient encouragement for Jane to go on.

"I think you have been there, Miranda, you know what I'm talking about."

Miranda was baffled, but not bewildered; she was picking up something ominous and a sense of shared vulnerability.

"Miranda, I," Jane stopped herself. She reached out and took Miranda by the hand and led her to the staircase where they sat down, side by side, half way up. "When I first started working with Dieter Kurtz I was... I wrote my honours paper for Dieter... I came to him a wounded child in a ravaged body. No, trust me, at twenty I was ... damaged and grotesque.

"Early in my fourth year, I went into his office at Jesus

College. He told me to sit down, then he brushed by me and closed the door. I knew it was university policy for male professors to leave the doors open with female students. He sat down behind his desk and folded his hands in front of him.

"'So you want to write about Francis Bacon?' he said.

"I told him 'yes.'

"'You want to work with the notorious Professor Kurtz?' he said.

"Without flinching, I told him I did.

"'There are conditions,' he said. 'Expectations.'

"I had heard rumours, Miranda, but I had made myself so unattractive—I was sloppy, a mess, I wrapped myself in a cloak of hang-dog slovenliness—I could not believe he would be interested. In fact, I thought myself clever to have access to him where more desirable students might not.

"Apparently I was mistaken; apparently being repulsive did not afford immunity. I started to get up.

"' Sit!' he snapped, and I sat.

"'I will work with you, young woman. I will, and you will become very accomplished in your field. You will go next year to Oxford, and you will stay there until you have completed your Doctorate, I know people at Oxford, and then you will come back here, perhaps even to this college, and you will be a professor, yes!'

"He spoke with such authority! I stared at him, not knowing how to escape, and the scene imprinted itself in my brain, this man, taking charge of my life!

"'And my conditions? You will dress properly. You will

attend the gymnasium. You will walk straight. You will be a woman, yes! You will be proud. Nothing more I ask.'

"I stared at him—his statement was like a revelation, the one great revelation of my life, the one we dream will come, and fear will never come.

"'I will work on your mind,' he said. 'You have much intelligence. I have watched you for three years. You were abused, yes. By your father. You are deeply ashamed. You are very angry with yourself. With *yourself*! That is over, yes. The child is mother of the woman. No! The child is dead, and in the gymnasium and in the clothing boutiques and under my supervision, the woman is born. You have no money, yes. I will see that you have money. You may dress by convention or you may dress like a woman of the streets, I do not care, but you will never dress again like you are ashamed. Never. No more!'

"I looked down at myself. My clothes and my body were a grotesque disguise.

"I started to explain. I wanted him to understand.

"'No,' he said. 'No, no, no. I do not want to know things more than I know, Jane Latimer.'

"I was stunned. I did not even know he knew my name.

"'Jane Latimer, you will make us both proud.'

"I started to thank him, I wanted to explain, to justify, to clarify, he cut me off.

"'You will tell no one of this talk. It would ruin the reputation of the notorious Professor Kurtz. Here is your reading list. I have prepared it for you already. Go away now.'

"He was right about you, wasn't he?" said Miranda.

"That I had potential? Yes, apparently. That I had been abused? Yes, since I was nine, by my father."

"How did he know?"

"How do we know anything! He observed. That is the Prime Directive from Bacon, himself. All knowledge comes from observation."

"And about me," said Miranda. "You knew that I was abused. You knew."

"Yes, love, I observed."

"Not my father." Miranda turned and gazed into Jane's eyes. *Yes, no. Another time.*

"We will talk whenever you wish, or if you wish, never."

"And you became a new person," Miranda said.

"No, Professor Kurtz was wrong about that. I am the same person, an older version of the girl I was." She looked down at her breasts on display and continued. "I dress like this, I thrill to the display of my own sexuality, I flaunt my body, always in a context defined by Dieter Kurtz. He made it safe. He made being a woman a joyful thing and the hell with good taste. Miranda, vulgarity can be deliciously empowering. Some people counter their conventional lives in the privacy of prayer, or drink, or masturbation, or dreams. For me, this," she ran her hands up the length of her body, and when they passed over her breasts and reached her face she threw them apart in a gesture of triumph, "this is my version of prayer!"

"Born again, in the church of Kurtz," said Miranda.

"Not rebirth but redemption, Miranda, the damaged little girl was redeemed."

Miranda leaned back against the wall and gazed, trying to envision Jane as a dowdy frumpy down-at heels morose young woman, or as an innocent child. Jane stood up and shivered as if so much self-revelation had given her a chill. Her perfect body pushed against her clothes from the inside, and despite the wine her eyes flashed with intelligence. Miranda rose to her feet, together they stood arm in arm for a moment, then descended the stairs and went their separate ways.

In any other context, this woman would be my close friend, thought Miranda. She walked straight to where Lionel and Felix were standing, near the French doors leading into the dining room. They adjusted their positions to accommodate her presence but kept on talking. She listened intently, confused by the amiability of their conversation. After a few minutes she withdrew and they adjusted their postures again to absorb the space she had temporarily occupied.

She looked across the room to catch Morgan's eye. She intuitively knew where he was, she always did, monitoring his activities the way she would a child or a lover. He was briefly on his own. She sidled up to him.

"So," she said, "what do you make of that?"

"Of Swan and Webb?"

"Yeah, thick as thieves. Given the Rector's been sent to Coventry and his lordship's the one to send him there, you'd think they'd be hostile. Reserved, at the very least."

"And there they are, best friends."

"Maybe not quite, but."

"But, turn things around. Let's say Swan is truly in disgrace, then perhaps Lionel has used his good offices to intervene and save what's left of his reputation so he can get another posting."

"Morgan, you're right, of course. What seems bad from one perspective, from another is quite noble. Good old Webb. Good old good old Morgan."

"Miranda, you're not driving home tonight."

"No? Okay. We'll stay here, Jane would love to have us. *She's* my new best friend."

She looked around and spotted Yijun Sung talking to Hermione the spy. Suddenly, she stepped directly over to him and taking his arm pulled him aside.

"I figured it out," she whispered.

"What, Miss Quin?"

"Your riddle."

"My riddle?"

"Yes?"

"Do you want me to tell you, Mr. Yijun Sung?"

"Please. I would be most relieved."

"Li Po was addressed as your uncle but he was not your uncle. You were closely related. Li Po was your father!"

"Very interesting, Ms. Quin."

"Your parents, they were not married."

"They were colleagues."

"And Li Po was your father?"

"That is what you have said."

"But when you applied for immigrant status, his

historic involvement with the Party threatened to undermine your qualifications. Back then, it might have been a problem."

"Very interesting, Detective. Rather unlikely, however."

"Then it was your birth out of wedlock, this the Canadian authorities might have found difficult to deal with? Back then."

"If, indeed, my father and my mother were not married, Canada at the time would have been concerned about that. Yes, that might be true."

"Ha! So they were unmarried colleagues, unmarried, and you… ?"

"Yes?"

"Marie Lachine is your sister."

"As you say, it is possible."

"And?" said Miranda.

"What?" said Yijun Sung. "Does this provide illumination? Have you now solved the murder of Professor Kurtz?"

Miranda tried to penetrate the man's ironic gaze. Even if the koan were resolved, there was no-where to go with the resolution. Another koan? "I'm sorry Li Po is dead. He was a very nice man."

"Thank you."

"Did you have the funeral already."

"The cremation, yes. It was my responsibility to press the switch and witness his burning."

"Because you are his son?"

"Because it is how we honor the dead."

"I thought it was Hindus who did that, lighting the fire. You are not Hindu?"

"No, Detective."

"Yijun Sung, why do you think your uncle, Li Po, your father, was Professor Kurtz's friend?"

"That is an impossible question. Who knows what binds people together?"

"Sometimes it can be terrible things," Miranda suggested.

"Yes, there is friendship in evil and in suffering as well as in good."

"And where did their friendship begin? What bound those two together?"

"The work camps."

"Where life was precarious."

"Life was incidental, I believe. Dying was real."

"That could be a description of the human condition."

"You are very morbid, I think, if you believe that."

"No, I probably don't," said Miranda. "It's what you make it."

"What?"

"Life. I'm quoting Jean Paul Sartre, more or less. Or Oprah Winfry. *Reality is whatever you choose not to doubt.*" Miranda was quite pleased, poised between appearing foolish and being profound.

Yijun Sung smiled at her and she thought she saw in his features the face of Li Po as a young man, perhaps when he and Hermione were lovers.

"Dieter Kurtz turned Li Po over to the authorities for helping him escape," she said.

"Dieter Kurtz turned Li Po over to authorities who removed him from the death camp, who sent him to Beijing where he was re-evaluated for his contribution to the revolution and sent to Lanchou. In short, Ms. Quin, Dieter Kurtz saved my uncle's life."

"You father's."

"As you wish."

"Thank you."

"For what, Detective."

"For our conversation."

Miranda had nothing more to pursue; she was fascinated by the positive twist Yijun Sung had put on Li Po's story, as well as by the uncanny way he made facts seem ephemeral and the intangible real. As she moved away, the young man began talking again with Hermione Mac, who had stood back when Miranda approached them, but not so far that she missed the gist of their conversation. Miranda returned to Morgan, who had been observing her from a vantage with his back to the wall. She winked and flashed him a seductive shrug. He was amused by her lack of inhibition. She was not much of a drinker.

"Time to go?" she said amiably.

"I'll drive. If you trust me."

"With the Jag or with me?"

"Both."

"Yeah, well, okay. We'd better—look who just came in!"

"Who?" said Morgan, without turning around.

"I don't know," said Miranda and smiled.

Morgan knew it must be Susan.

David Jenness was coming through the foyer with his mother. He had slipped out to pick her up in the limousine.

Morgan turned and nodded warmly. Susan waved him a cheery greeting. As he took Miranda by the arm to introduce them, Susan veered off to the side and into the arms of Simon Sparrow, who embraced her with a lingering kiss.

Morgan was stunned. He blushed deeply.

"Is that her?" whispered Miranda.

"Yes," Morgan mumbled.

"Lady Jenness, David's mother?"

"Yes."

"Your Susan?"

"Apparently not."

chapter thirty
Leaving Jesus

Saint Augustine gazed down from his perch on the roof-top parapet of the Toronto Police Headquarters, sheltered from the wind in the lee of the great blue dome. He was admiring the monumental grace of the architecture below when Morgan sat down beside him, dangling his legs into space. Beyond the splayed planes of pink granite under their feet was the spinning Earth.

"Well," said Morgan, "do we fly?"

"You must be mad," said Saint Augustine. "There's nowhere to go but down."

"You're a fatalist," said Morgan.

"I'm a realist," said Augustine.

"I thought you knew things."

"About what?"

"I don't know," said Morgan. "I just thought you

knew."

"About the streets of heaven? They're paved with the dreams of the living. About the joys of denial? Wake up, my friend: *a little delayed gratification is one thing, abstinence is another!*"

"Yes," said Morgan, who thought Saint Augustine sounded curiously like Miranda, despite the flowing white beard and glittering eye. "Am I asleep?"

Saint Augustine placed his hand on Morgan's knee and hoisted himself into the air where he hovered.

"I'm out of here," he said, and slid away into the clouds.

Morgan looked down and he could see an architectural stream flowing into the streets of Toronto at the base of the building. Carefully, he swung himself around on the parapet to stand on the roof. He looked at his feet. The building had disappeared. He was on the street, walking towards the Starbucks at College and Yonge. There was nothing profound about that, he thought, as he pushed open the door and woke up.

The telephone was ringing.

"David."

The image of Susan in Simon Sparrow's proprietorial embrace came crashing around him like a billboard toppling on a hapless pedestrian.

"David?"

"Yes."

"I'm sorry I didn't tell you."

"Tell me what?"

"Oh come on, David. Your response wasn't exactly

subtle."

"What? I walked out, I went home."

"I didn't meet your partner."

"She's not my partner—of course, she's my partner, but not that way."

"What way, David? She is absolutely fabulous."

"Absolutely fabulous! You talk like that now, do you?"

"How?"

"'*Absolutely fabulous*,' you say things like that."

"David, I didn't mean to hurt you, but."

"Simon Sparrow! For goodness sake."

"Simon Sparrow, yes, David. I am a widow, I have a right to choose my own lover."

"Lovers, apparently. Plural, simultaneously."

"You and I, in some dimension or another, we will always be lovers, David, but in parallel lives imagined on lonely days."

"Yesterday the parallels converged."

"Yes they did, at the vanishing point. And we were so much better than when we were children together."

"We were never children together. We were young."

"And clumsy and generous."

"You were generous, Susan. I was clumsy."

"And yesterday was beautiful."

"And brief."

"Oh no, David. We made long languorous love, my darling."

"What was it all about, yesterday?"

"David, it just was. Don't spoil things by searching for meaning. It felt right for both of us. Think of it as parenthetical."

"And Simon Sparrow, he's not *parenthetical*?"

"Simon is right for me, right now. It's not like we're getting married, David. And don't you dare condescend. He is much too much like you, he is what you were, only you grew up. He's my Peter Pan, he'll never grow up."

"I hadn't thought of him quite that way," said Morgan, pleased he could latch onto something to be amused by. Then, suddenly, it hit him: "What the hell do you mean he's like me?"

"Like you were, David. He's trying to find himself, he will spend his whole life trying to find himself. That's how you were then, when we were together."

"I thought I was trying to lose myself."

"It is exactly the same thing, David. And were you successful?"

"At losing myself? Or finding myself? I don't know. I guess I just got tired."

"Never, David! Not you. But you've grown up. Simon will never grow up. Right now I need someone like that in my life."

"Someone *like* that!"

"Simon, yes. My Nigel was a wonderful man, David, but he was mature from the age of three. His old Nanny told me that! His whole life, he was an adult." She paused and the silence hung between them. "David, you would have been terrible for me. We would have been a disaster together. But now, damn you, when I might have been ready for you, you aren't."

"How do you know?"

"You're not who you were."

"And Simon is?"

"Yes, Simon is. I've been having fun. I haven't had fun in a long time. I have been happy, but that is different, of course. Fun, and being happy are different."

"You sound very grown up, yourself, Susan."

"Call me Sue. One last time, call me Sue. Please."

"You're leaving?"

"Yes, I'm off to the airport in twenty minutes. David is taking me out in Lionel's limousine. I'm sorry to make love and run, dear love, but life is in a count-down mode."

"A count-down mode? Parenthetical? Do you really think we would have been such a disaster?"

"Yes, of course. We arranged our lives to protect each other from ourselves."

"You've only been here a couple of days."

"Three, I'll be home before jet lag catches up to me."

"I thought you were here to see David, for a bit of a visit."

"I was, I am. Now I'm going back. You take care, David Morgan. I must run. Take good care of yourself."

"Have you known him a long time?"

"Simon? Dieter brought him around. I found him amusing. And no, I did not cheat on my husband. Sometimes I pleasured myself and daydreamed of you."

"I thought you thought we were clumsy together."

"Deliciously. I love you, David. Bye-bye."

"Sue?" He heard a sharp intake of breath, a click, and the phone went empty.

Miranda had dreamed restlessly, and in her dreams she envisioned herself tossing about, unable to sleep, so that, although she actually slept deeply through most of the night, she felt exhausted as she shuffled into the bathroom and addressed the mirror in search of a familiar face.

The telephone was ringing.

It was under a pillow in her bedroom and the sound was distant but persuasive. She splashed cold water on her cheeks and peered into the mirror. She smiled at herself and her reflection smiled back. She felt better. How long had the phone been ringing? She sprawled across her bed to answer.

"Yeah?" she said in a grumpy voice.

"Good morning, Miranda."

"Is that you, Ellen?"

"The same. Ellen Ravenscroft, Medical Examiner, female *extraordinaire*."

"What d'you want? It's still, it's only, my God, it's nine-thirty."

"Out late, were we? Are you alone?"

"Yes, I'm alone! And I was working last night. Didn't get in 'til midnight."

"Said the bishop to his confessor."

"Pardon? I'm not awake."

"Any chance you can drop by."

"Yeah, sure. About Kurtz?"

"Yes, I think we overlooked the obvious."

"We?"

"Come on over, we'll talk."

"He wasn't murdered?" Miranda suggested, wondering why whatever Ellen had to say couldn't be said over the telephone.

"Oh, he was murdered, for sure."

"Ellen?"

"See you when you get here." The telephone clicked and Miranda was left staring at the silent phone as if somehow the technology had failed her.

Morgan decided to spend the morning on his computer at home, pursuing Francis Bacon on the internet. He stared at his own reflection in the blank screen. Superintendent Rufalo was getting impatient and they had come up with nothing substantial. The news media had lost interest, apart from a couple of tabloid columnists who refused to believe a murder with Lionel Webb among the dead man's closest associates would be entirely without a redeeming scandal. Hardly a case to boost circulation, but with sufficient notoriety to get off a shot or two at the establishment and drop a few zingers about police inefficiency. Rufalo was ready to downgrade the file to what was euphemistically called 'an ongoing investigation.'

Still in his pajamas, Morgan gave Miranda a call.

"I was just on my way out," she said. "What's up?"

"Nothing."

"Nothing?"

"That's just it, nothing," he said.

"Morgan, meet me, I should be at the office by noon.

I'll see you then. Let's brainstorm."

"Yeah, for sure."

"It could be Dieter Kurtz."

"What?"

"Telling the story."

"Interesting. See you later."

"Gotcha."

"Oh, hey, how're you feeling?"

There was a delay, then Miranda answered cheerfully, "Never better, why do you ask?"

"No reason. You take care."

"I'm off to the Coroner's Office. Ellen Ravenscroft called. I'm going to stop in and talk to Jane Latimer on the way. There's something odd about things she told me last night."

"What things?"

"I'll tell you later."

"What did Ellen want?"

"I'll tell you that, too. We'll have a lot to talk about. Bye."

"Bye," he said into the empty phone.

From the dingy corridor on the second floor of Jesus College, Miranda could see through Jane Latimer's open office door that she was in conference with a student. Miranda was about to leave when Jane called out to her.

"I'll only be a minute."

"Okay," she answered. "I'll go down and see if the Rector is in."

She descended the dreary stairwell and came out

opposite the Rector's Offices. He was talking to a secretary at her desk but when he glanced up he motioned Miranda to join him in his inner chambers. He closed the door solemnly behind him.

"We'll have some privacy."

"Good," said Miranda, taking her cue to be forthright. "I understand you are leaving Jesus."

"Ah, you've heard. Next spring. And not sorry to go."

"You don't like it at Jesus? I thought you relished the trappings of authority, Felix."

"Oh, I do, I do. You are very prescient, dear Miranda. But life here is too complex, more complex than I care to deal with."

"Do I detect the whiff of a scandal?"

He looked at her apprehensively. His florid face tightened and then relaxed. Clearly, he did not know how much she understood of his situation.

"I believe I will secure a good position at a smaller university. It will give me a chance to get back to my first love, and put aside all this administration business."

"Your first love?"

"Books. Bacon. Philosophy and literature."

"Not little boys?"

Sweat burst out of Felix Swan's facial pores and beaded and rolled down his thick neck into the flaccid gap around the collar of his shirt.

"You are unkind," he said.

Knowing she had the advantage, Miranda pressed him. "Do you want to give me your version." She said this as if she had another version in mind.

"I thought you might be here to talk about this. It has nothing to do with the case, with Dieter's murder. Not directly."

"If he was blackmailing you, that would be pretty direct."

"Blackmail. No, my dear Miranda, no, no, no. No one understands."

"Why don't you explain."

"Yes, I think I shall."

He drew in a series of deep breaths.

"Go on," she said.

"Yes, I think I shall."

"Please do."

"Many years ago, when I was a student here, some very bad things happened."

He adjusted his heavy frame in his oversized deskchair and leaned forward in a confiding posture.

"Miranda, I grew up in a very sheltered home. I am going to talk about sex, I hope you don't mind. Well, I had none. No sexual experience. And frankly I had very little interest. Then one night I was walking alone through Philosophers Walk. A small band of street urchins cornered me. Boys, fourteen or fifteen years old. One held a knife to my throat. I was, as I am now, a big man, I have a big soft body, and they forced me to take off my clothes. I was crying, they made me crawl on my hands and knees, and they sodomized me. Repeatedly, they sodomized me."

He looked across the desk at Miranda. His hands were shaking and his voice was tremulous.

"They called me Piggy and they sodomized me. You know what's pathetic. I kept flashing on scenes from that movie."

"Deliverance?"

"I couldn't even animate my own nightmare. I was Piggy from *Lord of the Flies*, and yes I was Ned Beatty squealing in *Deliverance*. My own experience was so limited, I had to borrow images to make what was happening seem real. When the scene plays back in my head, I hear dueling banjos."

"Really!"

"No. That's a sordid joke. Then, suddenly, in the melee, there were flashlight beams and two policemen practically stumbled on top of us, they thought it was kids playing games. I bucked and rolled over in terror, in abject humiliation. One boy, he was sodomizing me, I rolled onto his leg, he was pinned to the earth. The others whooped and ran off. And there was I, Fexlis Swan, a fat soft naked grown-up man crushing a fourteen year old boy with his trousers around his ankles, both of us weeping.

"The police unkindly held their flashlights on me while I scrambled around on the ground to find my clothes. They held their lights on me while I got dressed. A small crowd gathered, mostly students, but among them was Professor Kurtz. He stepped forward and urged them to allow me the privacy of darkness while I struggled to put on my clothes.

"They were very annoyed with him for interfering. The young boy bolted, disappeared into the darkness.

"And there we were. Professor Dieter Kurtz and I, held together in the flashlight beams while the policemen tried to figure out what to do next. The boy was their only witness. I was a pederast, a pedophile. I was contemptible. They could hardly bear to address me.

"Quite unexpectedly, Dieter Kurtz pushed himself between me and the police. Then, in a very calm voice, he told me to leave. I hesitated, then started to walk away. I do not know what he said to the policemen, they shouted after me, but they did let me go. Perhaps he simply told them they had no case. Perhaps he challenged their jurisdiction on university grounds, perhaps he cast doubt—I don't know. I left him amidst cross-currents of light beams and fled to my room.

"And what happened to Professor Kurtz?" said Miranda.

"Nothing. Not directly. Rumours built up around campus that he had been arrested for raping a boy in the bushes. No charges were laid. He took the fall, as they say. He shifted the dreadful rumours onto himself.

"Why?"

"I do not know. He was my mentor, but when I next went to his office on academic business we did not speak about the night of my humiliation. I think others thought we were somehow degenerates together.

"My reputation was tainted by the time I spent with him! That was one of the lesser ironies of the whole grotesque affair. He never talked about it. Not ever. And never again in my life have I had a sexual experience."

"That was not sex, Felix. That was assault."

"Is there a difference, Miranda?"

"Felix, what is happening now, why have you been asked to leave?"

"It is a funny old world, Detective. Since Dieter was killed, his reputation has grown like a cancer, especially among the powers-that-be. Not his scholarly reputation. The story began circulating about his having been arrested as a pederast in Philosophers Walk, being caught in the midst of buggering an innocent child. Circulating! I should say, *re-circulating*."

"And did you try to dispel the myth, is that what happened?"

"I was summoned before the College Board of Directors. They had to consider: given he was dead and a Professor Emeritus, should Dieter Kurtz be honoured? I was asked to verify the sordid past. To verify! They wanted the gossip to be true, to be done with him and his unseemly death. They wanted to wash their hands of the whole nasty business."

"And?"

"I sat before that august body, Miranda, and only Lionel Webb among them knew better. Professor Kurtz's death had unleashed a monster and it fell on me to bring it to ground. It was up to Felix Swan to slay the dragon."

"And did you?"

"Yes, Miranda, I did. It is the one good thing I have done in my life. I told them it was me that evening in Philosophers Walk, that Professor Kurtz had merely passed by. Lionel tried to intervene, but even Lionel had trouble believing that I was attacked, that the boy pinned against the earth by my bulk was not the victim."

The Rector stared at his hands. Miranda gazed at him, waiting for him to look up into her eyes. When he did, there was no question in her mind he was telling the truth.

"To the Board, my crime was twofold: concealing the truth and being raped in the first place."

"Good God."

"Not always, Miranda."

"Even so, Lionel went to bat for you."

"Yes, even so, he has gone to bat for me. I will get another appointment. Lionel will see to that. I will return to the lecture hall, to the seminar room. I will be happy."

"I hope so, Felix."

"Thank you, Miranda. Anything I have said is of course open to your discretion; what is not useful, please, say nothing about it. Except to your partner, of course. To no one else. It is not about pride. Yes, yes it is about pride. Thank you."

"Felix. I'm puzzled. Why do you allow Dieter Kurtz to be—I was on my way to ask Jane Latimer the same question—I thought you loathed the man. I thought you all despised him."

Felix Swan looked up at her and his Buddha face, swathed in sweat, softened into a sad smile.

"Is that a question, Detective? Or an observation?"

"A point of confusion, Felix. Perhaps you could clarify."

"Probably not. You had better speak to Jane for yourself. As for me, I found the man difficult. I found him detestable in some ways. It was nothing he did, at least not to me. It was not even what he knew. It was what he endured. I realize my feelings for him were inseparable from my loathing for myself. I know that. And yet, I could not help myself. He carried the burden of my public humiliation; but my private shame—"

"For being assaulted—"

"Raped, Miranda, face down in the dirt, squealing like a pig—the only way I could endure those depravities that played over and over in my mind was to disengage from myself, to dissociate from what happened, to project my self-loathing onto Dieter Kurtz, to imagine it happened to him. He virtually invited it. The more willing he was to accept my shame as his own, the easier it was to despise him. I don't know whether that makes any sense. What I hated about Dieter Kurtz was his capacity for evil."

"*Your* evil?"

"Yes! For taking it on as his own."

"But you did nothing wrong, you were a victim."

"Miranda."

"Yes."

"I think I enjoyed it."

"Enjoyed it?"

"The humiliation. The pain. The buggery!"

Miranda gazed into the porcine eyes, narrowed in a suffering confusion of fear and self-contempt.

"And you hated Kurtz for knowing that?"

"Yes. It makes no sense."

"It does. In a strange way, it does."

"I have never had another sexual experience."

"So you said." She paused. "Felix, you have never had a sexual experience, period. Not if that was it! And, if you want my opinion, I don't think you enjoyed being raped. I really don't. I think, after the fact, you feared you *might* have enjoyed it. The more you feared that, the more real it became as a possibility. That happens, Felix. Rape victims routinely blame themselves. The more you recoil in horror at yourself, the more inviting, to have someone like Dieter to take up your burden; someone to resent. It is a vicious circle, Felix, but it's broken now. It's over. He's dead. And you have tried to take back the crime as your own, you have done a very good thing. Sometimes, refusing to be the victim isn't the answer."

To Miranda's surprise, the big man reached across his desk for one of her hands, which she extended and let rest loosely between his sweaty palms.

"I am a Freemason," he said, with the sepulchral aura of someone making a significant announcement; part declaration, part confession. "And a Rosicrucian."

She looked at him quizzically. It was apparently important for him to tell her this. He was taking her into his confidence. It was his form of conferring gratitude for her understanding, to share something intimate and vaguely illicit.

"Being a Mason, I have brothers beyond the grave, we are bound by secrets. But I am not a man with friends, Miranda. I belong to the Bacon Society and I would die for any of the others, but our bond is not friendship. It was Dieter's knowledge of our hidden lives that held us together. It's funny how secrets work. Perhaps we will disperse, now. But I will still be a Freemason."

"And a Rosicrucian."

"The Ancient Mystical Order of the Rosy Cross."

"Rosy cross?"

"*Rosae Crucis*. The rose and the cross. The cross is the body of man, and the petals of the rose are the unfolding consciousness as the mind connects with absolute being."

"And why are we telling me this?"

"Because I belong, I am shaped and contained by arcane knowledge. I do not want you to feel sorry for me."

"I don't, Felix. I feel compassion. Empathy."

"You cannot know what it is like."

"To be you? No, but to be me, yes. The rest of us, in the world surrounding you, we are equally human, Felix. I may not need mysterious rituals and mystical beliefs to connect with my own humanity; but if you do, that's fine. And if you think that I don't know what it's like to carry the burden of guilt for my own suffering, well, you're wrong. Still waters run deep. I am equally human. That might be a good thing for you to try and understand."

He released her hand and sat back in his chair. Clearly, he was trying to sort out an appropriate response.

"You are so very very kind, Miranda. You are wonderfully perceptive." As he talked on, adding honey to vinegar, Miranda realized that she had perhaps shared the one true moment in Felix Swan's life when he had opened to another person, and that moment was gone.

She stood up.

"I had better catch Jane before she goes out."

Fexlix Swan, the Rector of Jesus College, stared down at some papers on his desk and smiled.

Miranda found Jane Latimer's door open. She knocked. Jane was leaning back in her chair with her legs hoisted up on the desk. She was about to swing down into a more genteel posture when she saw it was Miranda. She settled back comfortably.

"You want to know why I hated Dieter, don't you?"

"Pardon?" said Miranda. "You're ahead of me."

"When you catch up, that'll be your first question."

"Really? Okay, why did you hate Dieter Kurtz?"

"The answer to your question is, I did not hate him. There. That's finally out of the way."

"Jane. You gave us the very clear impression you found him an odious little vermin."

"Vermin is plural, Miranda. There was only one of him and he was not little. He was average size, maybe bigger when he was young."

"I only knew him dead, and people have a way of diminishing in size after death, although they often gain stature."

"Dieter was not an easy man to like. That doesn't mean I hated him."

"You gave the distinct impression any of you in the Bacon Society might have wanted him dead."

"Yes, and each of us for our own reasons."

"What would yours be?"

"My reasons? Dieter empowered me."

"And therefore you killed him?"

"No, of course not. But he exacted a heavy price for

my freedom."

"Ah, this is the part you left out last night."

"Last night. Too much wine."

"His price?"

"A relationship. His friendship."

"What?"

"Dieter Kurtz never talked to me again after that special day. We worked closely while I finished my honours thesis, but very impersonally. That seemed appropriate. We never talked about my transformation. He had done his bit; it was up to me to do mine. Then, when I went over to Oxford, it was as if I had flown off the edge of the planet."

"That doesn't make sense. When you came back, he was your mentor, you became colleagues, you were his 2-I-C in the Bacon Society."

"Two-eyes-see?"

"Second in command. I was a Mountie for a while. Very military."

"A Mountie! I can't imagine. Yes, but I was invariably reduced to my function. It was strange sometimes being alone together. As a person, I wasn't there."

"Why do you think that was?"

"Oh, I know why it was. That didn't make it easier. He was making damned sure I wouldn't rely on him emotionally. In a single act, he had set me free. He wasn't about to let me fall back."

"Would you have fallen back?"

"I couldn't, he left me nowhere to fall. The singular of vermin is varmit, in Bacon's tme it was varmint. There was something very animalistic about how things were between us."

"Animistic?"

"*Animalistic*. Like animals: tossing their fledglings out of the nest to fly on their own. No looking back and no looking down, you might plummet to the earth. Animism, that's something else, it means all things have souls. I'm not sure Dieter had a soul of his own. He borrowed ours."

"Last night you would have said he gave you your soul as a gift."

"Do you know what a succubus is?"

"Something sinister, like a vampire?"

"A demonic woman who has sexual intercourse with sleeping men. She sucks out their vitality through her loins, she pleasures herself while he dreams of other things."

"And you are a succubus?"

"Yes. All of us are."

"The Bacon Society?"

"Yes."

"And he was left depleted, an empty vessel?"

"No. That's just it, he seemed to have an infinite capacity to feed others from his strength, and for that he was hated."

"I take it the succubus does not respect her lover the morning after?"

"Something like that. So, to me, he remained the slumbering man, my lover, my enemy."

"The more you felt in his debt, the more you despised

him."

"And the more I loved him. You cannot separate hate from love."

"Did you kill him?"

"No, of course not. You know that or we wouldn't be friends."

"Are we friends?"

chapter thirty-one
The Crypt

Morgan was on the net when the telephone rang. He was reading about the Ancient Mystical Order of Rosae Crucis, or AMORC. He was fascinated by a contemporary group of self-described mystics who trace their lineage from ancient Egypt through Greece and Rome to medieval Europe and a flowering in Germany during the Renaissance down to the present day. There was something seductively calming in the Rosicrucian web-site and he was both relieved and annoyed at the interruption.

"Hello," he said.
"Mr. Morgan?"
"Yes."
"Detective Sergeant Morgan?"
"Yes."

"This is Pearson Airport Security."

"What can I do for you?"

"We're holding three people, they gave us your name?"

"Yes?"

"They gave us the name of Lionel Webb. We do not know Lionel Webb. They gave us your name."

"You don't know me, either."

"You are a cop."

"Yeah, who is this, what's this about?"

"It is Airport Security. We are holding three people."

"So you said."

"They gave us your name."

"You said that as well, and why would they do that?"

"We are holding a woman and two men. One is called Simon Sparrow. The woman is Susan Jenness. Her passport says she is a Baroness. The other man claims to be her son, his passport says Baronet."

"Very interesting," said Morgan. "I didn't know they put that kind of thing on passports."

"It is under 'occupation.' Where there is a line for occupation, hers says *Baroness* and his says *Baronet.*"

"Interesting."

"We are holding them."

"Yes," said Morgan.

"The woman is trying to leave the country with stolen property. The men are her accomplices. Possibly she is carrying for them."

"You're holding all three?"

"Yes."

"Good for you."

"Thank you."

"Okay, where are you? Terminal Three?"

"Terminal Two. Shall we expect you? Do you know who these people are, sir?"

"Yes, expect me. I'll be there in an hour. Make them comfortable, but don't let them out of your sight."

"Thank you, Detective."

"No, thank you for your very good work. I will be there as soon as I can."

Miranda decided to walk from the university over to the Coroner's Office. She wandered out of Jesus College and doubled back along Philosophers Walk to Bloor Street. When she stepped through the gate onto the public sidewalk her eyes grazed over a sign and then did a double-take. Of course. Philosophers Walk is spelled without an apostrophe—but the e-mail sharing the news of Kurtz's death with the members of the Bacon Society, it had spelled Philosopher's in the possessive form. Whoever sent it was not an academic. Anyone familiar with the university would not have made such an error, trivial as it was. So, who does that eliminate? Nearly half of them—Jane, Felix, Jennifer and Lionel are familiars, Marie has an academic background. That leaves Simon, David, Hermione Mac, the D'Arcys. And Li Po? Unlikely; he was a scholar. Hermione M? Possibly. Maybe it was nothing, but the misappropriated apostrophe played on her mind as she stopped off to have a sandwich in the Indigo bookstore and browse through the tables of remaindered best-sellers.

Morgan strode into the Security Offices at Terminal Two, projecting the air of someone with a lot of authority and not much patience. He was shown immediately into a windowless room where Simon, David, and Susan sat along one side of a table with their backs to the door. Morgan nodded to their interrogator who got up to greet him.

"Do you know these people?" the officer asked. All three swivelled in their seats and looked sheepish. Morgan nodded gravely to each of them.

"Yes," he said. "What seems to be the difficulty?"

"This woman was trying to leave the country."

"Is that a problem?"

"We picked these two up loitering around the security gate."

"Loitering?"

"They were assisting her."

"In leaving the country? But they weren't leaving?"

"No, definitely not. They weren't going anywhere." The officer seemed quite pleased with his declarative statement.

"So, she was leaving alone."

"With stolen property."

"Really," said Morgan. "I'm very disappointed."

He looked sternly at the three miscreants, then back at the security officer. "What were they smuggling? Is that it?" He gestured towards an elk skin Roots carry-on bag, a match for Miranda's chocolate brown travel bag, lying open on the table. "May I look?"

"Yes, of course. When we realized what we had here, we put everything back in the bag so as not to disturb the evidence. And then we called you."

"I thought you called me at their request."

"Yes, but since your name is on the warrant, the lady gave us your number."

"The warrant?"

"There is an item in the lady's bag which is wanted in your criminal investigation."

"A book?"

"Yes, an extremely valuable contraband book."

"Well," said Morgan. "That would be *Sylva Sylvarum*."

"Yes, David," said Susan as a medley of subtle emotion played across her face, ranging from fear to anger to amusement. "But it's not stolen, it was Dieter's."

"Please, madam!" said the security officer."

"It's all right," Morgan reassured him. "Let's hear what she has to say."

"May I, Detective?" said Susan, reaching over to open her bag.

"Of course, Lady Jenness," said Morgan.

"You do know her, then?" said the security officer.

"They are, all three, known to the police," said Morgan.

David Jenness had visibly relaxed after Morgan entered the room and seemed to be enjoying the procedure. Simon Sparrow was more wary.

"Ah," said Morgan, as Susan removed three heavy plastic folders from the bag and opened one of them.

"The *Sylva Sylvarum*." He took the proffered book in his hands and examined both sides of the title page. "This is not a first edition, officer. It is old, but of virtually no value. Perhaps a clever ruse to mislead us, yes, but there is nothing illegal, here."

"It's fake?" exclaimed Susan. "You're joking."

"Not at all, Lady Jenness. It is not a fake, it is merely a later edition from the same printer. The authentic first edition has been found." He turned to the officer. "Very good work on your part, I'm sorry for your trouble, we just recovered the genuine article and haven't delisted it yet. This one is of no consequence, a sixth edition. Still, if you don't mind, I think I will hold onto it for the time being."

Susan glowered at him and smiled.

"Yes, of course, Detective. It's all yours." The security officer nodded assent.

"It's Lionel's," offered David Jenness with offhand authority, as if the entire situation could now be seen as no more than a trifling nuisance. "It was Dieter's, I believe. Lionel gave it to mother."

"Then it will be hers again," Morgan responded. "But I'll just keep it for now."

Morgan turned his attention to the other two folders. "Now, let's see, what have we here?"

He knew before opening the second protective folder what would be inside—the only extant copy in the world of Bacon's *The New Atlantis!* Since it was being returned to England where it belonged, Morgan saw no reason to confuse the issue by acknowledging its inestimable value.

"No," he said. "This is not something we're looking for."

He placed the book carefully back on the table and picked up the third folder. Opening it, he was surprised to see a bound handwritten manuscript, apparently in medieval German. It seemed to be of great age; the pages were brittle and gave off a musty odour. He turned it over carefully in his hands, then closed the protective plastic around it.

"This," he said, "we'll keep. It may prove significant. Officer, if you will arrange for me to sign it off, I'll just take it with me, as well." Simon Sparrow flinched. Morgan continued, "she's carrying nothing of value as far as I'm concerned. I see no reason to hold her. These two," he nodded toward David and Simon, "her accomplices, I think it would be safe to release them. I know where they can be reached if the need arises. Thank you so much for your very good work."

"David," said Susan. "You can't keep that."

"What? *The New Atlantis*, no. The other two items, yes, of course I can. This tatty old manuscript will be turned over to its rightful owner in due course. The sixth edition of *Sylva Sylvarum* will go where it should. I hope the rest of your journey is uneventful."

He permitted himself a slight smile, then nodded to David and scowled at Simon before striding off to the outer office. He shook hands with the security officer who had accompanied him to the door and reiterated his appreciation for the good work.

Ellen Ravenscroft led Miranda into the stainless steel crypt. She swung open a thick door and drew out a flat drawer on which lay the covered icy body of Dieter Kurtz. She drew back the shroud and Miranda shuddered at how unreal he looked. There was none of the translucence found on living flesh, only a dull sheen. She wanted to leave, but Ellen had brought her here for a purpose.

She picked up Kurtz's medical profile and thumbed through it while Ellen watched her.

"Interesting," said Miranda.

"He was quite the boy, wasn't he?"

"Apparently."

"A ravaged body, Miranda. This guy's been through the works. Malaria, V.D., he's been mutilated, traumatized, brutalized, by man and nature, you name it, he survived the lot. And then, and then…"

Ellen pulled one arm of the corpse away from the body enough to expose the inner wrist.

"See those marks."

"Yeah, mosquito bites?"

"Here," she handed Miranda a magnifying glass. "Take a closer look."

"A bee sting! Two of them, side by side."

"Exactly, and how do we know that?"

"I can see the stingers, still with little gobs of bee guts." She moved the magnifying glass back and forth. "Ripped their little bottoms off. You wouldn't notice if you weren't looking."

"Well, it's my job to look. And I missed them.

Mosquito bites! I wasn't looking for bee stings. Sorry."

"So what does this mean."

"Well, we know he died of asphyxia." She moved up to his neck area. "Definite damage here, but he wasn't garroted by his cravat. The injuries to his throat and esophagus were *post mortem*. There's a little tissue damage but no swelling. The blood had stopped flowing."

"Thus we came up with death by cunnilingus."

"You came up with that, Miranda. I merely suggested suffocation. You put the sexual spin on it."

"Yeah, based on a pubic hair in his beard."

"And a sordid imagination."

"And a sad little penis protruding from his pants."

"From his underwear, love."

"His pants were unzipped with care and discretion."

"Discreetly unzipped, how quaint."

"And now? You think he died from a bee sting."

"Anaphylactic shock. Yes, from a couple of bees."

"Very unusual, that they would sting so close to each other."

"I'm only giving you the cause of death, love."

"Revised version."

"*Mea culpa*. The cravat damaged his throat sufficiently to obscure the constriction from anaphylaxis. I would check out your suspects for the bee wrangler among them, if I were you."

"Ellen, bees didn't put this guy's corpse on display. This doesn't change anything. Kurtz is just as dead, his death is just as whimsical."

"Whimsical?"

"In a perverse sort of way, yes."

"Do you think you were supposed to come up with the cunnilingual ploy?"

"Likely, yes. Someone was controlling the variables."

"Including us?"

"Yeah, in murder, cops and coroners are variables."

"Depressing, isn't it, love."

"No. That's what makes it exciting."

Four versions of Francis Bacon's *Sylva Sylvarum* sat on Miranda's desk. One was a facsimile, a self-proclaimed copy. This had been in the hands of the corpse. Another was a fraud, passing itself off as original. This one was brought from the dead man's house. The third was the real thing, recovered from her own living room in Waldron. The fourth, which Morgan had just brought in from the airport, was a later printing and worth relatively little.

In addition, there was a musty sheaf of ragged papers bound between untooled leather boards. She reached over tentatively and drew it towards her. Opening the sheaf carefully she tried to make out writing that declared itself to be in a cursive hand untutored by the refinements of English script—or so she imagined, since Morgan had informed her on the basis of having taken German for two years in high school. Teutonic, he declared, heavy-handed, and very old.

When he returned with a couple of coffees, she rolled the back of her hand over the manuscript pages in a beckoning gesture, asking him for further elucidation.

"I know what it is," he said. "I'm pretty sure."

"What, Morgan. You don't read medieval handwriting, you don't understand German. What's happening here? We're accumulating a library."

Alex Rufalo looked out from his office and catching Miranda's eye gave her a slightly derisive salute. She shrugged ingenuously and nodded towards Morgan, as if the library acquisitions were his doing and she was powerless to keep him in check.

"Okay," said Morgan. "The sixth edition, why was she carrying it? I'd say it was meant as a distraction. She was being used as a courier by Lionel Webb. He brought the one and only extant copy of *The New Atlantis* across the pond specifically to show it off to the Bacon Society— that tells you something of the man, doesn't it; with his billions, he still needs to curry the approval of a clique of intellectual misfits and ruffians."

"Quaint, Morgan! Li Po, the Hermiones, ruffians?"

"Misfits?"

"Possibly."

"There you go. My point is, bundling the only extant copy of *The New Atlantis* with a book of the same general age, by the same author, but of little relative value, Webb assumed no one would even notice it. And they didn't. They picked up on that damned *Sylva Sylvarum*—which means, literally, a 'treatise on trees.'"

"Susan was being duped. Lionel wanted to get it back to England. He used her."

"Yeah, he did."

"And what about this," she said, splaying her fingers

over the open pages of the manuscript in a delicate gesture, as if she might feel the letters and absorb their meaning.

"You shouldn't really touch it."

She recoiled as if it were fiery hot, embarrassed at being gauche.

"I wasn't," she insisted.

"If I'm right," said Morgan, "this is a remarkable document. It's the legend to the map, the key in the lock."

"Morgan, you're being elliptical."

"The manuscript. Lionel Webb wanted this manuscript out of the country. Why? What difference could it make, why risk parceling it with *The New Atlantis?*"

"To reinforce the diversion, same as with the sixth edition of the tree book."

"*Silva Sylvarum* is not about trees. It's about knowledge, the tree of unlimited knowledge, how humans can know all things not subject to revelation. Through the powers of the mind. No, it's valuable in its own right. There can't be many manuscripts of this age floating around."

"How do you know how old it is."

"I don't, not exactly. But from what Jennifer Pluck was telling us about old paper, and from the feel and smell, it reeks of authenticity. So, why would it be of interest to a pathological Baconian?"

"Pathological?"

"Webb brought *The New Atlantis* all the way over for show and tell!"

"Yeah, that's pretty extreme."

"And now he wants to spirit a rare manuscript out of the country. Why? There has to be a Bacon connection. I'd say it's because...are you ready for this?"

"Very."

"This is the foundation document of the Rosicrucians. Don't you remember, the Bacon people were debating whether or not Bacon himself was responsible for the renewal of interest in the Rosicrucians during the Renaissance. There was a treatise by a German, or apparently by a German, that brought the ancient and mystical order up to date. Many have argued that the treatise was actually the work of Francis Bacon."

"This is Bacon's own handwriting!"

"It could be. That would make it more precious by far than *The New Atlantis*. Can you imagine, the document itself is worth a fortune; the proof of Bacon's authorship would be an astonishing revelation in intellectual history. Imagine, it's like finding an original play-script of *Hamlet* in Bacon's own handwriting."

"Or the seventeenth Earl of Oxford. I'm in the Oxfordian camp."

"I actually think Christopher Marlowe wrote Shakespeare, after faking his own murder. But the question here is, why would Webb want this manuscript in England? How did it get to Canada in the first place? Would it provide a sufficient motive for murder? Remember, Kurtz was working on precisely this. Jane Latimer told us, his focus within Bacon studies was on the Rosicrucian connection."

"Fama Fraternitatis."

"Yeah, I think what we have in our hands is the original manuscript for *Fama Fraternitatis* in Christian Rosenkreuz's own handwriting."

"Proving Bacon's authorship. That he was Christian of the rose and cross."

"Otherwise, why would Lionel Webb risk packing it off to England like that."

"And you don't think Susan knew?"

"No. Webb would assume ignorance is the best cover. And it might have worked, except we didn't get around to delisting *Sylva Sylvarum*."

"There honestly didn't seem much urgency, Morgan. How many books by Francis Bacon are floating around?"

"More than we thought, apparently."

The telephone rang and they both reached for it. Morgan deferred and Miranda answered.

"Miranda?" It was Ellen Ravenscroft.

"Yeah, what's happening?"

"Things are dead around here."

"I know, but people are dying to get in."

"You've heard all the dead jokes?"

"Yeah."

"Somebody's finally put in a claim for the Kurtz body. Are you through with him?"

"Yeah, sure. I'll send over the papers. Who?"

"Who?"

"Who wants him."

"A man called Simon Sparrow."

"Really?"

"You know the guy?"

"For sure. It wasn't whom I expected."

"*Whom!*" said Morgan and Ellen Ravenscroft simultaneously.

"It wasn't whom or who I expected."

"Give Morgan my warmest regards."

"Yeah, I'll get the papers off to you in the morning."

"Bye, love."

Miranda hung up the phone.

"Simon Sparrow has claimed Kurtz's body."

"Funny, I thought it would have been Webb, or even Hermione Mac. Can he do that?"

"What? Claim the body? Yes, of course, if there's no family. It saves the city the cost of going after his estate for expenses."

"Curious, eh?"

"Yeah," said Miranda. "I suppose he could be acting for Webb. My God, you don't think they're going to have Dieter Kurtz stuffed like poor old Jeremy Bentham."

"Now that would give Webb's cabinet of curiosities a whole new dimension."

"One desiccated body and a bunch of skulls, it's a museum of wonders. Two bodies, one relatively fresh, and it's a crypt."

Morgan sat back in his chair and surveyed the books on the double desk between them.

"It's time for another meeting of the Bacon Society," he announced.

"Agreed," said Miranda, with equal authority.

"Tonight. At Lionel Webb's."

"Why not," she said.

"We'll tap into the Bacon Society's chat room."

"We can do that?"

"Maybe with a little help."

"And convene an urgent meeting. Lovely."

"They'll come. This bunch can't resist."

"Let's go for it, Morgan. It's almost time for the denouement."

chapter thirty-two
Wunderkammern

The e-mail notice asked the Bacon Society to convene at seven-thirty. Miranda and Morgan fortified themselves with cafeteria sandwiches and coffee, then signed out a car and headed over to the Bridle Path. Before approaching the door, they locked their Glocks and cuffs in the trunk of the car, along with their bullet-proof vests. It was an unspoken gesture that affirmed their commitment to a reasonable outcome.

On the way over, Miranda had told Morgan a story:

"I once had a boyfriend called Allan," she said. "He was easy-going, clever, and droll, and his favourite expression was, 'damn them all but six and save them for pallbearers.' But you know what? You only need one, Morgan."

"Pallbearer?"

"We live in the age of cremation. One, to carry the pot full of ashes. Damn the rest."

He thought for a moment, wondering if this was an affirmation of their singular friendship or the threnody of a congenial cynic, a declaration of trust or a premonition of doom.

"Your friend Allan didn't say 'damn them all,' did he?"

"No, he said, 'fuck 'em all.' I cleaned it up."

"Why?"

She smiled and the dash lights cast an eerie sheen on her features. *Sometimes things just come to your mind and you want to share them,* she thought.

"What happened to Allan?" he asked.

"Nothing."

And that is the point of the story.

Now, they paused between the soaring Corinthian columns while they collected themselves, unsure of their reception. After comparing notes at Police Headquarters, each had made assumptions. Miranda trusted Morgan needed only to confirm his suspicions by testing them in the presence of the entire Bacon Society before revealing the killer. Morgan assumed Miranda had garnered sufficient facts from the day's events that she needed only to confront the killer in the most appropriate context to make confession inevitable.

Each felt the other was in charge.

The door swung open and a very different Jennifer Pluck greeted them. Virtually overnight, she seemed to have acquired the grace of a young chatelaine. Gone were the quick mannerisms and unusual clothes. She appeared to the manner and the manor born as she welcomed each of them in turn, although just underneath the charm there might have been an almost imperceptible chill.

"Lionel told me you would be first," she said as she ushered them into the grand foyer.

"Really," said Morgan.

"You did send out the invitations, Detective."

"How did you know?" said Miranda.

"Technology. We used the telephone and called around."

Miranda laughed, while Morgan looked uncomfortable but managed a gracious shrug.

Lionel Webb came out of the library and greeted them with surprising cheerfulness, as if it were a festive occasion.

Chimes sounded and without waiting for anyone to respond, Padraig and Ralph surged through the door like errant boys returning to the classroom, the short one with a swagger and the lean one enigmatic.

"You!" said Padraig, pointing to Morgan. "This is your idea."

"Porrig, be quiet," said Ralph.

"Rafe, darling, piss off." He closed in on Morgan. "Do you realize what you've done?"

Morgan looked at the tubby little man with puzzled amusement.

"You have ruined a perfectly good evening. We were invited for a sail."

"A garage sale!" chimed in Ralph.

"Don't be silly, Rafe, we don't even need a garage!"

"What kind of sale?" said Miranda.

"I think perhaps a sail on Lake Ontario," offered Lionel.

"From the Royal Toronto Yacht Club, no less," said Padraig.

"Lionel's club," said Jennifer.

"I belong," said her paramour. "But I don't sail."

"Why on earth not," Padraig demanded.

"No boat," said Lionel with sufficient alacrity to fend off the awkwardness.

Lional had been a sailor, once, but since the death of his wife he used the club only for social occasions. Padraig seemed caught between vulgarity, referring to their host's illimitable financial resources, and insensitivity. He blushed deeply and had the good sense to let the matter drop.

For a moment, there was an awkward silence, then the chimes announced the newest arrivals. As the others moved into the foyer and milled about in the embrace of the twin staircases rising on either side of the room, Morgan sidled close to Lionel Webb.

"I believe we have something of yours," he said.

"Really," said Lionel Webb. "What would that be?"

"I think you know. Where's David, I'm sure he's already told you. Or Simon."

"They're both in David's apartment. They'll be over in a minute. And what do they have to tell me, Detective?"

"Didn't you hear about their adventure at Pearson?"

"At the airport, yes. I'm so glad you were able to work

things out for them. It pays to have friends in the police department."

Morgan was relieved that Lord Ottermead could be gauche, himself. "And Susan went on her way," Morgan added, somewhat cryptically.

"Yes, she did, on a later flight. Apparently she had to travel tourist class."

"I'm sure she managed," said Morgan.

"Yes, of course. It was not an overnight flight. I can't imagine sitting up all night," said Lionel Webb, indicating that he never had.

Morgan glanced over at Miranda who nodded encouragement, knowing he must be making significant connections.

"She was carrying things for you?" he said.

"Yes. A couple of books."

"Not just any books."

"No, one of them was *The New Atlantis*. It was a favour, she was returning them both to their rightful home."

"Your collection."

"England."

"Them. Plural. The other book?"

"A curiosity, a later edition, of no particular value."

"And the manuscript?"

"The manuscript? What manuscript would that be?"

The man appeared so genuine, Morgan faltered for a moment, then decided to proceed on the assumption they both knew Webb was dissembling.

"Well," said Morgan, "does the name Christian Rosenkreuz mean anything to you?"

"Yes, of course," said Felix Swan who had slipped unobtrusively into their conversation, a not easy feat for such a big man.

Webb ignored Swan. Morgan turned to him with sufficient menace, the erstwhile Rector backed off a pace, but not so far he would be out of hearing.

"Everyone knows Christian Rosenkreuz," said Lionel Webb, forgetting, for a moment, the larger world.

Morgan smiled. It was not often Lionel Webb made such a cavalier slip.

"Bacon aficionados and Rosicrucians," said Webb, recognizing the arrogance of his assumption. He went on to explain, without apology. "And medieval scholars, of course, they know the name as a pseudonym for the author of *Fama Fraternitatis,* a book sometimes attributed to Francis Bacon, which would make him responsible for the Rosicrucian revival."

"Revival?"

"The movement is said to have started 3500 years ago with Pharaoh Thutmose III. I have several artifacts from his tomb in my Cabinet. It nearly died out during the so-called Dark Ages."

"And the manuscript?"

"What manuscript?"

"A manuscript of *Fama Fraternitatis*, proving Bacon's authorship, wouldn't that be worth even more than your first edition of *The New Atlantis?*"

"Handwritten? Yes, of course, if such a thing existed. That was Dieter Kurtz's great dream as a scholar, to prove Bacon wrote the *Fama*. For Dieter it was an article of faith that Bacon was the author. The rest of us aren't so sure, although it doesn't harm Bacon's reputation to think that he might have."

Morgan was at a loss. Clearly, the man had no idea Susan had been carrying a manuscript of incalculable value, parcelled in with the bundle she was couriering.

It occurred to Morgan he could be wrong, the manuscript might be of no consequence. But his instincts, a good eye for the antiquity of paper and script, and a powerful sense of narrative proclaimed it a significant item in the unfolding story.

If Lionel Webb were not the manuscript's owner, who was? It had to fit in, somehow. Arcane artifacts of incalculable worth don't just float around, especially when there is a murder involved.

He glanced at Miranda and she responded to his vaguely lost look by walking over and suggesting Lionel lead them into the library.

"Certainly," he said, smiling graciously. "It's your show. Only the theatre is mine."

As they filed into the room and arranged themselves among the ample furniture, singly and in pairs, David Jenness and Simon Sparrow entered through a side door, clearly familiars in what might have seemed a mausoleum were there not so many living people about. Libraries can be alive with the prospect of knowledge or they can seem like a crypt, a repository for words of the dead. On this particular evening, despite or perhaps because of a forced jocularity, death seemed ascendant.

Gazing at the funereal grandeur around her, Miranda

was grateful for the intimacy of her Isabella Street condo. She waited until everyone was seated except Morgan, then walked to the fireplace and leaned against the broad mantle, leaving her partner at centre stage in what felt strangely like theatre of the absurd. Morgan looked slowly about him, making eye contact with each member of the Bacon Society in turn. The suspense became nearly palpable and still no one spoke. He caught Miranda's eye and gave her an almost imperceptible wink.

Finally, in a soft voice, he announced, "Thank you so much for coming."

"It was a police summons," said Hermione. "You don't think we'd miss an occasion like this." She was sly, managing to acknowledge his authority and dismiss it in the same breath.

"My partner has a few things she would like to ask you," said Morgan, and took a place by the piano.

Suddenly, an invisible proscenium descended around Miranda as all eyes looked to her for whatever was about to unfold. She was on stage by herself. Taking her cue from Morgan, whom she would have liked to throttle at the moment, she let silence work in her favour.

Gathering her thoughts, she wondered where to begin. Clearly, Morgan had run into a dead end with Webb and the German manuscript. She looked to Jane Latimer, sitting in a deep leather chair, dressed demurely in unseasonable black although her skirt was a little short. Where to begin, she wondered? Then, without looking at anyone in particular, she spoke:

"Since you are what remains of the Bacon Society,

perhaps we should talk about Francis Bacon."

The room stirred. Some of them seemed relieved or amused while others bristled.

"He seems to have been a very odd person," she said. "Very difficult to know. Not because he was elusive, it seems, but because he was such a contrdiction."

"Yes he was," said Lionel, speaking for them all. "That is perhaps his paramount attraction."

"Both intellectually and psychologically," said Jane Latimer, the nominal leader of the group. "He was a mass of contradictions in his life and in his work."

"That is the power of his appeal," added Felix Swan, flushed with the possibility they were about to spend the evening in esoteric discussion.

"So, if I understand right," Miranda continued, "he was a gentleman courtier and a fawning sycophant, a brilliant man of letters, a rather nasty spy, and a miserable husband."

"Don't forget felon," Padraig proclaimed with an air of pride.

"Bacon's life and work," Jane Latimer said, "embodied paradox—"

"Not unlike Dieter Kurtz," said Miranda, interrupting her. She held up her hand to quell a rumbling from several quarters. People wanted to have their say about Bacon.

"Professor Kurtz seems to have been a comparable character," Miranda continued. "Now, he's as dead as Francis Bacon."

So, they were going to talk about murder after all, and

not the reconciliation of opposites, as the more scholarly among them clearly would clearly have preferred.

Was it possible, she wondered, that Kurtz and Bacon were not fragmented personalities but so wholly integrated as unified beings that no one could see inside.

Miranda glanced over at Morgan who nodded encouragement.

"Let's start at the beginning," she said. She knew this was arbitrary, since the beginning of something can only be known by how it ends, and they were not quite at the end of anything yet. There were still many beginnings.

"Dieter Kurtz was dead on the ground in Philosophers Walk. Simon," she turned impulsively to the person in the room who, in contrast to Kurtz, had the least integrated personality: "it is spelled without an apostrophe."

Simon Sparrow stared at his hands in his lap. Good, she thought, no response. The others looked puzzled, they had not expected the punctuation police. Morgan knew she was thinking the anonymous e-mail posting of Kurtz's death was probably from Simon. That would mean he had access to Kurtz's home computer.

"The learned professor was introduced to my partner and me by a killer with a sense of humour. But was it Professor Kurtz being ridiculed or death itself? There he was, after all, grasping a facsimile he would have disdained in life. There he was, with a pubic hair in his beard and his penis poking out of his fly."

There was an audible intake of breath.

"His penis?" Padraig exclaimed.

"A hair?" said Hermione.

"The old buggar," said Lionel Webb.

"We'll come back to that," said Miranda, glancing at Lionel and then at Felix Swan.

"Please do," said Ralph. "For Porrig's sake. He loves penis chatter—and a public pubic hair, my goodness."

"When we first talked to you, each tried to outdo the other in expressing your loathing for Professor Kurtz. Jane, you claimed to despise him. So did you all. Some of you went too far. All of you revealed more about yourselves than about Dieter."

"Why would we want to do that?" said Jane.

"Perhaps it wasn't a choice. Or perhaps to shield your misfit messiah."

"From what. Good grief, Dieter was capable of defending himself."

"After death? That's an interesting notion." Miranda paused to consider the implications of a dead man taking refuge under a shroud of disparagement.

"Perhaps," she continued, "because the Bacon Society was determined to be part of the murder investigation."

"And why would that be?" said Jane, with the air of someone on superior ground.

"His death brought your separate stories together. Alive, he held you like birds in a gilded cage, hanging in a pitch black room. Perhaps you thought his murder would let in the light, forgetting that light reveals and exposes, forgetting that Dieter Kurtz, even dead, still held the key to the cage."

"Interesting," said Jane. "A Metaphysical conceit, with a capital M.

"You gave me your membership list before we asked for it. The only way to ensure your presence throughout the investigation was to draw the police into your midst, and to engage and confound us by your strange blend of animosity and affection: for Dieter and for each other."

"And why would we do that?" said Jane.

"Place yourselves at risk of being accessories to murder? You tell me?"

"I wouldn't want to usurp your role," said Jane quite cheerfully. "It's your conceit."

"I don't think there's an answer," said Miranda. "That's the problem, we were looking for an answer where there isn't one." She paused. "You are the collective creation of a man who is dead." She paused again. "He seemed to control you all with dark knowledge drawn from your private histories and innermost selves, and I think he still does."

The implications of a collective entity, even more than of posthumous control, caused a stir, but she again held up a hand with quieting authority. Having them all seated while she and Morgan were standing gave her a rhetorical and physical advantage that no one was yet prepared to challenge.

"The more we were exposed to Dieter Kurtz," she continued, "the more unstable his image as a loathsome tyrant became. But as we got to know each of you better, another Kurtz came into focus. If he was the worst among you, the devil in your midst, sharing in your various sins, he also began to emerge as a savior of sorts, a good man among the fallen, there to support you and bear many of your burdens himself."

Miranda stopped talking. She had ventured from a Metaphysical metaphor into a quasi-religious analogy that made her uncomfortable. She looked to Morgan and he stepped forward and began talking.

"You can see our predicament," Morgan said. "The motives for murder have become increasingly complex and elusive. From the get go, we accepted the killer was one of you. You invited us to believe this. Why, I think, lies in the personality of the dead man."

Morgan looked over at Miranda for help, but she offered only a covert smile. Since his next thought was far from forthcoming, his thinking circled around on itself.

"Each disclosure of something sinister came with a countervailing revelation to draw our attention away from the crime. It has been very easy to lose track of Dieter Kurtz as a victim."

Stepping back, he deferred to Miranda.

"We do not wish to betray anyone's confidence," she said, immediately taking up the line he had tossed her. She looked around the room. These were friends, suspects in the murder of another friend, and that in itself made the notion of friendship absurd.

"Jane, you and I have talked, and I believe you would agree, your relationship with Professor Kurtz could be read as both very positive and very negative."

The others glanced nervously around the room, looking at each other but avoiding eye contact. They were confused, threatened by the allusion to Jane's indebtedness to her mentor. What they had seen was a man who treated her with such casual disdain they assumed she sometimes flaunted her perfect body just to arouse his annoyance, to irritate him with her impropriety. This endeared her to the rest of them.

"Felix," Miranda continued, looking at the Rector whose broad face flushed with anxiety. "Felix," she repeated. "Dieter Kurtz suffered a great deal for you and earned your resentment. Still, you stood up for the man when he could no longer speak for himself. You have, perhaps, settled your debt. Honourably, I think."

There was general confusion about this. Miranda had been as oblique as possible to protect Felix Swan's privacy, and doing so had opened his relationship with Kurtz to a welter of damning conjecture. Even Lionel Webb, who knew that the old professor had taken the hit for Felix, did not know that Swan had been raped. He shared the assumption that Felix had been protected by a man who shared his unpleasant predilection. The strange thing was, given the consensus that Felix Swan was a pedophile, they all liked him, and such affection made them uneasy.

chapter thirty-three

Further Revelations

Miranda gazed around the room like a raptor casting about for her prey. "What about you two?" she said, addressing the D'Arcys who were sitting side by side on a deep leather sofa, so close their legs touched from knee to thigh.

"Us?" said Padraig.

"You."

"There's not much to say."

"Is that right? Dieter Kurtz had so little impact on your lives, there's nothing to tell us about. Perhaps someone else could fill us in." She looked about the room, as if calling for volunteers.

"Well, no, now, just a minute " said Ralph. "Maybe you could, it could be said, Dieter brought us together."

"Rafe," Padraig cautioned.

"It's all right," said Ralph. "There's nothing everyone doesn't already know."

"Rafe," Padraig repeated, this time plaintively.

"Porrig doesn't like to acknowledge it, but I was a bit of a whore," said Ralph, sitting upright on the sofa so the ambient light set off his Errol-Flynn features. "I was what Robertson Davies called a bum-boy, what football players call a tight end; I was an intimate part of the decor for several summers at Briar Hill Island."

"Dieter Kurtz introduced us," said Padraig, addressing Miranda directly, as if they were having a private conversation.

"Dieter was a friend of Lionel's," said Ralph. Turning to Lionel Webb, he said: "Dear man, I don't want to expose your family."

"The skeletons in my family closet are marionettes, old Rafe. Dangle them from the strings of your wicked imagination," Webb responded. "We'll see if there's harm to be done."

"I believe Dieter was very influential in your life," said Ralph, first to Lionel, then addressing the room he continued: "They met, if I'm not mistaken, soon after he came to Toronto. Bacon brought them together."

"I outbid him at an auction," said Lionel Webb, rising to his feet from a Victorian settee he was sharing with Jennifer. "He insisted on knowing where the book was going. It was a rare 1622 copy of *The History of the Reign of King Henry the Seventh.* He virtually followed me home and demanded to inspect my storage facilities; and he had no hesitation about telling me how to improve them. My *Wunderkammern*," he nodded towards the massive door leading into his *sanctum sanctorum*. "It was virtually his design."

Lionel paced slowly as he gestured for Ralph to continue.

"You became friends," said Ralph, his eyes following Lionel's movements. "He accompanied you to Muskoka while your father was still alive. He saw me. He liked what he saw. We all, myself included, thought Dieter Kurtz wanted me for himself. But no. He had become fast friends with Kate Nesbitt, the cook. During long evening talks in the kitchen, he learned about Porrig's family, and his mother's connection with the Webbs."

"Rafe, please!"

"It's all right, Porrig. Dieter Kurtz was fascinated by Porrig's mother, by her being a Jew. As if he bore the guilt of the Nazi regime when death ruled Europe and he was its henchman, he took it upon himself to be her personal golem."

"Golem?" said Marie Lachine. "What is golem, a Jewish creation?"

"An avenger risen from the earth without a soul. And so he was, just that," said Ralph. "Dieter arranged—is that too kind a word, Lionel—he procured recompense for wrong done to Ruth Robertshaw and the Robertshaw family."

"Arranged would be a good word for it," said Lionel. "And golem, that would be apt, as well."

"And for Porrig," said Ralph, "for Porrig, he procured me."

"Procure, that's harsh," said Padraig.

"Not at all, dear Porrig. It is, as Lionel says, quite *apt*. Dieter picked me out of the crowd, he selected me, and the first time he and I talked, we stayed up until dawn. He excoriated my soul in one night, razed it raw and clean. The next morning, he introduced us, Porrig and me. He brought us together and demanded we be seated as peers at the dinner table that night. The old man had a fit. Our own Lionel, if I remember right, was amused.

"Dieter Kurtz was a man without conscience, he left the old man with no option. Dieter knew enough to bring him to ruin. The old man knew Dieter would stop at nothing. The first few meals together in the formal dining room were like roasting in the fires of hell. Then, as we all began to bask in the glow, it became somehow a feature of the festivities, that we were equals, damn it, whether we were equal or not.

"Ah, the old man adapted, and not long after he died. Lionel kept us on and we have been friends ever since. We even invested in a Bacon first edition on Dieter's advice. The Bacon Society is our common meeting place, our fraternal abode."

"Assembled as a body through blackmail and extortion," said Padraig, "but we are bound by affection and trust."

"And so say we all," said Lionel. Apparently not offended by the degrading light cast over his family history, he returned to the side of Jennifer Pluck on the antique settee.

Miranda shifted her stance to address their host

directly. The man seemed imperturbable, even though it was clear the next salvo would be at his expense.

"The fortunes of your family were shaped a great deal by Dieter Kurtz. I'm assuming you hated the man as much as the rest."

"Hate is not the right word. And I admired him as well. Dieter opened an ethical centre within my family. We were a succession of successful men, in worldly terms, with each of us wanting, lacking, a moral dimension to fill out our characters. And then came Dieter."

"You've obviously thought about this a good deal," said Miranda. "The man who had no conscience, himself, he instilled one in you."

"Yes. A sense of responsibility. I suppose that's all conscience really is. Dieter called the Webbs to account for the treatment of Porrig's mother, for the debasement of Rafe, and for much else, besides."

"Such as?"

"Jennifer," said Webb.

"Jennifer? Right, he helped you establish the Webb Foundation."

"Oh, more than helped, Detective. He insisted on it. It wasn't blackmail. It was in recognition of loyalty, Jennifer's mother was loyal to a fault. But much more than that, it was in acknowledgment of knowing the sins of my grandfather, the crimes on which the family fortune was built—there are no fortunes that are not built on moral compromise; she carried the weight of knowing and keeping such terrible knowledge to herself—Dieter convinced me that there are few burdens more loathsome than to bear the sins of another. Since she would accept nothing for herself, then her daughter became virtually my ward, with roots as deeply embedded in the compost of our family origins as my own."

He drew Jennifer close to him on the settee with an affectionate arm across her shoulders that she rose to, rather than sinking against, indicating not a proprietorial but a loving relationship. Miranda could not resist being impressed by how quickly the young woman had shed her foundling disguise. Having endured the humiliation all those years of being denied what she understood as her birthright, she now proudly held a legitimate claim on Lionel Webb through an affair of the heart. Miranda was pleased for both of them, in spite of the fact it seemed Kurtz's murder was what brought them together.

The others, including Morgan, waited. They all had the sense Miranda and Lionel were not finished, but no one was sure who would take the lead.

Finally, Lionel said, "You want more?"

"Yes," said Miranda.

"You see a pattern, an incomplete triptych? If Dieter addressed the sins of the fathers, what about the sins of the son?"

"Something like that," she responded.

"The assumption being, I, too, have done great wrong?"

"Yes."

"I am perhaps guilty of murder, of killing Dieter Kurtz."

"Perhaps," she said.

"You are on the wrong tack, Detective, It is nothing

like that."

"That's a nautical term, isn't it? On the wrong tack. I would have said, 'on the wrong track.'"

"Whatever, Detective. It makes no difference."

"Oh, but it does," said Miranda.

"You think?"

"Yes. I'll explain. It's not about Dieter's death. Your wife died in a sailing accident, I believe."

For the first time, Lionel Webb appeared disconcerted, but only momentarily. Miranda continued, for the most part flying blind. She was following up nothing more substantial than an odd turn of phrase, yet she was certain it would lead to some sort of breakthrough. Information from the file of newspaper clippings they had assembled, that until now had seemed extraneous, surged forward in her head.

"Your wife died on Lake Ontario. You used to sail out of the RTYC. You had a sloop brought over from a shipyard in Cowes."

"On the Isle of Wight. You have a very good memory, Detective."

"For esoteric details, yes. I learned the need for that from my partner. Perhaps Detective Morgan would like to take over, here?"

"No," said Morgan. "You're doing just fine."

The truth was, neither of them knew where to go next. Lionel Webb did not know this.

Jennifer Pluck got up from the settee but seemed uncertain what to do next and remained standing as Lionel rose to his feet beside her. Drawing himself to his full height, he squeezed Jennifer's hand briefly and picked up the narrative.

"She was hit on the head by the boom as I jibed. It was a bit of bad seamanship that turned brutal, I'm afraid."

"And she was very sick at the time," said Morgan.

"Yes, she was dying."

"A miserable death."

"Yes," said Lionel. "Miserable, a miserable dying."

"And she asked for one last sail?" said Miranda.

"Yes," said Lionel. "One final outing. She loved the water, sailing away from the sunset, coming back to the city past Gibraltar point."

"And Dieter Kurtz was with you?" said Morgan.

"Yes, he was. She was very weak. I could not have managed without Dieter."

"And when you emerged through the Eastern Gap and cut across to the yacht club, the wind caught your mainsail and—"

"We were scudding through, wing and wing with an easterly wind at our backs, and as I rounded up towards the Island the mainsail crashed across the cockpit, and it smashed Clara's skull."

"She died instantly?"

"She was knocked overboard. I dove in after her. By the time Dieter got the boat around and hove to, she was dead."

Miranda moved closer to Lionel Webb and Jennifer stepped away from his side.

"She was in a great deal of pain, wasn't she?" said Miranda.

"Intolerable," said Lionel.

"You loved her very much," said Miranda.

"I could not protect her."

"And so you delivered her from her pain."

"Perhaps."

"But you couldn't do it yourself."

"No."

"She knew what was happening, didn't she?"

"Yes."

"You held her in your arms."

"I held her."

"But Dieter Kurtz killed her."

"He was at the tiller, he jibed. I couldn't—"

"She knew it was coming?"

"Possibly."

"And when the boom stunned her, you took her into the water—"

"She fell in."

"You held her under."

"She drowned in my arms."

The bookshelves wavered in Miranda's peripheral vision; the room seemed now an intimate place.

"You loved her very much."

"Yes."

"And Dieter Kurtz, he was there for you both."

"Yes he was."

"Did you love him?"

"Not then. Later perhaps. He was simply a part of me after that, like a vital organ: you do not love your heart, but you could not live without it."

If you listen very carefully, Morgan thought, you can hear the hearts of everyone in the room beating in a sympathetic cadence with Lionel's own.

For a moment, the air between Miranda and Lionel seemed intolerably charged, then she smiled and turned to Marie Lachine. The attention of the room shifted. "Dr. Lachine. Dieter Kurtz apparently knew more about you than you did," she said. "Usually, power over a person derives from the threat of revealing secrets the person already knows. But he kept yours hidden even from you."

"He brought us together," she responded, surprised the inquiry had suddenly turned towards her. "Within the safe perimeters of the Bacon Society. Perhaps he knew better than we did how much we could bear. Perhaps he was right."

"You don't seem angry with him," said Miranda. "The death of your parents seems to have mellowed your feelings."

"I was furious with him for such a long time. I knew we were being manipulated, but I did not know how. That can be difficult, especially for someone like me, all my life out of step. I felt at the mercy of some terrible knowledge he held, that we were the prisoners of his very dark world."

"And now?"

"In Muskoka, I learned that knowing can be an awesome responsibility. Dieter had brought us together, Detective, and protected us. And when the time was right, in the aftermath of his death, revelations about the strange intricacies of love were exquisitely liberating. My mother died fulfilled in the arms of her beloved, after a lifetime apart. My father died at peace, refusing guilt. When we were lovers, we were not father and daughter, and when we became father and daughter, we were not lovers. And Yijin Sung, he is my brother. My father died knowing this, of course, but it was only at my mother's wake that we discovered it, ourselves. The expatriate *separatiste* has a home, now, in Chinatown. *C'est bon, n'est pas?*"

"Yes," said Miranda. "So it would seem. Your family was brief in duration, but infinite in complexity."

"The inscrutable satisfactions of enduring brevity: yes, very Chinese, quite appropriate to my revealed identity."

"Yes," said Miranda. She was thinking of her own family, dead or dispersed. Even Jill, bound to her by torment shared, was a boarder at Branksome Hall. Miranda did not live the kind of life appropriate for a teenage girl. It was, in every way, too adult. She envied Marie Lachine, who now had a history, not merely a past, and a future defined by her newfound identity. Miranda felt a wave of loneliness sweep through her, as she gazed about this roomful of improbable friends.

Morgan shifted his weight from one foot to the other. He was impressed by how Miranda was leading the sequence of revelations, although he was unsure where she was going. Since she seemed at a temporary standstill, he picked up the initiative. Hermione MacGregor interested him in the context of new insights into Kurtz's character.

"Hermione," he said. "Does everyone know about

your special relationship with Dieter Kurtz?"

From the collective gasp, he realized a secret was hovering on the verge of exposure. Miranda grimaced at her partner's lack of subtlety, but Morgan felt no sense of betrayal. It was Kurtz who had chosen to keep the wartime affair a private thing. Morgan suspected it was he who had wanted to protect their privacy and not Hermione. The old woman gave Morgan a sweet smile, casting her eyes demurely to the floor, then flashing them up at him, dared him to continue. He did.

"You sometimes speak fondly of Professor Kurtz," he said. "This is a man who violated you at seventeen. He tortured you, he raped you, he betrayed you, he turned you over to the enemy for execution. How is it possible not to hate such a man? Is affection perhaps a perverse disguise, Hermione, to protect yourself from the terrible memories you were confronted with, every time you saw him."

"Ah, Detective. Life is more complex." The diminutive old woman smiled again, this time to reassure him that she felt no animosity for his disclosure of their private conversations.

"Than what, more complex than what?" Morgan asked.

Only Miranda knew fully what they were talking about, although several of the others suspected a wartime romance, and Lionel seemed familiar with the overall shape of her story. Young David Jenness listened in fascination. Jennifer Pluck had moved back closer to Lionel so that they touched, standing side by side against the bookshelves near the door into the Cabinet of Curiosities.

"There is never one story, Detective. Each time it is told, it swallows the ones preceding, it becomes another story and another and another. I have rehearsed the story of Dieter and myself so many times, and each time I am different for telling it, even to myself."

"And?"

"Dieter had the power to kill me, he had the authority, I was a spy, it was quite legal under the circumstances. He chose to let me live. And yes, he betrayed me. But, Detective, it was necessary. You say he turned me over to the enemy. Yes. But you are caught up in only one story. He was a Nazi, an SS officer; the Soviets were his enemy, not mine. When the Soviets rolled into Berlin, Dieter knew his fellow Nazis would try to kill me. Death, because they were about to die! The Soviets, of course, would have killed me as well; they raped and murdered the women of Berlin. It was part of their military strategy. So why would they pick me out to be spared, unless Dieter could convince them I was an Allied spy, captured by him and brought to Berlin for interrogation.

"The Soviets tortured me, not because I was their enemy, but to affirm Dieter's story that I was their friend. When they realized I had nothing to hide, they sent me home."

Each of the others in the Bacon Society, even Lionel, stared at Hermione MacGregor in astonishment. This tiny old lady in their midst, who had been old when she was first introduced to them by Dieter Kurtz, had lived a life of terrible adventure none of them knew anything about, beyond their wildest imaginings. From what they could piece together, and each of them came up with a different version, they were moved, and moved deeply, by their own ignorance, that they had taken for granted her life had been no more eventful than their own. 'Hermione the Spy' had been a nickname, a cavalier term of endearment. Not real.

"Well," David Jenness spoke up, "it seems appropriate at this time to declare my own indebtedness to Professor Kurtz."

"David?" said Morgan.

"Dieter Kurtz was a friend of my family. I knew him as an eccentric elderly uncle. Not genetically, um, yes, you understand about uncles. He introduced me to Lionel before I came down from Cambridge. We had dinner at Claridges several times. Nigel and my mother, myself, Dieter, he insisted I call him Dieter, and Lionel. After Nigel died, Lionel suggested I come and work for him in Canada. Actually, it was Dieter's idea. He wanted me to live in Toronto for a bit. He seemed to feel it was important. My mother loved the idea. Toronto, yes, it seemed exotic and strangely familiar."

While Miranda thought immediately that Kurtz's irrepressible propensity to orchestrate lives had been instrumental in connecting Morgan with his son, Morgan himself warmed to the idea that Susan might have encouraged David to come to Toronto out of romantic nostalgia. Neither she nor Dieter could have known the actual course of events that would bring them together. Miranda knew equally well that Kurtz's machinations could not have been prophetic but must have found the retroactive inevitability of their meeting attractive, a convergence of lives that cast the old man in a flattering light. There is no such thing as coincidence.

"In Toronto," David continued, "I became a provisional member of the Bacon Society and have been swatting quite diligently to catch up on our eponymous knight." Who, thought Morgan, but a Cambridge graduate with a title of his own would refer to Francis Bacon as *our eponymous knight*?

"And here I also discovered the complexity of Dieter Kurtz. I was fascinated. He was the same avuncular man I knew through my childhood, and he was a fiend—mind you, not one I feared. I realize others did. But he was also my mentor. His ambivalent roles in the lives of his friends enthralled me. I enjoy puzzles and labyrinths. I enjoyed knowing the minotaur. I think perhaps I was the only person who truly grieved at his passing.

"And your mother," said Morgan, who was thinking about his own fondness for labyrinths.

"Yes. And my mother. We grieved unequivocally."

"Perhaps," said Miranda, "because only you, of everyone here, did not anticipate his death."

"Miranda?" Morgan interjected.

"Apart from Morgan and myself," she added.

Where was she going with this? The implication that Kurtz's death was by committee had come up before, but never as a serious consideration. Miranda had made an intuitive leap, with no landing place in sight. She might have conspiracy in mind but, so far as Morgan knew, no theory, nothing more than a notion of collective responsibility.

He was accustomed to free-falling. When she looked at him with a plaintive gleam in her eye, he started speaking:

"That leaves Simon," he said, drawing attention away from Miranda. "You seem to be the only one not accounted for in this reckoning."

"What about Jennifer?" Simon retorted.

What an odd response, Miranda thought, but it gave her a place to land, back at centre stage.

"Jennifer's story is clear enough," said Miranda. "Yours is still very obscure."

This was an unsettling blow to Simon Sparrow. His lifetime had been devoted to rescuing himself from obscurity.

"I don't hide behind disguises," he countered.

The others glowered at him. Curiously, Miranda felt called upon to provide a defensive response.

"I think, Simon, if you mean Jennifer, it was not a disguise but a costume; she was dressing the part of a waif, perhaps, an emotional foundling, and she did so with style. If you're referring to Jane, well I think it was you, Hermione, who once said Jane makes you feel *damn* good about being a woman."

"And if you mean us?" said Morgan. "Cops disguised as human beings? Masks sometimes allow us to be who we really are, Simon. Of course, masks sometimes simply conceal, don't they?"

"I do not own a book by Francis Bacon," said Simon, his urgency catching everyone off guard. "I do not have a museum. I am not really a part of this group. I have an alibi."

"I imagine you do," said Morgan. "It would not surprise me if you all have alibis."

"Morgan..." said Miranda, and let her voice trail off.

"Each of you had an explanation for where you were at the time of the murder," he said. "Curiously, every one of you could explain, but none could confirm."

"And?" said Lionel Webb. "What do we make of that?"

"Here's what I think," said Morgan. "I think, if and when charges were to be laid, then previous explanations would vanish and a rock-solid alibi would appear as needed."

"Interesting," said Lionel. "So now, perhaps, you would like to hear Simon's alibi."

"Yes please," said Miranda.

Lionel Webb reached up and took a folder from the bookshelves behind him and opening the folder removed one of a dozen files. He handed it to Simon. Simon passed it on to Miranda, who glanced at it and turned it over to Morgan.

Inside, was a passenger manifest declaring that at the time of the murder Simon Sparrow had been airborne in a corporate jet owned by Webb Enterprises, on his way home from Vancouver to Toronto via St. John's, coast to coast and half-way back again.

"That would keep you in the air quite a while," said

Miranda when Morgan shared Simon's absurd itinerary, "passing through six or seven time zones—ten, if you count doubling back."

"Saint John or St. John's?" asked Padraig ingenuously. "Here we go with the damned apostrophes again."

"You tell us, Porrig," said Miranda. "I'm guessing you were on the same flight."

"Was I? I was indeed. I get them confused; one's with an apostrophe and the other spells out the word s-a-i-n-t. And one's in New Brunswick and one is the capital of Newfoundland."

"And which one were you re-routed through on your way home from Vancouver?" asked Miranda.

"Vancouver?" Padraig said, dubiously

"Vancouver," affirmed Ralph, forcefully.

Miranda shrugged and turned to Lionel Webb. "Why that particular route, and why only Simon's name on the manifest."

"Because it is an overnight flight and doesn't cross international boundaries. A separate form was made out for each passenger."

"Is that customary?"

"Not necessarily."

"But let me guess," said Miranda. "There are twelve of them, including one for Sir David. You are all covered in the same way."

"Quite possibly," said Lionel Webb. "If the need arises."

Miranda gazed around, her eyes making contact with each member of the Bacon Society in turn. She caught a glimpse of herself in the glass doors of the conservatory. Blended among the reflections of books and people she could see orchids illuminated by light coming in from the library and a faint bit of movement like a punctuation mark hovering.

chapter thirty-four

Arcana

"Bees and apostrophes," said Miranda. Being enigmatic gave her a certain indefinable power, as if she knew things beyond the comprehension of the Bacon Society, things about mysteries and murder that only a detective would know. In spite of their varying degrees of knowledge about the arcane practices of Rosicrucians and Masons, they seemed to her to be intellectually fragile. They knew about wonder in the Renaissance and rationalism in the Age of Reason, and were devoted to a mystical humanist in whom the two eras merged, but they seemed curiously unsophisticated about their own world. Even Lionel Webb, who had resumed his seat with Jennifer on the Victorian settee appeared content to let events unfold at her command.

"The penis was an accident," she said, thinking out

loud, "or possibly an afterthought."

Morgan stared at her. *Is this pronouncement a feminist take on Creation?*

She glanced at him and smiled confidently, unnerving everyone else in the room.

He smiled back.

"I really do have an alibi of my own," said Simon Sparrow.

"Another one," said Miranda.

He looked confused.

"Actually, one is enough," she said.

"I was out of town that night."

"So it appears."

"No, I mean really I was."

"Simon," said Miranda, "I believe Lionel has you covered. And I'm sure he has gone to a great deal of trouble to make sure the facts will stand up to scrutiny."

"Unassailable," said Lionel Webb. "And facts don't lie, do they, Detective?"

"But people do," she responded, not taking her eyes off Simon. "Tell us, Simon, where else were you the night Dieter Kurtz died?"

"I was in Peterborough."

"Peterborough?"

"It's an hour and a half east of here."

"I know where Peterborough is?"

"I was with a young lady."

"Well, good for you, Simon. But as you said, you were only an hour and a half away."

"We went to the Canoe Museum."

"Really?"
"Yes."
"How very unusual."
"Then we went out, we had too much to drink."
"Not so good for you."
"I think we passed out."
"Both of you?"
"Yes."

"Nasty business," observed David Jenness, obviously thinking of how his mother was compromised by her lover's sleazy behaviour.

"What?" said Simon. "Oh, no. It wasn't like that. I hardly knew her."

"Really!" said David. "Well then it hardly counts, does it?"

"No, no" Simon exclaimed. "She's just someone I knew, we went on a canoe trip together. A reunion. All very innocent. We both fell asleep. She can verify it."

"Well, even if she can," said Miranda, "poor Simon, it's not much of an alibi."

"No?"

"The Canoe Museum," said Lionel. "A wonderful place. They've got things there I'd love to have for my cabinet. I think I served on the board of directors. Why else would I be in Peterborough? Apart from its proximity to Lakebridge."

"Things for your cabinet?" said Miranda. She had almost forgotten the Webb family fortunes began near Peterborough.

"Old canoes," said Lionel.

"You collect canoes?" said Miranda.

"I collect," said Lionel.

"I met her on a canoe trip on Baffin Island, the Soper River," Simon interjected, and as no one seemed inclined to explore further the acquisitive propensities of their host, he continued: "The night Professor Kurtz died, we had a little too much to drink, maybe food poisoning."

"Simon," said Miranda. "It's the oldest trick in the book."

"What? There's no trick."

"Slip her a sleeping potion, duck out, do what you have to do, sneak back in beside her, she swears you were there all along. I've seen it several times on *Law and Order* and *Masterpiece Theatre*. Inspector Lewis, I believe it was."

"Oh."

"And if you weren't with her at all—if it was a bit of emotional extortion or a discrete sum of cash. No, Simon, stick with the alibi Lionel has gone to so much trouble to give you. It'll stand up better in court."

"In court! Am I being charged?" He paused. "Really?" He was nervous, but he was beginning to appreciate the occasion. Never before had he been the focal center of their group activities. He rose from his chair and began walking about, yet there was nowhere to go, and nowhere else he apparently wanted to be.

"Do you know how Professor Kurtz died?" Miranda addressed everyone, but her voice connected to the peripatetic Simon. He stopped and turned to her.

"Everyone does," said Simon.

"Do you know what killed him?"

No one, including Simon, responded. Morgan wondered if she wasn't about to reveal too much, too soon. Miranda walked over to the conservatory doors and opened them. The secretive aroma of orchids entered the room and quickly dissipated into the ambient odors of a library filled with old books and people.

She turned dramatically to face her audience.

"Bees," she said. "He was stung by bees."

"Really?" Hermione exclaimed. "Was it an accident, then?" Her voice betrayed a hint of disappointment.

"No," said Miranda. "Considering the whimsical presentation of his body, it was no accident." Had she seen a bee through the glass, among the orchids? Or had she imagined it?

"Then who? What?" said Hermione. She clearly was curious about details that until now were unknown, at least to her.

"It would have to be done by someone experienced with bees, wouldn't it? Someone might have captured a couple with a sugar cube and boxed them up. Think of a pill box with a slide. Hold it against the skin, the soft part of the wrist to avoid swelling, directly over the arteries, not bone—pull back the slide, tap the box, frighten the bees, they sting, side by side, now remove the box, the bees drop and their little abdomens rip away from their bodies."

"Gruesome," said Hermione, who had the imagination based on her own experience as a victim of torture to envision the drama in miniature.

Simon said nothing.

"There are only two people in this room, to my knowledge, who know very much about bees," said Miranda.

"And you're one of them," said Jane Latimer, recalling the incident with the bee the first time they met. "What about Morgan?"

"Simon is the other," said Morgan.

"Anyone can learn about bees," said Simon.

"Not Kurtz," said Miranda. "He would want to keep his distance, he was anaphylactic."

"That's hard to believe," said Hermione. "He seemed invulnerable."

"Yes, until his natural immunity broke down," said Miranda. "I believe that can happen. Perhaps it was the malaria."

"Malaria?" said Morgan. He wanted to keep up.

"It's in his medical profile at the morgue."

"Yes," Morgan agreed.

"Did you know he had had syphilis?" she asked Hermione.

"No, he certainly did not, not when I knew him."

"He must have picked it up in the brothels of Southern China. Who knows?" said Miranda.

"But he didn't—" Lionel Webb started to proclaim something, then stopped.

"No, I believe he cured himself," said Miranda.

"How—" Lionel again stopped short. He thought he had known Dieter Kurtz.

"Syphilis can be cured by malaria," said Morgan, who had read this somewhere. "Malaria will knock it out of the system—works better than penicillin, except the after-effects are pretty raw."

"Exactly," said Miranda. "The cost of the cure, having survived malaria, might have been susceptibility to anaphylactic shock. Bee venom became lethal. He would have known that. So would his killer."

Hermione beamed. Her one-time lover had proven himself strangely, indomitably, heroic. Exposing himself to malaria to rid his body of syphilis! The brothels of Shanghai! Miranda looked at her, trying to imagine what might be going through her mind. Did hearing of his exploits perversely make her remember what it was to feel young?

No one else said anything. Miranda was clearly revealing a sequence of deductions in the order of her own choosing. Morgan appreciated her method, although he suspected she was no more certain where this was leading than he was.

Miranda suddenly turned on Simon who was leaning against the frame of the conservatory doors. She move towards him. Affecting nonchalance, he at first held his ground. As soon as she started talking, however, he edged around the room to the massive door beneath the bust of Pallas. Behind him, the sprawling *Wunderkammern* lay both hidden and known, familiar to them all.

"Simon," she said, following close enough to unnerve him. "Why did you take it upon yourself to announce Dieter's murder?"

"I…" He couldn't get beyond the first-person singular.

"You sent the e-mail from his home."

"No, I."

"You?"

"What if I did? What does it prove?"

"It proves," said Morgan, stepping forward, "that you were responsible for substituting the fake copy of Kurtz's *Sylva Sylvarum* for the authentic copy which you removed from his house."

Miranda was pleased. She had not made the connection, although she was certain, on the evidence of the apostrophe, that Simon had sent the message.

"No, no," Simon sputtered, "you're wrong."

"And then," Morgan continued, "for some reason, which I'm sure you will want to share with us, you planted the stolen copy at my partner's place in the village of Waldron. You drove all the way up to Waterloo Country and staged a break-in, just so we'd recover the damned thing."

Morgan realized he was very annoyed with Simon for compromising Miranda.

"Why would you do that, Simon? Why would you steal it from Kurtz and then return it to us?" said Morgan. "What are we missing here?"

"I wanted to get it into your hands without you knowing where it came from."

"He didn't steal it," Lionel Webb interjected. "It wasn't stolen. The original edition belongs to me, I bought it from Dieter. Simon was working for me."

"You what?" exclaimed Jennifer Pluck. Other heads nodded in mutual confusion.

"I bought it. Dieter needed money, quite a large sum.

I paid him very well. The forgery was my gesture of good faith, an assurance I would return the original for the sum given him, on demand. It was Dieter himself who put the fake in his cabinet."

"So, the authentic *Sylva* was collateral for a loan," said Morgan.

"If you like."

"And sending me to pick up the fake?" Jennifer interjected with vehemence, for the moment forgetting that she and Lionel Webb were lovers. "What was *that*?" The word 'that' took in a multitude of sins.

"You know, dear Jennifer, how much Dieter admired a good forgery—to make such a book once, that is craft; to replicate it perfectly, that is art!"

"Do not patronize me, Lionel Webb. Why was I sent to retrieve a counterfeit book from Dieter's case? Did you think I wouldn't figure it out. My God, I worked on the original. I knew the touch and the smell of that text. Did you think I was so bloody stupid?"

"Not stupid—"

"Naïve?"

"No, that is not what I thought." He looked almost frightened of her, of losing her. "Yes, perhaps, perhaps it is. I'm sorry, Jennifer. When you turned the fake over to the police, I realized it wasn't as good as we had supposed—and what a formidable person you are. I had thought you were Dieter's graduate student, my arms-length ward. And suddenly, I saw you as my peer—my partner, if you would have me. And of course you very nearly wouldn't."

"Have you? Damnit, Lionel! Don't be so *quaint*." Her features contorted in a brief flurry of emotion and resolved into a flirtatious smirk.

"Why?" said Morgan. For a moment everyone in the room except Lionel thought he was commenting on their relationship.

"Why did I want the forgery?" said Lionel. "Simple, I had hoped to exchange them back without undue attention."

"Why?" said Morgan, again.

"Because I felt a moral obligation to keep Dieter's loan a private thing."

"An obligation to return collateral on a loan to a dead man?"

"Something like that."

"He requested secrecy?"

"Insisted on it, yes."

"Why not turn the book over to us. We're capable of discretion, you know."

"I'm sure you are," he laughed, "except when there's murder involved. After Jennifer discovered the forgery, I asked Simon to get the original into your hands anonymously. I gave no particular directions. Needless to say, I had not counted on Simon's appetite for adventure. Or irony."

By his facial expression, it was clear Simon saw nothing ironic about planting material evidence in a murder case in the home of an investigating detective.

"I wanted to be sure you'd find it," said Simon as he slouched against the door leading into the Cabinet of

Curiosities, torn between making himself inconspicuous and trying to hold their attention.

"What did Professor Kurtz need the money for?" Morgan asked.

"I really don't know," said Lionel with a jaunty chuckle. "It was related to his work on Bacon, that's all he told me. It did not seem appropriate to care too much. I wanted the *Sylva*, he was content for the while with the fake. And the money, I expect, was put to good purpose. Simon might help you on that."

Simon shrugged.

"I wonder if whatever the money was for was worth dying for?" said Morgan, looking first at Simon, then around as the mausoleum walls closed in on the members of the Bacon Society, and finally at Miranda. . Simon flinched. Lionel Webb's natural ebullience fizzled like domestic 'champagne.' The others shifted in their seats, oppressed by the mounting anticipation. Miranda seemed excited.

Morgan nodded to her and then towards his briefcase on the floor by her feet. She picked it up. He gestured with a lowering of his eyes and she opened it. He wanted the Bacon Society to think he and Miranda were working in perfect tandem. She withdrew a plastic folder containing the German manuscript and handed it across to him.

Morgan took the manuscript out of its folder and held it towards Lionel Webb, who looked at it with interest but did not reach out to take it. A shimmer of recognition crossed over his face, he smiled and stepped back. Clearly, he knew it was significant, but whether to the murder investigation or as an artifact, Morgan could not be sure.

"You recognize this," Morgan declared as he proffered the manuscript in a slow sweep of the room, as if expecting at least one of his audience to step forward.

Felix lifted himself ponderously from his deep leather chair, took the manuscript gingerly from Morgan's hands and laid it on a low table. As he hunched down, Jane Latimer hovered beside him.

"You know what this is?" Felix said to Jane, his voice quivering.

"Yes," she answered in a sepulchral tone. "I do, I think, if it's what I think it is."

"It is," said Felix. "I am sure it is."

The others moved closer, all except Hermione, whose interest in Baconian matters was secondary to her interest in Dieter and his cohorts, and Simon, who had already declared himself not to be a true Baconian.

"Where did this come from?" said Felix, addressing Morgan. He was speaking in the voice of a scholar, which somehow had a different timbre from his normal voice as an academic politician. "Do you know what you have here?"

"Yes," said Morgan. "I believe it is Bacon's original manuscript of *Fama Fraternitatis*, published under the pen name, Christian Rosenkreuz."

"Well, you have done your homework, Detective," said Felix Swan. Morgan could not restrain a muted grin.

"Not full marks, though," said Jane Latimer.

Miranda watched sympathetically as Morgan asked her to clarify.

"Well," said Felix, answering for her, "this is not Bacon's writing. It is another hand, altogether."

"Really," said Morgan, swallowing his disappointment. "But it is *Fama Fraternitatis?*"

"Oh yes," said Jane. You're dead right, there. It's the *Fama.*"

"In German?" said Morgan.

"Medieval German," she responded. "But it was written by a scribe. This is not the original text, it is a fine copy, a duplicate."

"Not a facsimile, not a forgery, not a fake, and not a later edition?" said Miranda, rhyming off possible variants.

"No," said Felix. "This is an authentic duplicate, the work of a very skilled scrivener."

"Not Christian Rosenkreuz?" Morgan asked.

"I have no doubt it was done *for* Christian Rosenkreuz, yes, almost certainly. It is a clean copy done no doubt from the original manuscript."

"So," Morgan said, feeling vindicated, yet a little disappointed. "Why would Bacon, if it was Bacon who wrote it, why would he use a pseudonym, why would he write in German? Why isn't it in Latin?"

Jane smiled at his enthusiasm while continuing to examine the manuscript.

"A work like this," she said without looking up, "was conceived as a secular text. Latin was the language of divine authority. Latin was the language of scholarship;

this is a work of imagination."

"Why German?" Morgan persisted.

"Because," said Felix. "The author was trying to breathe new life into a work passed down through the ages, yet to distance himself—for modesty, propriety, and perhaps to avoid the Inquisition. How better than by using a vernacular language not his own."

"Except it is probably apocryphal," said Jane, "not passed down through the ages at all. I'd say it is medieval fiction which has been given the status of ancient truth with a smattering of arcane allusions. By an Englishman."

"As a Mason, I would suggest something more satisfying," said Felix, returning to the depths of the leather chair that even for him seemed massive. "*Fama Fraternitatis* is the remnant version of an authentic Egyptian text, transcribed by Christian Rosenkreuz before it was lost."

"Conveniently," said Jane. "Like Joseph Smith and the golden tablets."

"Plates," said Felix. "Golden plates. Mormons believe in golden plates and magic spectacles." Then, being a Mason and liable to charges of credulity on his own, he added in a fraternal aside: "But let us leave the Mormons alone. Their original text disappeared but manuscripts do get lost, after all."

"Conveniently," said Jane again.

"How did it fall into the hands of the police?" asked Felix.

Morgan considered for a moment, then answered with a forthright explanation: "Lady Jenness was carrying it in her hand luggage; she was bound for England this afternoon. I don't think she had any idea what it was. I had assumed she was carrying it for you, Lionel."

"Good Lord, no," said Lionel Webb.

"Well, she had a couple of other items of yours."

"Exactly. *The New Atlantis!* I would not have trusted it with anyone else, except possibly her son," he tilted his head in young David's direction and David Jenness grinned from the sign of approval. "As for the sixth edition, it was merely to provide something rigid so the *Atlantis* wouldn't bend. Nothing more devious than that. It seemed appropriate company."

"And this?" said Morgan, indicating the manuscript.

"No," said Lionel with the air of a man amused at the novelty of having his veracity questioned, "I have never seen it before."

"Then it must be yours," Morgan declared, turning to Simon. "Who else could get Susan to…" he searched for a word. The manuscript was not contraband. He was not sure of the legality of it being transported across international boundaries as personal property. *Did it fall into a tariff-exempt category as an antique?*

"Well, it could be David's," said Simon. He paused to reconsider his role. "But no, it is not, I asked Susan to take it. It never occurred to me there would be any problem. How was I to know she would be carrying Lionel's' *Atlantis* as well."

"I was there when he asked," said David who, in spite of the perfidy of his mother's lover with the woman in Peterborough, rose to Simon's defence. "She was happy to oblige. She had no idea there was anything questionable.

She was carrying a couple of books and some papers for friends."

"Not a problem, David," said Morgan. "She's not in trouble."

"I think we might all want to know how this came into your possession," Lionel Webb said to Simon as he reached over and touched the manuscript. It was open in front of Marie Lachine and she seemed to be reading. Then he added, almost as an afterthought, "I am assuming it belonged to Dieter. I am assuming this is what he bought with my money; I am assuming this is what he wanted to keep secret."

"Does any of this matter?" Simon responded. "Apparently it doesn't prove Bacon's authorship. It's worthless."

"Ah," said Felix Swan, rising back onto his feet in an ungainly flurry of movement. "You are wrong, Simon, wrong, wrong, wrong."

"Wrong?" said Miranda.

"Wrong, yes, this manuscript is of exceptional value."

"Care to explain?" said Morgan.

Felix looked to Jane Latimer, congenially deferring to her expertise, but it was Marie Lachine, the cipher expert, who stepped forward.

"The script, it is very old, older than Bacon. It precedes Gutenberg. Why have a professional scribe make a copy? Because it was written before the printing press, copied by hand, yes? Dieter Kurtz would have known its age immediately. I too would not be surprised if English is the author's first language. The words are German, the syntax, the pronouns, there is an English twist. The concept, itself, only an Englishman would condescend to play the role of foreigner; a self-confidence I abhor and admire. Plantagenet England, I would think." She looked around. No one was prepared to disagree. Still, she felt it necessary to qualify her judgment. "Possibly Lancastrian. Written during Henry the IV's reign at the latest." The academics among them nodded assent, the eyes of the non-academics, except Morgan's, glazed over. Sensing the disjuncture, she noted, "I agree with Lionel, I believe it must have been Dieter's. Are we right thus far, Simon, *mon cher*?"

Realizing any response from Simon was irrelevant, Morgan spoke up, asking Felix, "Why so valuable if it's not Bacon? And why hide it?"

"Because it is *not* Bacon!" said Felix emphatically. "Its early date proves absolutely that Francis Bacon did not write *Fama Fraternitatis*—he is not, he could not have been Christian of the Rose and Cross, he is not the founding father of the new Ancient Order of Rosicrucians."

"Do they care?" Morgan asked.

"Probably not. This find is of monumental importance for Baconites, but contemporary mystical orders will have no trouble shifting their paternity."

"There seems to be a pattern here," said Miranda under her breath.

"The value, then," said Morgan, "is for what it proves *not* to be true?"

"Exactly," said Felix. "Some would give their lives to

have found such a thing. And others, of course, might die, knowing it was found."

"That's worthy of Li Po," said Morgan.

"Thank you," said Felix, the flatterer flattered. "You can see the importance of a work like this. Everything we know will be realigned. As you must be aware from your own business, Detective, the past is provisional, subject always to change."

Felix returned once again to his chair.

"Simon, you were charged with the manuscript's care by Professor Kurtz." Miranda said this as a statement of fact, not as a question, and Simon made no effort to challenge her.

"And Simon was involved in the purchase of the manuscript, I believe," said Lionel Webb.

Simon looked cornered, but did not respond.

"Come on, Simon, we're in this together," said Lionel, somewhat cryptically. "No one is questioning your integrity."

"Really?" said Padraig.

"No one," said Ralph.

"I found it in a shop in Berlin," said Simon. "Off the Kurfurstendam."

"That's a very unlikely place," said Marie Lachine, who had done research in Berlin during her studies at the Sorbonne.

"No, not really," said Simon. "You haven't been there since the wall came down. Hordes of treasures from Soviet Europe are streaming to the west. Buildings built on the rubble of World War Two are bulging with the most tantilizing artifacts."

"And that's where you found this?" said Miranda, indicating the manuscript on the table. "A museum curator from the east bought his stake in the western world with an anonymous manuscript."

"Not a curator," said Lionel. "A professional would know its worth, it wouldn't end up among curios. I would say it came from someone's attic, an aristocrat, and was sold by a housekeeper."

"Interesting," said Miranda.

Now that he had begun talking, Simon was anxious to continue.

"It was in a shop down a small side street. I contacted Dieter. I thought he could advise me on how much to pay. I was after it for you, Lionel."

"Thank you," said Lionel. "I'm in your debt."

"When Dieter saw the pages I faxed him, he declared his own interest. The dealer wanted a small fortune, although he didn't know exactly what it was, and obviously neither did I. Dieter apparently did and he was determined to get it off the market as quickly as possible. He arranged for the payment and I brought the manuscript over directly. He seemed worried the German authorities might claim it as a national treasure."

"You smuggled it." Miranda said.

"No, not exactly. I simply did not declare its worth. I knew what I paid for it, but not how valuable it was."

"Did it occur to you to check with Lionel?" said Morgan. "He was your employer."

"I work free-lance, I was a picker for Lionel, and I

admire him, you, Lionel, very much. But Dieter had first claim."

"This bond with Dieter, your loyalty, where does that come from?" Miranda asked. There was an awkward pause while Simon seemed to be searching inside his head for an appropriate answer. Clearly, the strength of his feelings was difficult to articulate.

"He was…it was not an easy relationship," said Simon at last. "He was, I suppose, like a father, not someone so intimate but, you know, a father."

"Really," said Miranda. "Perhaps you could elaborate."

"From the first time I met him until the last moments of his life, he treated me as if my own life was genuinely interesting. He knew who I was. It was uncanny."

"And how much of himself did he show to you?"

"Not much. It was not a two-way street."

"But heavily travelled, nonetheless. And you despised him for that?" Miranda suggested. "For the lack of equity in your relationship. The father knows the son but does not allow himself to be known."

Simon looked confused, a little injured.

"Were you curious about the manuscript?" Miranda asked, swinging the inquiry back to the most tangible link between Simon and Kurtz's death.

"Not especially. I listen to all the talk about Bacon, but, well…"

"You listen but you don't hear," said Miranda. "A reluctant Baconian!"

"I have a lot of interests, I may have to spread myself rather thin at times. Dieter made me vow to tell no one."

"Tell them what?" said Morgan, irritated that Simon seemed irremediably obtuse. And solipsistic: his 'other interests' always came back to himself. Morgan did not trust his own judgment of Simon Sparrow.

"About the manuscript. What I paid, where I bought it, nothing, everything. As if it had never existed."

"He especially wanted *me* not to know," Lionel offered. A query, an observation, a complaint.

"Especially you," said Simon. "I think that was a mark of his respect. But he didn't want any of you to know."

"Why would that be?" said Morgan. "You must have thought about this."

"Not a lot. I really don't know," said Simon.

"Perhaps the Rector can explain," said Morgan.

"Certainly," said Felix, who had been waiting to jump in. "The early date of *Fama Fraternitatis* negated everything Dieter had worked for. It would have destroyed him." He paused, then added, redundantly, "His intellectual scholarly esoteric academic world would have been devastated."

"It is not about vanity," Jane Latimer countered. "It's never just about vanity." She lapsed into a contemplative quietness that seemed to include only ghosts and memories, then returned her attention to the manuscript.

chapter thirty-five
Wonder in a Practical World

Miranda gazed around the room at each of the surviving members of the Francis Bacon Society, repeating Morgan's question in her mind. *Why would Kurtz conceal his discovery from the very people most interested?* How was each of them coming to terms with his clandestine purchase, his secretive betrayal of trust, of confidence, of the bond among them.

Lionel appeared puzzled and hurt while Jennifer Pluck, standing close beside him, glowed with pleasure, contemplating the course of scholarly research opened by this turn of events. Hermione, too, seemed pleased, but for different reasons. She clearly found it amusing that Dieter could still command such attention after his death. Padraig was bored. He looked like a boy with a mouthful of gum trying to stifle his impulse to blow bubbles. Ralph appeared solemn, apparently with genuine concern for Kurtz's reputation that seemed to be hovering on the verge of collapse.

Miranda could not read Marie Lachine, who seemed to be simultaneously appalled and detached, like an astronomer contemplating an imploding galaxy.

Felix Swan and Jane Latimer were more intrigued by each other's response to the manuscript than with its significance in relation to Kurtz's death.

"I think," said Jane, as if she were responding to a direct question, "he would have kept it a secret for two reasons. One, dignity. He would not have wanted us to see his life's work compromised."

"You're not suggesting his scholarship was the source of his power over the group?" said Morgan. "I would have thought it was his knowledge of your most intimate secrets."

"No, it wasn't his reputation as a scholar that brought us together."

"But you admire his scholarship."

"Of course."

"Even when it's proven dead wrong."

"Yes, scholarship isn't about right and wrong."

"Then what has been compromised?"

"As I said, his dignity."

"And the second reason he would not want you to know about the manuscript?" asked Miranda.

"It's both extremely simple and really quite complicated," said Jane.

"Let's start with simple."

"Simply, all that he believed in collapsed with the discovery that Bacon could not have authored the Rosenkreuz manuscript. He would have felt he had disappointed us. That is a big word in the Kurtz lexicon. *Disappointed.* Something other people did." Jane Latimer looked not to Felix but to Lionel for corroboration.

Lionel nodded.

Miranda turned to Felix Swan.

"What do you think?" she asked him. "Do you agree?"

"I don't disagree." Felix smiled ingenuously.

"And the more complex explanation?" said Miranda.

"The same as the simple one," said Jane.

"You've been reading Saint Augustine," said Morgan.

"No," said Jane, bewildered by his unusual allusion. She looked at Miranda, who was not about to resolve one enigma by acknowledging another.

"Okay," said Jane, as if she had just lost an argument. She seemed for a moment to grope for words, then struggled to explain. "Dieter was enthralled all his life with Bacon as Rosenkreuz. In thrall. It was an idea that gave his life meaning."

"Why," asked Miranda. "In a nutshell."

"The reconciliation of opposites. Bacon was completely a man of the world. As the author of the *Fama Fraternitatis,* he was also profoundly a mystic. A worldly mystic; a really quite wonderful and revolutionary achievement."

"And if he did *not* write it?"

"Then Bacon's mystical bent wasn't a challenge to church authority, it was just conventional superstition."

"And this was a problem?" Miranda queried. "To Kurtz or to Bacon?"

"He wanted Bacon to stand for wonder in a practical world," said Lionel. "He needed that. Dieter abhorred religious doctrine, not unusual for a spiritual man. He despised religion for highjacking the mystery of being."

"He wanted to get Jeremy Bentham out from under the stairs," Morgan offered.

"And install him in a *Wunderkammern*," Miranda added with a sardonic smile. The others nodded, each responding to the astonishing busyness of the human mind.

Morgan remembered Dieter Kurtz throttling the lectern at the front of a lecture hall, his voice crackling in a raucous diatribe against—Morgan felt like he was landing safely after a long fall—against St. Augustine! Francis Bacon, the elderly professor had declared (even then he was old), Francis Bacon argued vehemently for the unity of body, mind, and soul. Bacon, himself, lived with body, mind, and soul in terrible glorious harmony. The reign of St. Augustine was over! The wicked Saint, Father of the Church, a brilliant man, a libertine, turned against reason, mortified the flesh through denial, sacrificed his humanity (the old man pounded the lectern), his humanity, humanness, his human *being*, for the sake of his soul, some spirit thing of his own creation. Such vanity! Such vanity, in the guise of submission! Aurelius Augustinus, Augustine of Hippo, invented original sin, and he deleted, and he erased (the old man spat the words into the air), and he annihilated the mystical trinity of passion, reason, and faith, I repeat (the Germanic barbs in his voice scratched the air), I repeat, the only true trinity, the mystical oneness of body and mind and holy spirit. He gave us incentives to die, and nothing to live for! Nothing! And then, then, after one thousand years (the lectern trembled under the weight of the old man's passion), Sir Francis Bacon, the mystic, the man of letters, the courtier, the spy, the secular messiah changed everything—a new age was born!

All this Morgan remembered in the instant between two moments of time.

"Where was the manuscript going?" said David Jenness. "Why was my mother carrying it? Why would Dieter not simply destroy it?"

"Or, make a triumphal conversion," said Jennifer Pluck. "He could have made quite a splash among his academic peers, reversing himself. It would have been a spectacular close to his career, like Einstein acknowledging there are some things that travel faster than light."

The library fell silent as thoughts skittered about in profusion, gradually coalescing on why Dieter Kurtz would choose to spirit the manuscript out of the country. Morgan loved the milieu; it was as if the splendid array of books all around them was pulsing in sympathetic response to so much conjecture, while in Miranda's mind the mausoleum aspects of the room were briefly displaced by the warmth of human concern.

Simon, finally, moved to the centre and spoke up.

"I expect he felt betrayed by history."

All eyes looked to him for an explanation.

"He wanted me to bury the manuscript deep inside the Jenness library in Knightsbridge. Lost among the books—no malice intended, David, nor to your mother, but rather as a compliment to your extensive holdings. It would languish for generations in a private collection and be rediscovered in a whole new world some day, when, to use the precise words of Dieter Kurtz, '*religion has died a natural death and gods walk again on the Earth.*'"

"Lovely," said Felix. "That's so much like Dieter. To be right and so wrong at the same time—to judge what will be better for us, to control what will happen to us, to anticipate destiny by determining its course."

"Well said," Morgan declared. "I'm not sure that you aren't elevating a simple act of intellectual piracy into something quite grand, but so be it. You are, after all, the Bacon Society."

"He was, after all, trying to hide evidence that would undermine his own reputation," said Miranda, likewise distancing herself from the strange cohort of eccentrics surrounding them. Thoughts of her old friend Allan and their revision of his practiced cynicism, reducing the company of necessary friends in the final analysis from six to one, passed through her mind. She glanced at Morgan who was scanning the room.

"The news would have blown his reputation out of the water!" said Ralph.

"Really," said Marie. "It would have."

"Well now," said Miranda. "We still have a murder only partially resolved.

"Perhaps I can help," said Lionel.

"I wish you would," said Miranda.

"Several nights before Dieter's death we gathered here for dinner. All of us except David."

"No," said David, "I was here, too."

Lionel Webb looked at him with affectionate exasperation.

"I notice you're not calling it a supper," said Miranda.

"He could, I suppose" said Padraig, clearly wanting to participate.

"The last supper, Porrig!" said Ralph. "I don't think so, dear heart."

"It was an unusual gathering," Lionel continued, "given that we were due to have a regular meeting only a few days later. Dieter requested it, although for the most part he didn't enjoy himself. After dinner we adjourned to this room as we usually did. David fetched the key from my den while the Rector recited Bacon's 1594 admonition that every man who would be truly informed should cultivate a garden, assemble a library, have a laboratory, and be possessed of a goodly huge cabinet—as you can see, I am only lacking the laboratory. And then we opened the *Wunderkammern*, my cabinet of curiosities." He rapped on the massive door behind him with the bust of Pallas Athena perched ironically overhead on the lintel.

"We all filed in," he continued, "all but Dieter who lingered behind. He had been unusually quiet at the table. Absorbed in other things, not part of the conversation. When I looked out through the vault door, he had gone into the conservatory, the lights were switched on and he was touching the orchid petals with his fingers. It was unusual but I thought nothing of it. Simon, I believe you went to get him."

Simon flinched, as if caught in an act of betrayal.

"Simon?" said Miranda.

"Yes."

"It's time."

"Time?"

"It's time to share with your friends. They need to know what happened."

Simon walked over to the door of the *Wunderkammern* and Lionel stepped aside. Simon turned and stared across the room as if trying to find words to match the images crowding his head.

"The dinner," said Simon. "It was unusual. As Lionel indicated, Dieter said little, but the old man was an overwhelming presence, more so than usual. Perhaps because his mind was focused on himself and we were accustomed to following his lead, however subtly he directed us."

"Yes."

"I did follow him into the conservatory. He was examining a few bees nestled into the hearts of several orchids. They must have entered through the sky-vents and been stranded when night fell, fooled by the artificial light which went out on a timer after dusk. They stirred when he turned the lights back on."

"Yes."

"Dieter had a small lacquer box. Chinese…" He paused, looking around at the others.

"Simon."

"Together, we herded several bees into the box. He put it in his pocket. He put his finger to his lips; our secret. We returned to the library. The others were filing back in. Dieter waited until everyone was here, and port was served, then he explained he was about to die."

Simon looked around for encouragement but the others averted their eyes. It was up to him, now.

"He announced his imminent death," said Simon. "No one disputed his authority on the matter. And as he talked, he seemed in better humour than he had been all evening. Li Po asked why? Not when or how, but why?"

"And did he explain?" asked Miranda.

"He said he had Alzheimer's Disease. We all spoke at once, denying the symptoms."

"*'That is because I did not want you to know,'* he insisted. *'The present is bleeding out into the past very rapidly. Soon I will be empty. My old man's disguise, it will be all I have left.'* He seemed almost amused. *'The procedures of my death are already in progress.'*"

"We were horrified at the possibility his diagnosis was true," said Lionel Webb. "For a man who lived so much in the mind, it is a terrible illness. But I venture to say each one of us was thrilled in anticipation of death so casually embraced."

"*'You will participate in my departure,'*" said Felix in a strange mimic voice. "That's what he told us. The old devil pronounced his passing a Bacon Society enterprise. And why not? We were his project, why should he not be ours. When Porrig asked how he would do it, Dieter's voice dropped to a conspiratorial whisper, he smiled: '*I will be murdered.'"*

"And then that ... man ..." Jane Latimer searched for an adjective. "That man got up," she said, "and walked over to me and kissed me on the forehead, I can feel his lips burning still."

"'*Do not be concerned*,' he said. '*Do not worry, my dear Jane. Each will contribute as the occasion arises.*'"

"Then everyone left," said Lionel. "Except Dieter. He and I talked for a couple of hours. About Bacon, mostly. About his reconciliation of the mystical world and the natural. And then Dieter left. I called David from the carriage house, he was asleep I'm afraid, and David drove him home."

"Is that when he asked you to prepare alibis? He knew the exact day?" said Morgan.

"The day, yes. The alibis? No, he did not directly ask me—what alibis, Detective. The Bacon Society went on a field trip extending from Vancouver to St. John's."

"And," said Miranda, "I'll bet some of your members have proof of being elsewhere as well. Like Simon does. A plethora of alibis."

"Simon was with me," said Lionel. "The woman in Peterborough slept through the night, she wouldn't have known whether he was there or not. A meagre alibi."

"Yes," said Miranda, smiling.

"The passenger manifest is actually a cluster of separate documents," said Lionel, indicating his folder. "Quite elastic, Detective."

"Clever, Lionel. Not quite as unassailable as you might think, though. You'd be surprised at what your loyal employees might reveal, interrogated separately, threatened as accomplices to murder."

"I'm not excessively worried."

"No, I don't suppose you are."

"Perhaps that's because it's looking more and more like assisted suicide," suggested Hermione.

"No, it was murder," said Miranda, "and Dieter Kurtz was determined it should appear to be murder."

She looked around at them. They were a strangely endearing group, and there was a shared energy among them that extended beyond their mentor or the exceedingly long reach of Bacon himself.

"Was it his one last effort to exercise power?" she said, addressing Morgan, for a moment excluding the others from the intimacy of their combined strategy.

Morgan wondered if he was himself an intentional beneficiary of Kurtz's peculiar death, bringing him closer to his son. He scowled:

"Perhaps he considered murder a bonding thing—a crucible to fuse them together."

Miranda turned back to Simon: "Tell us what happened."

He feels safe enough within the Bacon Society, Morgan thought, *to enjoy his position as central protagonist.*

"We met in his office."

"Dieter's office, the night of the murder?" Morgan asked, not wanting a confession without absolute clarity.

"Yes," said Simon. "He had the bees in their little cabinet. He had placed a sugar cube in with them and a few drops of water."

"How did he know to do that?" Miranda asked.

"He knew. I don't remember. Perhaps I told him. We talked through much of the night. We laughed. We quarrelled a little. We talked about adventures and how they can make life more intense, and how they can be a distraction. The hours flew by."

"Was that when he gave you the manuscript."

"Yes. He told me he wanted it secured in Knightsbridge. Although I had brought it from Berlin, I had no real idea what it's significance was. I asked him to explain."

"You were interested because it no longer had value." Miranda observed.

"I was interested because he was preparing to die."

"And did he explain?"

"He was cryptic. He said what I quoted before."

"*Religion will die a natural death and the gods will again walk on the Earth,*" said Morgan.

"More or less," said Miranda. "That doesn't help much. Simon, did you see Dieter Kurtz as a religious man?"

"No, definitely not. But spiritual, yes. He believed the mind could fly."

Morgan envisioned his flights with Saint Augustine.

"Really?" said Miranda.

"That's what he said."

"That night."

"That night. We talked a lot, then we walked out of Jesus College down onto Philosophers Walk. That was one of his favourite haunts, that tight scruffy ambiguous dividing line between the university and the museum. There was no one around, it was very late. And as I recall it was very hot. We found a nice place under some chestnut trees. He sat down on the ground. He leaned against a tree. He was cheerful, he laughed quietly to himself, I thought he was going mad."

"The book, the facsimile," said Miranda, "was that his idea?"

"Certainly not mine. It was given to me at the shop in Berlin, it was only a facsimile, a reward for buying the manuscript. I passed it on to Professor Kurtz but he treated it with disdain. After examining the manuscript, he was contemptuous of it as well. He told me Francis Bacon was not who he thought he was."

"Who Bacon thought he was, himself, or who Kurtz thought he was?" asked Morgan.

"I'm not sure," said Simon. "I think both."

"The facsimile?" Miranda persisted.

"He brought it along from his office. He asked to be posed with it while he died. I was puzzled. '*A dead man can't read,*' he said. '*Not when it's dark. But don't you see, my poor Simon. It's not real, I already know what it says.*' And of course I didn't see. He became angry. He clutched the book fiercely. '*The gods already walk free, my poor Simon. This will be my final derisive commentary on Francis Bacon. He has proven himself to be a great disappointment. As perhaps I am to him.*' Then he made a strange pronouncement: '*Dear Simon,*' he said, '*our beloved Mr. Bacon will survive Dieter Kurtz, even though my gesture of derision may endure to the end of time.*' As a sort of footnote, he added: '*What is last on my mind will last forever, you see.*' I did not."

"Using his own death as critical commentary," said Morgan out loud, to himself, with quiet admiration. "It didn't matter if no one understood."

"I'm sure he preferred it that way," said Miranda, thinking that Simon least of all would comprehend his gesture. Kurtz didn't want to destroy the Bacon Society, merely to establish a point of dialogue between himself and his nemesis, at the vanishing point where their lives converged.

Go on," she said, addressing Simon.

"Well, then he held the lacquer case out to me. But when I leaned over him to take it, he grasped hold of my locket." Simon pulled his silver locket from under his shirt and away from his collar.

Peruvian, pre-Columbian: Miranda had admired it on the beach at Briar Hill Island.

"It's empty," Simon announced.

"But it wasn't empty when Kurtz seized hold of it," Miranda declared.

Simon was slow to respond, but he knew it was necessary to account for a key piece of evidence—to prove, in fact, that it was not actually significant. It had nothing to do with the case.

"No, it was not empty. We had talked of this. He made me remove the contents."

"Ah," said Miranda. She suddenly understood. "A pubic hair. Jane Latimer's, to be precise."

"Yes."

"Dear God," Jane exclaimed. "Whatever for? Simon, what were you thinking?"

"Of you. Too much, apparently. According to Dieter. Dieter took it from me and flicked it into the air."

"All right, Simon," said Jane, exasperated. "You all need to know. Simon and I had a fling, more like a hop, skip, and a jump. One night only—you're quite the lad with one night stands. It was just after we met. A meeting of opposites. Quick as a wink, and over in a flash. Simon, why the hell were you keeping a souvenir?"

"I think perhaps it was an affair of short duration for you more than for him," suggested Morgan.

"I am not proud of this," said Simon.

"In any case," said Miranda. "You flicked it into the wind."

"Dieter did. There was no wind."

"And he set you free," Jane Lattimer observed.

Simon blushed as he struggled to pick up his story:

"All of a sudden, Professor Kurtz started struggling to his feet, bracing himself against me to get up. I figured it was over, that we were going home. He was stiff, I think; he had been sitting on the ground for maybe twenty minutes by then.

"'*Here, Simon, give me a hand*,' he said. He was struggling with his zipper.

"I balked…"

"'*My darling Judas*,' he said, '*I don't want to piss myself*.'"

"Well, I tried, it was awkward, he couldn't get it out of his underwear."

"He probably wasn't trying for the fly, Simon. He was trying for the leg-hole," said Miranda with beguiling authority.

"Have you ever tried to pull someone's penis out of his underpants?" said Simon. "Oh, sorry, no, well, yes, it would be, of course, no. I went in through the fly, yes. I'd never approached it quite that way before."

"And you had trouble tucking it away," said Miranda, ignoring his embarrassment.

"Yes, well, he didn't have to go, after all. And getting it back in is harder than you might think."

"Probably it is," said Miranda. *If there is so much as a titter, there will be an explosion of laughter.* Everyone was looking as sombre as possible, except Hermione and she was smiling.

Morgan nodded solemnly to Miranda and she continued.

"You say he called you his Judas?"

"'*The most beloved of Christ,*' he insisted. '*Without Judas, there would have been no story.*'"

"Interesting," said Morgan. "You were all right with that?"

"It was another self, one I hadn't thought of. Yes, I didn't mind."

"Story is important," said Miranda. "Li Po died because his own story had come to a natural conclusion."

"Yes," said Simon, visibly confused.

"Tell me, Simon, do you think Dieter Kurtz's life was complete?"

"No."

"Why do you think he embraced death?"

"Because."

"Do you think it was about Alzheimer's or about

Bacon?"

Jane Latimer interjected: "It was about losing control."

"Or keeping it," said Miranda.

Instead of reacting as if she had been contradicted, Jane nodded agreement.

"Li Po used to say that no one is dead until the ripples turn smooth." Everyone looked at Marie Lachine. "I think for Dieter Kurtz," she continued, "the shock waves left behind by his death were all that he wanted, a kind of limited immortality."

"A lovely paradox," said Felix. "*Limited immortality.*"

"Simon," said Miranda. "Back to the recalcitrant penis. What happened?'

"We got distracted?"

"You got distracted."

"We both did, I guess. It was dark. He tried to sit down again, so he did, but I had to adjust him, he had seized up a bit from the effort, we wanted to make him look natural, he grasped a firm hold on his book and then, well, then, the bees."

"Did you release the slide on the box or was it him?" said Miranda.

"Don't answer that," said Lionel in a clarion voice. "That's not something we need to know."

Simon nodded to Lionel a gesture of appreciation.

"And the paisley cravat? He was wearing it very tight that night, wasn't he?" Miranda knew she would get no response but none was needed. It was all part of Kurtz's plan. Simon Sparrow was his devoted acolyte, assisting in rites understood only by the master.

"What happened to the box?" she asked.

"It's back in Dieter's house," said Jennifer. I saw it by his cabinet. You saw it when you were there."

"Did I?" said Miranda. "The one you handed me, the one my partner and I admired, the one with layers of fingerprints, including our own?"

"Yes, I expect that is the box," said Jennifer.

"Returned when you went in to send the e-mail, Simon? Before his house was declared a crime scene. Very efficient."

"Yes," said Simon, "I tried to look after things."

"Including his body," said Miranda.

"His body? Oh, yes, of course. I claimed his remains on behalf of the Bacon Society."

"Not for display!" said Miranda with a profound shudder.

"No dear. We're going to give him a lovely funeral," said Hermione.

"And then cremation," said Felix Swan. "We'd like to avoid the putrefaction of flesh."

"Felix is a sensitive man," said Ralph.

"Hope you'll come," said Padraig, addressing Miranda and Morgan.

"What I don't understand," said Hermione, "is why he would want to be murdered."

"He insisted on it," said Simon.

"I would suggest the answer is academic," Jane Lattimer offered, smiling at their apparent naïveté.

"Please explain," risked Felix Swan, apparently willing to put his intellectual reputation on the line for the sake of clarity.

"Poor Dieter was crushed when his edifice of scholarship collapsed."

"No doubt. It must have been humbling."

"Dear Rector, I don't think the word *humble* was in Dieter's vocabulary. It was inspiring. He wanted to balance what he considered Bacon's monumental fraud with one equally monumental of his own."

"But it wasn't Bacon who claimed authorship of the *Fama Fraternitatis*. He never said he was Christian Rosenkreuz. It was all in the mind of Professor Kurtz."

"Supported by exhaustive research," Jane responded.

"Which proved to be greviously flawed. Rather ironic, isn't it. He was the consummate researcher."

"Indeed, he was," she admitted. "So he rose to the occasion, he constructed his death as an insoluable murder which implicated all of us in the Bacon Society."

"In his mind," said Lionel, who had no pretensions to scholarship, "he was matching Bacon's deception, as he saw it, with something equally grand and obscure."

"We solved it, didn't we?" Hermione proclaimed, looking around for the other Hermione to provide confirmation, before her features tightened into a look of deep concern.

"It was grand," Morgan noted. "No doubt of that. Quite grandiose."

"And obscure," Miranda added.

"Well, well," said Lionel, "that just about winds things up, then, doesn't it? Would anyone care for a drink? Dom Perignon? A tour of the *Wunderkammern*, perhaps? Or are we all out of curiosity for one night?"

Miranda and Morgan had moved around the room, so they were now side by side. The others watched them closely. Lionel was host but they were in charge.

"An unresolved case or not?" Morgan spoke to Miranda in a quiet but resonant voice.

"We can hardly lay charges based on who slid the cover off a lacquer box," said Miranda in an almost inaudible whisper.

Even the book-laden walls leaned closer.

"Euthanasia?" she suggested. She glanced around her, encountering the gaze of each of her listeners in brief flashes of empathy. "I think we had best stick to murder."

The walls retreated.

"It leaves the case open," said Morgan.

"Less complicated."

"An open file will discourage the Bacon Society from trying again."

"We hope."

"No fear," said Lionel, as the room assumed its former dimensions. "Without Dieter Kurtz to pull the strings, we're marionettes hanging on pegs in the closet."

"In the cabinet," Morgan amended.

"Perhaps you would care to join our cadre of eccentrics. we have several openings."

"Thank you," said Morgan.

"No thank you," said Miranda, firmly but with warmth.

The two outsiders made eye contact. *Life itself is a cabinet of curiosities*— the unspoken phrase passed between them like a secret, a bond, a gift, from the redoubtable Dieter Kurtz.

David Jenness approached.

"Is everything acceptable?" he asked.

"Yes," said Miranda. "Acceptable."

"I need to say goodbye, then," he said with a shy smile.

Miranda picked up on his solemn tone. "Are you going? Back to England?"

"Yes, actually, I am. Mother came to get me, so to speak. She wants me to take over the business. Without Nigel, it's going rather badly."

"And Simon," said Morgan, "is he going with you?"

"Whatever for? Oh, no. That's over, Detective—may I call you David?"

"Yes, David."

"I assumed you knew. She said she had been talking to you and decided to break it off with Simon. I must say, he's been a good sport about it all."

"Really," said Morgan. "A good sport."

Simon, who had been listening, blushed but appeared content. It was clear he knew nothing of Morgan's intimate life.

Miranda edged close enough that Morgan could feel her body heat through their clothes. The rest of the room was listening intently.

"This has been quite an experience," said David Jenness with an awkward kind of restrained grace. "I owe almost as much to the two of you as to Lionel."

"We're going to miss him around here," said Lionel, drawing Jennifer to his side and gesturing around the room to take in the rest of the Bacon Society, all of whom had been listening intently. Hermione gave David a little wave across the room, Felix and Jane each made a thumbs up gesture, Porrig and Rafe grinned amiably, and Marie Lachine affected a slight bow from the waist. Simon squinted and winked.

Miranda grasped David's hand in both of hers and shook it, drew him close and kissed his cheek, put her arms around him and gave him a huge lingering hug, finally releasing him with an inexplicable hint of tears in her eyes.

David Jenness was confused but accepted her affection with élan, as if he knew there would always be things in life he could not completely understand.

He turned to Morgan.

"David," he said.

"David."

"Good luck with your running."

"I'm looking for another sport, something less cerebral."

"It's been nice to meet you, sir. If you're ever in England."

"You too, David. My love to your Mom."

"From both of us," said Miranda.

"Yes," said Morgan. "From both of us."